1

When I met Liselle Vila at the wedding reception, I had no idea that she was going to kill her date right there on the dance floor. I could even see the alleged murder weapon, but I didn't realize that's what I was looking at and, to be honest, I wasn't looking that closely.

Other people were apparently a lot more discerning than me, or maybe just less discreet, because they testified later that it was obvious what she was doing. It seemed to me that most of them were just taking credit for perception after the fact and that, if they had really seen it coming, they would've stopped it. But they didn't.

I had already left the reception so I didn't see it happen. Instead, I had to piece it together later through the eyes of dozens of witnesses who each perceived the events through very different lenses, like witnesses always do. Though people disagreed about how it happened, they did agree on two things.

Liselle Vila had a weapon. And they saw it kill Richard Phillips.

TRUE INTENT

A NATE SHEPHERD NOVEL

MICHAEL STAGG

True Intent

A Nate Shepherd Novel

Copyright @2020 Michael Stagg

All rights reserved

All characters in this book are fictitious. Any resemblance to an actual person, living or dead, is purely coincidental.

For more information about Michael Stagg and his other books, go to michaelstagg.com

Want a free short story about Nate Shepherd's start as a new lawyer? Hint: It didn't go well. Sign up for the Michael Stagg newsletter here or at https://michaelstagg.com/newsletter/

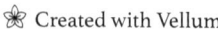 Created with Vellum

LEAVES

2

THE BRANSON-PHILLIPS WEDDING WAS THE BIGGEST EVENT THE city of Carrefour had seen in more than a decade. I was invited because the bride, Ellie Branson, was the little sister of one of my best friends, Matt.

Ellie was marrying Jake Phillips, a young man from St. Louis whose family had descended upon Carrefour, if the rumors were true, in not one but two private jets. The wedding was quite the affair—a cathedral, a trolley, pictures at every scenic area within a twenty mile radius, and, because no venue was quite right, the absolute biggest, tallest, most elaborate tent you'd ever seen, complete with a hardwood floor, four bars, and a stage for a band that had opened for Ed Sheeran and the Foo Fighters.

I was sitting at a table with Zach Stephenson and his wife, Mandy, who were also two old friends. The mother of the bride had been kind enough to rearrange things and seat me with them after I'd realized that I really didn't have a plus one.

Zach picked up the placard with the menu and whispered out of the side of his mouth, "What the hell is truffle oil?"

"Something you season food with when you decide you have too much money," said Mandy.

I chuckled. "You guys want a drink?"

Mandy twirled her near-empty glass. "Pinot?"

"You got it. Zach?"

"Think they have Jack here?"

I smiled. "I think you're gonna have to make do with Johnny Walker Blue or some Irish nonsense."

"Fine."

"Mind him," I said to Mandy.

"Always," she said with the air of someone mentioning a full-time job.

I excused myself and headed up to the closest bar. There were only a few people in line and I hadn't been waiting more than a second before a couple came tumbling up behind me. The man was tall and trim, with perfectly cut black hair that had a sprinkling of gray. He wore a tailored black suit that was cut slimmer than was usual for a man his age, which was probably explained by the woman leaning into him and whispering in his ear.

She wore a black sleeveless dress that shimmered just a little and contrasted sharply with blond hair that was so pale it was almost white. She wore extraordinarily high heels that let her whisper in the man's ear without him ducking his head. The man smiled at whatever she said and then held out his hand to me. "So, do you know my nephew or his new wife?"

I shook it. "Grew up with the bride's brother. Nate Shepherd."

"Richard Phillips. Groom's uncle."

I smiled. "So part of the St. Louis contingent. Trip okay?"

"Fine, fine," he said. "We got a later start than we wanted but we were able to actually land here. I thought we were going to have to go to Detroit."

"I told you," said the woman, smiling.

"You did. That'll teach me to listen to you."

"It should. It should also teach you to introduce me." She smiled as she said it and it was clear she wasn't offended in the least.

"Of course." Richard flashed a smile, more for her than me, and said, "Nate, this is Liselle."

"Hi, Nate," she said and her smile remained playful. When her smile got bigger, I realized I hadn't said anything.

Rather than get offended, Richard chuckled.

"Hi, Liselle," I said. Brilliant recovery. "Are you from St. Louis too?"

"A small town just south," said Liselle.

"She's with the Forest Service," said Richard.

"That's great work," I said.

"For very little money," said Richard. "I'm trying to talk her into coming over to the dark side."

"Which is where?" I said.

"Our company," he said and he paused as if I would know what he was talking about.

I didn't. "What company is that?"

Richard raised an eyebrow. "Really?"

Liselle smiled and leaned on his arm. "We're not in St. Louis, Richard."

"No, I suppose we're not," said Richard. "The Doprava Company."

An earlier conversation with Matt came back to me. Ellie was marrying into a family that owned a multi-billion-dollar multi-national company that did multitudinous things. Uncle Richard ran the whole thing. "I'm sorry," I said. "I should've remembered."

Richard waved it off. "How about you?"

"Lawyer. Here in town."

"Sir?" came the bartender's voice over my shoulder.

It was my turn. I ordered a Pinot, a Johnny Walker Blue, and a Miller Lite appeared by magic. I balanced three drinks in two hands and said, "Great to meet you both."

"You too, Nate,' said Richard. "I'm sure we'll see you around."

Liselle smiled at me and said something to the bartender that was lost in the rising tide of music.

As I brought the drinks back to Zach and Mandy, Zach said, "Who in the name of God's green gravy was that?"

"Who?"

Zach pointed.

"Richard Phillips and Liselle...I don't know her last name."

"Jesus," he said, still looking.

Mandy stared at Zach. "She is half his age, Zachary."

"Come on now, darling," said Zach, smirking. "Not everyone can be as lucky as you, finding the man of her dreams in high school. Some people have to keep looking."

"Right, that's exactly what I am," said Mandy. "*So* lucky."

Zach pressed his lips against Mandy's cheek and she scowled and then she smiled and then she kissed him on the lips and then she punched him in the arm.

The wedding went as weddings do. There was a dinner and there was a toast and I'd have to say that the maid of honor's was just a little bit better than the best man's but both of them were funny with just a drop of poignancy at the end. A cake was cut, a garter was tossed, and after all of those preliminaries, Ellie Branson, now Ellie Phillips, danced with her father. And after Ellie danced with her father, the wedding party danced with each other, and the rest of the guests were invited to join in. The band —who it must again be mentioned had toured with Ed Sheeran *and* the Foo Fighters and did *not* normally do weddings but was there only out of an abiding love and respect for the Phillips family and a check the size of three concerts—began to cut loose, and soon most of the guests were on the hardwood dance floor, spinning under the high-ceilinged tent in the flickering faux candlelight. Later, I decided that the flash of pale blonde I saw spinning by must have been Liselle and Richard, but at the time, all I really noticed was the bride and the groom and their parents and a mass of dancers that I thought of as the private jet contingent.

I sipped a beer and spoke to Zach and Mandy, but eventually she prevailed on Zach to get out there with her and it was just me and the other single person at the table, a woman in her thirties who the mother of the bride had placed on the opposite side of the table so that she wasn't being too obvious.

It had reached the point where it would be rude not to talk to her, so I moved and took a seat next to her and we talked about how I knew Matt and how she knew Ellie and how we actually had quite a few friends in common. It turned out that she was an accountant from Kalamazoo and she was very pleasant and I was very nice and after about twenty minutes, we both reached the conclusion that we had spoken long enough to appease Matt and Ellie when they asked us later what we thought of each other. I offered to get her a drink, she said she was still working on hers, and so I excused myself and went back to the bar.

Matt Branson was waiting for me when I got there. As a member of the wedding party, he'd been wearing a tux but the jacket was now gone and his tie was loose as he gave me a big hug.

"Shep!" he said, drawing it out. The wedding party trolley had been stocked with booze, as was proper. "Having fun?"

"You bet. Family holding up?"

"Much better. Nerves had them like jellyfish on a cactus yesterday but the pressure's off now."

The band stopped playing and announced that all of the married couples should come to the dance floor so they could do the dance where they kept reciting the number of years that people had been married until the couple who'd been together the longest was the last one on the floor.

Matt shot me a glance. I smiled and said, "You'd better find Beth."

"Got that right." He finished his drink. "Don't leave without saying good-bye."

"I won't."

He nodded and went to find his wife.

I almost left then but I decided to wait until after I saw that Mr. and Mrs. Rooker had been married sixty-four years—two years longer than the runner-up. After that, I caught up with Mr. and Mrs. Branson, who hugged me happily, and Ellie and Jake, who thanked me for sharing their special day, and Zach and Matt, who called me a candy-ass of the highest order for leaving before the tequila. I agreed and headed home around ten-thirty.

I was asleep two hours later.

MY PHONE BUZZED AT THREE THIRTY-NINE. THAT'S IN THE morning. I answered.

"Shep?" came a voice.

I hadn't had much to drink but three thirty-nine is three thirty-nine. "Yeah?"

"It's Matt, Branson. I need you to come back here."

"It was a great party, Matty, but I'm cooked."

"No, not to the reception. To the hospital."

I sat up. "Are you okay?"

"I'm fine. It's Jake's Uncle Richard. He's dead. We could use your help."

I got out of bed. "I'll be right there."

3

I found Matt Branson in the ER waiting room sitting by a stained, white coffeemaker. The room wasn't too crowded and consisted of exactly what you'd expect in the middle of a weekend night: a few stitches from a party mishap, a minor car accident, and a young couple hunched worriedly over a baby. On the far side of the room, opposite Matt, sat a woman in a shimmering black dress with pale blonde hair. Her hands were folded in her lap, her ankles were crossed, and she was looking down.

Matt came straight over. "I'm sorry, Shep. Thanks for coming. I didn't know who else to call to help us work through this."

"Work through what?"

"Did you meet Jake's Uncle Richard?"

The woman sitting across the waiting room helped me make the connection from Uncle Richard to Richard Phillips. "Briefly."

"He collapsed at the end of the night. His brother is the groom's father, Steve. He brought Richard's kids over and I brought Liselle."

It took me another moment to remember that was the blond woman's name. Then what Matt said struck me. "They didn't come together?"

"Small car. And it didn't seem like a good idea."

"How many kids?"

"Two. Bre and Andrew."

"Where are they now?"

"In back. Saying goodbye."

"You're sure he's passed?"

Matt nodded. "The doctor told us about half an hour ago. That's when I called."

We didn't get any farther as two men in tuxedo jackets and a woman in a knee-length peach dress came down the hallway. The men were tall and looked alike except that one had salt-and-pepper hair and the other's was dark brown. They were on either side of the woman, who looked to be in her mid-twenties and was leaning hard on the older man, crying.

As soon as they entered the waiting room, the younger man walked toward the far corner. Toward Liselle.

"Come on," said Matt and went over there. I followed.

Before we reached them, the older man grabbed the younger man's arm. "Not now, Andrew," the older man said.

"She fucking killed him, Uncle Steve," Andrew said. "You saw it!" The young woman cried harder.

"Calm down, Andrew," Stephen Phillips said.

"Fuck that. She fucking killed my Dad!"

Liselle didn't move. Her hands remained folded in her lap, her ankles remained crossed, and she just looked down, unflinching.

Matt positioned himself between Andrew and Liselle. Andrew tried to push through Matt. That wasn't going to happen so Andrew bent his head around Matt and said, "Are you fucking happy? Did you get what you wanted, you fucking bitch? My dad is fucking dead."

At Andrew's words, the woman on Stephen Phillips' arm collapsed into him. The sick baby on the other side of the waiting room began to cry.

Stephen Phillips glanced that way then said, "This isn't the time, Andrew."

The young man's eyes went wild. "So when is the time, Uncle Steve? My dad's already dead so just when is the right fucking time?"

"Andrew!" Stephen Phillips said. "Outside!"

Andrew didn't seem inclined to listen so Matt took him by the arm, carefully, and led him out. Matt was whispering so I couldn't hear what he said, but whatever it was seemed to work and Andrew let himself be guided out of the waiting room.

Liselle sat there, still.

Stephen Phillips caught my eye. "Nate, right?" he said.

We'd met a few times over the course of the weekend. I nodded.

"Matt said you would know who to talk to before we can take him home?"

I nodded again.

"We would like it to be as soon as possible."

"Of course. I'll talk to the coroner and let you know."

"Thank you. Matt has my number." Stephen Phillips started to lead the young woman away when Liselle said, "I'd like to see him."

Stephen Phillips froze. The young woman raised her head from her uncle's shoulder, focused her bloodshot eyes on Liselle, and said, "Don't you fucking dare."

Stephen Phillips' voice was calm but his eyes were not as he said, "I don't think that's a good idea, Liselle."

"Please."

Stephen Phillips' eyes were hard. "No. And I think it's best that you make your own way home. I'll pay for the flight."

Liselle raised her chin. "I can pay my own way."

Stephen Phillips didn't argue. Instead, he nodded once and led his niece outside.

Liselle looked up at me. In the bright lights of the emergency room, her eyes were a startling light green. "Can they do that?" she said.

"Are you married?"

"To Richard? No."

"Those were his kids, right?"

She nodded.

"Then I'm afraid so."

Liselle looked over her shoulder down the hall for a moment, then said, "Can I get an Uber here this time of night?"

"I'll drop you off at the hotel."

"Thank you."

I offered her my hand. She took it and glided to her feet.

As we walked towards the exit, the doors slid open before we could trigger them and a man in a solid blue suit walked in. We went to go around him, but he shifted slightly and blocked the way, raising one hand. "Excuse me, Ms. Vila?"

Liselle stopped and seemed uncertain.

"Officer Nicovitis of the Carrefour police," he said. "I need to speak with you for a moment."

We stepped out of the doorway and Officer Nicovitis looked at Liselle in a way that wasn't quite lecherous but was too long just the same. Liselle seemed a little stunned, so I stepped forward and said, "How can we help you, Officer Nicovitis?"

He noticed me for the first time, then said, "Were you at the wedding too?"

I realized our clothes made us an odd pair. I nodded. "I'd gone home. What does the Carrefour police need?"

"We had a detail working at the wedding. We need to file a report."

I pointed a thumb. "The ER doc is back there. His kids and brother are out in the parking lot."

Officer Nicovitis nodded and turned to Liselle, ignoring me. "Are you related to the vic—to the gentleman who passed as well?"

Liselle's eyes dropped. "I was his date."

"I'm very sorry for your loss."

"Thank you."

Officer Nicovitis's voice was sympathetic but his eyes were calculating. "So what happened at the recep—"

"Officer Nicovitis."

He stopped and looked at me.

"Her date died tonight. It's four o'clock in the morning."

"Of course, of course. You have my sympathies Ms. Vila but—"

"Thank you, Officer. I'm sure the ER doc can talk to you now."

Having failed twice, Officer Nicovitis said, "Do you have a number where I can reach you, Ms. Vila? In case I learn anything that you might be interested in?"

"Do you have a card, Officer?" said Liselle.

"I do." Officer Nicovitis pulled a card out of an inside pocket and handed it to her.

"Thank you. I'll call if I need anything." Then Liselle nodded to him and left.

"Night, Officer," I said and followed her.

It's a tough thing being with someone who's just lost somebody. I've been on both sides of it and it seems like people take one of two approaches—either they ask a lot of questions about it and relate it to similar things that happened in their own life or they make small talk and avoid it completely until the grieving person brings it up. I tend to be in the second category so, as we drove back to the hotel, I asked a couple of questions about where she was staying and whether she wanted to stop at a drive-thru to pick up something to eat. All she told me was the name of the hotel and that she wasn't hungry. The rest of the drive was quiet; I watched the road, which had virtually no traffic on it, and she stared out the window, not crying, not fidgeting, just staring. The quiet was neither comfortable nor uncomfortable. It was just quiet.

As we pulled into the hotel, I said, "Do you need anything?"

"No, thank you." She got out of the car.

As she did, I realized something. "Did you have a purse with you, Liselle?"

She turned and bent down a little bit so she could look back in. "No, Mr. Shepherd. I'm sorry we bothered you tonight."

"It's no bother. Good night."

She closed the door and I waited to make sure she made it in. As she passed the front desk, the night manager glanced up then watched her walk all the way across the lobby.

When she turned down the hallway, I left.

As I pulled away, I realized I had no idea how Richard Phillips had died.

4

I found out on Sunday afternoon, from my mother of all people.

I slept in for a couple of hours on Sunday morning because of the interruption overnight then drove up to the state recreation area near my parents' house. It had a series of trails that wound through woods and around lakes that made it a perfect place to run. It was also one of the places where my wife Sarah had done research before she died.

I found that I enjoyed running there very much.

I picked the Pine Way trail, which was a little under five miles, and took off. It was early fall so it was sunny but cool and the leaves were just starting to turn so it was beautiful except for the fact that I was running. The trail was an out and back loop marked, as you might guess, by a series of white pines. I saw two mountain bikers and another runner and that was about it. When I'd finished the loop, I got back into the car and went to my parents' house.

My parents lived in a small house on Glass Lake, about twenty-five minutes north of Carrefour. A Chrysler mini-van and a Ford Expedition sat in the driveway so I knew my brothers' families were already there. As I climbed out, my mom was standing on the front porch. She gave me a quick hug and a sniff and said, "Run, dear?"

"I'll hop in the lake before I come in."

"That would be nice. You've got about fifteen minutes before the game starts." She gave me a pat on the shoulder and I walked around back.

As I walked down the grass to the lake's edge, I saw my dad nosing his fishing boat up to the dock. "I got it, Dad," I said.

"Thanks, Son." He lined up the bow and gunned the boat up onto the lift. Once it settled on the padded rails, I turned the winch to raise it out of the water.

My dad gathered his things and slipped on a Detroit Lions pullover, the Honolulu blue a vivid contrast to his shock of white hair and skin like a weathered hickory plank. "Did you go to the Branson wedding last night?" he said.

"I did."

"How's Matty doing?"

"Good. Said to say hello."

"Your mom said something happened."

"How'd she know?"

"Retirees don't play bingo anymore. They gossip on Facebook."

"I thought they fished?"

He flashed a white smile. "The smart ones do."

I finished cranking the winch and locked it and my dad hopped out.

"Does she know what it was?" I asked.

"I'm sure she does."

"What?"

He smiled again. "I store the Facebook stuff in her head."

"Seems efficient."

He checked his watch. "Game's about to start." Yes, he still wore a watch because the radio waves from cellphones scare away the fish. Just ask him.

"Be right there." I went back to the shore, dumped my stuff, and walked into the lake. The water was cool, but there was still plenty of sun during the days and the nights weren't too cold so it felt pretty great. I took a quick swim to the raft and back, toweled off, and made my way into the house to join my family for our traditional Sunday cook out and the heartbreak that was watching the Detroit Lions.

As I walked in, three kids walked out—my nieces Taylor and Page and my nephew James. "Where you headed, trolls?" I said.

"We're biking down to the Groves, Uncle Nate," Taylor said.

"Do your parents know?"

"Of course. Bye." The three scrambled to the garage where their grandpa kept the bikes. He'd even named them and before long, I saw Taylor, Page, and James, ride off on Xbox, Wii, and Switch.

He's a wicked man, my dad.

I went into the cottage to a sea of Honolulu blue and silver. The rest of my family was already there—my mom and dad, my older brother Tom and his wife Kate, and my younger brother Mark and his wife Izzy. Tom and Kate had three daughters—Reed, Page, and Taylor—and a son, Charlie, who was three years old and sitting on Kate's lap. Mark and Izzy had three boys, the three J's—Justin, James, and Joe. Everyone was there except for

Page, Taylor, and James, who were biking to the Groves on the other side of the lake.

A sectional couch, an easy chair, and the chairs from the kitchen were set up around a low coffee table facing a TV screen showing the final stages of the Fox pregame show. A collective lunch spread of sandwiches and chips was laid out on the kitchen table (my contribution was a three-foot sub this week), which my dad would follow up with a dinner of barbecue chicken after the game. I had just picked up a plate when I heard, "Jesus, it's about time, Nate." My sister-in-law, Izzy. "We've been waiting to get the scoop from you all morning."

I held up a spoon. "Buffalo dip or French Onion?"

"Funny, asshole. About the wedding."

Kate was sitting next to Izzy on the couch. Both waved me over. I collected a sandwich, chips, and water and headed over.

Izzy had frizzy blond hair and mischievous green eyes. Kate had athletically cut brown hair and a sense of placid calm that came from corralling four kids and a football coach all day. They separated on the couch and patted the space between them so that they had an equal opportunity for inquisition. I sat.

"Two things," said Izzy. "Did you take a date and did someone really die?"

"No and yes." I took a bite of sandwich.

"What happened to Jessica?" said Izzy.

"Who died?" said Kate.

"I didn't ask Jessica to go and a guy named Richard Phillips."

"Why not?" said Izzy.

"Who's he?" said Kate.

"I didn't know how long I was going to stay and the uncle of the groom."

"Did you meet someone at the wedding then?" said Izzy.

"What happened?" said Kate.

I looked up at my brothers who were sitting off to the side

watching the pregame, munching sandwiches with a contentment that was infuriating. "A little help?" I said.

"We weren't at the wedding," said Tom.

"And we're all dying to know what happened," said Mark without taking his eyes off the screen.

"Totally," said Tom.

Mark extended the top of a beer bottle. Tom clinked it with his and went back to munching. Bastards.

I turned to Izzy. "Matty tried to set me up with an accountant from Kalamazoo. She had less interest in me than I had in her."

I turned to Kate. "I don't know exactly but I think he died at the end of the night. I'd already left."

"He died on the dance floor." We all stopped and turned as my mom "tsk'd," shook her head, and scooped some French onion dip onto a chip.

"How do you know, Mom?" said Kate.

"Betty Langshied was there. She posted pictures."

"What?" we all said.

"Not of the body, of the dancing." My mom pursed her lips. "The woman seemed much younger."

"You know we've been waiting for the scoop all morning!" said Izzy. "Why didn't you tell us?"

My mom smiled. "You didn't ask."

"How'd it happen, Mom?" I asked.

"This Mr. Phillips was making a fool of himself is what happened," said my mom. "Dancing all night with a woman half his age."

"That's it?"

"Apparently, that's enough," said Kate.

"Enough chirping, Uncle Nate," my eight-year-old nephew, Joe said. "The game's about to start."

My dad sat behind Joe with a straight face, pretending to chew his sandwich.

"Got it, Joe," I said. "Is Davis active?"

Joe glanced at my dad, who put his sandwich in front of his mouth. A moment later, Joe shook his head and said, "Game time scratch. They're starting Tavai. They'll be okay though."

So we watched to find out.

I GOT BACK HOME EARLY THAT EVENING, FULL OF MY DAD'S barbecue chicken and joy from the Lions' victory over the Vikings. I parked my Jeep next to an empty black rectangle in the driveway that was a little darker than the surrounding asphalt. As I went into the house, I was deciding whether to pull out my tablet and get a jump start on Monday morning's work or watch the Sunday night game instead. The Sunday night game was winning when my phone buzzed.

I didn't recognize the number. I sighed and answered. "Nate Shepherd."

"Mr. Shepherd, it's Liselle Vila."

"Liselle? Is everything okay? Well, I mean I know everything isn't okay. But what's wrong?"

"Detective Pearson has asked to interview me."

"Makes sense."

"Why does it make sense, Mr. Shepherd? His card says he's in charge of serious crimes."

"Call me Nate, please. Pearson is the local officer who deals with the coroner most often. I'm not surprised that he would be investigating."

"Does he investigate all deaths from natural causes in Carrefour?"

A point. "No."

"I assume he investigates killings?"

"Sure. And accidental deaths."

"But not purely medical ones?"

"I suppose it depends on the context. What do you need, Liselle?"

"I think I need a lawyer. Matt suggested I call you."

"Why would you need a lawyer?"

"You saw Richard's children last night?"

"I did."

"Then I need you to keep this Pearson honest. And I'd feel better if I have someone looking out for me if he goes too far afield."

"Okay. When does Pearson want to meet?"

"Tomorrow at ten. He asked me to come down to the police station."

"Are you at the same hotel?"

"Yes."

"Then I'll pick you up at nine o'clock and take you down."

"Thank you."

"I'm sure he's just dotting his i's and crossing his t's, Liselle. You'll be able to give him a statement and go on your way. When were you planning on leaving town?"

"When Rich does."

I paused, then said, "I understand. I'll see you tomorrow morning."

"Thank you, Mr. Shepherd."

"Nate."

"Thank you, Nate."

"No problem, Liselle."

I hung up and thought for a moment. It wasn't necessarily unusual that Pearson wanted to interview Liselle, but it wasn't necessarily usual either. Liselle was right: the police didn't get involved in checking on every heart attack that happened in Carrefour. Richard Phillips was a pretty big fish though and ran a multi-billion-dollar company. I suppose in that sort of case,

Pearson had to go through the motions even if he didn't believe there was anything wrong. Who knows, there might be insurance or other business reasons that would prompt an investigation. Judging from what I saw of Richard Phillips' son and daughter last night, Liselle was probably right to be cautious.

I went into the family room and watched the late game. When it was done, I watched a little SportsCenter, then turned off the TV and went to bed.

5

Mitch Pearson strode into the police station waiting room, hand extended. "Thank you for coming down, Ms. Vila. I appreciate you taking the time to..." Pearson stopped when he saw me. "What are you doing here, Shepherd?"

I shrugged. "Ms. Vila doesn't know anybody here in town. I gave her a ride."

"Are you here in an official capacity?"

I shrugged again. "As long as I'm here."

If that bothered him, he didn't show it. Instead, Pearson waved a hand and said, "Come on back then. This shouldn't take long."

Liselle and I followed Pearson back to his office. It wasn't much different than the last time I had seen it. It seemed like there were a few more case files on the floor but there was still the same picture of the family on the beach and the same triathlon medals on the wall. Pearson looked the same as the last time I'd seen him too; he was still tall and blonde and square-jawed like a World War II recruiting poster.

Liselle, on the other hand, looked very different. She was dressed in black yoga pants and an oversized Under Armor running pullover. Her hair was pulled back into a ponytail that stuck out the back of a St. Louis Cardinals baseball hat and she seemed fragile and tired, which was hardly a surprise.

Pearson indicated the chairs in front of his desk and offered us something to drink, which we both declined. He sat down crisply and said, "Thanks for coming to see me, Ms. Vila. I don't expect to take much of your time. I just need to have a brief report ready to pair with the autopsy results so that we can get Mr. Phillips back to St. Louis for services."

"I appreciate that, Officer Pearson."

I smiled behind my hand. Chief Detective Pearson hated being called Officer Pearson.

"Can I see your driver's license please, Ms. Vila?" Liselle handed it to him. Pearson wrote down her name, some numbers, and then said, "Is this your current address?"

"It is."

He handed the card back. "Thank you. When did you meet Mr. Phillips?"

"A little over a month ago."

"Down in St. Louis?"

"Yes."

"Were you dating?"

"We went out a few times."

"And were you here at the wedding together? As a date?"

"We were."

"How did you meet Mr. Phillips?"

"At a social gathering."

"Did he have any health conditions?"

"Not that I'm aware of—" she caught herself "—*was* aware of. I assume his children would be better people to ask about that."

"Probably. I was just wondering if you knew of anything."

"No."

"When did you get into town?"

"We came in on the second plane, Thursday night."

"The second plane?"

"The family flew in privately. Rich and I were on the second plane."

"When did the first one come in?"

"Monday. Some people made a week of it."

"What did you do here?"

"Wedding things. Rehearsal dinner Friday night, wedding Saturday."

"How about during the day Friday?"

"Rich and some of the family went golfing."

"You?"

"No."

"Spa day?"

Liselle raised an eyebrow. "I had business in southeast Detroit."

Pearson's brow furrowed for a moment before he said, "What kind?"

"I was checking certain trees there."

Pearson looked honestly quizzical. "Why did you do that?"

"I work for the Forest Service in cooperation with the Missouri Department of Natural Resources. I'm a biologist."

"Really?" Pearson said and immediately looked like he wanted to take it back.

Liselle stared at him.

"Right," said Pearson. He looked back at his paper and said, "Any indication that Mr. Phillips wasn't feeling well?"

Liselle shook her head. "None. We had a great time at the dinner Friday. He told me he'd golfed well that day. And we were enjoying ourselves at the wedding until…"

Pearson waited a moment before he said, "And you danced?"

Liselle's eyes didn't leave Pearson's. "We danced."

"Any indication he wasn't feeling well at the wedding?"

Liselle started to speak, stopped and cleared her throat, then said, "Not until he collapsed."

Pearson nodded and said in his best good-cop voice, "Can you tell me what happened?"

Liselle nodded back. "We had cocktails and circulated before dinner—there were a lot of people there that Rich wanted to see. We ate dinner and had some cake. We visited a little more after dinner and then when they opened up the dance floor, we danced. We were dancing toward the end of the evening and then Rich just collapsed."

Liselle paused.

Pearson handed her a tissue, but Liselle wasn't crying. She took the tissue, folded it in her hand, and said, "He was unconscious and we couldn't revive him. Then the ambulance came and took him away and..."

Pearson nodded. "Any complaints during the evening?"

"None."

"Notice anything unusual?"

"No."

Pearson checked some boxes, straightened some papers, then lifted his head and smiled. "Thank you for coming in today, Ms. Vila. Will you be staying in town for a little while yet?"

"Until..." She stopped, cleared her throat, then said, "Until Rich can go home."

Pearson stood. "That's all, Ms. Vila, thank you. And my condolences."

"Thank you, Officer Pearson." Liselle stood, nodded, and walked out.

I shook Pearson's hand and he was so busy watching Liselle leave that he forgot to try to crush it. "Let me know if you need anything else," I said.

"Hmm, oh yeah, right." Pearson pulled his eyes away and

came back to himself. "I doubt I will. Seems like the geezer bit off more than he could chew and his heart gave out."

"Right. See you." I left.

I didn't see Liselle in the lobby so I hustled out to find her standing outside, face tilted up to the sun. "Thought I'd lost you."

She smiled. "Not this time. So what happens next?"

"The autopsy will take another day or two. After that, the coroner will release the body and you'll be able to take him home."

"I won't be taking him home," she said. "But I want to make sure he's on his way."

Judging from what I'd seen of Richard Phillips' kids last night, I thought she was right. "What are you going to do until then?" I said.

"Work. I brought my computer and there are a couple of things I can check out here."

"Like what?"

She shrugged. "Biology stuff. I'm a woodland biologist so I thought I'd check out Groves State Park."

I stared at her. "Really?"

She nodded. "It'll give me some perspective on what I'm doing back home. Why?"

"I just...I know someone that worked there, at the park."

"Oh? Doing what?"

"A lot of monitoring—water quality, invasive species, tree health."

Liselle looked at me directly for what felt like the first time. "Could you put me in touch with them? I'd love to pick their brains about what they've done up here."

"It was my wife."

"Perfect. Can you introduce me?"

"I'm sorry. She's passed."

Liselle looked embarrassed. "I'm sorry, you're still wearing..." She trailed off and pointed at my hand.

I smiled. "Not quite ready to take it off."

She looked at me seriously before she nodded and said, "I understand. I'd love to hear about what she was working on though, if you don't mind. Care to join me for lunch?"

"Sure. What are you in the mood for?"

"Anything." She smiled. "As long as we can eat outside."

I DECIDED TO TAKE HER TO THE RAILCAR, A RESTAURANT THAT HAD been renovated out of the remnants of a used brick waystation on an abandoned spur of railroad. The Railcar had a back patio that overlooked a stream (that the railroad had used to supply the water tower that filled the steam engines) and the woods beyond. Add to that the smell of hickory smoke and just about the best barbecue you could find and you had an outstanding outdoor dining experience.

"How's this?" I said as we picked a table.

"Perfect." She took the seat facing out toward the woods and smiled. "Where are we?"

"We're up about twenty minutes into Michigan. Two-thirds of Carrefour is in Ohio and the northern third is in Michigan. We're just outside the northern city limits."

"It seems quieter," she said.

"It is. Greener too."

"I can see that. How far is the state park from here?"

"Only another twenty-five minutes or so. The hills start just outside of town."

The waitress gave us waters and menus and left us to look. As she opened the menu, Liselle asked, "So what did your wife do?"

"She worked for the Michigan Department of Natural Resources. She checked the water quality of the lakes and rivers, originally. Later, they had her assess tree health and do what she could to enforce wood quarantines."

Liselle's eyes became intent again. "Wood quarantines?"

I nodded. "About five years ago that was all she was doing. The emerald ash borer started in Detroit not too far from here and she did her best to keep it from spreading for a long time."

I stopped because this was usually the point where people asked what an emerald ash borer was. Instead, Liselle's strange intensity deepened and she said, "Are you serious?"

"Why wouldn't I be?"

"Because that's what I'm working on."

"What do you mean?"

"I mean I work for the Forestry Service and the State of Missouri down near the Mark Twain National Forest. We've been quarantining our woods against the emerald ash borer. It's not in all the counties yet, but it's close. I'm doing all I can to keep it out."

It was my turn to stare at her. "Really?"

"Really."

I shook my head and laughed. "I did not expect to be having another conversation about that stupid bug."

"She talked about it?"

"A lot."

"Does she have any research, anything they tried?"

"I'm sure her work has something. I have to warn you though, it wasn't very successful."

She shook her head. "We haven't been either. But we have to try." She thought. "Are there places I can go look?"

"Of course. We're not fifteen minutes from one of the biggest ash groves you've ever seen."

Her face fell. "Are they all dead?"

"Pretty much."

I can't describe the look on her face then except to say that it seemed that she went very far away for a little bit. I let her be and looked at the menu although I already knew what I was going to have. Eventually, she came back and said, "How many days do you think it'll be before…Richard can go home?"

"I think it will be another couple of days yet."

She nodded. "That'll give me some time to explore. I'm sorry your wife can't show me around."

"Me too." I pointed at her menu. "The beef brisket is delicious."

6

AFTER WE ATE, I DROPPED LISELLE back at her hotel and went to the office. My office was located on the Ohio side of Carrefour in a professional building made of glass and steel and brick that was the home to small practices of doctors, lawyers, and accountants. It didn't have a high-rise view and it wasn't a quaint old building; it looked exactly like what it was, a functional, professional office space.

After we'd handled a murder case this past summer, my associate Daniel Reddy and I had taken over a suite of three offices and a conference room that made up the bulk of the third floor. It was overkill for the two of us, but it was paid for through the next year so we'd found ourselves staying up there. Danny was waiting for me when I arrived. He was tall and thin and I'm pretty sure the latter was the result of constant, nervous motion. Case in point, he was flapping a sheaf of papers as I entered.

"The Jackson brief is due today," he said in greeting.

"Did you finish it?"

"Yes."

Danny could handle a motion like that in his sleep but he didn't believe it yet. "I'll look at it."

"We only have a couple of hours."

"I know. I'll take care of it."

"What were you doing?"

"Emergency meeting with Pearson this morning."

That broke through the Jackson-brief-feedback-loop and he made a face. "Lucky you. What for?" Danny's face grew stern. "We're not doing another criminal case, are we?"

"No. Just baby-sitting a witness interview. An old guy died at a wedding this weekend. The Chief Detective in Charge of Serious Crimes for Carrefour, Ohio was just interviewing the man's date."

Danny cocked his head. "How'd he die?"

"Heart attack is my guess."

"And Pearson was interviewing people?"

"I should have said rich, old guy. Pearson knows people will be asking for an official cause so he's covering his bases. Nothing major."

With that path traversed, Danny started shaking the papers in his hand again.

"Got it, got it," I said. "Did you email it to me?"

Danny nodded.

"I'll get it done so you can file it."

"Thanks," Danny said and went back to his office.

I was just turning on my computer when my phone buzzed. Matt Branson.

"Hey, Matty."

"Hey, Shep. I'm sorry to bother you. Do you have a second?"

"Sure. What's up?"

"My sister's new family is freaking out about how long this autopsy's going to take. Ellie and Jake already left on their honeymoon so you can guess who they're asking."

"Lucky you."

"Exactly. You know the coroner, right?"

"I do. Want me to call him?"

"Could you?"

"He won't give me the results but he'll let me know when to expect them."

I heard Matt sigh. "Anything to call off the dogs, man. Jake's parents are fine but Richard's kids …"

"I've met them."

"That's right, at the hospital. They haven't calmed down. I think they've gotten worse."

"I'll call the coroner right now and get back to you."

"Thanks, Shep. Beer's on me."

"Don't worry about it."

We hung up and I pulled up Ray Gerchuck on my contact list.

Ray Gerchuk was the coroner for the city of Carrefour. Although we had most recently been on opposite sides of a case, Ray was a true professional and called things exactly like he saw them. He was an altogether cheerful and pleasant man in a way that you didn't expect from a coroner and you could hear it in his voice when he answered his phone.

"Nate? I hope this is an invitation to go fishing before it gets too cold."

"Hi, Ray. You know my dad will take you out on the boat anytime."

"I'm gonna have to take him up on that. U of M has a home game this week but maybe next weekend."

"You know he'd love it, but you're going to have a hard time getting him to take Michigan's schedule into account."

"Such a good man but so misguided. Don't know how he ever stumbled into that whole Spartan thing."

"You know, you pay enough in tuition and it has a way of changing your view of things."

Ray chuckled. "I suppose that's true. So, if you can't take me fishing, what can I do for you?"

"I'm calling on the Richard Phillips case."

"I didn't realize there was one."

"No, not a criminal case, I meant the autopsy. Are you doing it?"

"I am."

"I'm friends with Matt Branson and the Phillips are now his sister's in-laws."

"Oh right, right."

"I guess the Phillips are getting antsy because they don't know what to expect timing-wise so I said I'd call you and find out."

"Sure. I expect to be done in a couple of days. Maybe even tomorrow. Matt can call me anytime for a status update if he wants."

"That's about what I thought. Toxicology will be another six to eight weeks?"

"Look at you, Mister Lawyer. It's like you're reading my emails. That's exactly what it'll be." Ray paused. "I can't give out any preliminary results."

"I wouldn't expect you to. I was just calling to find out when the family could expect to hear from you. I'll have Matt email you with who to contact."

"Perfect. How are things otherwise?"

"Better now that I don't have to go up against you on the stand again."

Ray laughed. "I told you, I'm neutral so we weren't against each other. Besides, you won, so it's bad form to complain."

I laughed. "I guess so. I'll tell my dad to call you."

"Excellent. Take care, Nate."

I hung up then texted Matt the information about the autopsy results and toxicology tests. I gave him Ray's contact info so the family could let Ray know who should receive the test results.

Matt texted me back within seconds. *Thanks, man! I know what a dog's rawhide feels like right now.*

I laughed and sent him a GIF of a dog delightedly chomping on a huge bone then turned my attention to Danny's brief. That pretty much took me the rest of the day.

∽

I was at home reading that night when I got a text with a 573-area code that said, *Was your wife Sarah Shepherd?*

It was jarring. I felt a surge at Sarah's name and confusion at the text out of the blue until I realized that I'd received a text earlier from the same number.

Liselle. Apparently, I was going to have to add her to my contacts.

I texted back. *Yes. Why?*

I've already read three of her papers. We've been studying everything they did up here, in Michigan. I didn't connect the names when we were talking earlier. Stupid.

That brought back a lot of late-night conversations, some of them filled with frustration and anger.

Not much worked up here, I texted.

True.

But the borer had a pretty big head start by the time they found it.

That's what we're hoping.

Three dots blinked on my phone, then another text from Liselle popped up. *She writes about Groves State Park. Is that the place you were talking about yesterday, with the ash grove?*

Yes.

Could you take me there?

I thought and closed the text app so that she couldn't see the telltale dots that I was thinking. I thought for a little longer then reopened the app and typed, *Sure.*

Thanks! When?

No problem. I thought about my schedule. *Tomorrow afternoon?*

Perfect.

I'll text you when I'm finishing up.

Great. Thanks!

I closed my phone and reopened my book. A few minutes later, I started to read.

7

The next day, I squeezed a day's worth of work into the morning, attended a pretrial by phone right after lunch, then changed clothes and picked Liselle up from the hotel. She wore a heavy blue denim shirt, jeans, and hiking boots, which was exactly what you'd expect to traipse around in the woods on a sunny, cool day in Michigan. Her pale blonde hair was loose and a little curlier than it had been at the wedding. She hopped into the Jeep and we took off for the state park.

"I'm sorry I was so blunt last night," she said. "When I looked back at my text this morning, I realized it must've come out of the blue."

"A little. But it made sense once you told me what was going on. You've really read Sarah's work?"

"The whole series. Four years ago, right after she published it. The invasion hit Michigan about ten years before us."

I thought about the ash trees that we were driving toward. "Are you sure you want to see this then?"

"I've seen dead ash trees before," she said.

"I'm sure you have but this is...concentrated. It's pretty

jarring." I bit the inside of my cheek. "It upset Sarah every time she went back."

"You should always know what you're fighting for. And against."

"I suppose so."

Liselle pointed at the sunroof. "Do you mind? It's beautiful today."

"Go ahead."

Liselle opened the sunroof and I had to admit that the wind and the sun felt good after being cooped up all morning in the office. We had a little bit of time before we got to Groves State Park, so I said, "Biology, huh?"

Yes, I am that smooth.

"Yes."

"Do you have a specialty?"

Her hair was whipping around her eyes so she pushed it back and said, "Woodland management is the technical term. Basically though, I like working with trees. Always have."

"Did you grow up near the woods or in the city?"

"I'm from a little town down by the Mark Twain National Forest, just south of St. Louis."

I thought. "I don't know that area. Is that in the Ozarks?"

She nodded. "It is. The Forest isn't as big as some of the other national parks but there's mountains and woods and some of the most beautiful springs you'll ever see."

"Did you study down there too?"

She nodded. "I did. Went to Washington University right there in St. Louis. What about your wife?"

"Michigan State. She wanted to stay close to home."

"Me too. I was the first Vila to come down out of the mountains and go to university. I found I didn't want to go too far away either."

I smiled. "You can take the girl out of the woods…"

Liselle smiled back. "But she won't enjoy it." She looked out the window.

"Is that where you live now?"

"I live in Fredericktown. Far enough away that we're right there in the Forest but close enough to St. Louis that I can get there when I have to."

"Is that where you grew up?"

"In a smaller place if you can believe it, farther west and farther in." Her eyes narrowed and she pushed her hair back again. "That's why this invasion matters so much to me."

We drove on until I saw the little brown and white sign identifying the turn-off for Groves State Park and I took it. About ten minutes later, after we'd driven north on a quiet road through some hills and trees, we came to the park entrance and wound our way to a parking lot, which was mostly empty since it was a weekday afternoon.

"How long a walk is it?" Liselle asked as she got out.

"About a quarter of a mile to the trail. See that lake there?"

She nodded.

"That's Glass Lake. There are trails that run all the way around the lake and connect to other lakes and woods for about a seventy square mile area."

She shaded her eyes and smiled. "Perfect."

So I led her to the trail that went through the Groves.

∼

ON THE NORTH SIDE OF GLASS LAKE, THERE IS A GROVE OF TREES. That's not unusual for Michigan as most of its lakes are surrounded by woods, at least until cottage-makers clear them. What is unusual is that this particular grove is made up of seven individual types of trees that have grown in clusters, forming seven smaller, distinct groves of trees. There's White Pine, Sugar

Maple, Red Oak, Black Cherry, Quaking Aspen, Eastern Hemlock.

And Ash.

Each section of the grove is comprised of trees of only the one type which, in these days of planting and husbandry, wouldn't surprise you—except that the Grove is not the result of the Michigan DNR or Michigan State University's famous horticulture department. By all accounts, the Grove is natural and unexplainable. Legend has it that when French explorers found Glass Lake about three hundred years ago, the Grove was already there and that, when they learned the language enough to ask, members of the First Nations told them that it had been there as long as they remembered too. A theory popped up now and then about how the soil in each area of the Grove was conducive to that particular tree, but that really didn't explain it. Eventually, the state stopped trying and simply embraced it, made it part of a state park, and built a walking trail so that people could enjoy it.

At the head of the trail, there was an eight-foot-tall sign letting us know that we were about to enter the Groves Trail, identifying the seven trees, and giving a brief history. Sarah and I had long since stopped reading it but Liselle had never been here, so we paused, and she read, and I turned my face up to enjoy the fall sun. There weren't any other hikers on the trail just then, which was nice because the quiet made it even more enjoyable. Liselle didn't say anything as she finished and walked on. Her eyes were intent as she looked around, as if she were devouring every bit of information the trees could give her.

I had seen that look before.

Though her eyes were intense, her pace was relaxed as she took it all in. "The White Pine is first then?" she said.

"Yep."

As we walked into the first layer, pine trees towered almost one hundred and fifty feet above us. The canopy was solid but not overcrowded and we walked easily down the path among the trees.

"How far north do the trees go?"

"Almost a mile."

Her eyes widened. "Each section?"

I nodded.

"Amazing."

"It is."

She didn't seem inclined to go off the path just then. She simply walked and looked from side to side. Glass Lake was visible through the trees on our left, about a hundred feet away. On the right though, it was pines as far as the eye could see.

We walked for a time, easily and quiet. Then it changed. There wasn't a hard, straight line, but in the space of no more than fifty steps, the towering white pines gave way to the dark green leaves of sugar maples. Now Liselle did leave the path and she went over and put her hand on one of the trees. These were shorter, closer to one hundred feet, and Liselle shook her head. "This must be beautiful later in the fall."

"All orange and yellow. They're pretty brilliant."

"So old," she said.

"How many years do you think?"

Liselle looked up and reached around the trunk with both arms. "They can live over four hundred years. Some of these are close."

She patted the tree and we continued to walk along the path. It was darker in this section, as the broad green leaves blocked out more of the light than the pine needles had.

"I can't believe no one ever logged this," she said.

"Sarah said that the logging was always farther north and the farmers never got this far. Then, by the fifties, no one wanted to see it destroyed."

"No, you wouldn't think so."

"MSU led an effort to preserve it and a state park was born."

"That was well done."

We walked for a time and again the trees changed over the course of about fifty steps. The trees grew shorter again, to maybe seventy-five feet or so, and the smell of cherries and the chirping of birds became pronounced. Now Liselle couldn't contain herself. She went right over to a tree and ran her hands along the trunk. "Black cherry," she said. "This really goes on for a mile?"

"All the way to the Cache River Rapids."

"What a sight this must be in the spring."

"White flowers everywhere."

She smiled, joyful. She moved to a tree with a branch hanging low enough to reach up and grab a handful of the small, dark cherries. "Not quite in season," she said but she took a bite anyway. She ate four in quick succession, then puckered at the sourness and laughed. "Should have known better," she said, wiping a little juice from the side of her mouth. "Had to try them, though."

I smiled and she wandered a little ways off between the trees, putting one hand out and then the other.

"Do you have anything like this in Missouri?"

"Not with so many separate groves. Usually it's just one." She shook her head. "I just don't see how it's possible."

"Sarah told me that the people of the First Nations said that this was how the trees chose to grow. The French explorers told tales of dryads guarding the Grove and trappers went missing just enough to encourage them." For some reason, recounting this made me hear Sarah's voice fairly clearly for a moment. That was getting harder to do. I paused, then said, "She thought it was as good an explanation as modern science had found."

"A spirit protecting the trees would solve a lot of problems," Liselle said, and came back to the path.

We walked on. The trees were shorter and the leaves farther apart in this section so it was noticeably lighter than in the other two. The sun shone through in one of those picturesque views where you can actually see the rays of light between the trees. We walked through it and I enjoyed the smell of the cherries and the songs of the birds and the rays of light that blinked through to warm my skin after weeks of sitting in a cold antiseptic office surrounded by plastic and metal. And, if I was telling the truth, I enjoyed walking next to someone who was so clearly enthralled by the beauty of the woods. We walked for a time and then, as before, over the course of about fifty steps, it all changed.

Everything was dead. Every single tree for as far as the eye could see.

The ash trees.

The trunks were tall and the branches were bare and the ash trees stretched far into the sky like dirty bones. No leaves blocked the sun so that its rays cast shadows on the bark, making the grooves seem like gashes in the bone. In the space of one hundred more steps, we left the cherry trees behind and were left standing in a silent graveyard.

Liselle stopped. Her face was horrified, her stance rigid. She just stared and I had to admit that, even though I'd seen it many times, the impact of going from the other trees to this was stark and brutal.

"It's one thing to read about it," I said. "It's another to see it."

She still stood there, staring. Finally, she said, "A mile?"

I nodded. "Just like the others."

And then, if possible, her face got worse. She looked at me with what I took to be pain and it seemed that her light green eyes became a pale silver. "Except it's not just a mile. It's the whole state."

I nodded. "They killed almost every one."

She looked back at the dead trees. "When?"

"For these? A few years ago."

She took a step forward and put her hand on a trunk. She pulled her hand back as if it'd been burned. "These are dangerous."

"I know. But with the budget crisis, people don't want to pay to have them removed or to replant with something else. There are too many in neighborhoods and more public areas that take priority."

Liselle put her hand back on the tree, focused. "Have any of them been studied?"

"Quite a few. Follow me." I'd been this way with Sarah many times so I guided Liselle farther up the path to where it bent around a particularly large, but still very dead, ash tree. We went around the tree to the side away from the path where a section of the bark had been stripped away. A swirl of trails and crisscrossing paths, lighter than the flesh of the tree, swirled around the trunk. Liselle bent down and put her hand on it.

"They monitored the trees to mark the borers' progress," I said. "In the space of a year, they went from one tree in twenty being infected to all of them."

"There was nothing they could do?"

"Not here. The borers had already taken hold by the time they were found."

"So your wife just had to watch them die?"

I nodded. "She fought them in other places. But there was nothing to be done here."

"That must've been terrible for her."

There are worse things. "It was."

"But she kept fighting them?"

"She did."

"She sounds like a good woman."

"She was."

"I would have liked to have met her."

"I wish you could. You'd have a lot to talk about."

We started to walk again and it turns out that a grove of dead ash trees and the mention of my wife Sarah gave us both something to think about so we didn't talk. Instead, we walked, each weighed down by a stark reminder of loss.

As we walked, the trunks changed from gray to white and the leaves gradually returned. The trunks on the new trees were pale with knobs of black on them, as if they had survived the carnage next to them, but just barely.

"Quaking Aspen," she said and put a hand on a tree and I swear it seemed to me that she took comfort from the fact that it was alive.

She pushed off then and we walked down the trail until eventually we were surrounded by green leaves and pale trunks. Where she had wandered around before, she now walked with a more purposeful stride, barely looking at the surrounding trees.

"How far along are you in Missouri?" I said.

She didn't look at me. "It's just starting."

We didn't say anything else as the trees grew taller and the pale bark changed to dark and the leaves grew more lobes and the trail became shadowed as red oak trees blotted out the sun. The strength of those trees after the devastation of the ash was palpable. Liselle's interest seemed to be piqued again but much of the wonder she'd displayed on the first half of the trail seemed to be gone.

We walked through the section of red oak and entered the last section of the Grove, which was eastern hemlock. The great old trees grew well over one hundred feet tall, were eight to ten feet around, and had what non-woodland biologists would think of as soft needles rather than of leaves.

"So bounded on each side by hemlock and pine?" said Liselle.

I nodded. "With the cherry and ash in the middle."

"That's all of it?"

"It is."

She looked around. "Our car is at the other end of the trail."

I nodded. "The trail loops around."

"So we have to go back through again?"

"Yes."

Panic is too strong a word for what flashed across her face; it was like right before you rip off a Band-Aid or swallow some particularly bitter medicine. Whatever it was, purpose quickly replaced it. "Let's go then."

We followed the path as it looped around away from the lake and back through the Grove. Liselle was still attentive, but we were walking far more quickly now and she seemed focused in a different way. She continued to stop here and there, but now it was if she was looking for specific things. As we came back to the section of ash, she didn't hesitate and strode through, taking it all in. As she looked at the trees beyond me, I caught a glimpse of her face.

It was ferocious.

We went back through the cherry and the sugar maple and the pine and then left the trail and got into my Jeep. We didn't talk as I drove her back to her hotel and, honestly, I didn't mind. As we pulled in, she said, "I appreciate you taking me out there today. Very much. I realize it couldn't have been easy."

"It was actually. It was nice to be back out there. It's been awhile."

We said good-bye and she got out of the car and closed the door. She turned back then and made a gesture for me to roll down the window. I did. She leaned in far enough that her pale blonde hair hung inside the car. "Do you mind if I get in touch if I have to follow up on your wife's research?"

"Not at all. I don't know much about it, but I can put you in touch with people if you need me to."

"Thanks." She stood up and tapped the car roof and I rolled up the window and pulled away.

When I checked the rearview mirror, she was gone.

8

I had just arrived at my office the next morning when my phone buzzed. Mitch Pearson, Chief Detective in Charge of Serious Crimes for Carrefour, Ohio.

"Nate Shepherd," I said. Why let him know I had him as a contact in my phone?

"Nate, it's Mitch Pearson."

"What's up, Mitch?"

"The Phillips autopsy has been completed. I think that the family is going to take him home today."

"Great. Do you need Matt's contact information to let them know?"

"No."

"Thanks for letting me know then."

"This isn't a courtesy call, Nate. I'd like to talk to Ms. Vila."

Shit. "Sure. Why?"

"I have a few more questions for her."

"About?"

"I'll explain when you come down here."

This, as you might imagine, was not good. "When?"

"Before she leaves. Anytime is fine. Just let me know you're coming so that I'm here."

"No problem. What did the autopsy show?"

"It's all doctor stuff. I'll give you a copy when you come down."

"All right. I'll get a hold of her and let you know."

"Thanks, Nate. I'll see you then."

I hung up and dialed Liselle. "Hi, Nate," she said.

"Two things. The autopsy is done so they'll be releasing Richard's body today. I assume the family will be going back now."

"Okay."

She didn't ask what the autopsy found. I took that as a good sign.

"Second, Detective Pearson wants to talk to you again."

Silence. Then, "Why?"

"He didn't say."

"Should I do it?"

"I think we should go down and see what he wants. I'll go with you and cut things off if things don't seem to be going well."

"All right. When?"

"I'll pick you up in an hour. Sound good?"

"Perfect. I'll see you then."

We hung up. I immediately called Ray Gerchuk. I'll be damned if I was going to walk into Mitch Pearson's office not knowing what the autopsy had found.

"Nate," Ray said when he picked up the phone. "Is this my fishing invitation?"

"Afraid it's work again, Ray."

"All of this work is getting in the way of a reduction in the bass population."

"My dad awaits your call. I heard you finished the Phillips autopsy?"

"I did."

"What did you find?"

"Why do you ask?"

"Pearson called me and said he'd give me a copy but that he didn't want to explain all the doctor stuff on the phone. So I thought I'd call the doctor about the stuff."

There was silence for a moment before Ray said, "I'm not going to ask if he's going to give it to you as part of questioning of a witness since that's not relevant to my finding."

I didn't say anything.

"So, since an autopsy is public record, I will tell you that the cause of death was likely a heart arrhythmia."

"Yeah?"

"Yeah. It doesn't look like there was a blockage or a heart attack. His heart was enlarged from a lifetime of high blood pressure and it appears that he was taking some blood pressure medication to control it. I think he sustained an irregular heart rhythm and died. He was a pretty fit guy and he was relatively young—" he chuckled "—or at least fifty-nine seems young to me now but, given the celebration that weekend, I'm not surprised. It happens more often than you think."

"Hmm. So natural causes?"

"Looks that way to me."

"Thanks, Ray."

"I'm not kidding, Nate. The next time you call me it had better be to let me know when the winch on that boat is dropping."

"Got it. Take care."

I hung up and thought. Fifty-nine-year-old man. Heart arrhythmia. Natural causes. It all seemed pretty normal. Tragic, but normal.

So why did Pearson want to question Liselle again?

I didn't know. So I emailed Pearson to let him know when we'd be there and left to pick up Liselle.

∼

"I'm sorry to ask you back down here again," said Mitch Pearson. "Thanks for coming."

The thing about Pearson is that he's a pretty good investigator, but he's a lousy actor. As we sat on the other side of the desk in his office, his manner was different than the first time we'd met. Before, he was asking questions by rote, without much care about the answers except that they were documented in his file. This time though, it was clear from the moment we walked in that he was focused and that he had a purpose.

"No problem," I said. "You mentioned that you'd have the autopsy for us?"

Irritation flashed across Pearson's face and was gone. I'd gotten the first question in and there was no good reason for him to refuse to answer it, not if he was going to continue to play good cop.

"Sure. Here you go, Nate."

He handed it to me and I scanned it to make sure the findings on the first page were "cardiac event, likely heart arrhythmia, natural causes." They were.

While I pretended to read it, Pearson said, "How long did you say you knew Mr. Phillips, Ms. Vila?"

"A little over a month. Six weeks maybe."

"Did Mr. Phillips ever discuss any health conditions with you?"

"His?"

"Yes."

"No. Wait, I take that back. I think he said once that his knee was bothering him and that's why he had switched to biking instead of running."

"You mentioned that you were staying with Mr. Phillips on this trip?"

"I don't believe I did mention that Mr. Pearson."

"You were though?"

"That seems personal."

"Okay. Family members of his mentioned to me that you were staying with him on this trip."

"His family certainly is going through a tough time. I'm glad you're helping them."

"In the six weeks that you knew Mr. Phillips, did you have access to his medications?"

"What medications?"

"Any of them."

"I'm not saying which medications, Officer Pearson. I'm saying that I didn't know that Rich took medications."

"So that's a 'no?'"

"That's exactly what I said."

"How did you meet Mr. Phillips?"

"A gala for Gateway Animal Rescue."

Pearson raised an eyebrow.

"It turned out we both love dogs. That's what got us talking."

"Do you have a dog?"

"Not right now. Mine passed last spring."

"I'm sorry. It's terrible when that happens."

"It is. Rich had a couple though. Ozzie and Tony. They're great."

"So you had been to Mr. Phillips' house?"

"Of course."

"I see. So you were a member of the Humane Society?"

"I am. They do good work."

"Are you a member of other organizations like that?"

"Of course. I work as a biologist so there are a number of groups that support woodland wildlife and the environment."

"The State Natural Resource Board?"

"For Missouri, yes."

"The Environmental Fund?"

"I've donated. I'm not a member."

"PETA?"

"I was once, years ago. They lost me when they started throwing paint on people."

"The Arbor Society?"

"Trees are the reason we breathe."

"The Last Auk?"

"Every day sees another species go extinct."

Pearson was nodding and writing. His face went casual, his voice nonchalant. "How about the Forest Initiative?"

"That's literally what I do, Officer Pearson. I work to save Missouri's forests."

"So, yes?" Like I said, Pearson was a shitty actor. His tone was that of a man checking the bet with a pair of pocket kings. Time to get involved.

"I'm not sure why all that's relevant, Mitch," I said. "I'm sure we can get you a resume if it really matters to you."

"That's not necessary, Nate. You know that Mr. Phillips was the head of Doprava Company, right, Ms. Vila?"

"I'm from Missouri, Officer Pearson. Everyone knows that the Phillips run Doprava."

"You know that a lot of these groups you're a part of have a problem with Doprava?"

"These groups are big organizations, Officer Pearson, and that's a very general question."

"They see Doprava as a bad actor against the environment, don't they?"

"I don't know who the 'they' is that you're talking about."

"The groups that you're part of."

"I would assume that all groups have things they agree and disagree on."

Pearson nodded his head. "Tell me about Ribbon Falls."

"What's that?" I said.

Pearson didn't look at me. "Your client knows."

I didn't know. And I'd be damned if I was going to have my client answer a question I didn't know the answer to in front of the Chief Detective for Serious Crimes of Carrefour, Ohio.

"Well, Mitch, my client has a plane to catch. I'm afraid we're going to have to get going."

Pearson raised an eyebrow. "The Phillips told me that their planes weren't leaving until later tonight."

"I'm not going with the Phillips," said Liselle.

"No, I don't suppose you are. I'd like you to stay in town."

"I have to get back to work."

Pearson smirked. "Biology emergency?"

"Actually, yes."

"It would be better if you stayed."

"Interesting," I said. "Did I miss the part where Ms. Vila was arrested?"

"No one's talking about an arrest."

"Well, then your request has been respectfully declined because Ms. Vila is going home."

Pearson nodded. "Saving the environment is a never-ending job, isn't it?"

"For which we can all be grateful." I stood. "Thanks for the autopsy, Mitch. I'm sure it's hard for the family, and for my client, to lose someone unexpectedly to natural causes like that."

Pearson nodded his head and because he was who he was he couldn't stop the smirk. "I'm sure I'll be back in touch. Probably in about six weeks."

"I look forward to it."

Pearson offered his hand and Liselle beat me to it and shook it. If Pearson tried to squeeze her hand, she showed no sign of it.

He tried it with me again, as always. The man really did have issues.

"See you, Mitch," I said, and we walked out.

"It seems to me that we need to have a talk," I said.

Liselle's eyes were green calm. "If you think so."

"Let's get lunch. Then I'll take you to the airport."

"I liked that Railcar place. Let's eat outside."

So we did.

9

"A venison Philly?" said Liselle as she scanned the menu. "That sounds good."

"Bow season hasn't started yet," I said. "They're not serving it for another couple of weeks."

"Too bad. I'll have to come back for it."

"Pearson said you might have to."

Liselle didn't take her eyes off the menu. "Pearson said a lot of things."

"He was interested in the groups you're a member of."

She nodded. "He was. I'd bet your wife was a member of half of them too."

"I'm sure she was. But she wasn't dating the head of a large industrial company either."

Liselle raised her eyes. "Are you going to climb into my bed now too? Because I didn't care to have Officer Pearson in it."

Trial lawyers don't blush so I didn't, but her blunt gaze was still disconcerting.

"No. I'm not. But Pearson seems to think it's important so he's working what he thinks is an angle. Are any of those organizations directly opposed to Doprava?"

Liselle returned to the menu. "It would be crazy to go against Doprava. They own half of St. Louis."

"That doesn't answer my question."

She folded her menu. "Nate, I care deeply about the environment in general and for the woods and forests of Missouri in particular. I'm sure my position diverges from Doprava and Rich sometimes. So what?"

I nodded. "So I know Pearson. Those questions were focused on building something."

"What could he possibly be building?"

The waitress came and we both wound up ordering a beef brisket sandwich and coleslaw. By the time she left, I decided not to answer her question and instead said, "He thinks he might find something in the toxicology report. That's what the 'six weeks' reference was to."

She sipped a sweet tea. "The doctor said Rich had an arrhythmia, so why is Pearson so interested?"

"My guess is that the family is chewing his ear pretty good." My next comment was delicate, but it had to be said because I was sure it was affecting the dynamics. "And that he's prejudiced enough by the optics to take a look."

She raised a pale eyebrow. "The optics?"

I shrugged. "There are dozens of movies and hundreds of books where the beautiful young girlfriend is the suspect in the death of the rich older man. A stark difference in philosophies between you and Richard only accentuates that perception."

Liselle folded her hands and when she spoke, her voice was cool. "That's a pretty offensive cliché to someone with a Ph.D., Nate."

"I didn't say I think it, Liselle. I'm saying that those optics and the kids' pressure are driving Pearson's investigation."

Liselle shook her head. "We weren't dating long enough for Bre or Andrew to resent me."

I figured it would mostly be Bre doing the resenting but I kept that observation to myself. "As long as we're on stereotypes, can I assume that since you only dated a month that you're not in the will?"

"I'm sure I'm not. And I wouldn't want to be."

I nodded. "Good. So what's this Ribbon Falls thing he was asking you about?"

Liselle took another sip of tea before she said, "Doprava is one of the largest land-owners in Missouri. It was going to lease some of that land for fracking. People protested it at Ribbon Falls."

"You went?"

"I did."

"Why?"

"Do you have any idea what fracking does to the surrounding area?"

"I can guess."

"This site was right next to Ribbon Falls. It would've jeopardized the water supply for the whole southwest section of the state, including the national forest. With my knowledge and my job, it seemed important for me to be there."

"Any violence?"

"Not by me."

"By others?"

"There were demonstrations, blocking equipment, that sort of thing. But Nate, what in the world does that have to do with Rich's death?"

"Nothing. It's goes back to the optics if something does come up."

Liselle raised both eyebrows. "You don't have witchcraft trials here, do you?"

I smiled. "Not recently. Why?"

"Men's hearts stop, Nate. It doesn't mean a woman did it."

"Agreed."

The brisket arrived and we began to eat and I managed not to drip tangy sauce and brisket juice onto my tie. Liselle dove right in, raising my opinion of her.

We got through a healthy portion of the brisket, with suitable expressions of reverence, when Liselle wiped the edge of her mouth with her napkin, pointed at the river, and said, "This is a nice place."

I nodded. "I like it."

"Not just here, the whole area. The hills, the lakes."

"Still flatter than what you're used to, I imagine."

"It is. A little closer to cities too. But the water and the trees make everything so green. I can see why your wife liked it."

I nodded.

Liselle started on the coleslaw before she said, "There're some sprays out of Wisconsin that have had some success with slowing the ash borer down. I may head up there later in the fall."

"Hope it works," I said, and meant it.

"Me too. I may stop in Carrefour on the way."

"We're not on the way to Wisconsin."

"I want to take a real dive into your wife's research then spend some time here on site to correlate how things progressed."

"She was thorough."

"And I'd like to see the Groves in the fall."

I nodded. "That's one of the best times."

The rest of our conversation was small talk. We'd talked so much about her that it only seemed fair when she fired back with questions of her own about me. We talked about my four nephews, my three nieces, and my two brothers. I told her about my mom and my dad and their place on the other end of Glass Lake and she commented that I was lucky to have them around and I agreed. She seemed particularly interested in the time my dad spent fishing and hunting and told me that I should try to get out there and do it more, which I couldn't really disagree with. When I told her about our weekly cookouts, she smiled and said that it sounded like fun.

She didn't offer any comments about her family and I didn't ask since I felt like I'd dug far enough into her personal life as it was. Soon enough, the brisket baskets were empty and Liselle took her last sip of sweet tea and said she really needed to go to the airport. I offered to drive her, which she accepted, and I drove her back to the hotel to pick up her things. I caught up on email and made a few calls while I waited and, a short time later, she came out with a bag that was smaller than I'd have expected for a woman gone on a long weekend to a wedding. I drove her to the Carrefour airport and the drive went quickly.

When she told me to go to the commercial departures entrance, I said, "They really made you book your own flight?"

Liselle nodded. "Steve told me again when we heard that the autopsy was finished. So Southwest it is."

I switched lanes so that I could take her to that terminal door. "Seems a little harsh."

Liselle shrugged. "They're grieving. I'm an easy focal point."

I pulled up to the curb and got out of the car. She was nice enough to let me get her bag for her out of the back. When I set it on the ground, she said, "Do you still have my number for when the toxicology results come in?"

I nodded. "I'll let you know."

"Let me give you some more digits," she said and held out her hand.

I coded my phone open and handed it to her. She bent her head down as she thumbed her way into my contacts and, after a few moments, straightened, pushed her hair back behind her ears, and handed the phone back. All the boxes for Liselle Vila—cell, work, home, email—were filled.

As I backed out to the home screen, Liselle leaned in close enough that her shoulder touched mine and said, "Is that her?"

Sarah's picture was the background on my phone.

"It is," I said and tilted it to her.

Liselle smiled. "She's beautiful."

"She is."

"You are a lucky man."

"I was."

"No, you are. No one is worse off for having someone like that in their life."

I smiled. "That's true."

Liselle smiled back. "Thanks for your help these last couple of days. You made a hard situation easier to deal with."

"No problem. I'll let you know when I hear something."

"Thanks." Liselle grabbed the handle of the bag and rolled her way toward the terminal. Two porters leapt forward to see if she needed help. She shook her head and went inside.

I hopped into the Jeep and left. On the way home, I stopped to get gas. As the dollars and gallons ticked off on the pump, I realized it had been a long time since I had spent most of the day with just one person, talking. It was different. Not good. Not bad. Just different.

The pump clicked off and I re-racked the nozzle. As I pulled out of the gas station, I decided to go in a different direction.

Half an hour later I was at Grove State Park. I got out of the car and decided that it was a beautiful day for a walk.

So that's what I did.

I lingered for a while beneath the sugar maples. They had been Sarah's favorite. They hadn't started to turn color yet, but they were close.

Fall was coming.

BRANCH

10

I was working in my office later that week when I received an email from Liselle.

> *Hi Nate, I just finished going back over Sarah's second paper. She really had some great ideas. It seemed like it was too late to implement some of them up in Michigan since they didn't know what they were fighting for so long. We may have more time here. She was something!*
>
> *Also, I received a call from the membership coordinator of the Forest Initiative today. She said that a police officer named Pearson had contacted her and wanted to know how long I'd been a member and if I was still active. What's with this guy? Should I be worried? Sorry to bother you.*
>
> *Lise*

I thought for a moment before I replied.

> *She was, Liselle. Hope her research winds up helping. She'd be glad.*

Pearson can be aggressive but your membership in an organization won't change the autopsy. Hopefully once the toxicology report comes back, he'll stop. Be careful in the meantime though and don't talk about it to anyone without a lawyer.

Take care.
Nate

I was pretty sure I was right. If the toxicology report was clean, I didn't see why Pearson would keep chasing his tail. There was nothing to do but wait.

I looked at the email a moment longer then decided that maybe there was something to be done. I pulled out my notes from our meeting, made a list of the organizations Pearson had questioned Liselle about, and added the Doprava Company to the bottom. Then I printed out the list and went to the Brickhouse.

~

THE BRICKHOUSE IS A GYM IN A RENOVATED BRICK WAREHOUSE that shares a parking lot with the Railcar. Actually, 'renovated' is too strong a word—unless by renovated you mean that the inside had been gutted so that it was all cement floor and brick walls and well-worn equipment. The only soft thing in the place was the mat in the back which the owners had eventually conceded was necessary, sometimes, for proper training.

Those owners were Olivia and Cade Brickson. As I entered the gym, Olivia was standing behind the desk. She had short, bleached white hair that swirled down in front of her left eye and the semi-reflective glasses she always wore. She was dressed for a class in black training pants and a red tank top that revealed a tattooed sleeve on her left arm. Her brother Cade was off to the side, filling an honor-system fridge with water and chocolate milk. He was a huge man with wide shoulders and traps that bulged like baseballs under his shirt. Cade looked exactly like what he was, the most fearsome heavyweight wrestler that Carrefour North had ever produced. Cade ran a bail bond company while Olivia did private investigations. Those businesses paid the bills but the gym was their passion.

Olivia put her hands on her hips as I entered. "Well, look who's here," she said. "You taking my class today, soft stuff?"

"I'm not man enough, Liv. You know that."

"You just gonna throw my weights around again?"

"Yes, ma'am."

"You shirk you shrink. Get after it."

I smiled. "I feel so motivated."

"Are you here by yourself today?"

I cocked my head. "I usually am."

"Not always, I hear."

"What are you talking about?"

The glasses always made reading Olivia's expression a little difficult but it was easy to see her smirk when she said, "Word has it that just a few short days ago, at the restaurant in this very complex, you were seen in the company of a woman ... How did they put it, Cade?"

"Way above his pay grade," said Cade and kept right on loading the chocolate milk into the refrigerator.

"That could be just about anyone," I said.

"Pale blonde hair," said Olivia. "Light green eyes. One theory was that she was a supermodel doing community service."

"I heard she'd lost a bet," said Cade.

I shrugged. "Just doing a favor for a friend."

"Somebody certainly owes somebody a favor," said Cade.

Sometimes diversion is the only tactic. "I have some research for you if you're interested," I said to Olivia. Besides being the owner of the gym and a master tormentor in the name of fitness, Olivia did research for me. Just last summer, she'd put in a lot of time on a murder case I'd defended.

"Always," she said. "What are we checking?"

I handed her the list. "Some organizations, mostly environmental-related, I think. And a company."

She scanned it. "No problem. Depth?"

"Surface. Just want to know what they're about, what they do, that kind of thing."

"You can't do it? Slow, soft, and lazy is no way to go through life, son."

"I want you to have a start in case I need more later. And fat, drunk, and stupid is what you want to avoid."

She rolled her head. "I was tailoring it to the situation. And sure."

"Thanks."

"No problem." Olivia gave me a wicked grin. "You up for a Spartan Race next weekend? There's one at the track."

"I would but I saw that it's sold out."

"I know but Abby had to cancel. Turned her ankle. You can take her spot."

"Ooooo, yeah, sorry, I'm working then."

"At seven Saturday morning?"

I grinned. "I'll make sure of it."

She smiled back. "I'm calling you now, you know."

"I'll be waiting. Thanks, Liv."

"Sure." She gestured. "Are you ever going to work out?"

"I was on my way but somebody kept asking me personal and prying questions."

"Sorry for being concerned about your welfare."

I bowed and walked to the locker room.

"I *suppose* she could have been blind," Cade said as I passed.

11

The next day was Saturday, which meant my nephew Justin had a football game. I was just walking out the door when my phone buzzed. A text from Liselle. *Can I call?*

I called her back and as she picked up, said, "Is everything okay, Liselle?"

"Hi, Nate. Yes, everything's fine. I'm sorry to bother you."

"Has Pearson called again?"

"No, no. I'm sorry, I should have thought of that. That's not why I'm calling."

"Oh. Okay. What's up?"

"Remember how I said I might take a trip to Wisconsin to talk to the manufacturer of a spray that shows some promise?"

"I do."

"They had another successful test so I'm planning on going up to Madison to check it out."

"I see."

"I was hoping to stop in Carrefour on the way back."

"Really?"

She talked a little faster now. "I've gotten through all of Sarah's articles again. I wanted to stop in the Groves to match the actual land features to Sarah's descriptions of how it progressed."

"Okay."

She paused. "I know it's a lot to ask, but do you think you could show me some of the places?"

"Liselle, I really have no idea where Sarah worked."

"No, I know that, but you know the area. I thought you would know the landmarks to help me find the places she describes."

If you know any lawyers, you know they have this annoying habit—when you suggest doing something, they immediately think of all the other things they have to do for other cases. I did the same thing now.

"It's a little hard for me to get away during the week, Liselle."

"Right, right. That's why I thought I'd come in on a Saturday."

"When were you thinking?"

"Three weeks from today. I'm making the arrangements now."

Notwithstanding my earlier conversation with Olivia, it was hard to raise a good work excuse on a Saturday.

"Sure. Just let me know when you're confirmed and I'll show you around that day. I'm booked that Sunday though."

"Saturday will be more than enough. Thanks, Nate, I really appreciate it. We're at the front end of the fight here and I'm hoping that with this head start we might be able to slow it down."

"Sure. Just let me know before you head up, okay?"

"I will."

"No calls or contacts on the other thing?"

I heard her enthusiasm dampen on the other end.

"No. I haven't talked to anyone since I got back." She paused. "They didn't let me go to the funeral."

"I'm sorry."

"It's okay. I just would've liked a chance to say good-bye that wasn't so...rushed."

"I'm sorry," I said again.

I heard her shift gears.

"Well, I need to book this flight before the price goes up. Thanks, Nate. I'll let you know when I'm confirmed."

"Talk to you soon."

I hung up. It took me a moment to realize what I'd just done. I took a moment more to realize that I was a little uncomfortable about it. But then, the more I thought, the more I realized it was just an afternoon and it was just showing a scientist some of Sarah's work so that she could build on it.

I decided that was okay. Then I checked the clock, swore, and hustled off to my nephew's football game.

∼

As I pulled into Ashland Park, I saw that both fields were occupied with twelve-year-olds running around in football helmets and pads. I hurried over to the south field to a cluster of parents wearing blue and orange. There weren't any bleachers so parents were scattered along one sideline, divided by which team they were rooting for. I saw my sister-in-law Izzy's shock of curly blonde hair next to my mom and my other sister-in-law Kate, all sitting in a row on pop-up chairs with my dad standing next to them. I said hi, kissed my mom on the cheek, and took a position between my dad and Izzy.

"Did they just start?" I asked.

"We kicked off," my dad said. "Held them to three and out and they just punted."

"Justin at linebacker?"

Izzy nodded. "Mark said he was going to alternate the kids

by quarter so Justin will play linebacker first and third and running back second and fourth."

My dad smiled. "The coach is a moron."

The coach was my brother, Mark. He was clapping and shuffling players in and out on the far sideline as we spoke.

"Where are the trolls?" I said.

"James, Taylor, and Page are over on the playground," said Izzy. "Joe is helping his dad."

I glanced over and saw Taylor, Page, and James sitting on the very top of the monkey bars, which made sense since all three climbed like monkeys. I looked across the field and smiled as I saw eight-year-old Joe standing near my brother Mark, holding a carrier with four water bottles in it. Right on cue, I heard a high little voice say, "Let's go, Cougars!" with fiery, squeaking intensity. With three-year-old Charlie on my sister-in-law Kate's lap, that meant all of us were here except my brother Tom, who was busy coaching the varsity football team.

We watched the organized chaos that is twelve-year-old football and clapped as the Cougars got a first down. As the kids went back to the huddle I said to my dad, "Ray Gerchuk said to say 'hi.'"

My dad nodded. "Where did you see Ray?"

"Talked to him on the phone the other day."

"Work?"

"Yeah. He wants to know when you two are going fishing again."

Although we were in the first days of fall, my dad was still the weathered brown of a hickory plank from fishing just about every day. "Whenever he gets his lazy ass out to my cottage is when."

"That's what I told him."

My dad looked at me.

I smiled. "Essentially."

"Talking to the coroner?" Izzy looked up from her chair, her eyes mischievous. "You're not representing rock stars again, are you?"

"No, my rock 'n' roll days are done."

"Movie stars then?"

"No."

"That's not what I heard," she said.

"What do you mean?"

"I've heard that you've been out and about with a movie star. Or someone who looks like one anyway."

"Blonde," said Kate. "Stunning. Not from around here."

Jesus Christ, Carrefour was a small town sometimes.

"That was for work," I said.

"New case?"

"Doesn't look like it." I realized that if Liselle was going to be in town three weeks from now, I needed to take some preemptive steps. "She's a biologist from down south that's studying Sarah's work. They're dealing with some of the same stuff down there that Sarah was up here."

"Emerald ash borer?" my dad said.

I nodded.

"They're never going to stop it," he said.

"Apparently, they're trying."

It takes a long time for a twelve-year-old to run sixty yards in full equipment, even with eleven guys chasing him, but that's exactly what happened and we all cheered as the Cougars' running back, Evan Green, did it. A chorus of "Good job, Evan" and "Great blocking line" followed as the kids lined up and tried, unsuccessfully, for a two-point conversion. That seemed to divert the conversation.

After the change in possession, the Cougars' defense trotted onto the field and I saw number 49 take his position on the right side behind the defensive line.

"Justin's wearing Uncle Tommy's number this year?" I asked.

"He insisted," said Izzy.

I smiled. "How did Mark take that?"

Izzy grinned. "He said that it's a great number."

"It's killing him, isn't it?"

"Absolutely."

Sometimes brothers' relationships are completely predictable.

"So, where is this beautiful biologist from?" said Izzy.

Apparently, the touchdown did not get me off the hook.

"Who said she was beautiful?" I asked.

"Literally everyone who told me about her. Where's she from?"

"Down south."

"Missouri?" said Kate.

Have I mentioned that my sisters-in-law are evil?

"Yes."

"Was she in town for the wedding?"

"Yes."

"Makes sense, that's where the groom's family is from, right?"

"They are."

I waited but they didn't ask the next question. Which was good since it meant that local people weren't associating Liselle with Richard Phillips' death. So I said, "I think she was killing two birds with one stone, going to the wedding and checking out the trees up here."

I paused, then I bit the bullet. "I think she's coming back in a few weeks to investigate some more sites."

All three Shepherd women turned.

"Really?" said my mom.

"Interesting," said Kate.

"You don't say," said Izzy.

Justin picked that moment to bail me out. He was dropping

back in coverage when a wobbly pass came over the middle. He jumped up, intercepted it, and ran down the sidelines. We all cheered and yelled as he scampered into the end zone for a touchdown. By the time they made the two-point conversion, I was able to turn the conversation to the high school's upcoming game with East Jackson.

I owed my nephew one.

When the game ended, the Cougars had beaten the Broncos 34 to 16, Justin had added one more touchdown, and my family was inoculated to the fact that I would be spotted in town with a blonde biologist at the end of the month.

It was far more pleasant than the next time we gathered together for one of my nephews.

12

I was at the office about three weeks later on a Friday afternoon when my phone buzzed. I saw the number for Ray Gerchuck and answered.

"So who won the Glass Lake bass championship, Ray?"

"Your dad and I both caught the limit so it came down to weight," Ray said. "Got him by half a pound."

"That explains why he wouldn't say when I asked him. I'll be sure to mention it to him this Sunday."

Ray chuckled. "Please do. I didn't just call to brag though. The toxicology report is back on the Phillips case."

I did the math. "Already? Shouldn't it be another couple of weeks?"

Ray paused before he said, "Let's just say that the subject's family has the means to accelerate things with the lab."

I suppose being the head of a Fortune 100 company had its perks. "What did it find?"

"Do you remember the autopsy report?" Ray asked.

"Cardiac arrest from a heart arrhythmia, right?"

"Right. The toxicology results and his medical records confirmed it."

"What did you find?"

"It's as much what I didn't find as what I did, Nate. Whenever an affluent person, especially an older man, dies like this, the first thing we look for is drugs. He was clean for all of the usual suspects—opioids, amphetamines, cocaine—anything that can cause an irregular heartbeat. Then I looked at his medical records which showed that he had a history of high blood pressure and was taking a beta blocker for it."

"What's a beta blocker?"

"A type of medication used to control high blood pressure. He was taking metoprolol. Lopressor is the brand name."

"I've seen the ads during football games. What does it do?"

"It slows your heart rate so that the blood pressure is reduced. According to his records, he had some episodes of irregular heartbeats about four years ago so that's why they put him on this particular medication. Once I found that in his records, we ran more tests and found trace amounts of the Lopressor in his system. Not as much as you would expect for the dose he was prescribed but still enough to show that he was taking his medication regularly."

"Anything else?"

"The last main thing was alcohol. It was an evening wedding, right?"

"Actually the wedding was early afternoon. The reception didn't start until six o'clock or so."

"So my guess is he did what people normally do in that circumstance—they go to the wedding and then start drinking in the afternoon. He had a fairly high blood alcohol level, about .18."

I nodded. "Too drunk to drive but not too drunk to function at a wedding reception."

"Exactly. Put all that together—high blood pressure, man in his late 50s, booze, and dancing, and you know what you get?"

"A fatal heart arrhythmia?"

"You got it. About as natural a cause as it gets."

I felt a sense of relief even though I didn't know Liselle well enough to have a reason to feel it. "Thanks, Ray."

"No problem, Nate."

A thought occurred to me. "Why did you call? I would've gotten the report eventually."

"I've been getting calls on this twice a day for three weeks, mostly from out of town folks acting like they can order everyone around."

"That sounds annoying."

"I'm not going to miss them. I'm going to call Pearson now and be done with it."

I chuckled. "Calling him second?"

"Did I mention I really don't like getting prodded?"

"I'll keep that in mind, Ray. Take care."

"You too. Say 'hi' to Mr. Second Place for me."

As we hung up, I thought for a moment. I knew the Phillips kids had an ax to grind with Liselle and I knew they wanted to blame her for his death but that should be the end of it. No matter how mad Bre Phillips was that her dad was dating someone her own age, there was nothing there.

I decided to call Liselle to give her the good news. She didn't answer so I left a message for her to call. I found that I was glad to be able to tell her that this was over.

～

AT THE END OF THE DAY JUST BEFORE I LEFT, MY PHONE RANG. It was Liselle. "Hey, Nate," she said. "Sorry it took me so long to call you back, I was in the air."

"You're here already?"

"I flew into Detroit actually. I have some sites to check out here then I'll drive to Carrefour late tonight."

"Really? Sites in Detroit?"

"That's where it started, in some neighborhoods near the ports where the ships carrying stow-away insects docked."

I heard the bustle of the airport in the background. "I won't keep you. I got some good news today and wanted to let you know."

"What's that?"

"The toxicology report came back. There was nothing unusual in it. The coroner is going to confirm that it was natural causes."

There was a pause before she said, "I'm not surprised since that's what it was but I'm glad the Phillips couldn't buy a different result."

"We have a good man up here. That was never a concern."

"Money can warp the natural order of things, Nate. I'm glad it didn't here."

"Well, that should be the end of it. Pearson is aggressive but there's only so much he can do with a report like that."

"That is good news. So are we still on for the site visits tomorrow afternoon?"

"We're on. Where should I pick you up?"

We made arrangements and then we hung up. I decided that was enough for the day and I went to the Brickhouse and then the Railcar and then home or, as I like to call it, Friday night in Carrefour.

∽

THE NEXT AFTERNOON I DROVE OVER TO THE BIOLOGY BUILDING AT the University, which was on the Ohio side of Carrefour. I texted

Liselle that I was there then watched as students went in and out. A minute later, she walked out. The student traffic at the door stopped for an extra beat, then started again.

She was dressed for the field, wearing faded blue jeans and a blue shirt along with hiking boots, and carried a backpack over one shoulder. She pushed her hair back and waved.

I got out of the Jeep and opened the rear hatch. After we exchanged greetings, I pointed at the backpack.

"Thanks," she said and handed it to me. The weight of it dipped my arm a little bit. "Geez," I said. "You got a body in there?"

She raised one eyebrow. "I'm a little sensitive to that kind of joke right now." Her eyes indicated she wasn't.

"Right. Bad form." I opened her door and she seemed surprised for a moment and then climbed in. I shut it and went around to the driver side.

"How'd the meetings go?" I said.

"Great. Two different professors made time for me this morning so it was worth the trip for that alone. They had some thoughts about where to go today too. They knew about Sarah's work, by the way, and spoke highly of her."

I nodded. "So where are we going?"

She pulled out a map and handed me one side. We held it up and she pointed.

"Sarah mentioned a heavy concentration here between Portage Lake and Round Lake. And then there was another grouping here, where they tried clear-cutting by Twelve Curves trail. Then I thought we could finish up at the Groves."

"Sounds good. Those are all within the state park." I took a last look at the map then pulled out of the lot. "It'll take forty-five minutes or so to get to the first place."

"No problem."

We exchanged pleasantries about flights and the hotel, and places to eat dinner when you were in the Carrefour. Finally, she said, "So that was good news about the toxicology report."

"It was. Although I really didn't expect anything else."

"I was a little worried," said Liselle. "The Phillips are pretty powerful in Missouri."

"I got the impression that they tried to throw their weight around up here but I think they just irritated the coroner." I remembered Ray's description of the daily calls. "Have they tried to contact you?"

"The family? Not since they told me that I wasn't welcome at the funeral."

"That seems harsh."

Liselle shrugged. "We hadn't known each other that long so I guess I shouldn't be upset about it."

"But still. I get it."

"And I would've liked to have taken in Mac."

"Mac?"

"The dog Rich adopted at the benefit when we met. I don't know what's going to happen to him. I've reached out but the family's ghosting me on that." Liselle looked up at the sunroof and said, "Do you mind?"

"Not at all." It was sunny that day with a crispness to the air that spoke of football and turning leaves. I hit the button and a rush of sunshine and cool air filled the cab.

Her hair whipped around and she smiled. "That's better."

We crossed the state line, then left northern Carrefour and soon the hills began and the trees crowded close to the road. Liselle's mood lightened with each mile until finally, when we reached the parking lot of the state park where we were going to hike to our first site, she seemed almost joyful. We got out of the car and I offered to carry the backpack which she accepted.

As we started up the path, I knew exactly where Liselle

wanted to go since Sarah had taken me there before. Liselle seemed hyperaware of everything and at one point said, "It's just so green here."

"More than Missouri?"

"We're in the middle of the Great Plains. Once you get out of the woods, a lot of the grasses are prairie brown. Here, it's green wherever I look. It's beautiful."

"We are spoiled a little bit. In the summer and fall anyway."

We didn't have to walk much longer before we came to the first area, a spot where the ash trees were scattered individually among pines and maples and oak. I stepped aside and let Liselle go to work.

I wasn't sure exactly what she was doing but it seemed like she was inspecting trees and cross-referencing against something on her tablet. Every once in a while, she would take a picture with her phone or scrape away some of the bark on the dead ash tree with a small knife.

It felt strange. I had walked this path with Sarah many times and seeing another woman going from tree to tree doing some of the same things with the same passion was a little disorienting. The constant sense of loss I felt rose up then but it was tempered by the memory of the time we'd spent here.

After a time, Liselle was done and asked if I could guide her to the next site. I led her past seven of the path's Twelve Curves to a small creek whose name escaped me but whose peaceful sound I recalled. Again, the dead ash trees were scattered among others that were thriving. Liselle went about her work again, which seemed to involve jumping back and forth across the water to measure the distance between dead trees with a nifty little laser. I took a seat next to the creek and watched it run. Sarah and I had eaten lunch here once and I remembered why we'd liked it.

Sometime later, I can't tell you how long, I felt a light touch on my shoulder. I looked up and saw not brown hair and brown eyes, but pale blonde hair and the lightest green. "You good for one more?" she said.

I smiled. "Sure. The Groves?"

"Please."

I stood and brushed off. "It's on the other side of the park. We'll head back to the car and drive over there."

We didn't say much as we walked back. I was thinking and she was doing something on her tablet. Finally, she slipped the tablet into her backpack and said, "I appreciate this."

"No problem."

She looked over at me. "Is it hard?"

"To go for a walk on a beautiful day? No."

"That's not what I meant."

I paused. She seemed serious so I said, "A little. But it makes me feel close to her."

Liselle nodded as if she understood. "The woods can do that."

We walked back to the car and didn't say much more but the silence was pleasant as opposed to uncomfortable.

What would have been a long trek on foot was a short drive in the car over to the trail that led to the Groves. We parked and she accepted my offer to carry the backpack again before we headed down the path into the trees. We passed the white pines and the sugar maples but stopped at the black cherries, where she took pictures and made notes on her tablet. I was about to ask why when I heard a sharp crack and a scream.

We both stood straight up, waiting. I couldn't tell which direction it had come from. Then a second scream ripped through the woods, raw and anguished. This one didn't stop. A moment later, two voices joined the screams.

The first voice was yelling for help.

The second voice was yelling, "James!"

I took off running up the path toward the voices of my nieces.

And the screams of my nephew James.

13

When I came to the grove of dead ash trees, I shouted, "Taylor! Page!"

They didn't hear me but they kept screaming. Their voices seemed like they were coming from the lake so I left the path and ran toward them. Three bikes laying on their sides told me that I'd guessed right. I kept running and yelled again. This time the girls heard me and yelled, "Over here! Over here!"

I dodged through the dead trees as their voices grew closer until I finally found them. When I did, though, it took me a moment to process what I was seeing.

Taylor and Page were standing on either side of what looked like a long, thick tree branch. Both girls were yanking at it but it wasn't moving. As I came closer, I saw that it wasn't a branch but half a trunk of a dead ash tree, split right down the middle. Then I heard more screaming and saw that James was underneath it.

I hopped over the side and saw that James's leg was caught beneath the tree trunk. Every time he moved, he screamed again.

"Uncle Nate, Uncle Nate, Uncle Nate," said Page.

Taylor kept pulling at the branches.

James kept screaming.

"Girls," I said and put a hand on each of them. "Stop."

They stopped.

I crouched down and put a hand on James's chest. He kept screaming and thrashing with his hands. I took a quick glance at the tree trunk. It was huge and it was laying squarely on the lower half of James's left leg.

"James," I said. "James, it's me. James, I need you to calm down, buddy. James can you hear me?"

James screamed again.

"Hey, Troll! It's Uncle Nate."

James screamed again, but then his eyes opened and he looked at me and I could see a little bit of the panicked haze clear. He cried and he whimpered and he nodded his head, but he stopped screaming.

"That's a boy. That's a boy, James." I kept my hand on his chest. "Can you feel your leg?"

My nephew nodded as his screams descended to sobs and tears poured out the sides of his eyes.

"I know it hurts but we're going to take care of it, okay?"

He nodded and kept crying.

"I need you to listen to me, Troll. Can you hear me?"

He nodded.

"I need you to hold still, okay? I'm going to get this trunk off you but I need you to hold still. Do you understand?"

"It hurts, Uncle Nate," he said around sobs.

"I know. But trolls are tough."

I looked up to tell Liselle what I was going to do.

She was gone. I didn't see her anywhere.

I swore and turned back to my nieces. "Girls, I want you to listen to me. I'm going to lift this trunk and I need the two of you to grab James under the arms, okay?"

The girls nodded, all eyes.

"If I say pull, you pull him out. But gently, understand?"

Taylor nodded. Page was crying now. "Page," I said.

She looked at me.

"It's worse for him. I need you to be tough."

She nodded.

"I know you're scared, but it's going to be all right."

She nodded again.

"I mean it. What does Pops say?"

Page didn't stop crying but she said, "A shepherd takes care of her flock."

"That's right. And we're going to take care of James. Ready?"

I went down to one end of the tree and bent down to get my arms around the jagged, dry trunk. I didn't know how much it weighed and I was worried that I was only going to be able to move it a little. It was going to have to be enough.

I bent down and wedged my hands underneath the trunk. I gathered my legs under me and prepared to lift. "Ready, girls? On three—"

"Wait"!

I looked over my shoulder. Liselle was running through the woods, her blonde hair flying behind her as she ran between the dead trees and leapt over falling brush. She sprinted up to us, her arms full of flowers.

I stared at her "What—?"

"I'll tell you after we get this off him."

I nodded. "Girls, you grab James under the arms. This nice lady is going to hold James's leg." I looked at Liselle. "Ease him out when I lift the tree?"

She nodded, dropped the flowers next to James, and guided the girls to either side of my nephew before she looked up and nodded. I crouched down into a deep squat, burrowing my hands into the grass and dirt to get my arms around the trunk.

"Ready, girls? 1-2-3!"

I lifted. At first, I didn't think it was going to budge, but then it rose, slowly, an inch, a little more, and I decided I was going to have just enough juice. I gathered myself, exploded upward, and then drove the tree forward with my shoulder like it was a football block. I sprawled face first into the dirt, pushing the tree away as I fell. It moved about three feet, which was just enough. I scrambled up and back over to James.

Liselle was crouched over his left leg, blocking the girls' view. Taylor and Page each held one of James's hands and were saying over and over that everything was going to be all right. I ran around to the other side of Liselle and I saw that it wasn't all right. It wasn't all right at all.

James's leg was broken clean through. Bone was sticking out of the skin from each direction and his leg was bent at an angle as if he now had another knee in the middle of his shin. It wasn't spurting blood, but it was oozing. An awful lot.

Liselle was cradling the leg, trying to keep it still. "Bring me the flowers and give me your pullover," she said.

I didn't hesitate. I grabbed the flowers, which looked like weeds you could find in any Michigan ditch, and yanked my pullover off. I gave her the flowers and I gave her the pullover and I handed Taylor my phone.

"Call 911, Honey," I said. "Tell them that your cousin's hurt on the path in the ash section of Grove State Park and that we need an ambulance right away."

Taylor dialed and I turned back to Liselle. She'd laid out my pullover and was crushing the flowers on top of it. "Put some of those on his leg," she said. "Then we'll try to immobilize it."

I started crushing flowers and sprinkling them on his leg.

"No, right in the wound," she said.

I raised an eyebrow.

"They'll help stop the bleeding. Get them right in there."

I put the flowers in the wound, avoiding the jagged bone that stuck out on either side.

Liselle was done. She had my jacket filled with crushed flowers. She looked at me, eyes intent. "You need to lift his heel and straighten his leg. I'll slide the jacket underneath. Then we'll tie it off to keep it from moving."

I heard Taylor begging the 911 dispatcher to hurry. I knew it was going to take time to get to us.

I nodded. "James? I'm going to move your leg."

He shook his head. "Please don't, Uncle Nate.""

"It's going to hurt for a second and then it won't hurt as much."

"Don't, Uncle Nate!"

Page grabbed his hand. "It'll be okay, James."

Sometimes a warning just makes it worse. I gave Liselle a nod, grasped James's heel as gently as I could, and straightened his leg.

He screamed with a rasp that went straight through my spine.

I didn't have to hold his leg up. The second Liselle saw me move, she whipped the jacket under the leg and immediately tied the sleeves over the top as I tied the tails at the bottom. We pulled the edges in the middle together and I slid my belt underneath it so that we could keep it together. I tightened it, not enough to cut off circulation but enough to hold the whole compress in place. Liselle had one too and she gave it to me and I did the same thing with it.

"Are they coming, Taylor?" I asked.

She nodded.

"How long?"

The dispatcher was still on the line. Taylor asked. She listened and then said, "Twenty minutes."

I thought that would be in time but then James began to

shiver and I could see he was going into shock. I went around to his head and sat down, gently putting his head in my lap while Liselle took off her own jacket and slipped it underneath his back to protect him from the chill of the ground. "It's going to be all right, Troll," I said. "The ambulance is on the way."

James wasn't talking anymore. He burrowed back into me and he cried and he cried and he cried.

Liselle put a hand on James's head and said, "Your uncle called you a troll?"

"He calls us all trolls," said Taylor.

Liselle ignored the girl and pushed James's floppy blond hair out of his eyes. "You don't seem like a troll to me. Trolls are nasty and gnarled and mean."

James's lips quivered and he spoke between sobs. "That's—what—Uncle Nate—says we are."

I smiled. "You should see him after a bowl of Apple Jacks."

Liselle smiled a little but she didn't take her eyes off James.

"You see, James, trolls like to dig in the earth, to hide in dark places."

"And under bridges," said Page.

"Yes, under bridges," said Liselle. "But I don't think that's you, James. I think you're the opposite. I think you like to climb as high as you can. I think you like to be near the sky."

"He does!" said Page.

Liselle glanced at the tree trunk. "I know he does. I think you're more like a falcon, James."

James's voice cracked and the space between sobs grew. "My mom says I shouldn't swear."

Liselle paused for a moment and then laughed. "No, James, a fal-con. A hawk."

"Oh." James sniffed. "I like hawks."

"I do too. I see them all the time when I'm in the woods. Have you?"

James nodded. "I see them circling sometimes."

Liselle nodded. "Here?"

"Sometimes."

"This is a good place for them. Lots of rabbits and mice, good thermals from the lake to glide on. Do you think we could find one?"

"I...I don't know."

"Well, let's look." Liselle made a show of looking up. "Beyond the trees there seems like a good place."

James pointed. "There?"

Liselle adjusted his arm. "Maybe more there. Over the lake."

I was still holding James's head in my lap and pulling the coat closer around his shoulders. He was still shocky, but he was calmer and I thought we were keeping his temperature up. Blood hadn't yet seeped through the jacket around his leg.

"Is that one?" James said.

"Hmm. I don't think so. I think that's a duck."

They looked. All four of them—James and his cousins and Liselle—craning their heads to the sky. James wasn't moving but his breathing slowed.

"What about that?" said Page.

"That's a black bird," said Liselle. "Keep looking though."

They saw a starling and a V of geese and then nothing for quite a while. I kept an eye on James as Liselle spoke to the kids, guiding their attention from one thing to the next, high, high in the sky, keeping their faces turned up and away, without realizing it, from the ground.

I looked at Liselle and then tracked a movement behind her shoulder. And there it was, sitting on a branch at the top of a dead ash tree.

It was big. It had a white chest and spotted, brownish-red wings. Its white face had a crown of darker coloring and it was looking not at us, but at the lake.

"James," I said.

"Yeah?" he said, eyes on the sky.

"Look over the nice lady's shoulder. Right there in the tree."

He looked. At that moment, the red-shouldered hawk swooped down out of the tree and skimmed away across the lake.

James gasped.

Liselle smiled without turning.

"He flew away!" said James.

"That's what hawks do," said Liselle. "He'll be back. You just have to keep an eye out for him."

James followed the hawk's flight, entranced.

A moment later, we heard the siren. James didn't notice it.

14

Izzy and Mark charged through the hospital entrance to where Liselle and I waited with Taylor and Page.

"Where is he?" she said as I stood to meet them.

"He's in surgery," I said.

Izzy's hand flew to her mouth. "Surgery? Before we got here?!"

"It was an emergency."

"Emergency surgery on what?"

"His leg. He was bleeding a lot and they were worried about nerve damage too."

I hesitated, but Izzy was his mom so she needed to know what James was facing. "They had to operate now to try to save his leg."

Izzy was not the gasping and sitting type but she wobbled for a moment before her eyes came into focus. She instinctively grabbed Mark's hand. "He could lose his leg?"

"They took him back right away to make sure that didn't happen."

"What happened, Nate?" said Mark.

So I told them how I had been showing Liselle the Groves

and how we had heard James scream and how we found him beneath the split trunk of a dead ash tree. I told them how we had moved the trunk and how the girls had been a great help and how James had been very brave as we waited for the ambulance together. I told them how much better James had seemed after he received some pain killers and had his leg stabilized and that the paramedics had been great. I told them how I had ridden in the ambulance with James and Liselle had followed in the car with Taylor and Page and how we had all arrived at the hospital at about the same time.

"They rushed us right through the emergency room," I said. "The ER doc took one look at it, got the pediatric orthopedic surgeon on the phone, and sent James straight to surgery." I looked at them both. "I told the doctors that I was his uncle and that I consented to the surgery, but I'm sure they'll want you guys to follow-up."

Izzy waved a hand. "Of course. How long has he been back there?"

"Only about twenty minutes." I thought of James's leg. "I think we're going to be waiting a while."

"Thanks, Nate," said Mark. "Let's check in, honey."

I showed Izzy and Mark to the information desk, which then directed them to the processing desk where an administrator led them through the paperwork guaranteeing that they were good for the small fortune their son's surgery was going to cost.

I left them to it and arrived back in the waiting room right as Tom and Kate walked in. My older brother looked like he had come straight from football practice and Kate had the ever-present three-year-old Charlie on one hip. "Where are the girls?" Tom said.

"They're here," I said. "They're safe. They're both fine."

"What happened to James?" said Kate.

So I told them the same story. This time I emphasized how

helpful and brave the girls had been, but Tom wasn't having any of it. "I've told them not to climb those dead trees."

"Now is not the time, Tom," said Kate. "Let's worry about James right now."

I nodded. "He's in surgery. It's going to take a while." I looked at Tom. "The girls really were great."

Tom nodded, it seemed a little reluctantly, and said, "Where are they?"

Kate looked over my shoulder. "Who is that with them?"

I glanced over to where Liselle was sitting with the girls over in the corner. She was waving her hands and appeared to be telling them some kind of story. "She's the biologist I told you about. I was showing her some of Sarah's sites when we heard the kids."

Tom and Kate nodded and made a beeline straight to them. Liselle looked up as they approached and the girls followed her gaze. When the girls saw their mom and dad, they jumped up, ran over to them, and were swept up into two big hugs. Page, the youngest, started talking a mile a minute in an unbroken stream about bikes and trees and broken legs and sirens. Taylor, being older and knowing her dad, squeezed him very tight and said, "I'm sorry, Daddy."

Tom bent down and squeezed her back and said, "Uncle Nate said you were very brave and helped your cousin very much. I'm proud of you." Then Taylor began to cry and Tom hugged her close and kissed the top of her head.

My mom and dad walked in then and found us right away since our growing group was hard to miss. My mom bustled right up to the girls and Charlie with juice boxes and cheese snacks at the ready. My dad came over, shook my hand, and said, "James in surgery?"

I nodded. "Just started."

"I imagine that'll take a while."

I agreed.

"An ash tree?"

I nodded. "Split right in half."

My dad shook his head. "One came down a couple of weeks ago on the Sampson's garage during that storm."

"I heard about that."

"They need to be taken down but it's so expensive the county can't afford it." He shook his head. "I climbed those trees when I was young. It's a shame."

"It's a crime." I looked; Liselle had joined our conversation. She practically spat the words.

My dad's mouth barely twitched, but his eyes twinkled. "Son, I don't believe you've introduced me to your friend."

"Liselle Vila, this is my dad, Dave Shepherd."

Liselle's anger evaporated as she held out her hand. "I'm sorry, Mr. Shepherd. All that destruction gets the better of me sometimes."

"Don't apologize. I feel the same way when I'm on my boat looking over the lake at what's left of the ash grove." He gestured at the hospital waiting room. "Even more so now."

Liselle shook her head. "The same people who say it's too expensive to clear out and replant are the same ones who can't be bothered to inspect or quarantine ships when they dock to make sure they aren't carrying a non-native species that destroys our whole ecosystem. One person cuts a corner and millions of our trees are destroyed. It's as if..." Liselle stopped, smiled, and ducked her head. "There I go again."

I smiled at my dad. "Liselle is a biologist from down near St. Louis. She's doing some of the same work that Sarah did."

My dad nodded, his weathered face expressionless. "Well, it sounds like you were in the right place at the right time for my grandson today. Thank you."

"Your son did all the hard work, Mr. Shepherd. Nate, can I talk to you for a second?"

"Sure."

My dad nodded and smiled at Liselle. "Good luck with your research."

Liselle and I moved over to the side of the waiting area. "I really need to get back to the hotel. My flight leaves tonight."

"Oh, right. Let me say good-bye and I'll drop you."

"No, no," she said. "You need to stay here with your family."

"It's a quick trip. I can run you over and be back before James is out of surgery."

Liselle shook her head. "You don't know that for sure and they obviously need you here, especially if there's another emergency."

"They can handle it."

She looked at me directly. "Not as well as you." She looked down at her phone. "You can catch an Uber here in Carrefour, right?"

"Right."

"Then I'll be fine." She put a hand on my arm. "Thanks again for your help today. It would've taken me twice as long to wander around and find those places on my own."

"It was fun. Well, the beginning was. You know what I mean." Jesus, I sounded like Danny. "I'll walk you out while you're getting a car."

"Thanks. Let me say goodbye to the girls first."

With that Liselle went across the room to Taylor and Page. She leaned down and said something to both of them and I saw Kate assessing who Liselle was and how exactly she felt about it. She smiled though when Page reached up and gave Liselle a big hug around the neck and a kiss on the cheek.

The sliding door to the waiting room opened and I was

surprised to see Mitch Pearson walk into the room. Then I realized that the ambulance dispatch would've gone out over the radio and that the police station likely heard it. I was a little surprised that he was responding to an accident call rather than a uniformed officer but you never know what schedules are like on a Saturday.

I went over to meet him and held out my hand. "Hi, Mitch. James is still in surgery but his parents are right over there if you want to talk to them first." I pointed to Mark and Izzy.

Pearson's eyebrows raised a little bit. "What are you talking about, Shepherd?"

"James Shepherd, the boy in the accident? Those are his parents over there if you need to get any information."

Pearson's face was blank. "Accident?"

"The boy who had the ash tree fall on him? Isn't that why you're here?"

Pearson's eyes cleared. "Oh, right. I heard it on the scanner. No, that's not why I'm here."

At that moment, Liselle walked up.

"Okay, Nate, I'm ready—" She noticed Pearson and stopped. "Officer Pearson. Are you here about the accident?"

"No, ma'am, I'm not," said Pearson. "I'm here to place you under arrest."

"For what?" said Liselle.

"For the murder of Richard Phillips."

I glanced at my family. "Can we take this outside?" I said.

"I think right here is fine," Pearson said. Then he read Liselle her rights, put her hands behind her back, and cuffed her.

My family watched. Page started to say something. Kate shushed her.

When he was done, I said, "My client is exercising her right to counsel. She's not to be questioned without me present."

"Oh," said Pearson. "Are you her lawyer?"

Liselle looked at me, eyes wide.

"Yes," I said to him. I turned to her. "Don't say anything. I'll meet with you after you're processed."

Liselle nodded and looked down. Pearson stared at my family for an extra beat then led Liselle out by the arm.

I met my family's eyes. "I'll be back in a bit," I said, and left.

15

I stood in the Carrefour jail, waiting. Mitch Pearson was happy to let me.

"When will they be done?" I said.

Pearson shrugged. "When they're done."

"Helpful."

"Does it really matter? She's going to be spending an awful lot of time in here."

"I've seen the autopsy and the toxicology, Pearson. You're never going to make murder."

Pearson shrugged again. It was getting annoying. "The grand jury has already returned an indictment, Shepherd. Seems to me like we're halfway home."

"What's the murder weapon? What's the motive?"

Pearson smiled. "I guess you'll just have to wait for the press conference."

Motherfucker. "Press conference?"

"As soon as the prosecutor gets here."

"Why would you have a press conference?"

"One of the richest men in the country was killed right here in Carrefour, Shepherd. By your client. People want to know that justice is being done."

"Then I don't know why they'd be looking to you."

Pearson tsk'd, shaking his head from side to side. "Don't panic, Shepherd." He looked at the clock. "They should be done processing your hot little killer in about fifteen minutes. You can see her then." He smiled his big quarterback smile. "Of course, if you do, then you'll miss the press conference. Right next door on the courthouse steps."

In fifteen minutes it would be six o'clock, just in time for the local news. This had been in the works for a while.

"When do I get the file?" I said.

Pearson walked away with a wave. "Take it up with the prosecutor."

I needed to get that file right away to see what their theory was. Richard Phillips had died of a heart arrhythmia. I hadn't seen anything in the autopsy or toxicology report that indicated anything other than natural causes. How in the hell were they going to prove murder?

I decided to go to the press conference.

∼

Pearson was joined on the courthouse steps by a man and a woman. A lectern with microphones stood in front of six or seven reporters and a similar number of camera operators. Judging from the logos, it looked like all of the Carrefour outlets were covered. More importantly, since this was going to be about the death of Richard Phillips, footage of the announcement would immediately be strung out to the AP newswires to run anywhere and everywhere. I stood off a ways, over by the large white oak that grew on the west side of the courthouse lawn, close enough to hear but far enough away to avoid notice.

Promptly at six o'clock, the man stepped up to the lectern and said, "For those of you from out of town, I'm the Carrefour Chief of Police Jack LaBeau. Earlier this afternoon, the Carrefour Police Department arrested Liselle Vila for the murder of Doprava CEO Richard Phillips. Ms. Vila had been under suspicion for some time, and, when our department learned that Ms. Vila had returned to the jurisdiction for reasons which we do not currently know, we acted swiftly to bring about her arrest. For this, I would like to thank Chief Detective in charge of Serious Crimes for Carrefour, Ohio, Mitchell Pearson."

Pearson nodded. Dick.

Chief LaBeau continued. "This was a difficult case that required coordination between departments and we would like to thank the many people who worked hard to make this happen. Chief Prosecutor Victoria Lance will now discuss the charges."

Victoria Lance stepped up to the lectern. She wore a plain black suit with a gray shirt and you knew she was tall because Pearson didn't make her look short. Victoria had been the chief prosecutor in Carrefour for a good six or seven years now and had won her last election easily.

Victoria Lance nodded in acknowledgment to Chief LaBeau and said, "As Chief LaBeau stated, Ms. Vila had been a person of interest in this investigation for some time. We had intended to file formal charges against her next week and then begin the extradition process from Missouri, but when she returned to Carrefour, we agreed with the police department that Ms. Vila should be apprehended immediately and took steps to file an indictment and obtain an arrest warrant. My compliments to Chief Detective Pearson for carrying out that warrant efficiently and without incident."

Pearson preened as if he'd brought down a dangerous crime boss.

"Because of the police department's swift action, we have charged Ms. Vila with the first-degree murder of Richard Phillips. Once the case has been assigned to a judge, we will have a better idea of when the case will proceed to trial."

A reporter raised his hand and said, "Ms. Lance, what took so long to make an arrest?"

"This case required cooperation between several investigatory units," Victoria said. "It was further complicated by the fact that both the victim and the defendant lived outside of the state. All things considered, we believe that the investigation was concluded and the arrest made fairly expeditiously."

Another reporter. "Ms. Lance, it has been well-documented that Mr. Phillips died while dancing at a wedding. How does the state claim that Ms. Vila killed him?"

"It would be inappropriate for me to comment on the evidence at this time. Rest assured that we will present a case to the jury that we believe will lead to a conviction."

"Do you intend to seek the death penalty?" said another reporter.

"At this point, we do not," said Ms. Lance. "That could change if additional evidence is uncovered between now and trial."

Victoria Lance looked at Pearson and LaBeau, then said, "That is the only comment we have at this time. We'll issue additional statements when necessary."

It was clear that most of the reporters were in the middle of a live broadcast because, rather than shout more questions, they all jotted on notepads and tablets and phones, and scattered to their camera operators to set up for their live shots. Chief LaBeau and Mitch Pearson shook Victoria Lance's hand and walked down the steps. Victoria Lance went back into the courthouse, presumably to her office.

I decided I should follow her.

~

THE CARREFOUR COURTHOUSE HAD BEEN BUILT IN THE LATE 1800s so it was all stone columns and high ceilings and heavy wooden doors. I climbed the stone stairs to the second floor and went to the door that had "Victoria Lance, Prosecutor," stenciled on the frosted glass in black paint. The door led me to a secretarial station and counter which was empty since it was a Saturday. I walked around the counter to another set of double doors, which were open, and saw Victoria Lance standing behind her desk, folding a tablet and sliding it into a case. She saw me and smiled. "Hello, Nate."

Victoria Lance was a local but she was about ten years older than me, just old enough so that we really hadn't run in the same circles growing up. Plus she was a Carrefour South girl who'd stayed on the Ohio side of the line while, well, I'd spent most of my time in Michigan and parts north. I knew her from the time I had worked in the prosecutor's office right out of law school, but, with one exception, we hadn't dealt with each other much then either since I'd spent most of my time doing entry-level misdemeanors while she, being ten years older, was already handling felonies and murders.

Victoria had shoulder length blonde hair, neatly cut, neither pulled back severely nor too long. Her suit was perfectly tailored and perfectly neutral. She wore heels that were neither too high nor too flat and she shook my hand in precisely the right way. I knew her well enough to know that this was entirely by design. Not a single thing in her appearance would offend anyone so that she was free to convince them that the defendant sitting there in front of them was guilty as hell and deserved to be locked up for the rest of his, or her, natural life.

"I haven't seen you in a while," said Victoria. "Didn't think you'd be getting back into the criminal game after you left for the big time."

I smiled back and shrugged. "Life takes strange turns."

"It certainly does. Like when you returned out of nowhere to beat Jeff Hanson's ass last summer. Congratulations."

Jeff had been the prosecutor I'd faced on the Hank Braggi murder trial. "Jeff tried a great case."

Victoria's smile was winter. "Jeff lost."

I shrugged. "If you're not trying them, you're not losing them."

"True. Although as prosecutors, we get to pick the charge so we shouldn't lose the case. That's half the job."

"Speaking of charges, I saw the press conference."

She nodded.

"How is the prosecutor's office claiming that Ms. Vila killed Mr. Phillips?"

"Are you representing Ms. Vila?"

"I have been."

"That's nice. Are you representing her in this trial?"

I thought. "I don't know for sure yet."

"Well, if you do represent her, I'll be happy to share everything we have with you. If you don't, I'm afraid I have no comment." Victoria pulled a piece of paper out of her case. "Here's a copy of the indictment we filed. It's public record. Give it to whomever her attorney turns out to be."

I scanned it. "This just says she committed first degree murder, Victoria. It doesn't say what you claim she did."

Victoria gave me a smile that was all mouth and no eyes. "Have you been out of the criminal game that long, Nate? You know we don't have to say how the death was caused in the indictment."

I tried another tack. "I've seen the autopsy," I said. "I can't see how it's possible to support that charge."

Victoria zipped her tablet case shut. "We feel very comfortable that it is. We think that when we're done, a jury will too." She checked her watch. "My sitter made it very clear to me that she has a date tonight. Goodnight, Nate."

"Goodnight, Victoria."

"We might be spending a lot of time together," she said as she walked by. "Call me Vicki." Then she turned off the office light and walked out the door, leaving me there in the dark.

I didn't think that was a mistake.

I went back to the jail to see what I needed to do to release Liselle.

16

THE CARREFOUR JAIL WAS JUST FOUR BLOCKS AWAY SO IT DIDN'T take me long to get back there. I checked in and told the guard I was there to see Liselle Vila. The guard, who looked like a stocky, buzz-cutted stereotype of his profession, clicked his mouse and checked his screen with a bored expression before he said, "Is that 'V' as in 'Victor?'"

"Yes."

He clicked a couple of more times before his expression changed from boredom to interest. "She's been photographed and printed so it shouldn't be too much longer. You her boyfriend?"

"Lawyer."

He stood. "I'll go back and check on her for you."

"Don't you need to mind your station?"

He didn't take his eyes off the screen. "It'll only take a minute. Have a seat." Then he left.

I sat down and shot a text to Izzy, asking after James. I didn't get a reply right away. I glanced at the time and realized James might still be in surgery. I switched then to the newsfeeds and read about the press conference. They were filled with headlines about a beautiful young woman murdering a rich old man but had little in the way of facts.

About ten minutes later, the guard returned, knocked at the glass, and waved me through. On the other side of the door, he led me back to an interview room designed for inmates and their attorneys. When I arrived, Liselle was already there. She wasn't shackled, which I took to be a good sign.

I nodded to the guard, who stared at Liselle for longer than would be appropriate in the outside world, then left.

I needed to get Liselle out of here as quickly as possible.

"Did you say anything?" I said.

Liselle shook her head.

"Did they try to question you?"

"A little. On the way over here, Pearson kept asking a uniformed officer why he thought I did it."

"You didn't say anything, did you?"

She shook her head. "You told me not to talk."

"Good job. They held a press conference already."

Liselle's eyes widened. "What did they say?"

"Nothing really. Just that you'd been arrested."

"This is ridiculous. How are they even saying I killed him?"

"They're not. I tried to talk to the prosecutor, but she would only give me the file if I confirmed that I'm your lawyer."

It didn't seem possible but Liselle's eyes grew wider. "Aren't you?"

"Do you want me to be?"

"Nate, I don't know anybody else."

"I can find somebody for you if you'd like."

"But you handle these kinds of cases, right?"

"I have. But I can find you someone who's done more."

Liselle shook her head. "I trust you."

"Does that mean you want me to represent you?"

"Yes, please. What will it cost?"

I told her. I was coming to know Liselle but I really had no idea about her means or her attitude toward this kind of thing so after I told her, I said, "I can refer you to someone else if you'd like."

She shook her head. "I want you. Next week okay?"

"Yes. You'll have to post a bond too. It'll be high since this is a murder case."

Liselle looked around the cinderblock room. "Then I'll have to pay it. I'm not staying here."

"You'll have to until you're arraigned."

That got her attention. "How long will that be?"

"As long as three days."

"They can hold me here 'til then?"

"Maybe longer. It depends on whether you bond out. I'll get to work on that too."

"Nate, I need you to get me out of here."

"I'll try."

She looked at me then, right in the eyes for a good five seconds before she said, "I didn't do it."

"I believe you."

She looked at me a moment longer until she finally looked away and said, "How is James?"

"I'm not sure. I checked before I came in but Izzy hasn't gotten back to me."

"Will you let me know?"

"Of course. Are you going to be okay?"

"I'll have to be. I'll see that you're paid as soon as I get out."

"I'll have a bail bondsman at the arraignment."

"Good. Thank you, Nate."

"You're welcome."

The guard banged on the door before I could bang for him, letting us know that our time was up.

"We should be able to get you out of here," I said.

"Soon I hope," she said.

"Me too." I smiled and then I left.

～

It was getting late but I still hadn't heard from Izzy so I went back to the hospital. I found out that James was out of surgery and had been placed in a room so I headed up to the pediatric ward. My brother Mark was in the waiting room, sipping coffee, waiting for me.

"How is he?" I said.

"Out of surgery, sleeping now."

"How did it go?"

"As well as can be expected. They were able to save the leg, so that's good."

I remembered the shards of bone sticking out in both directions and it seemed to me that saving the leg was no mean feat. "Good."

"They put pins and a plate in. They're hopeful," he cleared his throat, "they're hopeful that it will heal straight. It's hard to tell right now. There were a lot of fragments. And the growth plate's involved at both ends of the bone so the doctor said it's 50-50 whether that leg grows to the same size as the other one."

"Just wait and see?"

Mark nodded.

I smiled. "He'll be climbing again before you know it."

"If he does, I'll whip his ass." My younger brother is a tool and die maker for Ford. He's quiet and he's by far the toughest of us three brothers, but when it comes to his kids? Well, with his kids, it's another matter entirely. He started to speak, stopped, took a sip of coffee, then said, "The doctor said he could've bled out, Nate. Thanks."

I waved a hand.

"I mean it."

"I know." I looked away. "Family gone?"

Mark nodded. "Mom and Dad stayed until he was out of surgery and in the room. Tom and Kate took the girls and went to pick up Justin and Joe for us. They're going to watch them tonight."

"You staying here?"

Mark nodded. "They only let two people back at a time. Do you want to see him?"

"Do you mind?"

He shook his head. "I'll go get some more coffee."

"Thanks."

He told me the room number and I found it just one bend of the hall later. James was lying in bed but I didn't realize it was him at first. What I saw was a contraption of pulleys with a black sling and steel pins and a small foot sticking out the end. I realized the contraption was elevating James's leg. Once I realized what I was looking at, I saw the blond hair and the pale face of my sleeping nephew.

I came around to the other side of the bed and found Izzy sitting in a chair next to the bed holding James's hand. She smiled a little, waved me over, and made me bend down so she could squeeze my neck with her free arm. "Thank you."

"He's a tough kid, Izzy."

"Don't deflect, asshole. Say you're welcome."

I smiled. "You're welcome. Has he been awake?"

Izzy shook her head. "They're going to keep him pretty doped up for a few days. The pain's going to be bad."

"Mark said the operation went well?"

"As well as can be expected," she said. She didn't seem to want to talk about it so I pulled up a chair and sat next to her. "Need a break?"

"Not now, thanks. Mark and I will switch off a little later."

We'd only sat there for a little bit when a small, spare man dressed in light green scrubs came into the room. He was short, barely five and a half feet tall, with salt and pepper hair and black glasses.

Izzy sat up. "Hi, Dr. Norton."

"Hi, Mrs. Shepherd." Dr. Norton came around and checked the monitors and the IVs before he took James's pulse in his wrists and his ankles. He spent a while checking James's elevated toes and leg. "I wanted to take one more look before I go home tonight but I'll be back in the morning."

Izzy nodded.

"We're going to be keeping an eye on these toes. A little swelling is normal but if you notice a lot of it, or redness or heat, I want you to tell the nurse, okay?"

"Yes." Izzy looked at me. "Dr. Norton is the surgeon who saved James's leg."

Dr. Norton nodded in my general direction while keeping his eyes on James. "We have a good team here, Mrs. Shepherd. Your son is very lucky he was brought here so quickly."

"I was just thanking my brother-in-law here for that."

Dr. Norton straightened and looked at me directly for the first time. "You're the one who found him?"

I nodded.

"Packing the leg with *Achillea millefolium* was an astute move, son."

"With what?" I said.

"With yarrow." My expression must have still looked confused because he said, "The flowers. It was hell to clean them out but they definitely slowed the bleeding. That made a difference."

I really didn't have anything to add to that so I nodded and it appeared that Dr. Norton's scientific interest in me had likewise departed. "I'll be back tomorrow Mrs. Shepherd," he said.

"James is going to be uncomfortable so we're going to keep the pain meds high for a while. Don't be afraid to ask for them."

"I won't. Thanks, Doctor."

Dr. Norton nodded again and scooted out.

Izzy immediately put a hand on James's toes and checked them.

"Take a picture," I said. "It'll give you something to compare with if you're not sure."

"Good idea." She pulled out her phone and readied the camera. "What's he talking about with the flowers?"

"When we found him, the woman I was with grabbed some yarrow and added it to the wrapping."

"That helps?"

"Apparently."

Izzy took a couple of pictures. "That the woman sitting with the girls when we got here?"

I nodded.

Izzy looked back at James. "Hell of a date."

I realized Izzy had been at the information desk when Liselle was arrested. "It wasn't a date," I said. "She's a client."

"Does that matter?"

"It does."

"Then you should have her get another lawyer."

"That's not going to happen."

"That's a shame. What kind of case?"

I decided now wasn't the best time to explain how I'd come to bring an accused murderer to help her son. "I'll know for sure in a few days."

My response barely registered as Izzy settled back in next to James. I put my hand on her shoulder and said, "I should let Mark back here. Let me know how he's doing?"

Izzy put her hand over mine. "I will. Thanks."

I put a hand on James's shoulder and kissed his forehead. "See you, Troll," I said and started out of the room.

James stirred. He opened his eyes a little, made a noise, and said, "Hi, Mom."

Izzy leaned forward and put a hand on his forehead. "Hi, baby. How are you doing?"

"Guess what?"

"What?"

"I saw a hawk!"

Izzy smiled and smoothed his hair. "You did?"

"Right there in the tree," James said.

"I'll go get Mark," I whispered and Izzy nodded without looking away.

I found Mark, let him know that James was awake, then left the hospital.

I had a bond to arrange.

17

It took two days for Liselle to be arraigned. I was waiting in court with Cade Brickson, who looked like he'd snuck softballs in under the shoulders of his suit. We were waiting in the gallery for the next group of defendants to be brought in for their individual arraignments, along with other lawyers and family members and staffers.

"A bond for murder is going to be expensive," Cade said.

I nodded. "She says she can pay."

"I'll need to confirm it."

"Of course."

The courtroom doors opened but it wasn't the defendants. It was the prosecutor. The Chief Prosecutor. Victoria Lance.

"Uh-oh," said Cade.

"Yep," I said.

Victoria Lance did not take arraignments. Normally, she would send one of her assistant prosecutors for this even if she were going to handle the trial. The fact that she was here didn't make any sense.

Until Bre Phillips arrived. The daughter of Richard Phillips walked into court and started to go through the swinging gate to the counsel table. Victoria whispered and motioned and Bre stopped and slid over to the front row for spectators.

A message was being sent—that this case had the full attention of the prosecutor's office and the support of the victim's family.

And I'd bet the support of the family's money.

A moment later, three uniformed officers came into the room leading six shackled prisoners. That was also unusual. Normally, there weren't that many and they weren't shackled. Either the six women were exceptionally dangerous, or another message was being sent. Liselle was the last one in the line. She still wore her jeans and denim shirt and they'd given her back her boots and laces for her court appearance. She didn't look any the worse for wear after spending two nights in jail, but she scanned the courtroom and her face lightened noticeably when she saw me. I waved and she nodded and we both stood as the judge entered the courtroom.

There was a great rustling as everyone in the court stood and then sat.

"Good morning, everyone," said Judge Dante French. Judge French was a good draw. He had been a bailiff before he had become a judge and he was known for being even-handed and thoughtful regardless of whether it was a criminal or civil case. He took his black-framed glasses between a thumb and forefinger and straightened them before he said to the bailiff, "First case please, Marty."

There were five cases before Liselle's. Two heroin possessions, one heroin trafficking, one breaking and entering that sounded like it arose from someone trying to get money for heroin, and a case of felony domestic assault that involved a baseball bat and a man in a coma. Each defendant pled not guilty. Each one of them was allowed to go free on a minimal bond, if they could post it.

"You bonding any of those?" I whispered to Cade.

"Not a chance."

"One more, Marty?" said Judge French.

"Yes, Your Honor," said the bailiff. "State versus Liselle Vila."

I stepped forward and stood at the defense counsel table while an officer led Liselle over to me. I stepped aside and indicated where she should stand. At the same time, Victoria Lance stepped forward and took the place of the junior prosecutor who had handled the other five cases. I glanced behind her and saw Bre staring, not at me, but at Liselle.

"Miss Lance," said Judge French. "A pleasure to see you today."

"And you, Your Honor."

"Mr. Shepherd, good morning."

"Good morning, Your Honor."

"Are both sides prepared to proceed?" asked Judge French.

"We are, Your Honor."

"Very good." Judge French was a big man and while his voice was not overly deep, it was smooth and he proceeded with an easy tone that was a stark contrast to the incredibly serious charges he read. "We are here this morning on the case of State versus Liselle Vila. The State has issued an indictment and Ms. Vila is charged with murder in the first degree of Mr. Richard Phillips. Does the defendant wish me to read the charge or do you waive reading?"

"We'll waive, Your Honor," I said.

"Very well. Ms. Vila, in response to the charge of first-degree murder, how do you plead?"

"Not guilty, Your Honor," Liselle said.

"Very well. Do the parties anticipate discovery?"

"The prosecution is prepared to proceed in the standard time-frame, Your Honor."

"The defense will need additional time for discovery, Your

Honor," I said. "The prosecution appears to be proceeding on a unique theory of the case that will require a non-standard evaluation."

Judge French looked up.

"My client was dancing with Mr. Phillips at a wedding when he died of a heart attack."

Victoria flipped a hand as if my comment were ridiculous. "The prosecution will show that the killing was intentional and satisfies the requirements of first-degree murder, Your Honor.'

Judge French raised a casual hand. "We're not going to litigate it now, counselors. Suffice it to say that discovery is required. Have you turned over your file yet?" he said to Victoria.

"No, Your Honor."

"Do that now, please. We'll set a trial date for eight months out."

"Yes, Your Honor."

"Bond?" said Judge French.

Victoria Lance straightened. "Your Honor, the state recommends that no bond be issued. This is a murder case and the defendant resides out-of-state. We believe she represents a danger and a flight risk.

"Mr. Shepherd?" said Judge French.

"Your Honor, Ms. Vila has no criminal record and the underlying actions claimed here were not violent."

"Except that my father's dead," came a voice from behind Victoria.

Bre Phillips.

Judge French looked at her. "Ms. Phillips, I realize that this is difficult for you. But you will remain quiet during these proceedings or you will leave. Do you understand?"

Bre Phillips kept her chin up and stared for a moment before she nodded.

"Thank you. You were saying, counsel?"

"Your Honor, Ms. Vila has no criminal history and the underlying facts claimed in this prosecution do not indicate that she is a danger to others. We would ask that the Court allow her to remain free on her own recognizance with such monitoring as the Court requires to ensure her attendance."

"Have you made arrangements with a bondsman for monitoring?"

I gestured. "Mr. Brickson is here today in that capacity, Your Honor."

"Ms. Lance?"

"Your Honor, the defendant stands accused of murder. We believe that this represents an inherent danger to our community and that someone who has been part of such a criminal enterprise should remain in custody."

Judge French looked at me.

"Criminal enterprise?" I said. "Your Honor, my client is a woodland biologist who went on a date to a wedding. No bond is required. A minimal bond at most."

Judge French nodded. "The Court finds that bond in this case is appropriate. While Ms. Vila has no criminal record and the facts of this case are not typical, the fact remains that she stands accused of murder, which has its own inherent assumptions of violence and the potential for flight. The Court therefore finds that bond will be set in the amount of five hundred thousand dollars. Should the defendant post this bond, she will be subject to community control to assure that she stays within the city limits of Carrefour, Ohio. Anything else, Marty?"

"No, Your Honor," said the bailiff.

"Then we are adjourned." Judge French stood.

"Your Honor," I said. "May I have a moment with my client before we are dismissed?"

"Of course, Mr. Shepherd. Officer, please wait until Mr.

Shepherd has conferred with his client before escorting Ms. Vila back to holding."

As Judge French left, I turned to Liselle. Her eyes were a little wide but overall she seemed calm. "You'll need to come up with fifty thousand dollars and produce collateral to guaranty five hundred thousand dollars if you don't appear at trial."

"I understand," she said.

"Can you do that?"

Liselle chewed momentarily at the bottom of her lip before she said, "I can come up with it, but I need to make a call."

"Of course. The sooner you can come up with the money, the sooner you can get out. I'm going to have Cade go with you right now so he can help you. He's the one who will be posting the bond so you'll need to make arrangements with him for the money and the collateral."

"I understand."

"I'm going to go over to the prosecutor's office and get the file so we can get to the bottom of this."

"Okay." Her eyes were big but she seemed to be keeping it together.

I put a hand on her elbow. "Just a little longer. You'll be out soon."

She nodded.

"You mean she just goes free?" said a voice.

I looked over my shoulder. Bre Phillips again.

Victoria Lance wasn't having any of it. "Come with me," Victoria said. "We'll talk outside."

"She just gets to walk?"

"Bre!" said Victoria.

Bre stopped, apparently reluctantly, and the two of them began to walk out.

"You in this morning, Vicki?" I said.

She shot me a glance and then nodded.

"I'll stop by for the file."

I looked at the officer then pointed to Cade. "Can he go with you?" I asked.

"He can meet us at processing," said the officer.

"Call me as soon as she's out," I said. Cade nodded.

I came back to Liselle. "Don't worry. We'll get this taken care of."

She nodded and the officer led her away.

Cade came up to me before he left. "She really has fifty grand and the collateral?"

"She said she had to make a call."

Cade shrugged. "Then we'll take care of it."

"Thanks."

I left the details of getting the bond posted to Cade. I decided to grab a cup of coffee to give Victoria time to deal with Bre Phillips and get back to her office. I stopped at the coffee shop on the first floor of the courthouse. I judge coffee by heat more than flavor but the cup they served there had plenty of both. I took a seat at a high-top table and thought about Victoria's presence there today. Victoria had become the chief prosecutor two election cycles ago. She'd taken on a male assistant prosecutor in her first election, beat his ass, then ran unopposed the next time. She had a year or two before she had to run again but, like most prosecutors, Victoria always had her eye on the next election, whether it was preemptively undermining opponents or notching big wins.

It appeared from her presence this morning that she had decided that this was going to be a big win. Great.

I shook my head. This murder charge just didn't make any sense. I was sick of operating blind. I needed to see what was in the prosecutor's file.

Once I thought I'd waited long enough, I went up to the big, old-fashioned office on the second floor and checked in with the prosecutor's secretary. I took a seat and, to her credit, Victoria came out of her office right away. "Nate," she said. "Come on back."

She led me into her office and walked behind the dark wooden desk that was as large as a small boat. She opened a drawer, pulled out a thumb drive, and handed it to me. It was labeled "State vs. Vila" and had the file number on it.

"That's all the paperwork, Nate. You'll find the police reports, the witness statements, the autopsy, and the toxicology. There's an inventory for all of the physical evidence that we found and, since we're a ways off from trial, that'll all be in the evidence room. Have you been down there lately?"

"This past summer," I said.

Her face flicked with annoyance. "Right. It's all electronic now, so just check in and the duty officer will get you any evidence you need to inspect. We require it to stay on site. If there's anything that you need to perform your own testing on or examine in a way that could change it, let me know and we'll arrange some sort of stipulation."

"Got it. Thanks."

I tossed the thumb drive up and down in my hand, the little piece of plastic that used to be eight or nine boxes of documents. Just a light little thing that now held Liselle's future in it. "Do you want to give me the short version?"

Victoria cocked her head to the side. "What do you mean?"

"I'll read everything in here, of course, but we both know what happened that night. Liselle Vila went to a wedding with a man whose heart stopped on the dance floor. That's unfortunate. That's not murder. And I know you have something more concise to tell to the jury or we wouldn't be standing here."

"It's all in there, Nate."

"I know. I'm still asking."

Victoria tapped a perfectly manicured fingernail of medium

length with neutral nail polish on the dark desk before she said, "Ms. Vila made sure Mr. Phillips' heart stopped."

I raised an eyebrow. "And how exactly did she do that?"

"A couple of ways."

I waited. Victoria didn't say anything more.

Finally, I said, "Victoria, why are we here?"

Victoria stared at me, that manicured nail tapping, then said, "We're here because of St. John's wort."

"What?"

"St. John's wort."

I didn't know what Victoria was talking about. "What does a skin tag on a saint have to do with anything?"

Victoria smiled. She pointed at the drive. "Why don't you read up? We have eight months to talk about it."

Right. While she got a jump on the press and the case. "This sounds pretty thin, Vicki."

Victoria looked unconcerned. "Read," she said again.

I sighed. "I will. And I guess I need to learn about St. John's wort."

"You do. You could start by asking an expert. Like maybe a woodland biologist."

Fuck.

I thought for a moment. "She's not in the will, you know."

Victoria blinked. "So?"

"So what's your motive?"

Victoria smiled. "I have to give you our file, Nate. I don't have to connect the dots for you."

"No, I don't suppose you do. Do you have a plea offer for me to extend to her?"

"Sure. Exactly what the indictment says. If she wants to plead to first-degree murder, we won't have to go through a trial."

"That's not an offer, Vicki."

"That's all there's going to be in this case, Nate. She pleads to murder or we convict her of it."

"For dancing. That's insane."

"For plotting and killing a man. And it's not." Victoria offered her hand. "I look forward to working opposite you on this, Nate. Call my office if you need to arrange anything with the evidence room."

"Thanks, Vicki. I'm sure I'll talk to you soon."

We shook hands and I left. This case just kept getting weirder. I had some research to do.

18

I called Olivia Brickson from my car. I'd asked her for some preliminary research a few weeks ago. It was time to get her more involved.

Olivia picked up right away. "This better not be a call with some soft ass excuse about why you're not lifting tonight."

"Nope, I'll be there. Calling with work."

"Hang on a sec." I heard some shuffling and a moment later the background radio noise vanished. "Okay, shoot."

"I just took on a new case. Your brother's serving as bail bondsman. I need some research."

"Sure. What kind of case?"

"Murder."

"Jesus, Shep, for a guy who doesn't have a criminal practice you sure know how to pick 'em."

Olivia had helped me with the Hank Braggi case last summer. "I know. This one's different though. I don't think there was a killing here."

"Uhm, in a murder case?"

"Okay, there was a death but I don't think there was a killing. You know the Phillips-Branson wedding?"

"Matt Branson is a friend but I don't know anything about Ellie's wedding."

"A woman was dancing with a man at the wedding and his heart gave out and they're accusing her of murder."

"You're kidding."

"I'm not. This is related to the research I asked for a few weeks ago about the environmental organizations and the Doprava Company. I need you to add research on my client and the victim now too." I gave her the names Liselle Vila and Richard Phillips, and she confirmed back to me the names of the organizations I'd given her before. Then I said, "You probably better see what you can find out about Phillips' kids, Bre and Andrew, too. It seems like the family might be throwing some money around on this one."

"They rich?"

"Very."

"All right, I'll get some preliminary work done today. You can pick it up when you work out and give me some more guidance."

"Can't you just email it to me?"

"You know the answer to that, Shep. Someone's always watching and if they're not watching now, they'll be looking at it later. Pick it up."

"Got it. Talk to you soon."

We hung up and I decided that the other Brickson may have had enough time to do his job. I called Cade. "Hey, Cade. She out?"

"Just finished, Shep. We got her processed and the Electronic House Monitoring Division has fitted her with an ankle monitor."

"So she was able to post bond?"

"She did."

"All fifty thousand?"

"They don't let you out for less."

"Where did it come from?"

"That's a question you will never hear me ask, Shep."

"What about collateral? What did she post?"

"Some family land in Missouri. A couple of hundred acres."

Interesting. "Can you drop her at my office?"

"Not yet. We have to arrange where she's staying for the next eight months and report that to the EHMD before we can get permission for her to go other places."

"Right. Can you have my office listed as one of the permitted travel locations?"

"Done. It will probably take a couple of days."

"Thanks. Text me where she ends up staying so that I can come out to see her."

"You got it."

"Thanks, Cade."

I pulled into the lot for my office building as I hung up. I headed upstairs to the third floor. As I walked in, Danny came out of his office to meet me with his typical expression that looked like a cat who had pulled his tail out from under a rocking chair.

I handed the prosecution's thumb drive to Danny. "Say hello to the next eight months of your life."

Danny took the drive, bobbled it once, then looked at the writing on the outside. "State vs. Vila. What's this?"

"The prosecution's disclosures in the new murder case we're taking on."

Danny's eyes widened. "Another murder case?"

"I know, my blood pressure had just returned to normal too. Download everything that's in here and then organize it how Cyn showed you on the last one."

"Got it. How soon?"

"Now."

Danny nodded his head and started toward his office before he stopped. "Hey, how's James?"

That surprised me. "How did you know about him?"

"My wife knows Izzy."

"The surgery went well. It'll be a long time before we know how his growth plate reacts."

"Tell them Jenny and I are praying for them."

"Thanks, Danny. Mark and Izzy will appreciate it." I pointed at the drive. "Once we get that organized, we'll meet with Liselle."

"Liselle?"

"Liselle Vila, our client."

Danny looked at me, then shook his head. "I'll go tell Jenny that she won't be seeing me for a while."

"Don't worry, Danny. It'll only take eight months."

"I don't think that's going to reassure her."

"I suppose not."

Danny saluted and took the drive to download it. I went to my office and caught up on all of the things that skitter out of control when you're out of the office for a couple of days.

∼

A FEW HOURS LATER, DANNY HAD THE FILE DOWNLOADED AND organized. It didn't take much. Victoria was true to her word and it appeared that her disclosure was pretty complete.

I went straight to the autopsy. I had read it once before but wanted to make sure that the version Ray Gerchuk had given me was the same as the one Victoria had. It was. Richard Phillips had died of a heart arrhythmia. That meant he didn't have blocked blood vessels and he didn't have unexplained bleeding and he didn't have a stroke. It meant that his heart was beating fine one minute and went into an abnormal rhythm that he couldn't recover from the next.

I turned to the toxicology report. I knew Ray had been thorough and, since this was also part of a murder investigation, that he had looked for poisons or other agents that would cause an irregular heartbeat. There was nothing. At least nothing that you would think of as a poison that someone would use to kill somebody. Instead, I found exactly what you'd expect to find in the blood of a middle-aged man who'd died at a wedding—alcohol and trace amounts of a beta blocker. The alcohol concentration was well above the legal limit but since Richard Phillips wasn't driving that night, that didn't necessarily matter. And the beta blocker was present but in a trace amount. I'd have to find out what that meant but, at first glance, neither of those things seemed to indicate murder either.

Based on what Victoria told me, I next went to the inventory of the belongings in the hotel room Richard Phillips and Liselle Vila had shared. I skimmed through the clothes and the money and the jewelry to the bathroom items. There was a bottle of Lopressor, the brand name for the beta blocker metoprolol, with Richard Phillips' name on it, along with a small plastic bag of unlabeled little blue pills, which anyone who had ever seen a commercial during an NFL football game would know was Viagra. There was also a box filled with plain white, unbranded tea bags.

And that was it. No arsenic, no strychnine, no cyanide. No gun, no knife, no garrote. Not even the St. John's wort that Victoria Lance had implied was the murder weapon. Nothing.

Even if you were under pressure from one of the richest families in America, this seemed like a stretch. Victoria Lance wasn't stupid; in fact, she was one of the smartest, most ambitious people I'd ever met. There was no way her case was this skinny. She was being coy on two things—the St. John's wort and the motive—so it was clear that I needed more information on those to figure this case out.

It was time to talk to my client to find out what she knew. And what she was willing to tell me.

19

I went to the address that Cade Brickson had texted me and found the townhouse in the southwest section of Carrefour that would be Liselle's home for the next eight months. As I went up the brick walk, I noted that it was a new construction with a stone front and white trim. It was nice; nicer than I would expect for someone who had just put up fifty thousand dollars to get out on bond.

I climbed the steps and knocked. A moment later, Cade lumbered out. Actually, that's not fair—Cade moved with the grace of a mountain lion but you don't usually describe someone that big as moving so smoothly. Lumbering was easy, lazy shorthand.

Unaware of my internal reverie about his physical prowess, Cade nodded and said, "She's all set up."

I put a hand on the stone-arched entrance. "Did she pay for this?"

"I'm not paying for it," said Cade.

"Who did?"

Cade sighed and stared at me.

"Right. So the court approved this living arrangement?"

Cade nodded and slid on wraparound sunglasses. "We wouldn't be here otherwise. She'll need to sit tight for a few days. I'll have her approved to go to court and your office next week. In the meantime, if you need to meet with her, come here." Cade started down the steps. "The Electronic Monitoring Housing Unit will do surprise visits. Tell her to stay put."

"Got it, Cade. Thanks."

He waved one massive hand and kept on walking.

I entered. Liselle was waiting for me in the hallway. I wasn't sure how much she'd heard so I decided to pretend she'd heard none of it. "Doing okay?"

"For being in jail for three days, I suppose so. Come on in. Want some tea? I was just putting some on."

"Do you have coffee?"

"I don't think so, not yet. I have to make sure to get the grocery store on my list of designated visitation areas."

I hadn't thought of that. "I suppose that's true."

She guided me to the kitchen and showed me to a seat at a perfectly functional kitchen table topped with pale wood. A red tea kettle was whistling on the stove-top over blue gas flames. She pulled two mugs out of a cupboard. "Sure you don't want some?"

"No, thanks. Water's fine."

Liselle pulled a teabag out of a plain white box, dropped it into a mug, and poured steaming water over it. She took the other mug to the tap, filled it, and set it in front of me as she sat down at the table.

I studied her to see how she was doing and decided that you'd never know that she'd just been in jail. No dark circles, no jittery-ness, just a woman casually sitting down to a cup of tea in her kitchen to discuss murder charges with her lawyer.

"So," she said, steeping the tea. "How can they charge me with murder? What in the world did I do?"

"Do you mind if I ask you some questions first?"

Liselle gave a slight smile but her green eyes hardened. "Are you testing me?"

"No. I just don't want to influence your answers."

"Fine. Shoot."

"Tell me about St. John's wort."

Liselle's brow furrowed. "What do you mean?"

"What is it?"

"It's an herbal supplement. Pretty common. Why?"

"The prosecutor says that's why we're here."

Liselle's look shifted from confusion to incredulity. "Over St. John's wort? You're kidding."

"I'm not. What is it?"

"It's a flower that's used in all sorts of things, Nate." She lifted her mug and I smelled a waft of peppermint. "It's in this tea."

I remembered that the inventory in the prosecutor's file included a plain white box of teabags. "Did you ever make tea for Richard?"

"Sure. He joined me quite a few times."

"And there's St. John's wort in it?"

She shrugged. "It's a common ingredient in wellness teas."

"Is it toxic?"

Liselle thought. "Not that I know of. You'd have to drink an awful lot of it and you'd show all sorts of other signs first. Now, are you going to tell me what this is all about?"

I thought for a moment and decided that was about as much blind questioning as I was going to get. "I'm not sure yet. The prosecutor told me that we're here because of St. John's wort and I know that the inventory of your hotel room included tea in a plain white box."

Liselle nodded. "That was mine."

"But I don't know how they're connected to murder."

"Don't they have to tell us?"

"Not directly. Not yet."

Liselle shook her head. "Giving him tea can't be enough for a murder charge."

"I agree, there has to be more." I tapped the table as Liselle put both hands around her mug and took a sip. "I've only just been able to skim the file. I'll get to work on the science and put it together from that end. There's a second thing that's just as important that they're not saying."

"What's that?"

"The why."

"Since I didn't do it, I don't know."

"I understand that, Liselle, but this is important. Is there anything out there that they could point to as a motive for why you'd want Richard dead?"

"I already told you I'm not in the will."

"I understand that, but that's only one possible motive."

"If you read the papers, it sounds like that's a few billion possible motives."

The mention of money reminded me of another topic. "How did you post bond to pay for this?"

"Can't a girl have her own money?"

"Sure." I left it out there.

Finally, she said, "None of it came from Richard."

"Fine. Where?"

"I make my own money, Nate."

"Great. How?"

"I'm a biologist, remember?"

"And biologists have fifty grand lying around to post bond?"

"Biologists have a lot of ways to make money today that have nothing to do with dating billionaires."

I sighed. "Liselle, the prosecution is going to investigate your whole life. I need to know what to expect if I'm going to defend you. One of them is to know where you get your money so that I can combat any claim by the prosecution that it came from Richard."

That seemed to satisfy her. "My job pays me a salary." She frowned. "Or it did. I'll probably lose it now."

"A government job? No one will believe it paid you that much."

"I live pretty modestly." She shifted a little, as if embarrassed. "And I have a couple of patents. A couple of biological processes that produce a pretty nice source of income."

That made sense. "And the Missouri property?"

"Is the land surrounding my mom's home. I wanted to make sure my family could always live out there in the way they chose."

Before I could ask another question, she said, "Besides, I'm not the one with the money motive."

"Who is?"

"The kids, Bre and Andrew. I'm sure they're pushing this. The sooner Rich's attorney can show them his will and show that I didn't take their place, the sooner this whole thing goes away."

"Do you think?

"Bre especially."

It didn't seem like this was going anywhere but I tried one more time. "This is really important, Liselle. What could the prosecutor think they have as a motive?"

"I have no idea what the prosecutor's thinking, Nate. None of this makes any sense to me."

I stared at her. She stared back. "The sooner I know, Liselle, the sooner I can deal with it."

"If I knew something, I would tell you, Nate. I have no reason to want Rich dead. We were good friends having a good time, which I was frankly sorry to see end."

"Okay. I'm going to get to work on this. Send me a list of

things you need from the store and I'll have someone pick them up for you. Don't leave until we get approval for you to go out."

"I understand." Liselle swirled the last of her tea in her cup, then drank it. "Are we going to win, Nate?"

It's never a good idea to tell a client that she's going to win and I didn't plan to start now. Still, this was the thinnest murder case I'd ever heard of, so I said, "Their theory seems like a stretch. I think we have a good shot."

"Great." She smiled and it made the room seem as bright as if we were outside. "How long am I stuck here?"

"About eight months."

She sighed. "Well, at least I can get some research done."

"You can but not at the Groves."

She raised a pale eyebrow.

"The Groves are in Michigan. You can't cross the state line."

For the first time the whole day, I saw irritation in her eyes. "Are you serious?"

"I'm afraid so. You have to stay strictly within the jurisdiction of the court and the court is in Ohio. Going over the line to Michigan is off limits."

"Well, they have ash borers in Ohio too, I guess." She shook her head. "I am really beginning to regret getting on that plane to come to this wedding."

"I bet." I didn't mention that Richard Phillips probably had the same regret. Briefly. "You good for tonight?"

She looked around and nodded.

"Good. Then I'll check in with you tomorrow."

With that I got up and left, without much more information than I'd had when I arrived.

20

Danny and I were sitting in the office conference room, divvying up the things to do in the case. "You go through the witness statements from the wedding," I said. "I'm going to handle the medical records and I've got Olivia researching Liselle and Phillips and Doprava. We've got some time but I don't want it to get away from us." I stared at my tablet screen. "You've been through the file once?"

"The headings," said Danny. "Not all the individual documents."

"Me too. I haven't seen any evidence of motive yet. You?"

Danny shook his head. "Me either." His expression lightened. "Isn't that good news though? If the prosecution can't prove motive, they're going to have a hard time convincing a jury that Liselle intentionally killed Phillips."

"That's the problem, Danny. There's no way Victoria brings this case unless she's got one."

"Even with pressure from the Phillips family?"

"Especially with pressure from the Phillips family. Nobody wants to look stupid in front of one of the richest families in the country. And Victoria is not stupid."

I tapped the pen on the folder. "I just don't like it. Keep an eye out and your thoughts open."

"Will do." Danny picked up his tablet and was headed back to his office when he said, "How's James?"

"Still in the hospital. They want to keep him another couple of days to make sure the leg's healing right before they send them home."

"Tough little guy."

"He really is," I said. "Thanks for asking."

"Sure." He hesitated, then left.

∽

As Danny returned to his office, I used my own tablet to pull up Richard Phillips' medical records.

Richard Phillips had been seeing the same doctor for more than twenty years. The arc was pretty typical for a man in his late fifties. Very few visits in his thirties, mostly weekend sports injuries, including a knee and a shoulder. More regular checkups in his forties, which was when it looked like the high blood pressure started. And then a cluster of conditions and medications in his fifties—front line blood pressure medications, a six-month prescription of antidepressants which appeared to be related to a divorce, and the eventual inclusion of Viagra in his monthly medications.

The Viagra started four years ago, a year after the divorce, so that really had nothing to do with this case. The section related to an irregular heartbeat was more important though. In his early fifties, his blood pressure had kept creeping up until he'd had a series of rapid heart rhythms that had sent him to the emergency room three times. Ventricular tachycardia they called it, where your heart beats too fast for no good reason. According to the records, he eventually got it under control with changes to his diet, exercise, and—after trying several other medications—the prescription of Lopressor. A quick look at Google told me that Lopressor was a beta blocker that would have lowered his blood pressure and slowed his heart rate. It appeared that all of those things were enough to control Richard Phillips' blood pressure and irregular heartbeat quite well.

Until they weren't.

All that reading about high blood pressure and arrhythmia and sudden death made me decide it was a good time to go to the Brickhouse. I'd be able to see Olivia to find out what her research had turned up and get a workout in to prevent me from going down the same road as Phillips. I let Danny know I was leaving and headed out.

~

I PARKED MY JEEP, IGNORED THE WAFTING SMELL OF HICKORY smoke from the Railcar on the other side of the lot, and went into the Brickhouse. Olivia Brickson was standing behind the front desk. She straightened her half-reflective glasses and said, "You know, I was just talking to my class this morning about jellyfish."

I smiled. "Interesting. Why would you bring that up?"

"No reason. Lifting first or info?"

"Info."

"Come with me." Olivia led me back to her office. It was a curious space for a gym, with floor-to-ceiling shelves stuffed with books on training and philosophy, a state-of-the-art computer system complete with enough monitors to guide air-traffic, and a battered desk that looked like it came from a gym teacher's office. There was a brown folder on her desk alongside a pile of paper that was about a foot and a half tall. Olivia was an investigative whiz and, because she was an expert at finding electronic secrets, was paranoid about emailing me anything important. "Here you go," she said, gesturing. "That's the basics on your client, Phillips, and his company. Hard copy and thumb drive."

I leafed through the top of the pile. It looked like a week's worth of reading, at least. "Can you give me the highlights?"

Olivia offered me a water, which I declined, cracked one for herself, and sat down. "We'll start with your client. Liselle Vila grew up in the small town of Poplar Bluff in southeast Missouri. Family lived out in a small place surrounded by the woods in the Ozarks. Unremarkable family. Lost her dad when she was young, mom worked in a small auto parts shop to keep the family afloat. Took up track in high school and turns out she can run like the wind. She parlayed that into a track scholarship to Washington University in St. Louis and studied woodland biology. Ran a fifth year and picked up a masters that led to a grad assistantship and a Ph.D."

"I feel dumber just sitting here. She said something about patents?"

Olivia nodded. "Three, all having to do with a process for crossbreeding trees and creating hybrids. Do you want the details?"

I thought. "Not right now."

"Good because I didn't understand a lick of it. As a result of it though, the University wanted her to stay and do research and a bunch of companies tried to bring her in house but by all accounts, she wanted to work out in the field so she moved back to southeast Missouri, essentially created her own position with the National Forestry Service and the Missouri Department of Natural Resources, and has been working in the Mark Twain National Forest ever since."

I nodded. "That's consistent with what she told me."

Olivia put down one manila folder and picked up another.

"Richard Phillips, son of Lawrence Phillips, and, along with his brother Stephen, the heir to the Doprava Company. He's worked at the company since he was young. Went to Penn and Wharton for his business training before coming back and working under his father until he took over and led the company to unprecedented prosperity. Under his watch, Doprava became an international conglomerate involved in everything from agriscience to plastics to pharmaceuticals. Personally, he was married for twenty-four years to his wife Sharon before they divorced five years ago. Son Andrew, daughter Bre, both currently in their twenties and waiting for their turn to manage the family fortune."

"So what does the company do?"

Olivia shook her head. "I couldn't begin to list it all." She held up a glossy magazine. "I got ahold of their last annual report which gives you a pretty good picture, but I'm not kidding —they're involved at every level of the supply chain of their products from R&D to manufacture to retail to delivery. It's literally a corporate maze."

I sighed. That reading was going to be dry, dry, dry. "And you checked out the organizations Liselle is involved in?"

Olivia nodded. "There were quite a few."

"Anything interesting?"

"Some are exactly what you'd expect. Gateway Animal Rescue is pretty typical. It's the one who held the Furball where Liselle met Phillips."

"The Furball?"

"A charitable gala to support the rescued animals."

"Ah."

"The State Natural Resource Board, also pretty typical and more of a government actor than anything else."

"Sound like typical organizations for a woodland biologist to belong to."

A pause. "True."

I'd known Olivia a long time. "It sounds like there's a 'but' there."

Olivia ran her hand through her spiked white hair but instead of pushing it out of the way, she teased it down around the left side of her face. "She's a member of the Forest Initiative. Has been for a long time."

"That's bad?"

"Not necessarily. It's one of those organizations with a reputation for extremism but not one that has ever been proven."

"Extremism?"

"Back in the seventies, they were rumored to be spiking trees to thwart loggers. When the logging industry in the US began to replant more aggressively, it seemed that those efforts faded away."

"Corporate change having been effected."

"Right. In the nineties and the aughts, it seemed that they shifted to fighting deforestation internationally. A lot of deforestation in the Amazon is done with fire and there was more than one incident of buried fuel cannisters blowing up and bulldozer treads being cut. The Forest Initiative was thought to be responsible again."

"What did they say to that?"

"That it was all propaganda ginned up by the big corporations to fight the effort to protect the forests and waterways. Again, the extreme stuff was never proven. Instead, the public face of the organization is that it's the leader in replanting trees in almost every state, including Missouri and Michigan."

I considered what Olivia had found. "How involved was Liselle with it?"

"There's no indication that she was ever involved in anything criminal. She's planted thousands of trees, though. By herself."

"Really?"

"Yep. She appears to be very dedicated." Olivia flipped through one more folder. "There are a couple more organizations but those are the main ones."

"Any of these ever come into conflict with Doprava?"

"Not that I can see."

I remembered my conversation with Pearson. "Pearson mentioned a protest at Ribbon Falls. Something to do with a fracking dispute. Can you check that out too?"

"Sure. Does it really matter?"

"I don't know." I told her about my concern about a lack of motive. "So I need to check everything they might use."

Olivia nodded. "I hear what you're saying, Shep. I didn't see anything on my first pass. I'll keep looking though."

"Thanks. Can I leave all this here until I'm done working out?

Lizzie smiled. "I insist. You going to take the class today?"

"Still not man enough. I'll stick with moving heavy stuff around."

"Your loss."

"I'm sure."

So the two of us stood up and got to work.

∼

I TOSSED MY GYM BAG AND THE FILE FOLDER FROM OLIVIA INTO the back of my Jeep. The thick brown folder seemed like a squat, ravenous beast, eager to devour a night of my life. Reading about a multi-national conglomerate didn't really seem like the best plan for a fall night. I decided I had a better idea.

I drove over to Best Buy, picked up three items and a gift bag, and then headed over to St. Wendelin's. I checked in at the information desk, found my nephew's room, and walked in to find

James with his leg up in a winch and my sister-in-law Izzy sitting in the chair next to his bed.

"Hey, Troll," I said.

"Uncle Nate!"

I had to say that, although his leg looked awful, James looked pretty good. His color was back and his eyes looked clear and he smiled which was—well, it was fantastic.

I pointed at his elevated foot, which had metal rods sticking out in a couple of directions. "Can you get the Lions game with that?"

"With what?"

"Those rods look like an antenna."

"What's an antenna?" said James.

Izzy laughed. "Yeah, old man. What's an antenna?"

Mid-thirties and over the hill already. Great. I held up the bag. "I suppose I could just take this to some other kid who has more respect for his elders."

James's face brightened. "You're the best old person I know."

Ouch again. I handed him the bag. "Have at it, Troll."

James dumped the bag upside-down and a couple of boxes that were half-assedly wrapped in tissue paper fell onto his lap. He went for the biggest one first and tore it away. "Mom! Mom, it's a Switch. Look!" He held out the box of the mobile game console.

"Wow," said Izzy.

"You don't have one, do you?" I said.

"No. Thanks, Uncle Nate!" He started ripping the box open.

"Nate..." said Izzy.

I waved. "A broken leg should be worth something."

He had the box partway open before he remembered the other package and ripped the tissue paper off it too. "Mario Kart!" James reached up and I leaned down and he gave me a pretty big hug. I gathered the paper off his lap, stuffed it into the bag, and said, "Mark working tonight?"

Izzy nodded. "He's pulling a double."

"Why don't you grab some dinner? I'll stick around and watch the virtual races for a while."

Izzy looked at James, who was busy trying to break the plastic seal on the game. She nodded and stood.

"Take your time," I said. "I don't have to be anywhere."

"Thanks," she said. "Need anything?"

"I already ate."

Izzy nodded again and left. When she was gone, I pulled an unwrapped box out of my jacket pocket and held it out. It took James a moment to notice what I was holding, but when he did, his eyes grew wide. "*Doomfarers?!* Is that for me too?"

"It is. Figured you'd have some time to unlock it all."

"Ha! I'll be the first one done. Brandon's had it for a week and he's only beaten one boss."

I helped James set up the Switch, which means he set it up and I took the cardboard, ties, and plastic wrap from him when he was done. Then he loaded up *Doomfarers* (again with assistance from me in disposing of the garbage) and together we set up a character with bright red hair who had unknown parents, strange dreams, and a magic sword that led him on a quest into the Dryad Wood.

We beat the first boss before his mom came back.

21

I DECIDED TO START MY MEDICAL RESEARCH BY CONSULTING Matthew Beckman, the toxicologist who'd helped me in the Hank Braggi case. It took about a week before he could fit me in to his schedule. You wouldn't think a toxicologist would be that busy but there you go. Fortunately, his office was right down at the University so when he finally had an opening, I made my way over to the Medical Sciences Building and weaved my way through a warren of small offices and secretarial stations until I came to the pathology department, where a middle-aged woman led me through two more corridors to Dr. Beckman's office.

It was a mess. Piles of folders and stacks of paperwork surrounded a cluttered desk with two computer monitors on one side and a whiteboard on the other. Once the secretary dropped me off, Dr. Beckman stood to meet me.

"Good afternoon, Nate," Dr. Beckman said as he unfolded himself from the chair. He was tall, with black glasses and stringy black hair that was combed over to the side and constantly fell in front of his eyes. He hesitated, then stuck out his hand as if he wasn't quite familiar with the gesture.

I grasped it and said, "Thanks for seeing me, Dr. Beckman. I've got an interesting one for you."

Dr. Beckman took two folders off the only other chair in the room, looked around a moment, then placed them in one of the only clear spots on the floor before he said, "Excellent. Not another murder, I hope?"

"Well." I smiled.

"Goodness," Dr. Beckman said and folded himself back into the chair. He hesitated then folded his hands on the desk. "So how can I help?"

"What do you know about St. John's wort?"

"It's an herbal supplement that's commonly used in a variety of remedies. Unlike a lot of these supplements, this one actually has a quantifiable effect. It's typically used for general wellness, anxiety, depression, that sort of thing."

"Is it a poison?"

Dr. Beckman started. "A poison? Goodness, no. It's used in all sorts of things."

"So what could she mean?"

"Who?"

I realized I was just confusing the good doctor so I backed up. I told him about the wedding, about Liselle Vila and Richard Phillips, about his collapse, and the coroner's autopsy and cause of death. I told him about Liselle's arrest for murder and the seemingly clean toxicology report. I told him how I'd asked Victoria Lance why we were here and her answer of "St. John's wort."

"Which is why I came to see you," I said. "So it's not a poison?"

"No, definitely not. It has side effects."

"Like what?"

"Like anything else, taking too much of it is bad. It can cause dry mouth, headache, fatigue, dizziness, even sensitivity to sunlight if you really go overboard."

"But not death?"

"No, no, not death. Certainly not by itself. The real problem with St. John's wort is its interaction with other medications."

Alarm bell. "Interactions? With what?"

Dr. Beckman pushed his hair to the side. "It's been a while since I looked at it, but if memory serves, it can interact with certain blood pressure and cholesterol medications."

Double alarm bell. "Interact how?"

"It can block their effectiveness."

"Certain blood pressure medications?" I asked. "Like beta blockers?"

Dr. Beckman snapped his fingers. "That's it." His grin at solving the minor problem faded awkwardly as he saw I didn't return it. "What? Does this have something to do with the case?"

"I'm beginning to think so."

I could see Dr. Beckman warming up to the problem. "What would you like me to do?"

"Two things." I handed him a drive with the medical documents on it. "I'd like you to take a look at the state's toxicology report and autopsy and make sure that there are no signs of any substance that we would traditionally think of as poison in Mr. Phillips' system."

"I can do that."

"Second, I'd like you to run an analysis on this." I handed him two white pouches dangling from strings.

"What are these?"

"Teabags."

"Do you have a label with the ingredients?"

"Homemade teabags. I'd like you to analyze what's in them."

"I see. Sure."

Dr. Beckman balanced the drive in one hand and the teabags

in the other hand, all sense of awkwardness gone. "And the state says these add up to murder?"

"Yep."

He smiled. "We'll see." He lifted one paper, then another, then another before muttering something about a damn calendar. "I'm a little jammed up right now. A couple of weeks okay?"

"That's fine. Trial isn't for a few months yet. I'd just like to know what I'm dealing with."

"I'll let you know as soon as I have results." He looked up and the awkwardness returned. "Would I have to testify again?"

"You might. It depends on what you find."

"Okay." He blinked a couple of times. "What happened last time?"

"What do you mean?"

"What did the jury find?"

It was my turn to blink. Dr. Beckman had testified for me in a murder case involving a famous rock star. Coverage had blanketed the local and national news for a couple of weeks. "You really don't know?"

Dr. Beckman shrugged. "I work a lot."

"Mr. Braggi was acquitted."

He blinked at me.

"We won. Your testimony was a very important part of that."

"Well, that's good."

Dr. Beckman seemed like he was done speaking then so I stood and we both awkwardly straddled files and stacks of paper until we shook hands and I made my way out.

Dr. Beckman really was a great toxicologist. I chuckled to myself. It was a good thing.

∼

On the way back to the office, my phone buzzed. Olivia.

"What's up, Liv?"

"A potential problem," she said.

"Better than an actual problem. What is it?"

"The Forest Initiative."

"The organization that Liselle belongs to?"

"Exactly. You know how Liselle was employed by the National Forest Service and the Missouri Department of Natural Resources?"

"I do."

"It looks like she was stationed in the Mark Twain National Forest."

"She's mentioned that."

"That forest is different from a lot of other federally protected areas—it isn't one solid stretch of land, like Yellowstone or Yosemite. Instead, it's made up of seven separate pockets."

"Okay."

"So that means it's got more borders that can be encroached upon."

"Makes sense."

"About five years ago, a huge deposit of natural gas was found on land adjacent to two sections of it. There was a pretty nasty fight over whether fracking on the private land should be allowed since it was so close to the national forest."

"Let me guess. The Ribbon Falls protest, right?"

"Well shit, Shep, if you already knew about it, why'd you have me spinning my wheels researching it?"

"Pearson mentioned it. I don't know the details though."

"Doprava owned the private land and wanted to exploit it by leasing it out for fracking. The Forest Initiative opposed it, claiming that fracking would destroy the adjacent woodlands and the Ribbon Falls water supply."

"Was it settled in court?"

A pause on the other end of the line. "Mostly."

"Tell me the rest."

"The surveying crew had an uncommonly difficult time marking out the official boundary of the Doprava land."

"How can that be?"

"Markers and pins kept going missing. Surveying equipment was mysteriously damaged."

"And this is relevant because?"

"While the survey was being delayed, the Forest Initiative made two public statements against Doprava's use of the land. The first statement was made by its national president. The other was made by a local expert with vast knowledge of the Mark Twain National Forest and the impact fracking would have."

Shit. "Liselle?"

"Bing. There's video from a local news conference and three articles that I've been able to find so far."

"Any proof that she did anything other than speak?"

"No."

"Any proof that the Forest Initiative was behind the surveying vandalism?"

"No proof. Only common sense."

I sorted it quickly and decided I agreed with Olivia. This was a potential problem but not an actual one, not right now. "Thanks for letting me know. Anything else?"

"You know there's actually a picture of when Liselle and Phillips met?"

"Really?"

"Yep. The society page. Took a picture of the two of them holding the Toller that they rescued."

"Toller?"

"Nova Scotia Duck Tolling Retriever. It's a pretty rare dog. It somehow wound up in the shelter there. Phillips hunted with them. That's why he adopted it apparently."

"The paper published the picture?"

"Yeah. The bitch even photographs like a knockout."

I decided to assume she meant the dog. "Can you send it to me?"

"Sure." A pause, and then Olivia said, "That's a rare dog, Shep."

"You say that like it means something."

"Those kind of dogs don't usually get dumped at shelters. The shelter's records aren't online. It might be worth looking into."

"Fine. Anything else?"

"Isn't that enough?"

"Just making sure."

"That's it. I'll follow up though."

"Keep digging. Thanks."

I hung up and a short time later pulled into the office. When I went in, I found Danny working at his computer, scrolling through something on the screen and then making notes on a legal pad. "What are you working on?" I asked.

"Witness statements." The young man shook his head and ran a hand through his thick mop of brown hair. "There's over one hundred of them."

"Literally?"

"Literally. Pearson and his boys went overtime on this one." He waved the notepad. "There's family, people at their table, people who talked to them or saw them or danced with them. I swear to god there's a statement from a guy who passed Phillips in the bathroom."

"No kidding."

"They even took statements from at least half a dozen servers and bartenders. It's ridiculous!"

Danny really did look frustrated so I thought for a moment before I said, "Okay, we know that Victoria isn't going to call all of these people. Let's put them in categories. One group is everyone who was sitting at their table. I bet that most of them are going to be called because they were closest to them throughout the night and at least a few of them aren't well-disposed towards Liselle. Let's put the servers in a category. My guess is that someone might have said something useful in front of them because people forget that the servers are there and can see and hear everything that's going on. After that, separate them between people who actually interacted with Richard and Liselle and those who just observed them." I eyed the monitor. "Have you been through them yet?"

"About half of them," Danny said.

"What's your impression so far?"

"Bre and Andrew hate Liselle's guts. Stephen seemed to be going out of his way to keep it neutral."

"And Stephen's wife Paulette?"

"Surprisingly kind."

"Interesting. What about the other guests?"

"There was a gap of about four hours between the wedding and reception so that the wedding party could ride a trolley around scenic Carrefour and take pictures."

"What a pain in the ass."

"You're InstaOld, Nate. In the meantime, there was a hospitality room set up back at the hotel for family and close friends. A dozen witnesses saw Richard and Liselle eating and drinking there for a couple of hours before they left to freshen up and head back to the reception."

Different jurors might make different assumptions about "freshening up." I let it pass for now.

Danny continued. "Anyway, after a couple of hours, they were seen leaving the hotel and arriving at the reception. There was a cocktail hour while they waited for the wedding party to arrive and by all accounts the two of them were feeling good but not excessively so."

"A variety of witnesses on that part, I take it?"

"Yep."

"They have dinner at the reception, there's all the usual wedding speeches and whatnot, they eat dinner, they drink, they dance, he dies."

I nodded. "Just wade through them for now. You never know what'll be important."

Danny didn't look thrilled at the prospect but he nodded. "What are you going to do?"

"I'm going to dive into Doprava's corporate history. This motive thing is driving me crazy."

"Okay."

"Lunch today?"

Danny looked down. "Jenny is coming in today."

"She bringing the little princess?"

Danny smiled and just about burst out of his chair. "She's crawling."

"That's exciting. Are you sleeping at all?"

"Here and there."

"You holding up?"

"No worries. Thanks."

"All right. I'll check in later."

"Will do."

I stopped at the door. "Oh, and flag anything you see about Tollers."

Danny looked at me and I had the clear impression that I'd just dropped the final straw on his bowed back. "What's a Toller?"

"A type of hunting dog. Ever heard of them?"

"No."

"Keep an eye out in the witness statements for any mention of them. Richard apparently adopted one at the gala when he and Liselle met. If there's a witness who knows about it, it could be important."

"Got it. Read every statement from every person at the wedding and flag anything that might be vital eight months from now, especially pets." He shook his head. "I'm glad I took out those student loans."

"You're welcome."

Danny ignored me and turned back to his screen. I left him to it.

TRUNK

22

Preparing a case is a slog of man-hours spent poring through files and memos and statements. It's your job to assimilate all of those facts so you can lead the jury through them and show them how everything fits together. Every trial lawyer would love a short cut and every one of them knows there just isn't one. So for the next month, that's exactly what Danny and I did. We devoured witness statements and studied pathology reports and combed through corporate filings, while taking care of our other cases too.

Life moved along during that time. James came home from the hospital but still couldn't go to school since he had to keep his leg elevated during this crucial time for healing. I took to stopping by on Wednesday nights so that Mark and Izzy could go to their bowling league and I could see James. Two things happened because of my regular Wednesdays with James and his brothers Justin and Joe. First, I became much better at Mario Smash Bros., particularly with Yoshi, so much so that I stopped randomly falling off of platforms after the second week. The trolls still destroyed me but at least I was able to stay in the game.

Second, I introduced them to *The Narnia Chronicles* by C.S. Lewis. We read *The Lion, the Witch, and the Wardrobe* out loud together, at first huddled around James's bed and later, when the doctors let him take his leg out of the sling, on the family room sectional couch. I thought they were just humoring me but, when Peter, Susan, Edmund, and Lucy took their final journey beyond the lamppost back to Uncle Digory's house, they wanted to know what happened next so we started *Prince Caspian*.

I'm embarrassed to say I lost track of Liselle in that first month. Not lost track exactly—I knew she was in her townhouse and she visited my office a few times to help explain some of the materials in the prosecution's discovery file, and I knew that her immediate needs, like getting to the grocery store, were being met. No, I mean I lost track of the upheaval in her life—of being placed under house arrest in a strange town, of being kept from a job you love, of being utterly without friends or family for support.

You'd think with my track record...well, you'd just think that I would have been more attuned to her distress. But I wasn't. Not at first.

I got the first inkling of what was going on when I received a call one morning at my desk, five weeks after Liselle had been arrested.

"Hi, Liselle," I said. "What's up?"

"Can I come over to the office?"

I looked at the clock. "I'm sorry, I have a deposition this afternoon."

"It won't take long."

"Today's not going to work, Liselle. How about tomorrow?"

"Oh. Okay. Sure."

Her tone caught my attention. I'd heard that kind of response before.

"Tell you what, my depo is out your way, why don't I stop by after?"

"You don't have to."

"It's no trouble. I'll already be over there."

"Thanks, Nate." I heard relief. "I'll see you when you're done."

"I'll text you when I'm on my way."

Seven hours later, after preparing, deposing, and traveling, I knocked on Liselle's door, a couple of coffees in hand. She answered and her smile was faint as she invited me in. As we sat down at the kitchen table, she handed me a sheet of paper and said, "Here."

I offered her one of the coffees, which she politely refused by lifting a cup of tea, and I read.

The National Forest Service had suspended her indefinitely from her job. Without pay and effective immediately. She was to remove her things from their office within fourteen days.

"Did you know this was coming?" I said.

"I knew they were uncomfortable but I thought they'd wait until after the trial."

I shook my head. "Eight months is a long time to be without an employee. They probably had to replace you."

"That's just it. Read the rest."

They weren't going to replace her. I shook my head. "What does it mean that your portion of the program is being suspended? Are they just going to let the ash borers invade?"

She shook her head. "I was the frontline, investigating and trying cutting edge solutions. They'll continue with traditional methods—quarantines, clear cutting, monitoring."

"All the things that didn't work up here."

"Exactly."

"I'm sorry."

Her hands were clenched around her mug. "Is there anything you can do?"

"I'm not going to be able to get your job back, Liselle."

"No, no. I know that. I mean to make them keep my program going."

I raised my eyebrows. "The federal government?"

"Yes."

"No."

"But the destruction!"

I raised a hand. "I understand, Liselle, I do, but you're talking about a government expenditure here. Sounds like you need a lobbyist, not a lawyer, and someone with feet on the ground in Missouri, not Michigan."

"If they don't keep looking for a solution, half the forest will be wiped out!"

"What about your forestry organizations? They have to have access to lobbyists."

Liselle looked stricken. "I've been trying to avoid them because of all...this."

"They're probably your best bet."

Through the steam of her tea, I saw Liselle's eyes begin to well up but it seemed more like frustration than grief. She took a quick sip and ducked her head behind the mug for a moment before she straightened and said, "My contacts with them dried up once I started dating Rich."

"This is different. They should still care about your work. Reach out."

She nodded. "I will. Thanks." She wiped an eye, sipped her tea, and shook her head. "I'm sorry to bother you, I just, well, there just isn't anybody here."

I looked around her house. It was fine but it was mostly empty and I was suddenly hit with a sense of oppressive isolation. "Where are you allowed to go?"

Liselle pushed her hair behind her ear. "The grocery store. Your office. Court."

"I'm sorry," I said. "I should've realized this before. Hang on."

I made calls in quick succession to Cade about the options for expanding where Liselle could travel and Olivia for some recommendations. Liselle watched me and sipped.

I hung up with Olivia and said, "Cade thinks I can get permission for you to go to the Indoor Botanical Gardens if you're accompanied. He thinks the Metroparks pose too great a flight risk. He also thinks we'll be able to pick one gym or fitness studio that's nearby. Olivia gave me some recommendations." I listed them off for her.

"What's closest?"

"There's an Orange Theory two blocks away."

The look she gave me was strange. "That would be fine."

"Great. I'll have Cade get to work on it." I stood, threw away the first coffee cup, and took the second with me as I made to leave. "I'll let you know. We'll get it taken care of so you can get out of here once in a while."

As I went to the door, she put a hand on my arm and said, "Thanks, Nate."

I waved her off. "No problem."

"I mean it."

"Me too. Talk to you soon."

I loaded up and pulled out of the driveway. She shut the door as I pulled away.

∼

I PAID MORE ATTENTION AFTER THAT AND WE ALL FELL INTO A NEW rhythm over the next few weeks. Danny and I worked on the case during the day, I continued to visit James on Wednesday nights, and I met Liselle at lunch time on Fridays at the Indoor

Botanical Gardens where I would update her on the case and she'd share her latest thoughts on her research. Even though she'd been effectively fired by the Forest Service, her mind kept working the problem and I didn't mind giving her a sounding board for her theories.

It seemed as if the weekly visits to the Garden, the daily visits to Orange Theory, and her immersing herself in her research lifted Liselle's spirits. She was invariably cheerful when we met and she seemed to take delight in showing me a new thing in the Garden each week. In retrospect, there were only two incidents that stuck out.

The first one was when she noticed that two plants from two different continents were being displayed next to each other at the Garden. Honestly, I don't know what plants and I don't know what the problem was. All I know is that Liselle was so outraged that she demanded to see the head botanist and lectured her on how that placement could cause a fungus indigenous to one land to spread to a plant from another and if so much as a single spoor ever escaped this facility, say on a shirt or a breeze or an errant hummingbird, some kind of mutated apocalypse would be unleashed on the Midwest. I didn't follow the conversation, even a little, but judging from the way that the head botanist went pale, gasped, and sprinted for a phone, I judged that Liselle was right.

The second one was a couple of weeks later when we both were a little busy and decided that, rather than walk the grounds, we'd sit on a bench and do some reading. Even though it was getting cold outside, the sun through the glass ceiling in the environmentally controlled building was pleasant and warm. I'd just finished a packet of research Danny had given me and glanced at Liselle. She was no longer reading the article she'd brought and was instead looking at a broad leaf on a neighboring plant where a silkworm was hanging by a thin, nearly invisible thread, spinning around as in a non-existent wind. She smiled.

"What are you thinking of?" I said.

"Richard," she said. She kept smiling. "Sometimes we'd talk about a complex problem, like my research or his company getting a new product to market. He had this amazing ability to step back and find solutions. Instead of struggling against the forces at play, he'd look for ways to work with them." She smiled and pointed as the swinging silkworm landed on a different leaf and began inching upwards. "Like that." She looked thoughtful. "That perspective really surprised me. It was inspiring."

"Do you miss him?"

Liselle stared at the silkworm. "I feel like there was more potential there, you know?"

"I do," I said, and then we were both quiet until it was time to go.

That's it really. That's all that stood out during those weeks when I was working and going to see James and going to the Garden. There was nothing interesting or surprising at all.

Until I received a call from Dr. Beckman.

23

"Hi, Mr. Shepherd," Dr. Beckman said. "I finally finished the testing on the herbal tea you asked for."

"Great. What did you find out?"

"I'll give you the good news first—"

That's never what you want to hear from your expert.

"—There's nothing in the tea that shouldn't be there, nothing that anyone would consider poison."

"Okay." That seemed like a pretty low bar to clear. "What is in it?"

"All of general herbs and supplements that you would find in any wellness tea on the market, chamomile, mint, ginseng, etc."

Still good news so far. "But?" I said.

"You said this tea was homemade?"

"Yes."

"By your client??"

"I believe so."

Dr. Beckman paused, then said, "I compared the composition of your client's tea to sixteen other teas on the market. The best sellers mostly. That's what took the extra time."

"And?"

"Your client's tea has more St. John's wort in it than any other tea I tested."

"How much more are we talking about here?"

"Than the next highest? I'd say on the order of fifteen times."

"And the lowest?"

"Twenty-three times."

"I take it that's significant?"

"I'm afraid that it is. I told you that St. John's wort can interfere with beta blockers, right?"

"You did."

"Did I explain how?"

"No."

"I'll give you the high points for now. Beta blocker medications are removed from the blood stream by the liver. St. John's wort speeds that process up so that that the liver removes the beta blocker from the patient's system quicker. Much quicker."

"So was the St. John's wort in the tea enough to have interfered with Richard Phillips' beta blockers?"

"More than enough."

I deliberately did not sigh. "But they found the beta blocker in Phillips' bloodstream in the autopsy."

"They did, but it was only a trace amount. I can say definitively that, by the time Richard Phillips died, the beta blocker wasn't regulating his heartbeat anymore."

There is a legal expression for this kind of news—great fuckety fuck-fuck.

"Anything else I should be aware of?" I said.

"What was he eating the night he died?"

"I don't know. Does it matter?"

"When you're taking St. John's wort, you shouldn't eat or drink foods with tyramine."

"Tyra-who?"

"Tyramine. Foods like aged meats, aged cheeses, red wine."

"Why is that?"

"Because it can raise your blood pressure to life-threatening levels."

Double the prior expression. "Anything else to avoid on St. John's wort?"

"Caffeine and alcohol."

"Do you know what a trifecta is, Dr. Beckman?"

"No. Why?"

"Because I think I just hit it. Anything else?"

"No, I think that's it. I'll email you a copy of my findings and the lab test results."

"Thanks. And send me a bill. I'm going to want you on standby. I don't know that I'm going to call you at trial but I'd like you to be available just in case."

"You know this could all be a coincidence, Mr. Shepherd. It takes a pretty deep dive to learn about these things."

"Got it, Dr. Beckman. Thanks."

I walked over to Danny's office. He looked like a soldier hiding behind a fortress of paper towers. "Have you been through all of the witness statements?" I asked.

"A couple of times, yeah."

"I want you to dive into everything Phillips ate and drank."

Danny grinned. "Sure." The grin faded as he looked at me. "Seriously?"

"Seriously. I want you to pay special attention to aged meats, cheeses, red wine, caffeine, and alcohol. Scour the statements for everything he was drinking, the meals he had, all the way down to the appetizers."

"At the hotel suite too?"

"Yep. Then, wherever we can, we need to identify the source of anything that went into his body—whether he ordered it, whether it was generally available. Pay special attention to any mention of Liselle ordering for him." I thought. "In fact, see if you can find Richard's RSVP for the meals he picked. I'd say start with the waitstaff and then move on to the other witnesses."

Danny looked flabbergasted. "That'll take a month."

"Good thing we have five. After we get through that—"

"We?"

"I mean 'we' in the royal sense."

"Got it. Anything else? Want me to count the threads in the tablecloth, interview the vintner who bottled the wine?"

"Great idea. You can do that when you're done."

Danny looked at me and it took him a few seconds to realize I was joking. He shook his head and said, "What's this about?"

"Medication interactions. I know this seems like busywork, Danny, but I think it's going to be vital. I'll explain later."

He nodded, gave me the look that I imagine Sisyphus gave Hades, and went back to work.

My phone buzzed on the way back to my desk. Olivia. "What's up, Liv?"

"You need to come over."

"Sure. I was planning on working out after—"

"Now."

"Really?"

"Yes."

"What's up?"

"I'll tell you when you get here."

"A hint?"

"You need to get something that rhymes with glass over here."

"On my way."

I let Danny know I was going to the Brickhouse and left.

∼

"You really couldn't talk to me over the phone?" I said as I closed the door and sat down in Olivia's office.

"Is your client accused of killing one of the richest men in America?"

"Yes."

"Then it can't hurt." She pulled out a folder and flipped it across her battered desk. "You have a problem. Two of them actually."

If I could keep it to two, I'd consider it a personal victory. "What did you find out?"

"Remember the fracking dispute?"

I nodded. "Doprava wanted to lease its land for fracking. The land was next to the Mark Twain National Forest and the Forest Initiative protested to stop it because the fracking would harm the woodlands."

"Right. And surveyor materials were vandalized and went missing."

"Right. But there was no connection to the Forest Initiative."

"There's a connection."

I breathed deep. "What?"

"Jeremy Raines. Second folder."

"C'mon. His name's Raines? Really?"

"Really. About six months after the last vandalism incident, he was picked up in Kansas selling stolen goods at a pawn shop."

"Those being?"

"Surveying equipment."

"Brilliant."

"Yep. Had the name of the surveying company right on it still. I didn't find it earlier because it was in a different state."

I looked at the picture of Jeremy Raines. Reddish-brown hair, freckles, thick beard, early twenties. "And does this criminal mastermind have a connection to Liselle?"

"Not that I know of."

"Small favors."

"But he does have one to the Forest Initiative."

"Member?"

"Yep. And a protester at the fracking site."

"Did he confess to stealing the equipment?"

"No. He claims he found the stuff in a dumpster and was just trying to make a buck."

"Did anyone believe that?"

"No. He eventually pled no contest."

"Conviction?"

"Thirty days and a fine."

I thought. "Okay. That's not great but it's manageable. Liselle is associated with the protest but protests happen all the time. Half the country is protesting what corporate America is doing to the environment and the other half is protesting fracking. She's not responsible for what some fringe jack-bag does."

Olivia's half-mirrored glasses and down-swept hair made her expression hard to read so I was glad when she said, "I agree. But it's closer to her than I'd like."

"True. I can manage that though."

"I'm sure you can. But you have a bigger problem."

Giddy up. "Bigger?"

She slid another folder across the desk. "Fourteen years ago in rural Missouri, a group of teenagers got busted by the police having a party in an empty barn."

"Sounds like good country fun."

"They got busted after paramedics responded to a 911 call that a boy had collapsed. It was serious enough that they wound up life-flighting him to St. Louis."

I didn't like where this was going. "Okay."

"That caused an investigation and the police found what you'd expect—beer, pot, and ecstasy."

"Alright."

"The boy eventually recovered. The police decided that he'd taken some ecstasy and then got dehydrated."

"That can make you collapse?"

"It can."

"So the problem is?"

"The boy's name was Nick Heyward. Liselle Vila's name was also on the list of teenagers who were at the party."

"We all went to parties we shouldn't have in high school. That's hardly a crime."

Olivia's face was unreadable. "The kids all had the same story."

"Okay."

"Liselle and Nick had broken up a few weeks before but the kids all thought they must have gotten back together."

"Why's that?"

"Because she danced with him all night. Until he collapsed."

24

There's an old legal saying that you can explain anything once, but if it happens twice, you're fucked.

All right, I just made that up. That doesn't make it any less true though.

"Well, shit," I said.

"Yup," said Olivia.

An even worse thought occurred to me. "He did live right?"

"He did."

"Do you know anything more than that?"

"That's all I could pick up from the police report and the witness statements."

"It sounds like I'm going to have to go to Missouri."

"It does."

"Do you have an address?"

"I do. It's in the folder."

"Thanks. I think I'd better go down there right away."

"I think you should too.

"I think I need to speak to my client first."

Olivia nodded. "I think you do."

"I'll be back later to work out. Thanks again."

"See you, Shep."

It had been about a week since I had visited Liselle. It was time to change that.

~

I texted Liselle that I needed to see her because even if someone is electronically confined to her house, it's still rude to just show up. She asked if I could give her a couple of hours. I said sure. She asked if I could bring dinner. I told her I didn't think that was a good idea. A moment later, my phone buzzed. Liselle.

"Please, Nate? I'm going crazy here. Cade or Olivia checks on me once a day but I'm literally here all alone all the time and I'm going nuts."

"Aren't you alone in the woods when you work?"

"Yes. *In the woods.* Not in a wood box with a brick face."

"I need to talk to you about the case."

"We can talk about whatever you want. Just come over here in two hours with dinner. Please."

"Okay."

We hung up. I decided against going back to the office and instead pulled into the farthest corner of the parking lot, right up next to the trees that lined the creek that ran past the Railcar, then took out the files Olivia had given me to read. The records she'd included were bare-bones but accurate. Jeremy Raines was indeed a member of the Forest Initiative and had been busted trying to sell surveying equipment that had been stolen from the Doprava fracking site at Ribbon Falls. I set that aside and went to the file that really concerned me.

I read about the night that Liselle Vila had been at a party where Nick Heyward had collapsed and been rushed by life flight to the hospital. Olivia had been thorough to pick up the bit about the dancing with Liselle. It was only mentioned in two out of the sixteen witness statements and it was tucked away between denials about who bought the beer and whether any drugs had been taken.

I read all of the witness statements from the party and by the time I was done, it was time to head for Liselle's. I stopped at a Mediterranean place along the way and, a little while later, climbed the steps to her townhouse and knocked.

Liselle smiled as she opened the door and, despite the concern that brought me there, I was involuntarily glad that she seemed happy to see me. "Nate!" she said. "Come in." She took the white plastic bag from me and dipped her head toward it. "Is that hummus too?"

"It is."

"It's like you read my mind." She touched my shoulder and guided me in. We went to the kitchen and fussed around with plates and silverware. She took some Greek salad, hummus, pita bread, and shawarma; I grabbed a gyro.

"Thanks for doing this," she said as she began to eat. "Eating alone all the time is the worst."

I left my gyro wrapped in front of me. "We have a problem," I said. "Two problems actually."

She scooped some hummus onto a wedge of pita bread and took a bite. "Mmmm. Like what?"

"Jeremy Raines for one."

Liselle's green eyes didn't blink. I know because I was watching. "Who?" she said.

"Jeremy Raines. Do you know him?"

"I don't think so. Should I?"

"Maybe. He's a member of the Forest Initiative."

"So are about twenty-eight thousand other people."

"He seemed to be based out of St. Louis."

"Then I should've run into him at some point. What does he look like?"

I showed her a picture. She set down her pita bread and stared at it for a moment. "He looks a little familiar but I don't remember ever speaking to him or anything."

"He was involved in the Ribbon Falls protest."

She nodded. "That makes sense if he's based out of St. Louis." She took another bite, chewed, then said, "But then again the whole national organization showed up for that one."

"Why?"

She smiled. "If you're not gonna protest fracking next to a waterfall in a national forest then I don't know why you would join an environmental organization."

"Did you know he was arrested?"

"No. But that happens sometimes with protests."

"Not at the protest. It seems like he stole some surveying equipment."

Liselle stared at the photo a moment longer before she pushed it back toward me. "Sorry. I don't think I've had any direct contact with him. How is that a problem?"

"Because it looks like the organization you're a part of committed a crime when it was protesting against Richard's company."

"The organization didn't commit a crime, Nate. And neither did I. I can't imagine that the prosecutor would be allowed to try and connect that with this case."

"She wouldn't. But if you have any connection with Raines, I want to know about it so I can deal with it."

Liselle looked me dead on. "Fortunately, I don't know him. What's the second problem?"

"Tell me about Nick Heyward."

This time Liselle reacted. Not much, but she lifted her

eyebrows and looked at me quizzically. "What does a high school boyfriend have to do with this?"

"Tell me about the time Nick was taken to the hospital after the party."

Liselle nodded. "It was out at the McKenzie farm. Gabby's parents were gone for a week so she had a massive party. People came from five high schools and because we were out in the country and far away from town, things got pretty wild. Nick overindulged and collapsed so we called the paramedics. They came, which meant the cops came too, which meant a bunch of people got busted, but I can't believe that I'm the only person who's been at a high school party that got broken up by the cops."

"No, you're not."

"Then why is that a problem?"

There was no way that Liselle was that dumb. She either knew and could see the connection or she'd forgotten what happened. I wanted to see what she would tell me. "What was Nick doing when he collapsed?"

Liselle scowled and she pushed a piece of bread into the hummus and she took a bite and she appeared to be thinking when her eyes widened and she dropped the bread. "Oh no," she said.

"Oh no what, Liselle?"

She looked at me and said softly, "We were dancing."

I nodded and I spent a good thirty seconds unwrapping my gyro. Then I took a bite, set it down, and said, "I think you'd better tell me what happened."

Liselle looked as upset as I'd seen her. She pushed her plate of hummus and pita bread aside and said, "This is terrible."

"Tell me."

She picked up a napkin and wiped the corners of her mouth. Then she set it down and said, "Nick and I dated for a while in high school. He was at the party too. We were all drinking and dancing and there was music playing, and someone had molly. I had never taken it before, most of us hadn't, but that was kind of the point of having a party out in the middle of nowhere. I took some, Nick took some, and most of our friends did too." Liselle looked down in a way that was almost shy. "And then we started to dance."

"Just the two of you?"

"No. There was probably at least thirty or forty of us."

"But the two of you were dancing together?"

She shrugged. "Sometimes? It's hard to say in that...state."

"So what happened?"

"We danced for a while and then Nick just went down. I don't think it was a seizure or anything, he just kind of passed out and fell to the ground. We felt him and he was really hot and he wouldn't wake up so eventually we called the ambulance."

"Did he wake up while you were there?"

"Not until the ambulance came."

"Did you stay?"

"I did. Most of the others took off."

"Did you ever find out what happened?"

"The paramedics said he dehydrated."

"Really? At a party filled with beer?"

She looked at me sharply. "Have you ever taken molly?"

"No."

"You get hot and can dehydrate so you have to be careful to drink enough water. We had some but he still dehydrated and passed out."

I nodded and thought. "Did you get along with Nick?"

"I did. We dated."

"Were you dating that night?"

"No. We had broken up."

"How long before that?"

"I'm not sure. A few months maybe."

"Any bad feelings there?"

"No."

I munched on my gyro. It wasn't exactly the way Olivia had told me the story, but it was close enough that there seemed like a good chance that Liselle was telling me the truth. "Liselle, I can't say this strongly enough. Don't mention this to anyone."

Liselle looked around the room. "Who am I going to tell?"

"Still. I mean it."

"I understand."

"You understand this is a huge problem if it comes up?"

"Will it?"

"I doubt the prosecutor knows about it. But if I found it, they might too."

"But I didn't do anything!"

"I understand. And I should be able to keep it out."

"But you might not."

"Anything's possible."

We ate for a time, not really saying anything. Eventually, I said, "I'm going to St. Louis and Fredericktown to investigate a few things."

"Good."

I could see Liselle thinking of something. "What is it?"

"I hate to ask but…could you pick up a few things for me?"

"What do you mean?"

"When the Forest Service suspended me, they packed up my things at the office." She raised her leg to show the ankle monitor. "I haven't been able to get it and they won't pay for shipping. Would you mind?"

"Where's the office?"

"Right there in Fredericktown."

I thought about what I planned to do on the trip.

"I wouldn't ask," she said, "except it's mostly research I don't want to lose. It's just a box or two and a small filing cabinet."

"Sure," I said.

"Great." She stood up, went back to her room, then came back a moment later and handed me a keychain that looked like an oak tree. "This one's the office. I'll send you the address."

"No problem." I wasn't quite done eating but I decided that dinner should be done anyway. "I better get going," I said and stood.

Liselle walked me to the door. She opened it for me and then leaned in a little as I went past. "I didn't hurt him, Nate."

I wasn't sure which one she meant. "I know. I'll call you when I get back from St. Louis."

"Okay."

She didn't shut the door right away. Instead, she stood there and watched as I backed out of the driveway. It wasn't until I turned the corner that she shut the door.

25

THREE DAYS LATER, I WAS DRIVING TO ST. LOUIS. IT WAS ONLY about an eight-hour drive from Carrefour and I figured if I was going to be bringing some things back for Liselle, I might as well load it in my Jeep rather than try to haul it back on a plane. I didn't mind the extra road-time; it was better than sitting in an empty house on the weekend.

I left after work on Friday, arrived in St. Louis a couple of hours after midnight, and stayed in a Marriott on the south side of town.

I slept in the next morning then drove another hour and a half south to Fredericktown, where Liselle lived and kept a small office. It was a tiny town of no more than four thousand whose primary attribute seemed to be that it was situated right in the heart of the Mark Twain National Forest. There were no hotels to speak of, which was why I had stayed in St. Louis.

My first stop was Liselle's office. I took the main road south through town then turned left down a private drive that was lined with ash trees.

They were still alive. It affected me more than I expected.

I came to a nice old colonial house that appeared to have

been converted to office space. A sign out front indicated it was the home of "Zane Borrune, D.C." and "MO Department of Natural Resources/Forest Service." I parked and went up to the "B" side of the office-house and let myself in. I felt vaguely uncomfortable being there even though I'd been invited. The air was a little stale as I went straight to Liselle's desk and computer station. Sure enough, there was a packed box sitting on the desk and a small, two drawer file cabinet next to it, just like she'd said.

I inspected the file cabinet. The top drawer was labeled "EAB studies." I opened the drawer and scanned the hanging files. One file was labelled "Michigan," so I picked it up and leafed through it. It was a history of the spread of the emerald ash borer across Michigan, from its arrival in the shipping containers in Detroit, to its discovery in 2002 in the Downriver area, and from there on to the woodlands across the state. The whole bottom drawer was labelled "Missouri" and was far more detailed. There were maps and geology surveys and quarantine plans and infected zones and clear-cut zones and chemical application theories and optimal replanting plans. From the little I could see, Missouri was losing the same way Michigan already had. I shut the drawers, picked up the file cabinet, and took it to the Jeep.

After the file cabinet, I loaded the box and then went back to the office to make sure I'd gotten everything. Sure enough, I'd missed one more map that was spread out on the desk itself. It seemed to show the year by year progress of the borer's voracious path across Michigan. I folded it up and prepared to leave.

A blinking light on the phone caught my eye. The phone was an older model and it looked like you could get voicemail just by hitting the lit button. I didn't know if Liselle could access the system anymore so I found a pad and a pen, hit the button, and listened to the messages over the speaker. Most of them were spam, but the eighth one was something different.

"Hello, Ms. Vila?" said the voice. "This is Missy Lincoln from Gateway Animal Rescue. Mac, the Toller that Mr. Phillips adopted, has been returned to us. I know you had some affection for Mac too so I was calling to find out if you'd be interested in adopting him. I'll be able to hold him for a week or so but after that I'll be posting him for open adoption." Missy Lincoln of Gateway Animal Rescue then left the number and address of the shelter with an invitation to call.

I wrote down the information and left.

~

MY NEXT STOP TOOK ME DUE WEST TO SPRINGFIELD, MISSOURI, which was about three hours away. That meant a drive through sections of the Mark Twain National Forest. It was late fall so there was still color; leaves of red and gold and green. At times, the trees were back a ways from the road and, at others, the trees came in and met overhead so that I was driving through a multi-colored, living tunnel.

At one point, I came to an area that opened into a valley so that I had a view of tree-covered hills for miles in the distance.

For the first time, I saw swaths of dead trees on the hillsides, like cancerous streaks amidst the greenery. The streaks were thin and you might not notice them if you weren't looking for them, but since I was, I knew lines of dead ash trees when I saw them. I traversed the valley and the trees closed back in, so close that the broader picture was hidden. But I knew it was there.

I arrived in Springfield around mid-afternoon and followed my navigation app to the southwest side of town to an industrial warehouse near Interstate 44. A weather-faded sign declared that I'd arrived at Ozark Components. I parked on the gravel because all of the spaces in the small asphalt section were filled. I'd called ahead and found out that the shift ended at four so I had a few minutes before the press operator I'd come to see got off work. I pulled out Liselle's "Michigan" file again and leafed through it.

I didn't have to read much to see that Michigan never stood a chance. In the early 2000s, people wondered why the ash trees southeast of Detroit were sickening. A lot of time was spent thinking it was a disease until a guy named Dave Roberts found larvae in a tree and sent it to a series of entomologists that led from Deb McCullough to Richard Wescott to Eduard Jendek, who finally figured out that an obscure bug from across the ocean was to blame. On July 9, 2002, they identified the emerald ash borer and quarantined the wood in five Michigan counties soon after. But it was too late. The borer had already spread and there was no way to stop it.

Little was known at the time about the emerald ash borer except that it was a burrowing pest that was indigenous to China. They eventually figured out that the emerald ash borers had hitched a ride to the port of Detroit in cargo ships and from there, disembarked to attack the woods in the surrounding Downriver area. In China, the ash trees had built up a resistance to the borers but the ash trees of Michigan? Well, those were fresh, defenseless meat.

The speed with which the borer spread was staggering. It's estimated that they first hit Detroit in the late 1990s but no one's sure since they weren't discovered until 2002. By the time my Sarah got involved in fighting the borer, it was 2007 and far, far too late. They tried everything: clearcutting, outlawing transportation of wood, you name it. But by 2014, almost every ash tree in the State of Michigan—damn near every single one—was dead. It had happened before we even knew it had hit.

I sighed and picked up a file labelled "Missouri timeline." Missouri had had warning. The first ash borer was found in July 2008 in southeast Missouri. By 2013, there had been a quarantine on ash wood in every single county in the state and in the city of St. Louis. But by August 2018, eleven more counties had reported finding emerald ash borers and where you found those, you found dead ash trees. I could see from the clippings and from her diligent journaling that Liselle had not given up, that she thought that there was an experimental pesticide being manufactured in Wisconsin that might give them a chance. But I could also see from her schematics and colored maps that the ash borer was making its relentless way through the state, and, from what I'd seen in Michigan, if you could see the results, it was already too late. I had a feeling that the ash trees in Missouri were seeing their last seasons. It was a bleak thought; the relentlessness of it, the remorselessness, the fact that there was nothing left to be done except watch all of these beautiful, century-old trees die.

A stream of men began to leave the building then and I tossed the ash borer apocalypse folder onto the front passenger seat. I got out of the Jeep and made my way toward the building as men filed out toward the forty or so cars in the lot. I saw the man I was looking for. He was a little over six feet, good size, with curlyish brown-blond hair. He had a few days' growth of beard and still looked as if he could run for a touchdown or knock down a pass, which he'd done as the star running back and safety for Poplar Bluff some years ago. He carried a small cooler and his Carhart coat in one hand as he pulled out keys with the other.

"Nick Heyward?" I said.

Nick looked up, cautious. "Yeah?"

"Can I talk to you for a minute?"

"Seems like you are."

I looked around the lot. "Is there somewhere to get a beer near here?"

His eyes narrowed. "That sounds like more than a minute."

I nodded. "Probably two beers worth."

"I don't have that kind of time, man." He clicked his key fob and the lights on a blue F-150 next to me blinked.

"It's about Liselle Vila."

Nick stopped. "What does she want?"

"She doesn't want anything. I need to ask you some things about her."

Nick's eyes darkened. "If she had a kid, it's not mine."

"She didn't and that's not it. Please. Two beers."

Nick was clearly torn. He looked at his truck then at me then back at the truck, as if he were picturing his exit. "Fine. Two beers. But I drink fast."

"Sure. Where are we going?"

"Follow me." I stepped back as Nick climbed into his truck, started it, and pulled out of his spot without waiting.

I hustled back to my Jeep and gunned it to follow him. I thought I was going to lose him until I saw the blue truck up in the distance pull into the Cardinal's Nest, which looked like Springfield's highway-side sports bar.

Nick's truck was already parked when I arrived. I parked myself and jogged inside.

Nick was sitting in a booth in the back corner, as if he were uncertain about being seen with me. That was fine because I felt the same way—I hadn't seen anyone follow me but still. As I slid into the booth, I saw that he had two long-necked bottles of Busch Light sitting in front of him and that one of them was half gone. "Nancy will get you a beer if you want since your tab is already open," he said. He took a long pull on the half-drunk beer so that now only a quarter was left. "So what does Liselle need with me after all this time?"

"I need to ask you about the party when you collapsed."

Nick half smiled and then took a sip. "Back in high school?"

"Yes."

"What do you want to know?"

"What happened?"

"There was a big party. I drank beer. I took molly. I collapsed and ended up in the hospital for three days." He took another long pull and set down an empty bottle.

I waved to the waitress and gestured for two more. "Did Liselle go to the party with you?"

"No."

That was a relief.

"We hooked up there."

Never mind.

"What do you mean?" I said.

"We had broken up a few months before and so we didn't really hang out anymore. But everyone we knew and a shit-ton we didn't went to that party so we both ended up there."

"Did you take the molly together?"

Nick shook his head and then took a drink. "I'd come with a group of eight or nine guys and girls. We all took it in a cluster and I saw other clusters of kids doing the same."

"How did you end up dancing together?"

Nick took a drink and smiled. "Have you ever taken molly?"

"No."

"We all ended up dancing together, right there in the middle of the barn."

"You remember dancing with Liselle?"

"I do."

"Did you mind?"

"Have you seen Liselle?"

"I have."

"Then you know the answer is fuck no, I didn't mind." Nick took a drink and I saw with some dismay that it was half gone. I looked around for Nancy and the next two beers but didn't see her yet.

"What happened?" I asked.

"That's kind of personal, isn't it?"

"I mean, do you remember collapsing?"

"No. I remember dancing with a bunch of people and I remember dancing with Liselle for even longer and then I remember waking up in the hospital and being told I was lucky I had avoided brain damage."

"Was it summer?" I asked.

Nick took another drink and made a face over the top of the bottle before he said, "Why the fuck does that matter?"

"Because I've read that one of the main risks of molly is overheating, that it raises your body temperature so you can dehydrate."

Nick smirked a little. "That is one of the risks. It's why people always make sure they drink water when they're tripping."

"So did the doctors tell you what happened?"

"They did."

Then Nick tipped the bottle, took five long swallows, and set down an empty beer. "Thanks, man," he said and stood. "Those hit the spot."

"Wait," I said.

"You said two beers, I drank two beers." He slipped his Carhart coat on and began to walk toward the door. Just then Nancy returned and set two beers on the table. "How about two more?" I said.

Nick turned and he stared at me for a moment and then he walked back. He picked up one of the beers, put it to his lips, and drank it in one continuous pull.

"Liselle said you were dehydrated," I said as the last of the beer glugged away.

Nick set down the empty bottle and belched. "That's what everyone thought because that's what the paramedics said when they showed up. That's not what happened though."

Nick looked at me then and the look was strange. A mixture of caution and rue. "It was the opposite," he said. "I had hyponatremia. Water intoxication."

"You had too much water?"

He nodded. "That happens too. She wouldn't stop giving them to me."

I kept my face neutral. "She?"

Nick picked up the last beer. "Liselle. She was paranoid that we would dehydrate."

"So Liselle gave you the water?"

Nick nodded. "Close to a dozen bottles of it. Bitch almost killed me." He paused. "But Jesus could she dance." He shook his head and raised the last beer. "I'm taking this one to go."

Shit. "Two more?"

"Bye."

With that, Nick Heyward walked out the door of the Cardinal's Nest. And I knew that if he ever walked in the doors of the Carrefour courthouse, Liselle Vila was doomed.

26

I paid for four beers I didn't drink and left. I didn't think I'd get another shot with Nick and I knew where he was if I had to subpoena him. Which I never, ever would.

I decided that Springfield had shown me all I cared to see and hopped onto I-44 to head back to St. Louis.

I'd logged a lot of time behind the wheel that day so I should have been tired but all I could think about during the three-and-a-half-hour drive was that it had happened before. Not exactly, maybe, but close. Fourteen years ago, Liselle had danced with a guy until he'd collapsed from hyponatremia.

I'd heard about people getting sick from drinking too much water, mostly because it had happened to some poor woman at one of Sarah's triathlons—the woman had been so worried about dehydrating that she'd drank herself to death. It sounded like the same thing had almost happened to Nick. He'd been worried about dehydrating when he was on molly so he'd drank too much water.

Correction—*Liselle* had given him too much water. While she was dancing with him. And this guy who had broken up with her a couple of months before had almost died.

I made myself pull back a little bit. This didn't look good from a practical level—if a jury heard it, they might make the leap that there was some kind of pattern. But this seemed to be an accidental overdose, *on water*, by young, stupid kids. There was nothing to show that this was anything but accidental and there was nothing to show that Richard Phillips' death was anything but natural and accidental. There was still no evidence that I could see of motive, of a reason Liselle would want Richard Phillips dead.

Still, I decided that more investigation down the Nick Heyward avenue wasn't helpful at all.

Sports radio seemed like a better option to keep me awake for the last hour of the drive. After forty-five minutes on the Kansas City Chiefs though, I found that there was a limit. I flipped through the satellite channels and found a station that happened to be playing a Lizzy Saint song off the *Ripper* album. I smiled, turned it up, and rolled the rest of the way back.

~

It was early evening when I got back to St. Louis and I realized that I hadn't eaten anything but gas station snacks and coffee all day and that I was starving. I decided it would be a waste to come all the way to St. Louis and not try some barbecue so I ducked into the hotel, asked the woman at the front desk where to go, and popped back out to my Jeep to head to Shorty's.

Most good barbecue joints run out during the day but the woman at the hotel had sworn that Shorty's had racks coming out of the pit until midnight and that Shorty took it as a personal offense if anyone went home hungry. I made the drive willingly and I'd only gone a few miles when I saw a simple, well-lit white sign with red letters that let me know that Shorty's ribs awaited.

The place wasn't much to look at from the outside; it was an old cedar plank construction with a metal roof, but it was in good repair and the dozens of cars jammed into the lot meant that decor didn't mean shit. That was confirmed when I got out of the car and smelled the smoke. It was pungent and delicious and I didn't recognize what kind of wood it was.

I inhaled, my mouth started to water, and I headed in.

The place was packed. There were a dozen people standing around the hostess stand and even more filling a bar in the center of the room, drinking and waiting for seats. I made my way up to the hostess who was busy marking off tables with a wax pen on a laminated seating chart. She looked up, harried, and then smiled.

"One for dinner, please?" I said.

She looked down at the chart. "It'll be about forty-five minutes," she said. "Unless you want to eat at the bar?"

"That would be fine."

She smiled and made a tick with the wax pencil. "Then follow me."

She grabbed a menu, smiled again, then led me through the crowd toward the back end of the bar. It stuck out like a rectangle into the middle of the restaurant with about ten seats on each long side and five on the side facing the door. She led me to a seat at the far left corner of the rectangle, right by the kitchen door, handed me a menu, and told me to enjoy my dinner. I sat down, the bartender took my order for a beer, and I took a look at the menu.

There were two choices, a half rack of ribs or a full rack. There were two sauces, Shorty's Special or Shorty's Extra. All the ribs came with coleslaw, beans, and a roll. The greatest choice was the drinks; there were five choices of soft drinks and three choices of beer. I looked again at the overflowing crowd. It seemed to me that Shorty had it nailed.

The bartender set my beer on the bar. "Ordering dinner?" he said.

"What's the difference between the Special sauce and the Extra?"

The bartender gave me a look that said no matter how simple we make it, somebody's always got a goddam question. "Extra is spicier."

"I'll take a full rack extra and another beer."

"You got it," he said, took my menu, and left.

A steady stream of platters was coming out of the back of the restaurant. Shorty must've had fifteen people running tables that night and they were all hustling. It smelled great.

I was halfway through my beer when a full rack of ribs appeared in front of me along with my sides and a second beer. The smell that wafted up reached into my soul and set my mouth to watering.

"Already?" I said.

"Already," the bartender said. He didn't appear too impressed with my grasp of the obvious.

I took a bite of the first rib and lost all track of space and time. The meat was cooked perfectly, tender so that you could bite it off the bone but firm so that it didn't fall off. There was the sharp taste of the smoke, a citrusy but spicy taste to the sauce, and a tang that made them just about the best ribs I'd ever had. I decided that the roll and the coleslaw and the beans were an evil distraction and focused solely on demolishing the ribs.

It took a while but I did it. I was just gnawing the last of the meat off the last rib bone when a man who was easily six foot seven and wearing a red shirt with a white apron came walking out the back and leaned over to whisper to the bartender. I waited until he'd stopped talking then said, "You must be Shorty."

The man regarded me with the same look the bartender had used. "I am. Why?"

"Because those are the best ribs I've ever eaten and I wanted to say thank you to whatever culinary god made them."

The man's expression changed to a smirk and he wiped his hands on a towel that was tucked into his waist. "That would be me."

I stuck out my hand. "Thank you."

The man took it and his fingers wrapped damn near all the way around my hand. "No problem."

"If you don't mind my asking, what kind of wood do you use? I didn't recognize the smell of the smoke."

"Red Oak," Shorty said. "Can't use anything but oak to smoke ribs."

"I've been using hickory. It appears that was a mistake."

Shorty smiled and looked beyond me at the crowded room. "Apparently so."

"And was there cayenne in that rub?"

Shorty looked at me sharply. "See, now that I do mind."

I should know better than that. Blame the ribs. "I suppose you would at that. Sorry, these were just fairly overwhelming."

Shorty nodded. "They do have that effect sometimes."

"Is this normal?"

"The crowd? For a Saturday. A little more since it was payday yesterday for the plant."

"Which plant's that?"

Shorty scowled at me. "The natural gas facility."

"That the plant that processes the gas from the Ribbon Falls site?"

"That's an interesting way to put it."

"How would you put it?"

"The plant just down the street."

"Ah."

Shorty eyed me from a considerable height and said, "You're not from here?"

I shook my head. "Michigan."

"What are you doing here?"

"In St. Louis? Work. In here specifically? Recommended by the clerk at my hotel's front desk who is going to get an enormous tip when I get back."

"What kind of work?"

No one wants to hear about a lawyer coming to their town and asking questions. "An errand for a friend. She left some things down here so I volunteered to pick them up. Have the protests finally stopped?"

Shorty wiped his hands on his apron. "Well, it's good to have you come all this way. Be sure to stop in if you ever come back. Enjoy the ribs."

With that Shorty disappeared back to his magical pit. I sucked the remaining meat off a rib bone and let it drop to the plate. The bartender walked back to me and pointed. "Need another beer?"

"Please."

The bartender reached into a cooler, pulled out a long neck, and popped off the cap on the opener attached to the bar. As he set it in front of me, he said, "Why do you care about the protests?"

I shrugged. "I don't really."

The bartender nodded as if that non-answer were an answer. "A lot of good jobs at the gas plant. A lot of good men have work." He pointed around the bar. "And spend money."

I nodded. "I can see that."

"We're not stupid, the forest brings in a lot of tourism dollars too. And damn near every man in here hunts those woods or fishes those rivers."

"Makes sense."

"Doesn't make sense to let some bureaucrat in Washington decide where we can work and where we can hunt."

"That is the truth."

"You sure?"

"Am I sure what?"

"That what I said is true?"

I took a sip of beer. "If you can't trust the bartender in Shorty's then I'm not going to answer the phone the next time my momma calls because she's a damn liar."

The bartender eyed me, processed, then barked a short laugh. "Damn straight," he said, then moved on to the next customer.

A moment later, I felt a heavy hand on my shoulder and a voice said, "Done with your ribs?"

I looked up and saw a man with about five days of growth on his face, brown hair, and green coveralls that said "Doprava Processing" on the left chest. He wore a baseball hat pulled down low so that his eyes were in shadow but I got the picture. "Almost," I said.

"No, I said 'done with your ribs.'" The man changed his inflection to make it a declaration.

I picked up a rib bone and began to gnaw. "I appreciate that. And I said almost."

He was standing right next to me so he couldn't really step closer so I guess it would be more accurate to say he loomed closer to me and said, "See, that's the problem with out-of-town folks. They don't know when supper's done."

"As well-traveled as you look, I can't believe that you know everyone in St. Louis." I took a sip of beer.

The man blinked. "What?"

"Maybe I'm from the north side. Do you ever get up to the north side?"

"No." The man blinked again. "Sometimes."

"Well, do you ever get to my neighborhood?"

"What neighborhood?"

"I didn't think so. See, you should learn your neighborhoods before you accuse people of being from out-of-town."

The man's eyes twitched back and forth before they stopped and narrowed. "I said, you're done with your ribs."

I was finding the people in southwest St. Louis to be fairly single-minded. I made a point of picking up another rib and gnawing it clean. I looked around the man's shoulder and saw two more men in green coveralls watching us from just a couple of arm's lengths away. This looked like it might go the route of being downright unsportsmanlike.

I held up one finger and made a point of biting the last bit of meat off the end of the rib. Then I tossed my rib bone into the air so that it flipped up end-over-end until it came down and landed with a clatter on my plate.

Coveralls Boy couldn't help it. He watched the bone arc up over the plate and then rattle home.

I stood up quickly and delivered an uppercut just below his ribs and to the left of his solar plexus.

Recently, I had spent a little more than a year working through some shit. A big part of that had been training with Cade Brickson. I had known my way around a fight before but Cade had taught me the unfettered joy of the liver punch. He would have been proud.

Coveralls Boy bent over and dropped to a knee. A second later, he puked on the floor.

I caught him with one arm and lifted him into my chair. "Hey, bartender," I waved. "I think this guy's had a little too much."

"Jesus, Randy, again?" said the bartender. I peeled off three twenties and tossed them onto the bar. I made a show of steadying Randy into my seat and patting him once on the back before I headed for the door. "Give my best to Shorty," I said and waved on the way out.

I kept a straight face and walked, neither fast nor slow, toward the doors. I heard Randy coughing and panting behind me. The other two men in green coveralls seemed confused, looking from me to Randy and back. I nodded, didn't speed up, and walked out the door.

Once I was in the parking lot, I knew it didn't do to linger. I hustled to my Jeep, climbed in, and drove back to my hotel.

I decided I felt better all the way around.

27

THE NEXT DAY I JUST HAD ONE THING LEFT TO DO. FIRST THING IN the morning, I drove to Gateway Animal Rescue.

I don't know what I was expecting, maybe a bunch of cages and a little mini jail for dogs, but it wasn't that at all. I found kennels and crates of all sizes, housing barking dogs and aloof cats and one potbelly pig of a surprisingly good disposition. I also found an exercise yard and an agility course and three climbing posts, along with what looked to be at least eight high school and college students feeding and grooming and exercising the animals.

I waved to a young woman filling the bowl of a forlorn Great Dane and asked for Missy Lincoln, the owner of the shelter who had left the message at Liselle's office. The girl nodded, scratched the chin of the Great Dane (who in turn rubbed his great head against her leg), and told me to wait just a moment. The Great Dane and I each stared with mutual curiosity about what the other was doing here, when a woman in her forties came over from the exercise yard. She had long, honey blonde hair with a streak or two of gray and she wore jeans, work boots, and a gray fleece that was, not surprisingly, covered in dog hair. She smiled and I was taken aback because it was about as nice and as forthright a smile as I'd ever been given.

"Missy Lincoln," she said. "Can I help you?"

She offered me her hand so I took it and said, "Nate Shepherd."

Her smile brightened even more. "I like the name."

"Thanks. This is a great place."

"We try. There's an awful lot of work to do." She slipped her work gloves off and gestured. "You'll have to excuse the mess; I was digging a post hole for a new obstacle in the yard."

I waved. "You can't do good work without getting dirty."

"Ain't that the truth. So what can I help you with?"

"You left a message for Liselle Vila about a Toller. I was following up."

A wave of something crossed Missy's face. "I did. I shouldn't have done that."

"Why not?"

"Because I didn't know what had happened."

"What do you mean?"

"Do you want some coffee?" Missy said. "It's still not noon and I'm still in the refueling part of my day."

"I'd love some."

She gestured for me to follow her and we went to a small kitchenette area with a microwave, a mini fridge, a sink, and most importantly, a large coffee maker. "Where did you find one that holds sixteen cups?" I said. "I haven't been able to find one of those anywhere."

"A special donation." She smiled. "Probably the best one we've ever received."

She poured me a cup and one for herself and left them both black which increased my admiration for her another notch.

The din of the dogs was a little less in here so that it was easier to hear her as she said, "It's kind of a long story."

I smiled and raised my mug. "I'm fully fueled to listen."

"You're a friend of hers?"

I nodded.

"I do feel like I owe her an explanation. I know she really liked the dog."

"I'll pass it along."

Missy took a sip of her coffee, then said, "We took ten dogs with us to the Furball last year for adoption. It's a great event for that, usually all of our dogs are placed with good owners. We'd had a Toller come in the week before, which is unusual because purebred hunting dogs don't end up here very often. Well, Richard Phillips bird hunts with Tollers so the minute he saw Mac, he wanted to adopt him on the spot."

Missy smiled. "Liselle had seen Mac first and had wanted to adopt him herself and the two of them had a good-natured battle over him. In the end, Richard convinced her that his two-hundred-acre estate, regular hunting, and two companion Tollers was the best possible environment for Mac. In exchange for visitation rights, Liselle conceded and played with him while Richard filled out the paperwork."

"You remember all that?"

Missy nodded and sipped her coffee before she said, "You don't often see a woman in an evening gown willing to get down on a knee and play with a dog." Missy smiled self-deprecatingly and gestured at her fleece. "I can appreciate that."

I smiled. "It's a rare gift."

"People are never ready to take the dogs home right then so we arranged for him to pick-up Mac the next day."

"Did you handle that too?"

She nodded. "I always do. These people are usually big

donors and I like to make sure that the dogs all get to their new homes smoothly. Richard came to pick up Mac himself and Liselle was with him."

"Oh?"

"I was a little surprised when they showed up together because I had the impression that they hadn't met until they were competing for Mac." She paused and took another sip. "By the time they left, I had the impression that the visitation might have started without him."

I let that pass.

"So about a month ago, a young woman I didn't know brought Mac back and of course I recognized him right away. I asked why she was bringing him here and she said that Mac was 'that woman's' idea and she could just take care of him. I didn't know what she meant because I tend to miss the news with all that goes on here. She left before I could ask anything else but it didn't take long to figure out that Richard Phillips had died and that there was no one to take care of Mac. My first thought was of Liselle. We'd spoken at the Furball about the fact that she worked in the Forestry Service and we had a lot of common interests so I didn't even think about it and called her office right away."

She took the pot off the burner and held it out to me. I nodded and held up my cup as she refilled it and then refilled her own. "Like I said, I don't follow the news much so I didn't know what had happened. Or about the arrest."

"Did that surprise you?"

Missy shrugged. "Animals are my life, Mr. Shepherd. I have a hard time believing that someone who loves animals that much could do something like that. So how do you know Liselle?"

I thought for a moment about being evasive but Missy didn't seem like that kind of person. "I'm her lawyer. I was down here picking up some things for her when I saw your message. She's pretty lonely and I thought that if the Toller was still here..."

"There are Toller rescue organizations that keep an eye out for purebreds like this that end up in shelters. Once I learned what had happened, I let them know and Mac was adopted within a week." She smiled. "He's in Washington State as we speak."

Missy took another drink before she said, "And I'll be honest with you, I don't know that I would've let you take him."

"Why is that?"

"His life had been disrupted enough. Liselle would've been great with him but if she's convicted..." She shrugged.

"I hadn't thought of it that way."

"People usually don't."

I thought. "Would you mind if I looked at the paperwork for Mac?"

Missy cocked her head. "Why?"

"Lawyer habits. Just to be thorough."

She looked at me and smiled, just a little. "Do those lawyer hands get dirty?"

I smiled. "Sure."

"I have three more post holes to dig for our mini bridge. Give me a hand and I'll have one of the kids copy the file while we work."

"Done." We shook hands, set down our coffee mugs, and went out to the yard.

~

AN HOUR AND A HALF LATER, I DUSTED OFF MY HANDS, ACCEPTED the manila folder with Mac's paperwork, and said goodbye to Missy Lincoln. I stared at the Great Dane for a while and he stared back at me, but I remembered that I was alone and that I was a lawyer and that I was gone for long stretches of days at a time. In other words, I'd be a pretty crappy dog dad right now. I felt a twinge of regret and an unexpected wave of missing Sarah and went out to the Jeep.

I got on the road and was about two hours out from St. Louis when I was hungry enough to stop at a drive thru. Apparently, I wasn't the only one because the line was long and it was slow and it didn't appear to be in danger of picking up anytime soon. I grabbed Mac's folder and opened it. I saw the transfer paperwork for the Toller from a few weeks ago showing that he was being adopted by the Collins family, who'd come all the way in from Washington. It had their address and the licensing information and the records Gateway had provided showing that Mac was current on all of his shots.

The drive-thru line crept forward. I turned to the next page, which showed the return of Mac to Gateway by one Bre Phillips. It was a brief one-page form that listed her name, address, and the reason for dropping off the dog. The form had checkboxes for age, disease, behavior, biting, or other. Bre had checked "other" and scrawled "owner died."

The next page was the paperwork from when Richard had adopted Mac at the Furball. Again, it had all of Mac's information and proof from the rescue that he'd received all of his shots and was licensed.

I turned to the last page in the folder, which was again the check-box drop-off form. I read it, read it again, and pulled out of the drive-thru line into a parking space. I put the Jeep in park and stared at the page.

The man who had dropped Mac off was listed as Jeremy Raines.

For a fleeting moment I hoped that it was a coincidence but then I saw that his address was an apartment in Kansas City, Kansas.

Jeremy Raines, protester at Ribbon Falls, stealer of surveying equipment.

And member of the Forest Initiative. The same organization Liselle was part of.

It was a long drive back.

28

It was late when I got to Liselle's house. I didn't care. I was carrying her file cabinet so I knocked with my elbow.

She told me to wait a moment through the door. When she finally opened it, she was barefoot and wearing blue jeans and a white, V-neck t-shirt. "Nate?" she said. "I wasn't expecting you."

"I just got back from St. Louis."

Her eyes lightened. "You got my files? Come in." She opened the door wider and stood aside and I brought the file cabinet into the kitchen "Right there by the table is fine," she said. She sat down, opened a drawer, and started leafing through the folders. "This is great. Great! I had some of these things online but I hadn't converted a few of the studies to—"

"We need to talk about the trial."

Liselle stopped, straightened, and closed the file drawer. "Okay."

"I'm not going to put you on the stand. You're not going to testify. That means the prosecutor isn't going to be able to ask you questions about what happened, or about Rich, or about your past."

"Fine."

"But I need to know the truth about those things so that I'm prepared to respond to them."

"Sure."

"I'm your lawyer, Liselle. You can tell me the truth."

Liselle looked confused. "Of course."

"How do you know Jeremey Raines?"

"Who?"

"The man from the Forest Initiative who was at the Ribbon Falls protest. The one who stole the surveyor equipment."

There was nothing but question in her eyes as she said, "The guy we talked about before?"

I nodded.

"I told you, I don't know him."

"He's a member of the same group as you."

"The Forest Initiative doesn't really have meetings. It's more of a society that you donate money to, get their newsletter."

"A society you protested with at Ribbon Falls."

Liselle shrugged. "With five thousand other people, Nate. I've told you that. I think I heard that it was one of the biggest protests the Initiative ever put on. I can't imagine that I knew more than a handful of the people who were there."

"So you're saying you don't know Jeremy Raines?"

"No, I don't."

"And you weren't involved in sabotaging any of the equipment at the fracking site?"

Liselle's brow furrowed. "Of course not."

"Even though it was right in your backyard?"

"I had other things on my mind, Nate." She tapped the file cabinet. "I was spending my time working on things I hoped I could actually change. Every day I did something else was another day that this burrowing plague had to destroy our forest. Sabotaging fracking equipment doesn't save ash trees." She pulled a leg under her. "Why do you care about this guy?"

"You got a call from Gateway Animal Rescue."

No flash of guilt or panic. Instead, Liselle looked at her phone. "I did?"

"At your office. I went to see them. Mac got returned."

Real dismay seemed to cross Liselle's face. "Richard's Mac? What's wrong? Is he okay?"

"After Richard died, Bre returned Mac to the shelter."

"Oh, no. Does he need a home? You have to help me get him!"

I raised a hand. "Missy found him a home."

Liselle visibly relaxed. "Missy is the best." Then real anger darkened her face. "He should be with the others, with Ozzie and Tony."

"Who?"

She smiled. "Richard's other Tollers. He was a real Cardinals fan." She scowled again. "Mac's had enough disruption as it is. Uprooting him again is cruel."

"Missy placed him easily. She said there are groups of owners that keep an eye out for Tollers like Mac that turn up at shelters. You know how unusual that is, right?"

"How unusual what is?"

"For a rare breed of hunting dog to show up at a shelter?"

"Absolutely. That's why I was so interested in Mac. He could've run with me all day in the field. If I'd known Bre had brought him back, I'd have taken him in a heartbeat."

I handed her the folder on Mac that Missy had given to me. "He's with a good family now. Here's his paperwork if you're curious."

Liselle opened the folder and read. "Oh, good. The family's in Washington State. It's beautiful out there."

"Uh-huh," I said and watched. She flipped the page then shook her head. "Bre returned him within a month? Mac must be so confused."

"I'm sure," I said.

She turned the page and then turned a few more in quick succession until she came to the last one. She froze. "Nate."

"Yes?"

She looked up, her eyes filled with alarm. "This says that Jeremy Raines abandoned the dog at the shelter."

I nodded. "It does."

"Nate, that looks awful!"

"I'm glad you see that."

"Who is this guy?"

"That's what I keep asking you, Liselle."

"I don't know!"

I stared at her. She was sitting there with one leg folded under her, giving off nothing but fear and concern. I wasn't getting a vibe of deception at all.

I suppose I wouldn't if someone was really good at it.

"That's a pretty big coincidence, Liselle."

"That's my point, Nate. It looks terrible!"

"So what's the explanation for it?"

"I don't have one," she said.

"That's not very helpful."

"Well, if I were involved in it, I'd have one. But I'm not, so I don't."

"I'm going to need to be able to explain this at trial."

Liselle looked all around the room, at Mac's file, at me, at the table. Her panic was palpable before she said, "Are you?"

"Am I what?"

"Going to have to explain it at trial?"

I was silent for a moment before I said, "Probably not. I only contacted Missy because of her message to your office. I don't know that the prosecution has tracked that far."

"Let's hope not because I can't explain it all," she said.

"You have some time to think about it," I said.

"Time to think doesn't change the truth, Nate. I don't know why this guy dropped Mac off at the shelter."

She got up and grabbed a couple of bottles of water out of the fridge and gave me one. I thanked her, left it unopened, and said, "I also talked to Nick Heyward."

She froze for a second, then cracked the bottle and took a drink. "How is Nick?"

"We didn't talk about his current life much."

"Where was he?"

"At a plant over in Springfield."

"And?"

"And he remembers you."

"Of course he remembers me! What did he say?"

"He remembers the night he took molly with you."

"And with about thirty other people," she said.

"And he remembers collapsing and waking up in the hospital."

Liselle shook her head. "They warned us, the kids who had taken it before. They told us that we could dehydrate and have heat exhaustion."

"That's just it," I said. "He didn't dehydrate."

Liselle cocked her head. "What do you mean?"

"I mean that Nick didn't dehydrate. He had hyponatremia. He had *too much* water."

"What?"

I looked at the bottle sitting on the table in front of me. "And he said you gave it to him."

"That can't be," she said.

"Did you give him the water, Liselle?"

"They said we could dehydrate!"

"Did you give him the water?"

"They said we could overheat and die."

"Did you give him water?"

"Of course I gave him water! I didn't want anything to happen to him!"

"Why did you tell me he dehydrated?"

"Because that's what the paramedics told us! That's what they told all of us!"

"That's not what Nick found out when he woke up in the hospital."

Liselle's eyes were wide. "I never saw him again, after he went to the hospital. His parents wouldn't let us see him in the hospital and he never returned my calls."

"Why did you give him the water, Liselle?"

"Because I thought I was protecting him!"

And for the first time since all this had started, Liselle began to cry. Not small tears gently rolling out of the corner of her eyes. No, she put her head into her hands so that her blonde hair tumbled around to hide her face and she sobbed. She wasn't loud but her breath came in ragged gasps and her shoulders trembled and her arms shook and, in that moment, she projected nothing but abject distress and utter vulnerability.

I stood up, put my water bottle on the counter, and picked up a box of tissues, which I set next to her on the kitchen table. Liselle took one, wiped her tears, then looked up at me, her light green eyes brimming and filled with fear. "I'm in trouble, aren't I, Nate?

"Yes."

"Can you help me?"

"That's what I'm trying to do."

"Thank you," she said and reached out her hand.

I stepped back. "No surprises, Liselle. If there's anything else I need to know, you need to tell me now, before trial."

She pulled her hand back. "There isn't anything else," she said and collapsed into herself a little bit.

"Then I'll talk to you tomorrow."

"Okay," she said quietly.

"I'll let myself out."

It's not natural to leave someone in anguish, to refuse to comfort them when they're afraid and distressed and alone. But it wasn't my job to comfort Liselle, even if she reached out to me. It was my job to save her, to win regardless of whether she had killed Richard Phillips or not.

And I found that right then, on that particular night, I had no idea if she had.

29

Over the next months, the prosecution's case became clear. Victoria Lance was going to argue that Liselle gave Richard Phillips a tea laced with St. John's wort that neutralized his blood pressure medication, fed him foods and drinks that would spike his blood pressure, and then danced with him until he went down. They would portray her as an environmental extremist upset over fracking.

The day for both sides to disclose our witnesses came. Neither Nick Heyward nor Jeremy Raines was on the prosecution's witness list. I breathed a little easier.

Danny and I prepared, with the occasional research help from Olivia. Liselle and I continued our weekly lunch walks at the Botanical Garden. I thought they might be awkward after our conversation when I returned from St. Louis but Liselle acted as if nothing had happened and she didn't break down before trial again. She continued her research and shared the latest with me and it lightened both of our moods when the weather grew warm enough that spring for us to move to the outdoor sections of the garden.

I continued the visits with James and Justin and Joe. Mark

and Izzy were more than happy to let me and bowling night became a couple's game night which became co-ed softball night as summer approached. The boys and I continued *The Narnia Chronicles* and, when we finally got to *The Last Battle* and the Pevensie children had gone farther up and farther in, I thought we might be done, but I still wanted to come over and they still wanted me to read so we started on *The Belgariad* by David Eddings. We eventually made it to where Garion had met the half-dryad Ce'Nedra when I told the boys that I had to stop and put the book aside for a few weeks, and met their protests with promises that yes, yes, we would start up again soon.

It was time to go to trial.

ROOTS

30

Danny and I had decided that jury selection might be the most important part of this trial. Apparently, Victoria Lance did too.

Judge French ran a good court. He'd been a bailiff before he had become a judge so he had an inherent sense of how these things should flow and he would accommodate almost any reasonable suggestion so long as it moved the case forward. At the same time, he wasn't shy about dropping the hammer, in the calmest, most courteous way, when an attorney or witness went too far afield.

We were approaching the limit of his patience by noon of the second day when he said, "Counsel, please see me in chambers before we break for lunch."

I let Liselle know I'd be right back. She sat at the counsel table, back straight, hands folded, and nodded. Danny and I followed Judge French back to his office.

Victoria brought her whole team. She had an associate—Carrie Landon, I think—and a man and a woman who looked to be in their mid-forties. I wasn't sure what their role was but they'd been passing notes to Victoria the whole time she was questioning jurors. The man's head had been buried in a laptop while the woman had been making furious notes on a tablet with a stylus.

The judge had three fabric chairs in front of his desk and a sagging couch on one wall. Victoria, Carrie, and I took chairs while Dan stood off to one side. The man and the woman hesitated, then took a step toward the couch.

"I believe I directed counsel to come back," Judge French said.

Victoria gestured. "Your Honor, this is David Jenson and Elizabeth Korzwyski from—"

"Are they attorneys representing the State?"

"No, Your Honor. They're jury consultants. I assumed we were going to talk about the jury selection process."

"We are. You're free to consult with them when you're done here."

"Of course, Your Honor." Victoria nodded to the consultants and they left.

When the door had shut, Judge French took one side of his glasses between his thumb and forefinger and straightened them. "Counsel, this has gone on long enough. We are seating a jury after lunch and we're going to have opening statements this afternoon."

Victoria straightened in her seat. "Your Honor, I'm certainly sorry that it's taken this long to seat a jury. I thought we'd be giving openings yesterday too. But we have a right to explore the jurors' beliefs so that we get an impartial panel."

I stayed silent.

Judge French sighed. "You're not trying to get an impartial panel, Ms. Lance. You're trying to seat older women. Mr. Shepherd is trying to seat men of any age. I'm not going to comment on whether such a strategy is sexist but I will say that I've reviewed the current pool of jurors, I've listened to their answers and there will be no more challenges for cause granted. After lunch, you're each going to get your three peremptory challenges to strike three jurors and we're going to get underway."

"Yes, Your Honor," we both said.

Judge French nodded and looked at the ceiling. "And, not that this would happen mind you, but if you strike three men, Ms. Lance, or you strike three women, Mr. Shepherd, it would seem to me that you better have a pretty good gender neutral reason for doing so or you're going to have a hard time overcoming a *Batson* challenge. Don't you agree?"

"Yes, Your Honor," we both said.

"Good. Now I'm going to get some lunch. Please be back in an hour."

We all stood and left. Victoria went straight over to her consultants, pulled out a chart of the jurors, and started whispering. Danny and I went over to Liselle, who still sat arrow straight at the table, her hands folded in front of her. She was wearing a conservative black suit that made her pale blonde hair seem almost white and she seemed nervous, which was to be expected given that we'd been sitting there for a day and a half picking the people who were going to decide whether she had committed murder.

I gestured and she followed me out into the hall, as did Danny. Olivia Brickson had been sitting in the back of the courtroom, and after a nod from me, she joined us as well.

"We're going to make the final jury selection right after lunch," I said. "We're not going to ask them any more questions. We're just going to knock out the three that we're the most uncomfortable with."

"Only three?" said Liselle.

I nodded. "And they can't all be women."

"Why not?" said Liselle.

"If we do, then the judge is going to assume that we're doing it because of their gender and that's not allowed." I handed Liselle the juror seating chart with their names and descriptions. "Think about it over lunch. Olivia, would you mind taking Liselle to grab something to eat?"

"Sure," said Olivia.

"I can't eat," said Liselle.

"Then get some water and eat a snack. You'll need it later in the afternoon."

"What are you going to do?"

"Danny and I are going to make sure everything is ready for opening statements."

Liselle eyes were a little wide.

"It's okay. Go with Olivia."

She nodded and the two of them went downstairs with Olivia saying something about the café on the first floor.

"What do you need me to do?" said Danny.

"Let's make sure everything's ready to go and then you can grab a quick bite too."

Danny nodded and the two of us went back into the courtroom.

Victoria and her associate Carrie were still huddled with the jury consultants. The man was animated, as was Carrie, who looked up when I entered and stopped talking.

In case you're wondering, this many people on the prosecution side of a case was not usual, not in Carrefour anyway. Having the chief prosecutor and an associate in court, another associate working back at the office, and two jury consultants was far beyond the usual budget for a case in a town like ours.

It was almost as if a billionaire had died.

Danny and I made sure our screen was up and our projector was working and that our trial presentation software was ready to go. Victoria and Carrie and the consultants seemed to reach an agreement on whatever they were debating and the four of them made to leave the courtroom. Victoria stopped at the gate and said, "Share the same screen, Nate?"

"Of course," I said. "I'll leave it up."

She nodded. "Thanks."

Once we were sure everything worked, we turned everything off and Danny went to get something to eat. I took my bag lunch, complete with the ever-exciting turkey sandwich and an orange, and went to a quiet spot on the fifth floor, where I ate my sandwich and went over my opening one more time.

At the appointed time, we met back in Judge French's chambers. This time it was everyone—lawyers and clients and consultants. Danny, Liselle, and I stood on one side of the judge's office while Victoria, Carrie, and the two consultants stood on the other. We each had a chart of the twenty-four jurors remaining in the pool. The first twelve would be our jury and the next two after that would be our alternates. Each time we struck somebody, the next one in line would move up.

"Ms. Lance, the prosecution may exercise its first peremptory challenge."

"Your Honor, the prosecution would thank and excuse juror number six."

Man, executive, married to wife number two. That moved up juror number thirteen, a married mother of two who had worked for fifteen years at a local bank.

"Mr. Shepherd, it's your turn."

I leaned in and whispered to Danny and Liselle. "Do we still agree on juror number three?"

Danny and Liselle both nodded.

"Your Honor, the defense would thank and excuse juror number three."

Divorced woman, fifties, husband remarried to a woman in her thirties.

"Very well," said Judge French, his face unreadable. "Juror number three is excused and juror number fourteen moves up." Juror number fourteen was a single man in his thirties who worked at the Ford plant as a line engineer.

"Ms. Lance?"

The prosecution team huddled and whispered. There again seemed to be a difference of opinion between Carrie and the male consultant. I'm not sure who won, I only know that Victoria straightened and said, "Your Honor, we would thank and excuse juror number two."

Man, fifties, divorced.

"Very well, juror number two is excused and juror number fifteen moves up."

Juror number fifteen was another woman. Thirties, two kids, homeschooling.

"Mr. Shepherd?"

We whispered and agreed to our predetermined second choice. "Your Honor, we will thank and excuse juror number five."

Juror number five was a happily married young nurse. However, she had repeatedly volunteered that her father had divorced their mother for a younger woman.

"Very well, that will seat juror number sixteen. Ms. Lance?"

This would be interesting. She either needed to pass or dismiss a woman.

The prosecution group whispered and this time it lasted longer. Judge French waited patiently.

Finally, Victoria said, "Your Honor, we would excuse juror number thirteen."

"That would be the woman who was originally the alternate?"

"Yes."

That was interesting. I would've thought that the woman they just dismissed would be in their camp, but then I saw that it moved a woman on who would, presumably, fit their apparent ideal-juror profile even more closely. And since they'd bounced a woman, I couldn't object that they were discriminating based on gender.

"Very well, Mr. Shepherd?" Judge French said.

I looked at the current alternate, a woman who'd given off such strong body language against our case that it had seemed like a beacon. If I struck anyone, she would move onto the jury.

"I think we stand pat," I said to Liselle and Danny.

"Why?" said Liselle.

I explained. "If we strike someone, this woman goes onto the jury."

Liselle nodded. "I don't see anyone worse either."

"Okay." To the Judge, I said, "Your Honor, we'll pass on our last peremptory."

"Very well. Ms. Lance, Mr. Shepherd, you have your jury. Opening statements in fifteen minutes."

"Thank you, Your Honor."

We walked out and Danny made a clean list of our jurors and then gave it to Olivia who would run a final check on all of them. We wound up with seven women and five men and a fairly even distribution of single, married, and divorced. I still thought the prosecution's case was thin and that Liselle's relationship with Richard and their age difference shouldn't matter but sometimes the smallest thing can turn a case.

After eight months, we were about to find out.

Once the jury was sworn in, there was some rustling over on the prosecution's side of the courtroom. I saw the jury consultants fall back into the gallery and two new people, who had the look of young attorneys, move forward into the first row, laptops in hand.

I leaned closer to Liselle. "Doing okay?"

She nodded.

"Good. Remember, keep your cool and don't show any emotion. This next part is going to be hard. They're going to portray you in the worst possible light."

Liselle nodded again.

I looked at Danny. "You ready?"

Danny tapped his laptop. "All set."

I nodded, crossed my legs, and faced the jury.

"Ms. Lance," said Judge French. "Is the State ready to proceed?"

Victoria stood. "Yes, Your Honor."

"Very well. You may give your opening statement."

31

Victoria Lance strode to the lectern without a note. She wore a finely tailored blue suit and moderate heels that attracted no notice. The only jewelry she wore were small gold earrings, a gold watch, and her wedding band. She walked right up to the jury as if she were meeting them at a cocktail party and said, "Liselle Vila killed Richard Phillips at his nephew's wedding. And she did it intentionally. For that reason, we're going to ask you to find her guilty of first-degree murder."

Victoria paused and looked at each one of the jurors before she continued. "This case is different, though, because I'm not going to be presenting you with a traditional murder weapon." She pointed to the evidence table where pre-marked items were arrayed. "I won't be showing you a gun or a knife or a baseball bat. I won't be presenting you with a car that a drunk driver got behind the wheel of or a swimming pool that someone left the door open to or the broken leash of a vicious dog that got loose."

"No, the evidence will show that a very different sort of murder weapon was used in this case."

Victoria strode to the evidence table and brought a cup and the teabag back with her. She put the cup on the edge of the jury box and dropped the teabag into it. Victoria let it sit there and moved back a couple of steps to give the jury room. "There are two murder weapons in this case. That bag of tea, which contains an herb called St. John's wort is one." She paused. Then she pointed at Liselle. "And the defendant, Liselle Vila, is the other."

She had the jury's attention.

"The evidence will show that the victim, Richard Phillips, had high blood pressure and an irregular heartbeat. In order to treat those conditions, he was given a common medication, a beta blocker called Lopressor. This medicine kept his heart rate low, kept his blood pressure low, and kept his heart beating in a normal rhythm."

Victoria stepped forward and tapped the edge of the teacup with her pen. "The evidence will show that the tea in this bag contains something called St. John's wort. Now, St. John's wort is a common herbal supplement that's used to treat anxiety and depression. But it has a side effect, a well-known side effect."

She paused.

"It eliminates the effect of beta blockers."

She let that hang out there for a moment. "You're going to hear from our experts exactly how that happens but for now, I'll just say that the evidence will show, conclusively, that St. John's wort prevents beta blockers from working."

Victoria lifted the teabag out of the cup. "This isn't a teabag you can buy in a store, by the way. It's homemade. The evidence will show that Liselle Vila made it. And the evidence will show that it contains fifteen times the amount of St. John's wort found in commercial teas. Let me say that again. The tea in this bag that Liselle Vila made contains fifteen times the normal amount of St. John's wort." The teabag spun on the string like a hypnotist's watch. Eventually, Victoria dropped it in the cup.

"The evidence is going to show that Liselle Vila and Richard

Phillips came here to Carrefour for his nephew's wedding and, throughout that whole weekend, Liselle Vila made sure that Richard Phillips drank plenty of this tea which was cancelling out the effectiveness of his blood pressure medication."

"That's not all that she did though. You're going to see that Liselle Vila left nothing to chance. You're going to hear that she also made sure that Richard ate and drank things that would stress his heart, spike his blood pressure. And then," she shook her head, "and then with his system incredibly stressed, Liselle Vila danced with him."

Victoria raised her hands, "Now, at first glance you may think that there's nothing wrong with that, but you're going to hear evidence that Richard Phillips asked to stop dancing, several times, but that Liselle continued to encourage him to stay out on the dance floor, just like she encouraged him to drink and she encouraged him to eat. And he did all of those things until he died."

Victoria stepped back a little bit. "Now, you may think those things are all coincidental. But we will show that, when you put it all together—that she made the tea that blocks the effectiveness of his heart medication, that she gave him tea and food and drink that encourages an irregular heartbeat, and then that she danced with him until he literally died of an irregular heartbeat—we think that you'll be convinced that it was not a coincidence at all. But just in case there's any doubt, we will present you with evidence that she had a motive to do so, that she regularly opposed the policies of the Richard Phillips' company, a company which he no longer runs now that he's passed away."

Victoria stepped forward and tinked the cup one more time with her pen. "This murder is unusual. The evidence that you will hear is unusual. But in the end, the result is not. Richard Phillips is dead. Liselle Vila killed him with malice and just as she intended. For that reason, at the end of this case we will ask you to find Liselle Vila guilty of murdering Richard Phillips. Thank you."

The jurors' eyes followed Victoria back to her seat. I checked Liselle quickly. Her face was composed and she'd met Victoria's accusations with a raised chin. I smiled and stood and walked over to the jury and said, "I think it's really important that we review what Ms. Lance said the evidence is going to be in this case." I counted off on my fingers. "Liselle Vila and Richard Phillips drank tea with an over the counter herbal supplement in it. They ate at a wedding reception. They drank at a wedding reception. And then, my goodness, they danced at a wedding reception."

I wiggled the four fingers. "That's it. That's how she says my client killed Mr. Phillips. And not accidentally. *On purpose*, because that's what first degree murder is, the purposeful killing of another. Ms. Lance is saying that Ms. Vila concocted this elaborate plan in which she ate and drank and danced with Mr. Phillips *knowing* that it was going to cause his death."

I paused.

"That's absurd. We ask that you listen closely to the prosecution's presentation for evidence that Liselle Vila put all this together as a scheme to kill Richard Phillips. We don't think you will."

I shrugged. "You know what evidence you will hear though? The evidence will show that Ms. Vila and Mr. Phillips met about six weeks before the wedding at a gala to help abandoned dogs. You'll hear that they enjoyed each other's company enough that Richard Phillips invited Liselle to his nephew's wedding here in Carrefour. The evidence will show that they went to the wedding events together—the rehearsal dinner, the morning brunch, the wedding, and the reception where Mr. Phillips tragically died."

I nodded. "You'll hear testimony that Mr. Phillips was fifty-nine years old with a history of an irregular heartbeat and you'll hear from an expert doctor," I pointed at Victoria, "their expert doctor, that he died of an abnormal heart rhythm."

I looked at the jury. "A man in his late fifties died of a heart arrhythmia at the end of a long weekend celebration. It's tragic for the Phillips family but we can't even say that's an uncommon occurrence. And we certainly can't say that it's murder. That's why, at the end of the case, we'll ask you to find that Liselle Vila is not guilty of the murder of Richard Phillips. Thank you."

As I walked back to my seat, I noticed Bre and Andrew Phillips glaring at me from the front row.

"Thank you, Mr. Shepherd," said Judge French. "Ms. Lance, the state may call its first witness."

Victoria stood. "Your Honor, the prosecution calls Dr. Ray Gerchuk."

I glanced back at the gallery again and remained standing. "Your Honor, may we approach?"

Judge French motioned us forward. Victoria Lance stared at me for a moment then followed me to the bench.

"Yes, Mr. Shepherd?" Judge French said.

"Your Honor, the prosecution has disclosed Bre Phillips and Andrew Phillips on their witness list and they are currently sitting in the courtroom. If the prosecution still intends to call them, I move for separation witnesses."

Judge French nodded and looked at Victoria. "Ms. Lance?"

"Your Honor, these are Mr. Phillips' son and daughter. They're entitled to watch these proceedings."

"I appreciate that Miss Lance," said the judge. "Do you intend to call them as witnesses?"

"I do."

"Then I'm going to order them to leave the courtroom."

"But Your Honor, they have a right to hear the coroner's testimony about their father."

"So if that's what you're worried about, switch them around and have the Phillips children testify first."

"But Dr. Gerchuk is only available today."

"Then it seems that you have a choice to make, Ms. Lance. What is it?"

Victoria only paused for a moment. "I'll be calling Dr. Gerchuk first."

"Very well. Please return to your seats."

As we made our way back to our respective tables, Judge French said, "Members of the jury, we had a housekeeping matter to address before testimony begins. There has been a motion to separate witnesses, which I have granted. Would anyone who is sitting in the courtroom right now who is going to be testifying at any time during the trial, please leave the courtroom and wait outside until you are called. Once you have testified, you're free to remain in the courtroom."

I watched Bre and Andrew as they sat there, seemingly deciding that what the judge said didn't apply to them. Victoria approached the rail, leaned over, and whispered to them.

"What do you mean we have to leave?" said Bre clear enough for me, and the jury, to hear.

Victoria whispered.

Bre turned her head and stared daggers at me. "But I want to hear what the coroner has to say!"

Victoria whispered again.

I wasn't watching Bre Phillips anymore. I was watching the jury. I hoped this tantrum lasted a little longer.

"Well, you best call us next then," Bre said as she stood. Andrew stood with her and the two of them filed out of the court room. Judge French waited until they were gone before he said, "Do you intend to call the same witness, Ms. Lance?"

"Yes, Your Honor. The prosecution calls coroner Ray Gerchuk."

32

One of the young attorneys went out to the hallway and, a moment later, the coroner for Carrefour, Ohio, Ray Gerchuk, strolled in.

Ray Gerchuk was the antithesis of what you thought a coroner should look like. He was in his early sixties but still fit, tall and slightly tan, even though we were barely past Memorial Day. He had blonde hair that was almost imperceptibly white at the fringes and a perpetually cheerful disposition that seemed out of line with his chosen vocation.

Victoria let him get settled in the witness chair before she said, "Could you introduce yourself to the jury please, Doctor?"

"My name is Ray Gerchuk."

"And what do you do, Dr. Gerchuk?"

"I'm the coroner for Carrefour, Ohio."

"You are a medical doctor?"

"I am. I went to undergrad and medical school at the University of Michigan and then went down to Ohio State for my residency where I trained in pathology."

"Given that background, Dr. Gerchuk, I think it's very important for all of us to know just who you root for in the big game?"

Dr. Gerchuck smiled. "I played for Michigan, so no matter how many years I trained down in Columbus, I'll always root for the Wolverines."

"Dr. Gerchuk, I'm afraid you just alienated half of the jury."

Two of the jurors smiled and gave exaggerated nods.

Ray Gerchuck smiled back. "My apologies."

Victoria smiled then put on her serious face. "Now Doctor, please explain to the jury what you do as a coroner."

"I examine the bodies of people who have passed away in order to determine a cause of death."

"And have you done a number of autopsies?"

"I have."

"About how many would you estimate?"

"I'm not certain but probably more than fifteen thousand."

"And how do you determine the cause of death?"

"I examine the exterior of the body and I examine the organs. If that's not sufficient, I also perform a microscopic examination of any relevant tissues and perform toxicology or chemical testing on the blood and organs."

"Dr. Gerchuk did you perform an autopsy on Richard Phillips?"

"I did."

"Tell us about it."

"May I refer to the autopsy report?"

"Of course."

Ray Gerchuk slipped on a pair of reading glasses and picked up the autopsy report that was a joint exhibit in the case. "Mr. Phillips was a fifty-nine-year-old man in reasonably good shape for his age. His external examination was unremarkable."

"Was that a surprise?"

"No. It was consistent with my understanding that he had collapsed and died at a wedding reception."

"What did you do next?"

"I moved on to an internal investigation. Because of the way Mr. Phillips died, I was most interested in his heart and vascular system."

"And what did you find?"

"I found that Mr. Phillips had an enlarged heart. Specifically, he had left ventricular hypertrophy."

Victoria smiled. "What does that mean for us lay people, Doctor?"

"It means that Mr. Phillips' heart was bigger and heavier and thicker than it should have been."

"And what causes that to happen?"

"It's a common finding in someone with high blood pressure. When someone has had years of high blood pressure, the heart tends to get larger because of the effort it takes to pump. I confirmed this fact when I dissected the walls of the heart and found that they were thicker than normal."

"Did you also examine the blood vessels leading into and out of the heart?"

"I did."

"And what did you find?"

"One of the first things I looked for was atherosclerosis. That's when you get a buildup of plaque in the blood vessels."

"And did you find any plaque?"

"I did not. Mr. Phillips appeared to have clean vessels for his age."

"What did you do next?"

"I examined the tissue of Mr. Phillips' heart. With a traditional heart attack, what's called a myocardial infarction, the blood supply to a portion of the heart is cut-off and that section of heart muscle dies. Here, Mr. Phillips' heart muscle was intact."

"So he did not have what we would think of as a traditional heart attack?"

"He did not."

"What do you think happened to him then?"

"Because there was no evidence of tissue death in the heart, and because we know that his heart rhythm was disturbed, I believe that Mr. Phillips died of an arrhythmia."

"Now what does that mean?"

Dr. Gerchuck leaned forward like an enthusiastic teacher. "Your heart runs on an electrical system. That's what makes it beat regularly. When you have an arrhythmia, those beats become irregular, and when the arrhythmia is severe, the beats are so irregular that the heart can no longer pump blood."

"And the person dies?"

"And the person dies."

"And do you believe that is what happened to Mr. Phillips?"

"I do."

"What's the basis for that opinion?"

"Well, we know from the paramedic records that he was having an irregular rhythm. The defibrillator machine that they used to shock him registered the heartbeat first and we can see from that record that Mr. Phillips' heart was not in sinus rhythm. When you combine that with my examination of his heart, which showed that there was no tissue death, the only alternative is that he had an arrhythmia."

"As part of your examination and investigation, did you check any of Mr. Phillips' medical records?"

"I did."

"And did those records support your opinion?"

"They did."

"How so?"

"I found that Mr. Phillips had been treating for high blood pressure for some years, probably close to ten, and that he had been treated for episodes of an irregular heartbeat. He was receiving a medication for both of those conditions."

"How do you know that he was receiving medication for an irregular heartbeat?"

"Two ways. His medical records state that he was being prescribed Lopressor and, in the toxicology tests I performed, I found the presence of trace amounts of a beta blocker in his system."

Victoria raised a hand and glanced at the jury. "I'm going to have to slow you down a little bit there, Doctor. What is a beta blocker?"

"A beta blocker is a type of medication that's used to treat high blood pressure and heart arrhythmias. Basically, it causes your heart to beat more slowly and with less force which in turn lowers your blood pressure."

"And you said Mr. Phillips was being prescribed a beta blocker?"

Dr. Gerchuk nodded. "He was. According to his records, Mr. Phillips had been taking one for about four years. It was a drug called metoprolol. The brand name was Lopressor."

"Is that medication a common treatment for high blood pressure?"

"It's not usually the first line of treatment but it is fairly common."

"Are beta blockers strong drugs, Doctor?"

Dr. Gerchuk looked over his glasses. "I'm not sure what you mean by that."

"You shouldn't stop taking beta blockers abruptly, should you?"

"No, you should not."

"Why is that?"

"Because you can have an irregular rhythm or a heart attack."

"Dr. Gerchuk, in the course of your practice, do you also study the interaction of drugs with each other?"

"Sometimes."

"You evaluate certain drug interactions when you're determining someone's cause of death?"

"If necessary."

"Do you also examine the interaction of over-the-counter medications or supplements with prescription drugs?"

"I do."

"Dr. Gerchuk, are you familiar with the herbal supplement St. John's wort?"

"I am."

"What is it?"

"St. John's wort is a common herbal supplement that people take. It's often used to treat depression, anxiety, or sleep disorders."

"Do you know how St. John's wort is taken?"

"It can be taken as a pill. It's also a yellow flower that can be dried and mixed as a tea."

"Dr. Gerchuk, does St. John's wort interact at all with beta blockers?"

"It does."

"How so?"

"Basically, St. John's wort speeds up the metabolism of your liver which speeds the elimination of beta blockers from your system."

"Could you explain that a little more please, Doctor?"

"Sure. Your liver processes the medications you take and removes them from your system. When you take St. John's wort, it speeds up the rate at which your liver gets rid of the beta blocker. For that reason, our current thinking is that you shouldn't take St. John's wort if you're taking a beta blocker because it speeds the beta blocker out of your system."

Victoria nodded and looked at the jury. "And when the beta blocker is out of a patient's system, the patient could be susceptible to high blood pressure or a heart arrhythmia, true?"

"That's true."

"So if a patient is taking a beta-blocker, he should not take St. John's wort, is that right?"

"That's the standard recommendation."

Victoria walked away from Dr. Gerchuck and glanced at the jury again. "Now Doctor, St. John's wort can also interact with other things besides beta blockers, can't it?"

"What do you mean, Ms. Lance?"

"For example, are there certain foods you shouldn't eat when you're taking St. John's wort?"

"Oh, yes, right. People taking St. John's wort shouldn't eat foods that are high in tyramine."

"Could you explain to the jury what tyramine is, Doctor?"

"It's an ingredient that's related to an amino acid."

"What are some examples of foods that have tyramine?"

"Aged meats like prosciutto, aged cheeses like brie or blue cheese, and red wine are the big ones."

"And why shouldn't a person who's taking St. John's wort eat those kinds of foods?"

"Because the interaction between the St. John's wort and the tyramine can cause a person's blood pressure to skyrocket to life-threatening levels."

"And that effect of St. John's wort is totally separate from the beta blocker effect?"

"It is."

"So are you saying that, even if someone has a perfectly healthy heart or has normal blood pressure, he shouldn't eat aged meats or drink red wine if he's taking St. John's wort?"

"That's right."

"Because he would run the risk of experiencing life-threatening blood pressure levels?"

"Right."

"And that risk would be even higher for someone with a pre-existing blood pressure problem, true?"

"That's also true."

"That person would have the double risk of eliminating the effectiveness of his blood pressure medication *and* ingesting a chemical that could spike his blood pressure, right?"

"That's right."

"So giving someone St. John's wort who is taking a beta blocker and eating prosciutto would be like putting a gun to his head, wouldn't it?"

I stood. "Objection, Your Honor."

Judge French didn't even look up from the brief he was reading. "Sustained."

Victoria nodded. "Let's go about this another way, Doctor. Someone who's taking a beta blocker shouldn't take St. John's wort, should he?"

"It's not recommended."

"Because it could spike his blood pressure?"

"That's correct."

"Or cause a heart arrhythmia?"

"True."

"And someone who is taking St. John's wort should not eat aged meats?"

"That's right."

"Or eat aged cheeses?"

"Correct."

"Or drink red wine?"

"Right."

"Or drink coffee?"

"They should avoid caffeine."

"All those things can cause a serious spike in blood pressure, right?"

"Right."

"All those things can cause a fatal heart arrhythmia?"

"Yes."

"Doctor, do you have an opinion as to what caused Richard Phillips' heart arrhythmia?"

"I do."

"What is that opinion?"

"Richard Phillips had an enlarged heart from years of high blood pressure and was taking a beta blocker to treat it. I originally thought that he just had a heart arrhythmia over the course of the long weekend. However, I was subsequently provided with evidence that he was drinking tea that contained St. John's wort. The St. John's wort would have eliminated the effectiveness of his beta blocker. I also understand that Mr. Phillips was drinking and eating foods high in tyramine. All those things together were a volatile cocktail which caused his arrhythmia."

"Doctor, do you hold that opinion to a reasonable degree of medical certainty?"

"I do."

"Doctor, would you say that, given the events of that weekend, Mr. Phillips' arrythmia was inevitable?"

I stood. "Objection. Calls for speculation."

"He can offer his opinion if he has one, Your Honor," said Victoria.

Judge French looked at me and then looked at Dr. Gerchuk. "Doctor, you may offer an opinion if you hold that opinion to a reasonable degree of medical probability."

Dr. Gerchuck tilted his head back for a moment as if thinking before he said, "I think that the combination of taking St. John's wort, eating high tyramine foods, drinking wine and caffeine, and physical exertion made a heart arrhythmia likely to occur in a man with a history of that condition."

"Could that result have been anticipated?"

"If you knew of all these factors, sure."

"You mentioned physical exertion. Do you consider dancing to be physical exertion?"

Dr. Gerchuk smiled. "Have you seen the way people sweat on the dance floor?"

Victoria smiled back. "I have."

"Then you know that, yes, dancing is physical exertion."

Victoria crossed her arms, acted as if she were thinking and stepped forward so that she was standing right in front of the jury box. "Now Doctor, to be fair, most people probably don't know all of these things about St. John's wort, do they?"

"I don't know what most people know, Ms. Lance."

Victoria smiled. "Fair enough. Doctor, would you be surprised if people didn't know about these interactions with St. John's wort?"

"I would not be surprised."

"However, people with a scientific background might know about them, right?"

"I don't know what other people know."

"You wouldn't be surprised if a biologist knew these facts about St. John's wort, would you?"

I stayed in my seat. An objection would only serve as an exclamation point to the answer we all knew was coming.

"No, Ms. Lance, I would not be surprised if a biologist knew those facts about St. John's wort."

"That's all I have, Dr. Gerchuk. Thank you for your time."

As I started to stand, Judge French raised his hand. "Counsel, we've been going at it for a while. I think we'll take our afternoon break now."

Victoria looked over her shoulder at the door. "Your Honor, if Mr. Shepherd isn't going to take too long—"

"Ms. Lance, I don't know if he needs a break but I certainly do. We will reconvene in fifteen minutes."

"Of course, Your Honor," she said. The jury was ushered out and Victoria hurried out the door as soon as they left.

I looked over to Liselle. "How are you holding up?" I said.

Her face was neutral. "Fine. For a murderer."

"Like I said, the beginning's the worst part. You did fine."

"Nate, I didn't know about it."

I nodded. "I know, Liselle. I'll bring it out."

"I didn't even know he was taking the blood pressure medication."

"There's no reason you would. I'll be right back." She nodded.

As I left the courtroom, I saw Victoria holed up with Bre and Andrew Phillips on the far side of the hallway. Bre was facing Victoria, standing straight, fists clenched. "I did not pay all this money to be sent to the hallway like some girl in detention."

"This is typical in a trial like this," said Victoria.

"Don't tell me about typical. We are not typical."

Victoria's eyes flashed at me, then she put a hand on Bre's arm and whispered.

"And I will not be shushed either!" Bre said.

I kept walking. When I hit the corner, I pulled out my phone and called Olivia Brickson.

"Hey Nate? How's Gerchuck going?"

"No big surprises. Got time for some research?"

"Always."

"I think that the Phillips family or their company or a charity is donating money up here in some way to help pay for the trial. Can you see what you can find out?"

"On it. I'll get back to you."

"Text me if you find something and I'll call you after we get out."

"Got it. Luck."

"Thanks." I hung up. By the time I returned a couple of minutes later, Victoria was gone and Bre and Andrew Phillips were sitting in the hallway on a bench. Bre glared at me as I passed.

I smiled, went back into the courtroom, and planned on keeping Dr. Gerchuk on the stand for the rest of the afternoon.

33

"Mr. Shepherd, you may cross-examine the witness."

"Thank you, Your Honor." As I walked to the lectern with my trial book, Ray Gerchuk smiled. The coroner could be counted on to be cheerfully neutral so the key thing was to know where his opinions supported my case.

"Dr. Gerchuk, let's start with where you left off. You mentioned that a biologist might know about the interaction of St. John's wort with a beta blocker?"

"I did."

"You don't have any evidence that Liselle Vila knew about that interaction, do you?"

"I do not."

"So the jury is clear, you were speaking hypothetically, weren't you?"

"I was answering a general question, yes."

"Right, generally, you wouldn't be surprised if a biologist knew about this St. John's wort interaction, true?"

"True."

"But you have no evidence, absolutely none, that Liselle Vila knew about this interaction, do you?"

"I do not."

New topic.

"Dr. Gerchuk, Ms. Lance said that the chemical process that causes the interaction between St. John's wort and beta blockers was complex, do you remember that?"

"I do."

"I'd like to get into that a little bit."

Dr. Gerchuck smiled. "Excellent."

"Medications like beta blockers are metabolized by the liver, aren't they?"

"They are."

"And by metabolized we mean eliminated from the body, correct?"

"That's correct."

"The liver does this with certain enzymes it creates, right?"

"That's right."

"Some of those enzymes are out of the cytochrome P450 family, am I correct?"

Dr. Gerchuk's smile broadened. "You are."

"You and I are going to be rattling off some number and letter combinations. I'm going to have Danny put them up on the screen, is that okay?"

"That would be most helpful."

Danny put two lines up on the screen:

CYP2D6-primary eliminator
CYP3A4-secondary eliminator

"Lopressor is primarily metabolized by the enzyme CYP2D6, isn't it?"

"It is."

"That means CYP2D6 is the enzyme produced by the liver

that does most of the work eliminating Lopressor from the body, right?"

"That's right."

"Now St. John's wort increases production of a different enzyme, right?"

"Yes."

"The enzyme stimulated by St. John's wort is CYP3A4, true?"

Dr. Gerchuk nodded. "That's true."

"And CYP3A4 is not the primary enzyme that eliminates Lopressor from the body, is it?"

"It is not."

"Just because both enzymes start with CYP doesn't mean that they do the same thing, does it?"

"That's right. They're in the same family but they don't do exactly the same thing."

"Danny," I said. A new slide came up:

CYP2D6-primary-no effect
CYP3A4-secondary-stimulated

I pointed to the screen. "So the jury understands, Dr. Gerchuck, St. John's wort does not have any effect on the main enzyme that metabolizes Lopressor, right?"

"That's correct."

"None whatsoever."

"That's right."

"Instead, it stimulates one of the many enzymes that play a secondary role in that metabolization, true?"

"True."

New topic.

"Dr. Gerchuk, I want to talk to you little bit about some of the health conditions that Mr. Phillips had."

"Okay."

"You mentioned that Mr. Phillips had a history of high blood pressure, correct?"

"He did."

"Men with high blood pressure have an increased risk of cardiac death, don't they?"

"There is certainly a statistical correlation, yes."

"Liselle Vila did not give Mr. Phillips high blood pressure, did she?"

"She did not."

"Mr. Phillips had a history of a heart arrhythmia as well, didn't he?"

"He did."

"Men with a heart arrhythmia are at increased risk for cardiac death, aren't they?"

"They are."

"I want you to assume Ms. Vila met Mr. Phillips six weeks before he died."

"Okay."

"If that's true, Mr. Phillips had high blood pressure and a heart arrhythmia years before he met Ms. Vila, right?"

"That's right."

"Mr. Phillips was fifty-nine years old when he died, correct?"

"He was."

"That is an age bracket that puts Mr. Phillips at an increased risk for sudden cardiac death, doesn't it?"

"It does."

"And of course, Mr. Phillips' age was not caused by Liselle Vila, was it?"

"Of course not."

"The fact is, men in their fifties die of sudden cardiac death every day in this country, don't they?"

"They do."

"Just because a man in his fifties dies of sudden cardiac death doesn't mean, by itself, that he was murdered, does it?"

"It does not."

"We are all at an increased risk of death as we age, aren't we?"

"We are."

"That is the natural way things work, right?"

"It is."

"In fact, your original autopsy stated that Mr. Phillips died of natural causes, didn't it?"

"It did."

"The autopsy was later amended though, wasn't it?"

"It was."

"Why?"

"Objection, Your Honor." Victoria was standing.

"Basis?" said Judge French.

I saw Victoria make the same calculation that I was making and come to the same conclusion. "Withdrawn, Your Honor," she said and sat down.

"Was your autopsy later amended, Dr. Gerchuk?" I asked.

"It was."

"It was amended because the prosecutor's office came to you and asked you to assume that St. John's wort had been given to Mr. Phillips, right?"

"That's right. I then verified the presence of St. John's wort."

"And even on your amended autopsy, you still stated that Mr. Phillips had a fatal heart arrhythmia, correct?"

"That's correct."

"You just removed the line stating it was from natural causes, right?"

"That's true."

"You did not however put anything in your report to say that the death was deliberately caused, did you?"

"That's true, I did not."

"And that's because you did not find any evidence in your personal examination of Mr. Phillips that his death was caused deliberately, did you?"

"That's also true."

"Now Dr. Gerchuk, you testified a minute ago that men in their fifties die of sudden cardiac death every day in this country, do you remember that?"

"I do. And I'm suddenly feeling less optimistic about going home today."

The jury chuckled.

I did too. "Dr. Gerchuk, St. John's wort is an herbal supplement, right?"

"It is."

"It's sold as a pill in grocery stores, drugstores, and health stores all across the country, right?"

"It is."

"Millions of units of that herb are sold in this country every year, true?"

"That's true."

"It is not poison, is it?"

"It is not."

"People take it for their health, don't they?"

Dr. Gerchuk thought. "I believe that people think that it helps."

"People typically take it for anxiety or to help themselves sleep, is that true?"

"It is."

"For that reason, it's also a common ingredient in herbal teas, isn't it?"

"It is."

"St. John's wort is a yellow flower, right?"

"It is."

"It's found naturally in the wild?"

"Yes."

"People have been drinking tea with it for hundreds of years, haven't they?"

"I imagine so."

"Dr. Gerchuk, you don't treat patients anymore, do you?"

"I do not."

"You're familiar with the basics of treating patients in the medical community though, right?"

"I am."

"Doctors tell patients about medication interactions all the time, don't they?"

"They do."

"And it is ultimately the patient's responsibility to abide by those recommendations, isn't it?"

"It is."

"It's ultimately the patient's responsibility to control what goes into his body, isn't it?"

"It is. So long as they know what they're ingesting."

New topic.

"Dr. Gerchuk, you did a toxicology test on Mr. Phillips' body, didn't you?

"I did."

"You took a blood alcohol level, right?"

"I did."

"You found that Mr. Phillips had a blood alcohol level of .18 when he died, didn't you?"

"I did."

"That's more than twice the legal limit for driving in this state, isn't it?"

"It is. Although it's my understanding that Mr. Phillips was not driving."

"One last question, Dr. Gerchuk. You aren't actually

surprised that a fifty-nine-year-old man with a history of high blood pressure and a history of a heart arrhythmia who drank enough alcohol to have a level of .18 and who was exerting himself suffered from a cardiac event, are you?"

Dr. Gerchuk paused. Then he said, "I'm not."

"That's all I have, Doctor. Thank you."

"Ms. Lance?" said the Judge.

Victoria was already on her feet. "Dr. Gerchuk, Mr. Shepherd talked to you about the enzymes that are stimulated by St. John's wort. Do you remember that?"

"I do."

"That was a very interesting scientific discussion but I'm going to ask you a simple question—do doctors recommend that patients refrain from taking St. John's wort when they are also taking a beta blocker?"

"They do."

"And is that because it can be dangerous?"

"It is."

"And do doctors recommend that patients avoid certain foods when they're using St. John's wort?"

"They do."

"And is that because it can be dangerous?"

"It is."

"There's no question about that in the medical community, is there?"

"There is not."

"It is dangerous to take St. John's wort with beta blockers."

"That's right."

"And if the person taking it doesn't know that he's taking St. John's wort, then he can't avoid taking it, right?"

Dr. Gerchuk cocked his head. "Can you say that again?"

Victoria smiled. "That was a bad question. Let's try again. A person can only avoid taking St. John's wort if he knows that St. John's wort is in the thing he's about to take, right?"

"That's right."

"So if you give someone something with St. John's wort in it, like say tea, and don't tell the person that it has St. John's wort in it, that can be dangerous, can't it?

"It can."

"And if a patient is being cautious and vigilant about his health, he can always read the label on the packaging and find out for himself what he's taking, can't he?"

"That's the wisest course, yes."

"Or in the case of tea, what he's drinking?"

"Yes."

Victoria went straight over to the evidence table and picked up a plain white box that I knew was filled with plain white tea bags.

Fuck.

She brought the box over to Dr. Gerchuck. "Dr. Gerchuck, what's in this box?"

Dr. Gerchuck opened up the box and pulled out a teabag. "It looks like some teabags."

"Will you please read the ingredients listed on the box?"

Dr. Gerchuck turned the box back and forth, showing the jury an expanse of blank whiteness. "There aren't any."

"Fine. Will you instead read the ingredients listed on the teabags themselves?"

He spun the bag like a rearview mirror ornament. "There aren't any."

"I see. So assuming this tea was homemade, how would someone find out the ingredients in it?"

Dr. Gerchuck shrugged. "I guess you'd have to ask the person who made it."

"I guess you would." Victoria took the box back and stood

there with it, holding it in front of the jury. "Thank you, Dr. Gerchuck."

Better hit this head on.

I stood. "Dr. Gerchuck, I want you to assume that the evidence is going to show that Ms. Vila made that tea you just examined, okay?"

"Sure."

"You don't know if Mr. Phillips asked Ms. Vila what was in the tea, do you?"

"I do not."

"And you don't know if he didn't ask what was in it, right?"

"I do not."

"He should have though, right?"

"Yes."

"Especially if Ms. Vila didn't know that Mr. Phillips was taking Lopressor, right?"

"Absolutely."

"Thanks, Doctor."

"You may step down, Dr. Gerchuk," said Judge French and looked at the clock. "That is all we're going to do for today. I will see you all tomorrow at eight a.m." Then Judge French gave the jury some closing instructions about not discussing the case and not researching things they'd heard and excused them for the night.

As we gathered our things to go back to the office, Liselle leaned into me and whispered, "I never told him exactly what was in the tea."

"I figured," I said. "But you told him it was herbs and that it would help him rest, right?"

She nodded.

"And he never told you that he was taking a beta blocker, right?"

She nodded again.

"Then it's not your fault. There was no way you could've known. It was up to him to ask you about ingredients that mattered."

Liselle looked unsure.

"Really," I said. "It's okay."

I hoped.

We finished gathering our things and headed back to the office. On the way out, I took some unprofessional pleasure in seeing Bre Phillips in the hallway stomp her foot—literally stomp her foot—because she wasn't going to testify that day.

34

Danny and Liselle and I stood outside the courthouse waiting for Olivia to pick Liselle up and take her home. It was the week after Memorial Day, which meant we were just making the turn into more sunny days than not and had abandoned our overcoats with impunity. At Liselle's suggestion, we waited under the great white oak tree on the courthouse lawn and there was a light breeze that rustled the leaves above us. I could see Liselle studying the oak as she said, "How did it go today?"

"How do you think it went?" I said.

"No way, Nate," she said. "I'm paying you to be my lawyer. That includes giving your legal opinion about how my murder trial is going."

I smiled. "Fair enough. I think the jury is as balanced as we're going to get. I thought the opening statements were fine, and by fine I mean there was nothing unexpected in them. I still think the prosecutor's case is a stretch after listening to it."

"I didn't know about the medicine he was taking," Liselle said.

I nodded. "That's what I'm counting on. All this business

about tea and food and dancing only matters if they can prove that you knew about his conditions."

Liselle took an oak leaf in her hand and rubbed it between her thumb and forefinger. "She made me sound like a monster."

"That's what she has to do to get you convicted of murder. They have to make the jury believe that you'd do it." I thought for a moment. "Both sides got things out of Gerchuck."

Danny bobbled a file and said, "I thought it sounded like Phillips was an old man who died of natural causes." A stricken look crossed his face. "I mean not old, old, I'm sure he was fine. I meant—" He bobbled the file again.

Liselle smiled. "I know what you meant."

"That's what we were going for, Danny," I said.

Danny regained his grip on the file. "Who's up tomorrow?"

"Family members mostly."

We moved to the curb as Olivia drove up in a bronze Chevy Tahoe. I opened the door for Liselle and she climbed in. Olivia motioned and I walked around to the driver side. "Do you have something?" I said.

Olivia handed me a folder. "Your instincts were right. We have a partial explanation for why our prosecutor might be bringing a thin case."

"What's that?"

"Two things. First, right at the end of last year, a series of donations flooded into the Lance campaign."

"She is up for reelection this year. Anything unusual?"

"There were a series of max donations, both individual and corporate. A super pac even got into the action. All St. Louis addresses."

"Really? Interesting."

"Ms. Lance is now sitting on a war chest that will destroy any local challenger. Looks to me more like an amount intended to propel someone to state office."

"Can they do that?"

"You're the lawyer. But yes, as long as their paperwork's accurate and the people donating are really the ones who donated."

"No shit."

"One of the advantages of being a billionaire is that you don't even have to use your own money a lot of the time. You make a suggestion and money flows where you tell it to go. Guess that explains why she wasn't willing to drop the case."

"Victoria's too honest to bring a baseless case. But that kind of money would make sure that ties go to the runner. What's the second thing?"

"Do you know about the state prosecutor internship program?"

"I didn't know there was such a thing."

Olivia nodded and teased her bleached hair down around her glasses. "There wasn't until about three months ago. A charitable foundation set up a program so that newly graduated law students can apply for a paid internship in a metropolitan prosecutor's office. The understaffed prosecutors get new lawyers who can help with their caseload and the new lawyers get training and a salary that's just as much as the prosecutor would pay. Once the new attorneys finish the program, they have an inside track on finding a prosecutorial job or they have good trial experience to go work on the civil side."

"Sounds like a great program."

"It is. The interesting thing is that most of the positions are in Ohio's larger cities: Columbus, Cincinnati, Cleveland, Akron, Toledo. Want to guess the smallest city to get lawyers from the program?"

"Would that be Carrefour, Ohio?"

Olivia nodded. "It would. Any guesses on how many positions it provides?"

I thought of the young attorneys helping Victoria. "How about two?"

"Bing. Again totally legitimate and by all accounts a great program but..."

I nodded. "But they're making sure there's plenty of resources for the prosecutor on this case."

"Exactly."

"Which would also explain why Bre Phillips was so pissed off when she had to leave the courtroom today."

Olivia cocked her head and I explained about the separation of witnesses and kicking her out of court. Olivia chuckled. "That had to have chapped her ass, paying all that money and not getting to see anything."

"Thanks, Olivia." I looked across the car to where Liselle was just staring at the oak tree. "I'll see you tomorrow, Liselle. Eight o'clock."

Liselle nodded. "I'm not going anywhere."

I tapped the car and Olivia drove off.

Danny said something.

"Sorry, what's that?" I said.

"You know she's eating alone every night, right?"

"What? Oh, Liselle? Yeah, I guess so."

Danny shifted his weight. "I'm just saying, we're working and she's nervous and she's all by herself in that house. It's got to be hard."

When I get going with trial, I don't tend to notice a lot of what's going on around me. This was one of those times and I felt embarrassed by it. "That's a good point, Danny. She doesn't really get to talk to anyone about her questions, does she?"

Danny shook his head.

"Tell you what, let's have her eat with us back at the office each night. She can ask questions and she might have contributions to what we're doing the next day. Do you mind taking her home if Olivia's not available since it's later?"

"That would be fine. I'm sure she'd prefer it."

I clapped his shoulder. "You know, Danny, for a lawyer, you're a pretty good guy."

"Sorry. I'll work on that."

I smiled and we drove back to the office.

35

Bre Phillips took the stand first thing the next morning. She wore an expensive suit and a jeweled watch as she sat in the witness chair, hands folded, back straight. "Could you introduce yourself to the jury please?" said Victoria.

She glared at Liselle for a moment before she said, "Breanne Phillips."

"You were related to Richard Phillips?"

"I am. I'm his daughter."

"Do you have any siblings?"

"My brother, Andrew."

"Thank you for being here, Ms. Phillips."

She glared at Liselle. "I wouldn't miss it."

"I know this may be difficult for you. Were you with your father the weekend he died?"

She lifted her chin. "I was."

"Was that here in Carrefour, Ohio?"

"Yes."

"What brought you here?"

"My cousin Jake's wedding. His wife Ellie is from this...place."

"How are you related to Jake?"

"My dad Richard has a brother, Stephen. Jake is Stephen's son."

"I see. Is your family close?"

"Very."

"Did you travel to the wedding with your father?"

"I did. By plane. We all flew out together."

"Were you on the same flight?"

Bre tossed her hair a little and smiled. "We own the plane."

"I see. And were you on the same plane as your father?"

"I was."

"Who else was on the plane?"

"My brother, Andrew. Daddy. Her." She pointed.

"By her, you mean Liselle Vila?"

"Yes."

"Had you met Ms. Vila before?"

"Briefly. At the fundraiser where Daddy met her."

"This was the first time you'd seen them together?"

"Yes."

"Ms. Phillips, did you make the hotel arrangements for your family?"

"I did. The wedding had arranged for a block of rooms so I reserved the rooms for my family."

"How many rooms?"

"Three. One for me, one for Andrew, and one for Daddy."

"Did Ms. Vila have a separate room."

"No."

"I apologize if this seems rude, but it's important. Where was Ms. Vila staying?"

"In Daddy's room."

"Thank you. I understand you arrived on Thursday night?"

"We did."

"What did you do the next day?"

"Daddy and Andrew and I golfed with some other family members during the day. The rehearsal dinner was that night."

"Did Ms. Vila golf with you?"

"No."

"Do you know where she was?"

"Daddy said she was looking at trees. Apparently, you have neat trees around here."

"I see. Did she join you for the rehearsal dinner?"

Bre lifted her chin. "It was supposed to be for family and the wedding party but Daddy insisted."

"How was dinner?"

"It was very nice. I was pleasantly surprised by the food. Aunt Paulette picked a great place."

"What kind of food did they have?"

"They had the usual appetizers—shrimp, stuffed mushrooms, some breaded thing on a stick. And they had a huge antipasti set up."

"Oh? And what was that?"

Bre looked at Liselle. "A full board of aged meats and cheeses."

"Did you see your father eat the appetizers?"

"I did."

"What did he have?"

"I brought him some shrimp. He was just finishing it when *she* brought him a plate of the antipasti."

"You actually remember that?"

"I do. *She* said the prosciutto was delicious." She paused. "So Daddy set the shrimp plate down and started eating the prosciutto."

"By 'she' you mean Ms. Vila?"

"Yes."

"Did you all eat dinner together?"

"We did. The wedding party wasn't that big so we were at one long table. I was a couple of places down from Daddy."

"Did you see what he ate?"

"No. I saw what he drank though."

"What's that?"

"When the server came around, Daddy asked *her* what she wanted. She said a Malbec and then Daddy said, 'two Malbecs.'"

"What's a Malbec?"

"It's a red wine."

"I see. Did you see how many he had?"

"No. But I saw them order a bottle later on and split it."

"And why do you remember that, Ms. Phillips?"

"Because Daddy never drank red wine."

"Was there anything else unusual that night?"

"No, it was the usual conversations and toasts. Jake was a little nervous, which was very sweet. The official dinner broke up a little early."

"Did you see any more of your father or Ms. Vila that night?"

"No. A few of us cousins stayed out, but Daddy and that woman went to bed right after dinner." Bre's face made it clear what she thought of that idea.

"Did you see your father the next day?"

"I did. He came down for breakfast at the hotel. It was a buffet style so I sat with him for a while." Bre appeared to choke up a little bit. "Just the two of us."

"And how did your father seem that morning?"

"He was in a good mood. He said that he'd slept like a baby. He said that *that* woman had given—"

I stood. "Objection, Your Honor. Hearsay. It's one thing to talk about what she was observing at the time. She's now relating her father's words of what happened outside of the witnesses's presence."

Victoria turned to the judge. "Under the dead man's statute, a decedent can speak about the cause of his death."

"Unless the prosecution is changing its theory to say that Mr. Phillips slept to death, it's not relevant. Also, that statute's not applicable to a criminal case in this circumstance."

Judge French touched the side of his glasses. "Sustained. The witness will only speak about what she observed."

Victoria turned back to Bre. "Did you see your father that afternoon?"

Bre shot Judge French an annoyed look before she said, "Not until the wedding. He and that woman had plans to go see something. I don't know what."

"Let's skip ahead to the wedding reception then. Did you see your father there?"

"I did."

"What did you see."

"I saw Daddy drinking and dancing with that woman."

"What was he drinking?"

"I remember red wine at dinner."

"And you said you remember them dancing?"

"I do."

"Why?"

Bre didn't just choke up this time. She started to cry. When she didn't stop, Victoria picked a box of tissue up off the counsel table and put it on the railing of the witness stand. After Bre had wiped her eyes and nodded, Victoria said again, "Bre, why do you remember them dancing?"

"Because they were dancing the whole time, through the whole reception." She took a jagged breath. "As soon as dinner was over, they started." She took another jagged breath. "They had to stop when Jake and Ellie did the garter and the bouquet." A jagged breath. "And I caught it. I caught the bouquet. And Daddy said to me—" a jagged breath "—Daddy said to me that he couldn't wait to dance with me at my wedding—" another jagged breath "—And I said why don't you dance with me now? And before I could, that woman, that woman right there, came up to him and said, 'You owe me a dance,' and Daddy looked at me and said, 'We'll save it for your wedding,' and they twirled away, and the next time I talked to him I was screaming at him because he was dead."

Bre broke down completely then.

Victoria looked at the judge. "Your Honor, perhaps this would be a good time to take a break."

Judge French started to speak when Bre waved a hand and said, "No, no let's get this over with. I'm fine."

Victoria waited for another minute until Bre looked up at Victoria and nodded. Then Victoria said, "Bre, did you know that your father took blood pressure medication?"

She nodded. "Everybody knew Daddy was on blood pressure medication. He was always complaining about it. He hated taking pills of any kind."

"Did you know that your father was taking St. John's wort?"

Bre wiped the corner of her eye one more time and said, "I don't even know what that is."

"I know this has been hard for you," said Victoria. "Thank you, Ms. Phillips."

Bre nodded. As Victoria sat, I stood and said, "Ms. Phillips, would you like to take a break?"

Her expression hardened. "No."

"Let me know if you do."

She nodded.

"Ms. Phillips, your father was a very successful man, wasn't he?"

"He was."

"He was the head of the Doprava Company?"

"The CEO, yes."

"He had been the CEO for over fifteen years, right?"

"Something like that."

"As the CEO, your father was the chief decision-maker for Doprava, wasn't he?"

"Yes."

"He made decisions for his company every day, didn't he?"

"I suppose so."

"Decisions that affected the jobs of thousands of people?"

"Yes."

"Decisions that controlled millions of dollars?"

Bre straightened. "Billions of dollars."

"I'm sorry, you're right, Doprava is a multi-billion-dollar company, not a multi-million-dollar company. Ms. Phillips, your father knew how to decide what he wanted to eat, didn't he?"

"Objection," said Victoria.

"Directly relevant to the prosecutor's theory of the case, Your Honor."

"Overruled," said Judge French.

"Your father knew how to decide what he wanted to eat, didn't he?"

"Unless someone else picked the menu."

"Ms. Vila didn't pick the menu for your cousin's wedding, did she?"

Bre straightened. "She did not."

"Or the rehearsal dinner?"

"No."

"Or the breakfast buffet you shared?"

"No."

"Ms. Phillips, you mentioned that you golfed with your father and your brother the day before the wedding."

"We did."

"Your father drank while he was on the golf course, didn't he?"

Bre hesitated before she said, "A little."

"Beer?"

She nodded.

"You have to say 'yes.'"

"Yes."

"Did you get your father a beer while you were on the golf course?"

Bre scowled. "What?"

"When you were on the golf course. Did you ever get a beer from the cart or from the cooler or from the clubhouse and hand it to your father?"

"I don't remember."

"I see. You testified that, on the morning of the wedding, you had breakfast with your father in the hotel?"

"I did."

"You said it was just the two of you at the table?"

"It was."

"What did your father order to drink?"

Bre's face was turning hard. "I don't remember."

"It was a bloody Mary and a coffee, wasn't it?

"It might have been."

"Ms. Phillips, you just said you knew that your father was taking blood pressure medication, right?"

"I did."

"You testified that everyone knew that your father took blood pressure medication because he always complained about it."

Bre nodded. "To anyone who would listen."

"Ms. Phillips, what was the name of the medication your father took?"

"It was high blood pressure medication."

"I understand that, Ms. Phillips. What was its name?"

"I don't see how that's important."

"I can see that. What was the name of the medicine your father took?"

"I don't see how that's relevant."

"It can be the brand name or the generic name."

She looked at Victoria. "Are you going to do something?"

I looked at the judge.

"Ms. Phillips," said Judge French. "Please answer Mr. Shepherd."

She straightened. "I can't think of it off-hand."

"So you knew he took medicine, but he didn't tell you what its name was, right?"

"I'm sure he did."

"So you either forgot what he told you or he never told you, right?"

"I suppose."

"Ms. Phillips, I know this is hard to talk about, but on the weekend of the wedding, your father seemed completely normal, didn't he?"

"What do you mean 'normal?'"

"I mean he was acting appropriately, wasn't he?"

"I hardly think dating someone your daughter's age is appropriate."

"Oh? Are you and Ms. Vila the same age?"

"I think we're only about four years apart?"

"And how do you know that?"

Bre raised her chin. "I checked."

"I see. Ms. Phillips, since your father passed away, you've learned about your father's will and estate, haven't you?"

"It's a trust. And yes."

"A trust. Thank you. Ms. Vila didn't receive anything from your father under this trust, did she?"

"I would think not. They'd only known each other six weeks."

"Exactly. Ms. Vila had only known your father for six weeks. It's fair to say that you knew your father far better than Ms. Vila, right?"

"Of course."

"And you don't know the name of his medication."

She stared at me.

"Thank you, Ms. Phillips. No further questions."

Victoria stood up. "Ms. Phillips, does the name Lopressor sound familiar?"

I laughed and stood. "Your Honor, that's leading. And outrageous."

"Yes!" said Bre. "That's it!"

"Move to strike, Your Honor," I said.

"Objection sustained." Judge French stared at Victoria. "The jury will disregard the witness's last statement. Do you have anything else, Ms. Lance?"

Victoria sat, unconcerned. "No, Your Honor."

"The witness may step down."

Bre Phillips left the witness stand and marched squarely between our tables, through the swinging gate to the gallery and sat down in the first row. Her eyes never left Liselle the whole time.

Victoria Lance turned to the judge and said, "Your Honor, the prosecution calls Andrew Phillips."

It was her brother's turn.

36

Andrew Phillips wore a slim-fitting gray suit of fine silk with a light blue shirt open at the collar and a matching pocket square. His hair was longish and overly styled and he looked exactly like what he was—an underemployed, billionaire's son.

"Please state your name for the record," said Victoria.

"Andrew Phillips."

"Mr. Phillips, you are the son of Richard Phillips?"

"I am."

"Now you weren't in here, but we've asked your sister a variety of questions. We're not going to ask you all the same ones."

"Good." Andrew gave the impression that there were a lot of other places he'd rather be.

"Did you come to Carrefour for Jake and Ellie's wedding with your father?"

"I did."

"And did you stay in the same hotel?"

"Yes."

"On the first night you were here, Thursday night, did you go out with some of your friends?"

"I did. I met up with my cousin Jake and some of our other friends and we went out for a few beers after Ellie went to bed."

"And did you return to the hotel that night?"

"I did."

"What happened when you came back?"

"Well, the bars had closed so it was a little after two. My dad had arranged for a 24-hour kitchen in one of the banquet rooms, so me and Jake and a couple other guys went in there to get something to eat before we went to bed."

"Was the kitchen actually staffed?"

Andrew nodded. "We were going to get a late-night breakfast."

"And what did you find when you got there?"

"My dad was sitting at a table, drinking some tea."

"How do you know it was tea?"

"Because I could see the little string connected to the bag hanging out of the cup. And because he told me so."

Victoria nodded as if this was a spontaneous discovery. "Why don't you tell the jury everything that happened."

"We all went over to the counter, and placed orders, and then we went over and sat next to my dad while we waited."

"Did you get along with your father?"

Andrew nodded. "Very well. And Jake got along with him really well too, better than his dad a lot of the time, so Jake was glad to see him."

"What happened next?"

"Now that we're all older, we don't see each other as much, so my dad had a lot of questions for Jake and our friends about what had been going on with all of us, so we talked until our food was ready."

"Did anything else happen while you were talking?"

"Uhm, not that I can think of."

Victoria smiled and nodded her head. "Did your father drink his tea?"

"Oh, yeah right, he did. He finished his cup and then he went and filled a new cup with hot water and pulled this white tea bag out of his pocket and put it in the cup and started bouncing around you know like..." Andrew held up his hand and jiggled it like he was moving a yo-yo.

"Did your father drink tea often?"

"No, that was the funny thing. I asked him what sort of sissy ass, uhm, I mean what kind of pansy drink he was drinking and he said it was tea."

"What else did he say?"

"I asked when he started drinking tea and he said that the woman he was seeing had turned him on to it."

"Who is that woman?"

"That woman right there," Andrew said, pointing. "Liselle Vila."

"Did he say why he drank it?"

"He did. He said that he had trouble sleeping sometimes and that she'd made this tea for him. Said it worked like a charm."

"Now Andrew, this is important. Your father actually said that Ms. Vila made the tea for him?"

"He did."

"Did that concern you?"

Andrew shook his head. "Not at all. I mean it was tea for Christ's sake. And Dad said it worked so, as far as I was concerned, it was fine."

"Did he say anything else?"

"No, about then our food was ready so we went up to get it and my dad said it was time for him to turn in, so he poured his tea into a 'go' cup and went back to his room."

"When you say he went back to his room, was he sharing that room with Ms. Vila?"

"He was."

"Mr. Phillips, did you know that your father took blood pressure medication?"

"Everybody knew that my father took blood pressure medication."

"Objection, Your Honor," I said. "The witness has no idea what everybody knows."

"Mr. Phillips, you will limit your answers to what you know," said Judge French.

Victoria shot a glance at me and said, "Mr. Phillips, did *you* know that your father took the high blood pressure medication Lopressor?"

"I did."

I let Victoria's naming of the medication pass.

"How did you know?"

"Because my father was always complaining about it to anyone who would listen. He couldn't stand the stuff."

"I see. And did your father drink alcohol?"

"Sure."

"What did he normally drink?"

"Pappy Van Winkle at home. Johnny Walker if he was out."

"You have to forgive me, that's…?"

Andrew smiled. "Whiskey."

"I see. Did your father drink red wine?"

"Not usually."

"What about over the wedding weekend?"

"He did drink red wine then. It was weird."

"When did he drink it?"

"When Ms. Vila ordered it."

"How do you know that?"

"I guess I didn't know it at the wedding. I know it from the rehearsal dinner because I saw him ask her what she wanted and when she said 'Malbec,' he said make it two."

"And did he have more than one glass?"

"He did. When Ms. Vila ordered another, he said, 'let's just get a whole bottle.'"

"And that was not his normal drink?"

"Not that I'd ever seen."

"Finally, Mr. Phillips, I know this may be difficult for you but did you see your father towards the end of the reception?"

"Before he died?"

"Yes."

"I did."

"What was he doing?"

"He was dancing."

"When was he dancing?"

"The question is when *wasn't* he dancing. He danced all night. She wouldn't let him off the dance floor."

I stood. "Objection, Your Honor."

"Sustained," said Judge French. "Again Mr. Phillips, you must limit your answers to what you personally observed."

"Well, I observed, Your Honor, that at one point my dad started walking off the floor and the band started playing some song by some country band that I'd never heard of and Ms. Vila over there grabbed him by the arm and said it was her favorite song and that she had to dance to it and he went back out."

"And you saw that personally?"

"I did."

"Thank you, Mr. Phillips. No further questions, Your Honor."

As Victoria sat down, I approached Andrew Phillips and set up right in front of the jury. "Mr. Phillips when you saw your dad on Thursday night when you came back from the bar, he seemed fine, didn't he?"

Andrew scowled. "What do you mean fine?"

"He wasn't flushed, was he?"

"No."

"He wasn't sweating?"

"No."

"He wasn't short of breath that you could see?"

"No."

"Instead, he was talking about having a little trouble sleeping, right?"

"Yes."

"And he had some tea and went to bed?"

"Yes."

"Did he seem fine to you when he left?"

Andrew smirked. "I still don't think we know what 'fine' means."

"Your dad didn't seem sick in any way when he left for the night, did he?"

"Other than having insomnia?"

"Yes."

"Then no."

"If it seemed like something was wrong with him, you would have called for help, wouldn't you?"

"Of course."

"You golfed with your dad on Friday morning?"

"I did."

"Did you give him a beer while you were on the course?"

Andrew made a show of thinking. "I don't think so."

"You didn't buy your dad a beer the whole time?"

"I don't think so."

I gestured and Danny popped a receipt onto the video screen eight feet tall. "If a receipt from the course showed that you bought a twelve pack of Stella Artois, would that refresh your recollection?"

Without a prompt from me, Danny highlighted Andrew's name on the receipt in yellow. He really was a good associate.

Andrew nodded. "Now I remember. I did buy a twelve pack."

"On the front nine. You bought another on the back nine too, right?"

Andrew's eyes flicked to the screen. "I believe I did."

"And did you share that with everyone who was golfing with you?"

"Yes."

"And did your dad have some of them?"

Andrew nodded reluctantly. "He did."

"You mentioned that you knew your dad had high blood pressure, right?"

"I did."

"And you said that's because he complained about taking the medication frequently?"

"He did. I remember him talking about it on the course that day."

"Liselle Vila wasn't on the course with you and your family that day, was she?"

"She was not."

"You also mentioned a moment ago that you heard Liselle Vila ask your father to go back on the dance floor at the reception when her favorite song came on, do you remember that?"

"I do."

"And you said you saw your father go back out on the dance floor?"

"He did."

"And that was one time for one dance during the course of the reception, is that true?"

"That I saw, yes."

"That's my point, you saw her ask him to dance one time, right?"

"Yes."

"That dance lasted what four minutes, five minutes?"

"It could have been longer."

"Fine. Let's say it was Bohemian Rhapsody. That would mean the song lasted about six minutes."

Andrew smirked again. "It wasn't Bohemian Rhapsody, though."

"Can we agree that the song was no longer than ten minutes?"

"I don't have to agree to anything."

"No, Mr. Phillips, you don't, but you do have to tell the truth. You golfed with your father on Friday, right?"

"I already said that."

"It was hot that day, right?"

"I don't remember."

"If the National Weather Service said it got up to eighty-eight degrees that day in Carrefour, Ohio, you wouldn't dispute it, would you?"

"I guess not."

"And it took you, what, five hours to play?"

"I don't know exactly."

"A least four hours, right?"

"I guess."

"And we know during that time that your dad drank beer, right?"

"Yes."

"And that you bought him beer, right?"

"Yes."

"And your sister's already testified that your father had a coffee to start the round, right?"

"If she says so."

"And you knew that your father had high blood pressure because he complained about taking the medicine all the time, true?"

"Yes."

"And yet you kept him on a golf course for over four hours in the eighty-eight-degree sun drinking beer, didn't you?"

Andrew ground his teeth a little bit before he said, "I didn't make him do anything."

"No, you didn't, did you. Because he made up his own mind to drink beer and golf, didn't he?"

"Yes."

"So when you gave your father beer and kept him out in the eighty-eight-degree sun for over four hours, you weren't trying to kill him, were you?"

Victoria stood. "Objection, Your Honor. That's a ridiculous, argumentative question that's completely disrespectful of the witness's loss."

I shook my head. "Your Honor, I agree that it's completely disrespectful to ask someone who cared about Richard Phillips if they were trying to kill him when they were clearly just drinking and having a good time but here we are."

Judge French did not look at all pleased with me but said, "Overruled, Miss Lance."

I nodded. "You weren't trying to kill your father when you drank and golfed with him all day were you, Mr. Phillips?"

"No, I was not. But that doesn't mean that she wasn't."

"Really? My client didn't get anything from your dad's trust. Did you?"

Victoria sprang to her feet. "Objection!"

Judge French raised his hand and stared at me. "Sustained."

"No further questions, Your Honor."

37

The last witness of the day was Paulette Phillips. Paulette was tall, slim, in her fifties, and had shoulder length blonde hair that was cut perfectly straight. She wore a suit, a strand of pearls, and a diamond ring that was large enough to be noticeable from across the courtroom. As she took the witness chair, she could just as easily have been taking a seat at a board meeting or a country club brunch as she raised her eyes expectantly to Victoria.

"Could you state your name please?" said Victoria.

"Paulette Phillips."

"And how are you related to all of the Phillips the jury has heard about today?"

Paulette smiled. "I'm married to Stephen Phillips, who is—who was—Richard Phillips' brother. The groom, Jake Phillips, is my son. Bre and Andrew, who you met today, are my niece and nephew."

"Thank you," Victoria smiled.

Paulette Phillips smiled in return and said, "It can be confusing."

"Mrs. Phillips, I will be brief. As the mother of the groom, did you arrange the rehearsal dinner the night before the wedding."

"My husband and I did, yes."

"Had you met Liselle Vila before that dinner?"

"I had not. Richard had RSVP'd some weeks before with a generic plus one so the first time I heard her name was a couple of weeks before the wedding when Richard sent us a note letting us know whom he was bringing. Steve and I came out on an earlier flight to take care of arrangements so the first time I met her was at the rehearsal dinner."

"What were your impressions of her?"

"She's stunning, obviously. She's also young, or at least thirty seems young compared to me or Steve or Richard. But you only have to speak to her for a little while to realize that she's also incredibly smart."

"Oh? What led you to that conclusion?"

"The small talk we had before we sat down to eat. Apparently, while Richard and Steve and the kids were out golfing, Ms. Vila was inspecting some nearby woods because they were related to work she was doing back home in Missouri as a woodland biologist."

"Did you know what that work was?"

Paulette smiled. "I'm afraid I'm not a woodland biologist. I do recall that I was impressed that she'd taken the time to fit in work while she was here. It struck me as being dedicated." She smiled a little. "And not entirely like other people that Richard had brought around."

"Other people?" said Victoria.

"Other dates. Richard had brought other beautiful women to events but I don't know that he'd ever brought one who was so dedicated to something beyond the society scene."

"Mrs. Phillips, did you coordinate the menu for the rehearsal dinner that evening?"

"I did."

"Did it include prosciutto?"

"It did."

"Aged cheese?"

"Brie and Romano, I believe."

"Did you see Richard eat any of those foods that night?"

"I didn't see him eat any cheese. I did see him eat a good deal of prosciutto."

Victoria smiled and walked towards the jury. "Now Mrs. Phillips, I have to ask you, with all that was going on for you at your son's wedding, how do you remember that your brother-in-law ate prosciutto as an appetizer at the rehearsal dinner?"

"Because I remember Ms. Vila bringing him a plate and telling him it was delicious and Richard asking where we got it. When I told him that it had been flown in especially from Italy for the event, Richard had wanted to know the name of the castle where it was aged and I texted it to him later that night."

Victoria stopped and turned. "The castle?"

Paulette shrugged and smiled and didn't look the least bit apologetic. "We have access to some means, Ms. Lance."

"I see," said Victoria.

"That's why I remember it though."

"Did you offer red wine that night?"

"We did. And I remember that Richard had some because he doesn't normally drink it."

"No?"

"No, he enjoys Pappy Van Winkle, which we'd brought in especially for him. He wound up drinking the wine instead."

"Is that why you remember it?"

Paulette smiled. "I'm afraid I must admit that I was slightly irritated."

"Anything else that stands out to you from the rehearsal dinner?"

"Richard drinking tea."

"Again, I have to ask, how can you remember that?"

"Because it was unusual. When we served coffee and dessert at the end of the meal, Richard asked if he could have a cup with hot water. That caught my attention because no one else wanted any. When the water came, he put a teabag in it. I asked him what he was doing and he smiled and said he was trying new things. I didn't think anything more of it."

"Did the restaurant provide him with the tea?"

"No."

"Who did?"

"I saw Ms. Vila give him the teabag."

"So that night you saw Ms. Vila recommend the prosciutto to Richard?"

"Yes."

"And you saw the two of them order red wine together?"

"Yes."

"And you saw Ms. Vila give Richard the tea that he drank that evening?"

"I did."

"Thank you, Mrs. Phillips. No further questions, Your Honor."

I stood. "Good afternoon, Mrs. Phillips."

"Good afternoon, Mr. Shepherd." She spoke as if she'd just run into me while we were both out and about.

"Your niece testified that you had other appetizers at the rehearsal dinner besides prosciutto. Is that true?"

"We did."

"Shrimp, stuffed mushrooms, olives, caviar?"

"There were a wide range of items, Mr. Shepherd."

"Richard was free to eat whatever he wanted, wasn't he?"

"He was."

"You're not suggesting that Ms. Vila made him eat anything, are you?"

Paulette Philip shrugged. "Men can be influenced."

"How so?"

"I think you know."

"Tell me."

Paulette Phillips glanced at Liselle and said, "Your client is striking, Mr. Shepherd. It's not a leap to think that men will try to impress her."

I decided not to ask if Richard had. I was certain it was true. I took a different tack. "Your brother-in-law ran a multi-billion-dollar corporation. He can make his own decisions, can't he?"

"He used to be able to. He can't anymore."

"You're close with Richard Phillips' ex-wife, Sharon, aren't you?"

"I am."

"Mr. Phillips was married to her for twenty-four years, wasn't he?"

"He was."

"And in those twenty-four years, you would have attended many things with Sharon, wouldn't you?"

"Of course."

"After Richard's divorce, you didn't care much for the dates he brought to family functions, did you?"

Paulette shrugged. "Some were better than others. I was optimistic about Ms. Vila until..." she shrugged again.

"Did you talk to the prosecutor before testifying today?"

"I did."

"How many times?"

"Three or four."

"When?"

"Shortly after charges were filed would've been the first time. A few more times closer to the trial."

"And the prosecutor told you her theory about the St. John's wort, didn't she?"

Paulette Phillips nodded. "She did."

"And the prosecutor's office told you about the significance of the aged meat and red wine, right?"

"She said it was a potential issue."

"That's why you remember it, isn't it?"

"I told you why I remembered it and when the prosecutor told me her theory, it fit. Perfectly."

I was making no progress here. I needed to get out of this line of questioning and scrambled for a solid finishing point.

"Richard Phillips was the head of a multibillion-dollar corporation who made decisions that affected himself and thousands of other people every day, wasn't he?"

"He was. We miss him very much."

"Thank you, Mrs. Phillips. That's all I have."

Victoria stood. "Mrs. Phillips, during your testimony, you weren't talking about Richard Phillips making business decisions that affected other people, were you?"

"I was not."

"I got the impression that you were talking about Richard's personal decisions that affected himself. Was I wrong?"

"No. That's exactly what I meant."

"No further questions, Your Honor."

I decided the best thing was to get Paulette Phillips out of the courtroom. "No questions, Your Honor."

"The witness may step down," said Judge French. Paulette Phillips left the stand and, unlike her niece and nephew, didn't look one time at Liselle Vila and left the court. When she was gone, Judge French said, "Members of the jury, that's all we are going to do today. We will see you tomorrow at nine a.m."

We were collecting our things when Victoria came over to me. "I had mentioned that we're calling Pearson and Stephen Phillips tomorrow."

I smiled. "We certainly don't want to leave any of the Phillips out of this."

Victoria shrugged. "They all saw important evidence. I wanted to let you know that we're calling Wrigley too."

I remembered a scientist buried around number eight-four on their witness list. "The toxicologist?"

She nodded.

"Didn't you cover that ground with Gerchuk?"

"Wrigley didn't examine Mr. Phillips. He examined the tea."

"Is that what he's going to talk about?"

"That's it. It'll be limited to the report we gave you. It shouldn't take long."

I kept my face straight. "What's he going to say?"

Victoria smiled a little. "You know. It's in the report."

I had read the report and had my own expert analyze the tea. I knew exactly what he was going to say tomorrow. "Thanks for the heads up."

"Sure."

I went back over to Danny and Liselle.

"What was that about?" said Danny.

"She's letting me know that they're turning up the heat tomorrow. Let's get back to the office."

I turned to Liselle. "Join us for dinner? It's just sandwiches and we'll be working but it's company if you want it."

Liselle smiled and nodded. "I do."

"Then let's go."

∽

DANNY, LISELLE, AND I WERE SITTING AROUND THE CONFERENCE table with Hungry Howie's as the sandwich provider of choice. I finished chewing and said, "So, tomorrow we have the investigating police officer, a toxicologist to talk about the tea, and Stephen Phillips."

"Okay," said Liselle.

"Pearson is going to talk about his investigation. You're sure you told him that you didn't know about the Lopressor?"

Liselle nodded. "I'm sure. We just didn't know each other that long." She took a bite of her Italian sub. "This is really good."

After this case, I was pretty sure I wasn't going to look at pepperoni and salami the same way. "Victoria is probably going to ask Pearson about the Ribbon Falls protest. You only went the one time?"

She nodded. "With about five thousand other people."

"And that was it?"

She chewed and thought. "That was the only time I protested the fracking publicly. I was preoccupied with the ash borer quarantine at the time. We were deciding where to impose it."

I nodded. "I've cross-examined Pearson before. I'll deal with anything else new that comes up. Tell me how you make the tea."

Liselle took another bite and held one hand up as she chewed before she said, "Does that matter?"

"It does. Their toxicologist is going to testify that the tea contains about fifteen times more St. John's wort than is present in other teas."

"Vicki told you that?" said Danny.

I kept my eyes on Liselle. "No. I had it tested myself."

Liselle's expression didn't change. "Sometimes I buy

processed leaves and sometimes I dry them myself. I can't tell you which batch this was. I didn't think it mattered."

"Why is it so high?"

"Don't forget you're not ingesting it directly. Because it's tea, it's diluted in the water; it can be weaker or stronger depending on how long it steeps. It needs to be more concentrated to be effective in the tea."

It seemed like she believed that but I wasn't sure it was true.

My expression must've shown because she said, "If he was getting too much St. John's wort, he would have shown signs of overdosing. Well, not overdosing, but being nervous and jittery and all the things that having too much St. John's wort does. He wasn't."

"That's a good point. I'll remember that. Finally, no interactions with Stephen Phillips other than the kind we heard today? Eating, drinking, and small talk?"

"That's all I can think of," she said.

"Do you have any questions from today?" I asked her.

Liselle kept her eyes down and, in that moment, she seemed particularly vulnerable. "I don't understand it at all, Nate. How they could think that I…"

I realized again that Liselle had been up here alone for a very long time.

Danny jumped in. "I'm still not seeing it either, Liselle. So far, it's seemed more the other way, that the family had more animosity toward you than you had toward Richard."

Liselle looked at me. I nodded. Then she looked back at Danny and said, "I'll just be glad when this is all done."

Danny leaned forward. "There'll just be another couple of days of their case. Then we'll put on ours and we should be done by middle of next week. Right, Nate?"

"Right."

Liselle nodded, gave Danny a little smile, then said to me, "How is James?"

"Getting better every day. Still in therapy, walking but not running yet." I smiled. "Izzy said he's obsessed with hawks. She had to get him a set of binoculars to shut him up."

Liselle smiled, the first truly joyful one I'd seen in a while. "They are beautiful."

"Yes, they are."

We were all finished with our sandwiches. "I'm afraid we have to get back to work," I said.

She stood. "Of course. Thank you. Both of you."

I waved. "Don't thank us yet."

"Still," she said.

I checked my phone. "Olivia is going to pick you up in a couple minutes and take you home."

"Okay. I'll wait out in the lobby."

A question I had from that day occurred to me. "Hey, when they were all golfing, the day of the rehearsal, where did you go?"

She smiled. "To southeast Detroit to see the neighborhood where the first ash trees had been hit by the borer. It's fairly well documented, in your wife's research and others', but I wanted to see for myself."

"Were you able to find it?"

"The neighborhoods, yes. The trees?" She shook her head. "Most of them weren't even there anymore. They had died and started to fall, so in a lot of places I just found stumps. It was almost worse." She shook her head again. "You can read about things like that but sometimes you just have to see it to really drive it home."

I gathered the sandwich wrappers. "Danny, could you wait with Liselle for Olivia? I have to get started."

"Sure," said Danny without looking at Liselle.

"Hang in there," I said to Liselle. "I'll see you tomorrow."

"Okay, Nate. Thanks."

Danny stumbled a little bit before he opened the door for her and then Liselle asked him about the picture of the cute little girl on his desk and Danny regained his balance as he spoke about his daughter on the way down to the lobby. Their voices faded and I got to work.

38

Mitch Pearson was the first witness called the next morning. He strode into the courtroom in his usual testifying uniform: a dark gray suit tailored extra slim so that it was tight enough to reveal his large frame and the gun he carried at his hip. He wasn't wearing his badge at his belt this time, though. This time, he was wearing it around his neck on a lanyard, like he'd just arrived on a crime scene, and as he sat in the witness chair, the badge was still visible for the jury to see, just above the railing. Pearson sat straight, folded his hands, and identified himself as Mitch Pearson, Chief Detective in Charge of Serious Crimes for Carrefour, Ohio.

After Pearson had introduced himself to the jury, Victoria said, "Detective Pearson, were you called upon to investigate the death of Richard Phillips?"

"I was."

"When?"

"The night that he died."

"How did that come about?"

"We received a call from a plainclothes officer that there had been a death at a wedding reception at the Forester Hotel."

"A plainclothes officer was there?"

"She was."

"Why?"

"We'd been advised that the Phillips family would be in town so we stationed officers near the celebration."

"Why is that?"

"Given the Phillips' profile, it seemed like the prudent thing to do."

"Could you explain?"

"The Phillips are a well-known, wealthy family. In addition, large companies like Doprava tend to draw extreme positions against their policies. We did not want anything to happen when the Phillips were in Carrefour."

"Were you aware of any threats against the Phillips or Doprava when you assigned the plainclothes officers to the wedding?"

"Not at that time, ma'am, no."

"So what happened next?"

"After I received the call, I went straight to the hotel to secure the scene."

"What did that entail?"

"I spoke to our plainclothes officers and to hotel staff. The consensus was that Mr. Phillips had had some sort of cardiac event on the dance floor so it did not seem like a crime scene to me at the time. I asked for the names of the staff working that night and a guest list and then obtained permission to search Mr. Phillips' room."

I stood. "May we approach, Your Honor?"

Judge French waved us up. Victoria and I went to the bench and I spoke quietly so that the jury couldn't hear me. "Your Honor, I renew our objection to any evidence garnered from the search of my client's hotel room. There was no warrant and she did not consent to it."

Judge French looked at Victoria.

"Your Honor, we briefed this at length before the trial and, consistent with your preliminary ruling, we point out that Bre Phillips consented to the search. Ms. Phillips booked this room along with the rest of the Phillips' rooms but, more importantly, since Mr. Phillips had died, Bre Phillips was his heir and authorized to act on his behalf as to his possessions and his room. For the reasons Your Honor stated in your preliminary ruling, we submit that evidence from the search is admissible."

I shook my head. "Your Honor, the fact that Ms. Phillips booked the room is irrelevant. If that were the case, a travel agent could consent to the search of any room he'd booked for a guest. Further, Bre Phillips was not authorized to consent to a search of my client's possessions regardless of her status as Mr. Phillips' heir."

Judge French waited until we were done before he nodded and said, "For the reasons set forth in my preliminary ruling, the Court finds that Bre Phillips was authorized to consent to the search. The Court agrees with Mr. Shepherd that the fact that she booked the room is not relevant. However, once Mr. Phillips died, the only practical way for Mr. Phillips' possessions to be removed from the hotel room and for his bill with the hotel to be settled was for his heirs to handle it. The Court will not allow evidence of a search of any of Ms. Vila's possessions that were in the room. For example, I will not allow testimony if Detective Pearson looked into her suitcase or her purse. However, he can testify about any of Mr. Phillips's possessions that are relevant and about anything that was in plain view in the room."

Victoria and I both nodded and she went back to the lectern as I returned to the counsel table.

"It's coming in," I whispered to Liselle. She nodded.

Victoria continued. "Detective Pearson, you said that you received consent to search Mr. Phillips' room?"

"I did."

"From whom?"

"From his daughter, Bre Phillips."

"And why did you obtain permission from Mr. Phillips' daughter?"

"Because at that point, Mr. Phillips was dead and she was acting on his behalf."

"Did you ask Ms. Vila if she consented to the search?"

"I did not."

"Why not?"

"Because she wasn't there and because I had no intention of searching her belongings. Instead, I wanted to see if Mr. Phillips had anything with him that would explain his collapse."

"Like what?"

"Like legal or illegal drugs."

"Wouldn't toxicology give you that result?"

"In six to eight weeks. But we wanted to have a better sense of what had happened right away, to see if there was any easy explanation for it."

"And what did you find, Detective Pearson?"

"Nothing that we thought was significant at the time."

"Is there anything that is significant to you now?"

"Yes."

"What was that?"

"Two things. We found a bottle of prescription pills sitting on the left side of the sink next to a drinking glass with toothbrushes in it."

"Did you take a photo?"

"I did."

A photo of the hotel sink went up on the screen. "Is this that photo?"

"It is. You can see the prescription bottle there in the upper left, next to the glass."

"Did you move anything before you took this picture?"

"I did not. That was what the sink looked like when we found it."

"And what was in the bottle?"

"A medication called Lopressor."

The picture was blown up so that the bottle was clearly visible. One of Victoria's associates highlighted the word "Lopressor" in yellow. "Is this a true and accurate representation of what you found?" asked Victoria.

"It is."

"Do you know what Lopressor is?"

"I didn't at the time. I now know that it is a beta blocker medication used for control of high blood pressure and heart arrhythmias whose industry name is metoprolol."

"And it was sitting there in plain sight?"

"I saw it easily."

"What else did you find?"

"The suite had a small kitchenette with a refrigerator, stove, and sink. It also had a coffee maker. Next to the coffee maker, we found a white cardboard box with teabags in it."

"Did you find any significance to that?"

"Not at the time."

A picture of the kitchenette went up on the screen. A white box was visible next to the coffee maker. "Is that the white box you were referring to?"

"It is."

"Did you find any evidence that any teabags had been used?"

Pearson nodded. "We found several damp teabags in the trash."

"Did you find any evidence of who might have drunk the tea?"

"Not from what we found in the room, no ma'am."

"Did you find anything else in the kitchen?"

"I found a bottle of Pappy Van Winkle and two bottles of red wine. All had been drunk to some degree."

"Did you question Ms. Vila that night?"

"No. It didn't seem appropriate and there didn't seem to be a reason to."

"Did you have occasion to speak with her again later that weekend?"

"I did."

"What happened?"

"I spoke to her on Sunday and asked in more detail about what had happened. She indicated that Mr. Phillips had collapsed on the dance floor which was consistent with what we'd been told by other witnesses."

"What happened next?"

"In the week following Mr. Phillips' death, while the autopsy was being performed, I received a call from Mr. Phillips' daughter, Bre. I assumed it was in follow-up to my looking in the room but instead she was asking me to investigate Ms. Vila."

"Why would she do that?"

"Objection, Your Honor," I said.

"I'll rephrase, Judge," said Victoria. "What did Ms. Phillips tell you?"

"She said that I should investigate Ms. Vila because she—"

"Objection. Hearsay once again, Your Honor."

"Sustained."

"Detective Pearson, as result of your conversation with Ms. Phillips, did you begin an investigation of Mr. Phillips' death?"

"Technically, I suppose there was already an investigation underway. As result of my conversation with her, I continued it rather than closed it."

"Did you take that request seriously?"

Pearson straightened and became his most Pearson-y. "I take

every investigation seriously, Ms. Vance. However, I did not think it likely at the time that it would reveal anything."

"So did you speak to Ms. Vila again?"

"After the autopsy was complete, yes."

"And what did you learn as a result of that conversation?"

"I asked Ms. Vila if she was a member of certain organizations."

"What organizations are those?"

"There were several. The Humane Society. PETA. The Last Auk. The most significant was The Forest Initiative."

"Why was her membership in the Forest Initiative of interest to you?"

"Because it had taken positions publicly that were in direct conflict with Doprava, the company that Mr. Phillips ran."

"And did Ms. Vila admit that she was a member of that organization?"

"She did."

"And did she also admit that she knew Richard Phillips was the head of Doprava?"

"She did. In fairness to her, she pointed out that everyone in Missouri knew that he was the head of Doprava."

"Did she tell you anything else?"

"She told me that she had known Mr. Phillips for a short time, several weeks, and that she didn't know of any medical conditions that he had."

"What did you do next in your investigation?"

"Several things. First, I ordered a test on the tea to find out what was in it. Next, I did background research on Ms. Vila. Last, I waited for the toxicology results from the autopsy."

"Let's start with the tea. Did you send the tea to Dr. Newt Wrigley for analysis?"

"I did."

"We'll be calling him later today and ask the specifics of

what he found. I have a report marked here as State's exhibit 49." She handed him a paper. "Did he give this to you?"

"He did."

"What was the primary thing you took from that report?"

"That the tea was an herbal tea with a variety of supplements in it."

"And was there more of one thing than any other?"

"I was told that it contained St. John's wort."

"You also mentioned that you did background research on Liselle Vila. What did you find out?"

"I confirmed that Ms. Vila was in fact a member of the Forest Initiative and that that organization had organized a protest against Doprava near the Mark Twain National Forest where Ms. Vila worked."

"What kind of protest?"

"Apparently, Doprava was going to allow fracking on property that it owned near the forest. The protest was purportedly organized to stop that."

"Objection, Your Honor," I said. "We can't take testimony on every organization that every witness is a member of."

"We are getting pretty far afield here, Ms. Lance," said Judge French.

"I'll narrow it down, Your Honor," said Victoria. "Detective Pearson, did you find evidence that Ms. Vila participated in that protest?"

"I did."

"And what evidence is that?"

"From photos on the Forest Initiative's website."

I objected and we approached and we spent the next fifteen minutes arguing about whether the photos from the website could come in. Eventually, Judge French ruled that sufficient foundation had been laid and allowed it.

When she started again Victoria said, "And what pictures of Ms. Vila did you find?"

"These," said Pearson and the first picture went up. It showed a woman, clearly Liselle by her blonde hair and light eyes, linking arms with eight others in front of a piece of heavy equipment. A second picture showed her with her fist up and her mouth open, clearly chanting or screaming.

She looked angry.

Victoria let the picture sit there for a while before she said, "So what did you investigate next?"

"So, after I had conducted this research, I waited a few more weeks for the toxicology results to come back. I spoke with Dr. Gerchuk about it once his results were complete."

"Now Detective Pearson, Dr. Gerchuk has already explained to the jury that the toxicology results found the presence of alcohol and metoprolol, a beta blocker, in Mr. Phillips' bloodstream. Did he relay similar information to you?"

"He did."

"And did you relate information to him?"

"I did. I told him that we had found an herbal tea supplement in the room that contained St. John's wort and other chemicals in it and I asked if that could have played a role in Mr. Phillips' death."

"And what did Dr. Gerchuk say?"

"He said he would get back to me."

"And did he?"

"The same day."

"Detective Pearson, Dr. Gerchuk has also explained to the jury how St. John's wort can speed up the elimination of a beta blocker from a person's bloodstream. Did he relay that same information to you?"

"He did."

"And what did you do?"

"I turned all of that information over to the prosecutor's office."

"I see."

Victoria was silent for a moment and walked over next to the screen, one finger on her chin. She stood there, as if thinking, and the jury's eyes naturally gravitated to the screen where Liselle stood, fist upraised, screaming, angry. Victoria stood there another moment, then pointed to her associate and the prescription bottle of medication popped up on the screen again. "And, just so the jury is clear Detective Pearson, this bottle of Lopressor, a beta blocker, was sitting in plain sight at the bathroom sink."

"It was."

"And there was only one sink in that bathroom?"

"That's right."

She started to walk away then she stopped and turned back to Pearson. "And how many toothbrushes were in the glass next to the sink, Detective Pearson?"

"Two, Ms. Lance."

"Thank you. No further questions, Your Honor."

"Mr. Shepherd?" said Judge French.

I stood. "Detective Pearson, your office doesn't investigate every heart attack that happens in Carrefour, does it?"

Pearson smirked. "Mr. Phillips didn't die of a heart attack."

"No, he didn't. Thank you for correcting me. Detective Pearson, your office doesn't investigate every sudden cardiac death caused by a fatal heart arrhythmia in Carrefour, does it?"

"We do not."

"Instead, you investigated this one because of Mr. Phillips' high profile, right?"

"I don't like what you're implying," said Pearson.

"I'm not implying anything, Detective. I am saying that six other people died of cardiac related causes over that weekend in

Carrefour, Ohio, the same weekend as Mr. Phillips, and you didn't investigate any one of those did you?"

"There was no implication of foul play in the other cases."

"How can you possibly know that if you didn't investigate?"

"Well, we didn't receive any complaints in any other cases."

"And that's exactly what happened here, isn't it?"

"Excuse me?"

"Bre Phillips called you and complained, right?"

"She did."

"And she encouraged you to search her father's room for drugs, didn't she?"

"That's standard operating procedure in a case like this."

"And you did not find any illegal street drugs in Mr. Phillips room, did you?"

"We did not."

"That's what you went in there looking for, wasn't it?"

Pearson's eyes hooded. "We were looking for anything that might shed light on the situation."

"At the time, there was no situation to shed light on was there? You just had a fifty-nine-year-old man who had experienced a cardiac arrhythmia, didn't you?"

"We didn't know that yet. The autopsy was still pending."

"So, at Bre Phillips' direction, you searched my client's room, didn't you?"

Pearson bristled. "With Bre Phillips' consent, we searched her father's belongings."

"And anything you thought was in plain sight."

Pearson smiled. "If it was in plain sight, we couldn't avoid seeing it."

I nodded. "You testified that there was a pill bottle sitting next to the bathroom sink, correct?"

"That's correct."

"And that there were two toothbrushes in the glass next to the sink?"

"That's right."

"You're implying that both Mr. Phillips and my client used that sink, right?"

Pearson shrugged. "It's not my place to say. What I can say is that there were two different toothbrushes that had been used sitting in a glass next to the prescription bottle of Lopressor."

"I see. You don't know when the bottle of Lopressor was placed next to the sink, do you?"

"I do not."

"You don't know who brushed their teeth first that morning, Mr. Phillips or Ms. Vila, correct?"

"I do not."

"So Mr. Phillips could have used the sink after Ms. Vila, correct?"

"That's true."

"In fact, it's possible that Ms. Vila could've used the shower first and then gone to the other room to do her hair and makeup while Mr. Phillips showered and brushed his teeth in the bathroom, correct?"

"I don't know what they did or the order they did them in."

"Exactly. You don't know who was in the bathroom first and who was in it last, do you?"

"That's what I just said."

"So there's a fifty-fifty chance Ms. Vila used the bathroom sink first, right?"

"I suppose."

"And if it takes Ms. Vila longer to get ready than Mr. Phillips, it's more likely that she was in there first, right?"

"I can't say that's true."

"You also can't say it's not true, can you?"

Pearson nodded.

"You have to answer out loud, Detective Pearson."

"Yes."

"And it's possible that Mr. Phillips didn't set the medication on the sink until he used the bathroom, right?"

"Not necessarily."

"You mean he could've set the medicine on the sink when he wasn't in the bathroom? How would he do that?"

"No, obviously he had to have been in the bathroom when he set the medication on the side of sink."

"So he might have set it there after Ms. Vila used the bathroom, right?"

"I don't know."

"Detective Pearson, you can't tell the jury for sure that Ms. Vila saw that medication bottle, can you?"

"For sure? No. I think it's likely though."

"Okay, Detective Pearson, why don't you tell the jury how you know it's likely."

"Well, because it was sitting right there."

"Ms. Vila didn't see you in the room, did she Detective Pearson?"

Pearson scowled. "Not that I know of."

"But you were right there by the sink! Next to the medicine bottle!"

Pearson didn't reply. I let it hang there for a moment, then said, "Detective Pearson, you mentioned that my client belonged to an organization, the Forest Initiative, that supports conservation, is that right?"

"Yes."

"And you found that the Forest Initiative opposed certain decisions and policies of Doprava Corporation, true?"

"True."

"And you were implying that my client has a motivation to

see Mr. Phillips come to harm, because an organization that she belonged to opposed his company, right?"

Pearson shrugged. "That's not for me to decide. I'm just saying that she protested against his company."

"Membership in an organization like the Forest Initiative is not illegal, is it?"

"No."

"In fact, it supports a variety of environmental causes, true?"

"From what I could tell."

"It seeks to preserve forests and clean water and wildlife, right?"

"From what I could see."

"That's entirely consistent with her job, isn't it?"

"I suppose."

"I see. You investigate a lot of murders don't you, Detective Pearson?"

"As many as we have here in Carrefour."

"You investigate motives for crimes as part of your job, don't you?"

"I do."

"On the night of Richard Phillips' death, Bre Phillips told you to search his room, right?"

"She consented to it."

"And Bre Phillips gave you information to start your investigation of Ms. Vila, is that right?"

"That's true."

"Who received Mr. Phillips' shares in Doprava when he died?"

"Objection, Your Honor," said Victoria.

"The jury has the right to know whether Ms. Vila received any monetary benefit from Mr. Phillips' death, Your Honor," I said.

"Overruled," said Judge French.

"It was Bre and Andrew Phillips, wasn't it, Detective Pearson?"

"As far as I was able to determine, yes."

"Ms. Vila did not receive any shares or money upon Mr. Phillips death, did she?"

"She did not."

"Detective Pearson, besides being the Chief Detective for Serious Crimes here in Carrefour, you also supervise the Carrefour Police Recreation League, don't you?"

"I do." Pearson straightened and looked at the jury. "I believe that by intervening early with schoolchildren, we can avoid drug overdoses and drug-related crimes later."

"As part of that program, you also provide sports equipment to kids in need, right?"

"We sure do. We donated over ten thousand dollars in equipment last year alone."

"That's great. And did the Carrefour Police Recreation League receive a donation of twenty-five thousand dollars late last year from the Children's Future Foundation?"

Pearson hesitated. "We did."

"I assume you're aware that the Children's Future Foundation is funded by the Doprava Company?"

Pearson cocked his head. "I didn't think it was directly."

"Oh. So you knew Doprava funded it indirectly?"

Pearson opened his mouth, shut it, and opened it again. "I guess I don't know where it came from."

"I see. That's all I have, Detective Pearson. Thank you."

Victoria stood. "Detective Pearson, was the bottle of Lopressor that you saw next to the bathroom sink visible from outside the bathroom?"

"It was. If you were standing in the hallway, you could see the sink."

"Was Bre Phillips ever a suspect in her father's death?"

"Absolutely not."

"Is that a ridiculous suggestion?"

"It certainly is."

"Did the donation to the Carrefour Police Recreation League affect your investigation in any way?"

"No, it did not."

"Thank you, Detective."

It was my turn. "You couldn't see in the bathroom if the door was closed, right Detective?"

"Obviously."

"And you couldn't see it if you were in the other room of the suite, right?"

"That's true."

"And it wasn't visible from the bedroom?"

"No, it was not."

"And you certainly couldn't see it if it hadn't been placed there yet, right?"

"I think we covered that, Counselor."

"So it should be easy to answer."

Pearson rolled his eyes. "No, you couldn't see it if it hadn't been placed there yet."

"Now Detective Pearson, I wasn't suggesting that Bre Phillips killed her father."

"Good."

"I was suggesting that you didn't investigate that possibility. That's true, right?"

Pearson glared. "That's true."

"You had different theories for why Mr. Phillips died throughout your investigation, didn't you?"

Pearson shrugged. "Investigations always evolve."

"Why don't you tell the jury the theory you told me the first time you met Ms. Vila."

Pearson's head jerked. "What?"

"You remember. The first time Ms. Vila and I came to see you at the police station so you could question her. You told me your theory about Mr. Phillips' death. Do you remember what you told me?"

Pearson ground his teeth. "I don't remember."

"Really? Let me find my notes." I went back to the counsel table, picked up a random legal pad, and leafed through it. "Ah, here. Ms. Vila walked out of the room, you watched her go, and you said ..." I looked up. "Well, why don't you tell the jury what you said."

I felt the jury's eyes swing to Pearson. So did he.

Pearson straightened.

I flipped the blank page in my hand. "Are you going to make me read it?"

He shot a glance at Liselle and said, "Seems like the old man bit off more than he could chew."

"Close but not quite." I shook my head and tapped the blank page. "Your exact words were 'seems like the geezer bit off more than he could chew and his heart gave out.' Do I have that right?"

Pearson's jaw muscle twitched. "I don't recall exactly," he said.

But he didn't deny it.

"Thanks, Detective. That's all."

Judge French said, "Thank you, Detective Pearson you may step down."

Pearson took a moment to regroup, buttoned his coat, and tucked his badge into it before he strutted out of the courtroom.

He didn't look at me as he left.

39

When Pearson was gone, Judge French said, "Are you prepared to call another witness before lunch, Ms. Lance?"

"Yes, Your Honor. I have a witness that needs to be done by noon."

"You may call him or her then."

"Thank you, Your Honor. The state calls Dr. Newt Wrigley."

One of Victoria's associates went out to the hall and came back with a thin, small man in a dark blue suit, stylish thick black glasses, and light brown shoes. When he sat down and was sworn in, Victoria said, "Sir, could you introduce yourself to the jury?"

"My name is Newton Wrigley. I am a toxicologist at the University."

Victoria spent about five minutes establishing his qualifications as a toxicologist and his experience for the past fifteen years in analyzing substances and their effect on the body and even managed to work in that the wiry doctor was a top marathoner in his age bracket. When they were done, Victoria said, "Doctor, did Detective Pearson request that you analyze some packets of tea that were found in Richard Phillips' hotel room?"

"I don't know where they were found but I did analyze some packets of tea at his request."

"And what did you find, Doctor?"

"I found that the tea consisted of components typical of many herbal teas that are commercially available."

"What about the ratio of those components?"

"That was not typical."

"How do you mean?"

"The level of St. John's wort in this tea exceeded that which is found in commercially available teas."

"By how much?"

"These tea bags contained fifteen times the dose St. John's wort typically found in commercial teas."

"Do you have an explanation for that?"

"I do not. I assume you'd have to ask the person who made it."

"Doctor, we heard testimony earlier from Dr. Ray Gerchuk stating that St. John's wort can interfere with the body's absorption of certain beta blockers. Do you have an opinion as to whether that's true?"

"I do."

"What is that opinion?"

"It can. And it does."

"Does this tea contain enough St. John's wort to interfere with the body's absorption of Lopressor?"

"It certainly does. It contains far more than what would be necessary to do that."

"That's all I have, Doctor. Thank you."

I stood. "Doctor, those teabags would have been diluted in water prior to their use, correct?"

"That's true."

"The amount of St. John's wort that was actually ingested would depend on how long the tea was steeped, right?"

"That's also true."

"In other words, if the person simply dipped the teabag into the water once and took it out, there would be very little St. John's wort in the water, true?"

"That's right."

"On the other hand, if one left the teabag in the water for hours, more St. John's wort would be absorbed, correct?"

"That's correct."

"Assuming Mr. Phillips drank the tea you examined, you have no idea how long Mr. Phillips allowed the tea to steep, do you?"

"I don't."

"That would have been entirely up to Mr. Phillips, right?"

"That's right."

"I understand you're only offering testimony about the composition of the tea, right?"

"That's right."

"You did not study Mr. Phillips' blood, true?"

"I did not."

"You did not study his medical history or history of cardiac arrhythmia, correct?"

"That's correct."

"You did not study the dose of Lopressor he was taking?"

"That's correct."

"You did not measure his blood alcohol or verify that it was at more than twice the legal limit?"

"I did not."

"And you are not offering any opinion here as to the effect which the alcohol and caffeine he ingested would've had on his heart, right?"

"That's right."

"Your opinion is limited to how much St. John's wort was in the tea, correct?"

"That's correct."

"But you have no opinion as to how much tea was actually ingested, right?"

"That's right."

"Thank you, Doctor."

Victoria stood. "Again, Doctor, you found that the tea you analyzed had fifteen times the amount of St. John's wort that is present in commercial teas?"

"I did, yes."

"So let's say, hypothetically, that a person always steeps their tea for three minutes."

"Okay."

"And that person drinks a commercial tea every morning and always steeps their tea for three minutes."

"Fine."

"And, one day, the person switches their commercial tea for the tea in front of you and steeps it for three minutes. Are you with me?"

Dr. Wrigley smiled and nodded. "I am."

"Is it reasonable to assume that the tea in front of you would have fifteen times more St. John's wort in it after being steeped for three minutes than a commercial tea that was also steeped for three minutes?"

"I think that's a reasonable assumption."

"That's all. Thank you, Doctor."

I rose. "Doctor, you have no evidence of how Mr. Phillips prepared this tea, do you?"

"I do not."

"And you have no evidence that he'd ever drank herbal tea before this tea, do you?"

"No."

"In fact, his children have testified that they'd never seen their father drink any tea before this. Are you aware of that?"

"No."

"Do you have any reason to doubt it?"

"I don't know why I would."

"Thank you, Doctor."

"You're excused, Dr. Wrigley, thank you," said Judge French. As Dr. Wrigley stepped down, Judge French said, "Members of the jury, let's break for lunch. Please be back in an hour."

Judge French wasn't a gavel-banger so instead we all rose and the jury left and we prepared for the afternoon. I looked at Victoria. "Who are you calling this afternoon, Vicki?"

"Stephen Phillips," she said. "I imagine that will take the rest of the day."

"Great. Thanks."

I sent Danny and Liselle off to get some lunch and went to a quiet floor in the courthouse to get ready to cross-examine Richard Phillips' brother and the current head of the Doprava Corporation.

40

Stephen Phillips looked like exactly what he was—the CFO and now CEO of a multibillion-dollar company. His concession to being in court was that he wore a finely tailored blue suit with a light blue shirt and a pocket square to match. He did not, however, put on a tie. His hair was turning white and it was tight on the sides and swept back on top and his resemblance to his brother was jarring. But where Richard had blunter features and exuded a sort of cheerful bonhomie, Stephen's face was leaner and sharper and he radiated a penetrating stillness, like a hawk on a branch.

He took a seat in the witness chair and was sworn in. After introducing himself to the jury and giving a little bit of his background—born and raised in St. Louis, away for an Ivy League education before he returned and worked his way up in the family business from the backlot warehouseman all the way to CFO before his brother's untimely death—Victoria said, "Mr. Phillips, could you explain the roles you and your brother had in the Doprava Company before he died?"

"Sure," said Stephen. "My brother was the CEO. He was the idea guy. He would come up with new product ideas or new manufacturing processes or a restructuring plan to make us more efficient. He was always creating or troubleshooting. I was the money guy. When he decided to do something, it was my job to figure out how to pay for it or, after an idea had been working for a while, it was my job to see if it was making money for the company."

"And was that partnership successful?"

Stephen nodded. "Once the two of us took on those roles, the value of the company tripled in less than ten years."

"You said Richard was an idea guy. Can you give the jury some examples of what you're talking about?"

Stephen appeared to think for a moment before he said, "Sure. I can think of two off the top of my head. One of our products had a component part that was only made by a couple of Chinese companies. When we weren't successful in getting the price we wanted, Richard orchestrated a purchase of one of those companies through a series of shells so that we could make the component ourselves and ship it here along with some of our other products. That's more common now but nobody was doing it then. It took that product from being a dog to a cash cow."

"What else?"

"Another example was we had a large number of real estate holdings from acquisitions our father had made back in the 1980s. When the shale boom started, Richard was smart enough to get ahead of the curve and sell drilling rights on some of the land to oil and gas companies. The financing is a little complex, but basically we turned the land into cash producing assets without having to give up ownership."

"And you played a role in that too?"

Stephen shrugged. "Sure. I figured out how to make the money end of it work. But the ideas were all Richard."

"On the topic of drilling, did there come a time when the

Doprava Company sought to lease lands for oil and gas exploration just south of the Mark Twain National Forest?"

I stood. "Objection, Your Honor. This is collateral."

"Your Honor, we will demonstrate that it goes to motive," said Victoria.

"You have a very small window here, Ms. Lance," said Judge French.

Victoria nodded and said, "Do you need me to repeat the question?"

Stephen shook his head and said, "We had five thousand acres in south-central Missouri that bordered the Mark Twain National Forest near a place called Ribbon Falls. We decided to lease the rights to that land, which we had purchased decades before."

"And did organizations protest this exploration?"

"They did. Several times."

"Were they successful?"

"I guess it depends on your definition of success. They certainly received publicity. They did not stop our company from leasing the mineral and gas rights."

"Did any of the demonstrations become violent?"

I stood. "Objection, Your Honor."

"Sustained."

"That's fair," said Victoria. "Let me ask you a different question. Did the Ribbon Falls demonstration where over five thousand people showed up become violent?"

"Objection, Your Honor," I said.

"Your Honor, the evidence has already shown that Ms. Vila was at this demonstration," said Victoria. "It's certainly relevant if there was violence directed at the decedent's company at a demonstration in which she participated."

Judge French thought. "Your small window has become a peephole, Ms. Lance."

Victoria nodded to Stephen Phillips, who said, "There was some of what I would think of as typical demonstration tactics. People laid in front of equipment or strapped themselves to trees. There was a fight at one point with some of the oil workers so that security forces had to use riot shields and mace to disperse the crowd. I think some surveying equipment and excavation equipment was damaged. That's about all that I remember."

"But that project went forward, didn't it?"

"It did."

"And that project was your brother's brain-child?"

"It was. He always tried to share the credit but Richard was the one who could figure out how to get these kinds of things done."

"Mr. Phillips, are you also on the Board of Directors of the Doprava Company?"

"I am."

"Shortly after that demonstration did you receive this letter?"

Victoria handed him a piece of paper. "For the record, this item has been marked as State's Exhibit 62."

Stephen Phillips looked at it then nodded. "I did."

"Could you read it to the jury please?"

Stephen Phillips held it a little farther away from his eyes and said, "It's addressed to all of the board members. It then says, 'For the past nine months, we have protested your proposed lease of the Ribbon Falls site bordering on the Mark Twain National Forest for fracking. As you well know, this will have a disastrous effect on the surrounding forest, water supply, and wildlife. We believe that your short-sighted exploitation of this site will cause harm that will last for generations. We will lobby our state and federal governing bodies to curtail this project and will continue to protest and resist your reckless development of the land at every opportunity. We have attached what is just the first of our petitions to this letter. We hope that you will have the foresight and conscience to curtail this monstrous project which will cripple our land, deplete our natural resources, and lay waste to our state's precious woodlands. Very truly yours, the Forest Initiative.'" Stephen Phillips looked up from the letter as if it tasted bad.

"Thank you, Mr. Phillips. There is a list of signatures attached to that letter, isn't there?"

"There is."

"Can you please go to the fourth page, the third column, line number 962?"

He flipped. "I'm there."

"Can you read the signature on that line, please?"

There was no surprise on his face as he said, "Liselle Vila."

"Was this letter addressed to your brother Richard as well?"

"It was. He was on the Board too."

Victoria nodded and looked at the jury as she slowly walked forward and took the letter back from Stephen Phillips. She waved it a couple of times before she said, "Mr. Phillips, had you ever met Liselle Vila before the weekend of your son's wedding?"

"I had not," said Stephen. "My brother had told me that he'd met someone at the Gateway Animal Rescue gala and that he was bringing her to the wedding but I didn't know who."

"When you met her, did she ever mention that she'd protested against your company?"

"She did not."

"Would it have surprised you if Liselle Vila had told you that she was a member of the Forest Initiative?"

"It would have."

"Why?"

"Because they were so aggressive in their opposition to our

company. They didn't stop at just protesting fracking. They arranged a boycott of our products as well."

"Was it effective?"

"We're a little too big for a boycott at their level to be effective. But it was noticeable."

"And she never mentioned it to you? That she was adamantly opposed to your company? Not once?"

"She did not."

"Mr. Phillips, did you see your brother dance with Ms. Vila at your son's wedding reception?"

"I did."

"When?"

Stephen Phillips clenched his jaw before he said, "For just about the whole reception."

"And why do you remember that?"

"Because as outgoing as my brother was, he hated to dance."

Victoria put a hand on her hip and gestured. "Hate is a pretty strong word, Mr. Phillips."

"Fine then, let's just say he never did it. My brother liked to have a good time and was always fun to be around but dancing just wasn't his thing."

"Why is that?"

"For one thing, he wasn't very good at it and he hated not being good at something in front of people. And for another..." he stopped.

"And for another what?" Victoria said.

"And for another his ex-wife didn't like to dance very much either so the two of them never did."

"Mr. Phillips, we've heard a lot of testimony during this hearing that your brother was an independent thinker who made decisions for his company all of the time. That's true, isn't it?"

"It certainly is."

"And yet were there times when your brother would do things that he wouldn't necessarily want to do?"

"Objection, Your Honor," I said.

"Mr. Shepherd opened the door with his questions about decision-making, Your Honor," Victoria said.

"I'll allow it," said Judge French.

"Yes, he would," said Stephen.

"When?"

"You had to understand my brother," said Stephen Phillips. "As powerful as he was, he always wanted people to be comfortable and he didn't like conflict in a social situation. He was always looking to diffuse things and was big on harmony, especially within the family."

"Did your brother say anything to you about dancing that night?"

"Objection, Your Honor," I said.

"Sustained."

Victoria tried again. "Did your brother say anything about dancing with Ms. Vila to keep her happy?"

"Objection, Your Honor."

"Sustained," said Judge French. "That's enough, Ms. Lance."

"So let me ask you this another way, Mr. Phillips. Did you hear Ms. Vila talk to your brother about dancing at all on the night of the wedding reception?"

"I did."

"What did she say?"

"They had just finished eating when Ms. Vila said to Richard, 'We're going to drink this bottle of wine and then we're going to dance until we drop.'"

"And that's exactly what happened, isn't it?"

"Objection, Your Honor."

"Sustained."

"No further questions, Your Honor."

I stood and walked over directly in front of the jury. "Mr. Phillips, there are seventeen hundred and thirty-two signatures on that petition, aren't there?"

"I wouldn't know."

I handed the letter back to him. "Why don't you look. They're numbered. Go to the last page."

He flipped and took a quick glance. "Yes."

"You're not accusing the other seventeen hundred and thirty-one people who signed this letter of having a motive to kill your brother, are you?"

"No. But they wouldn't have had the opportunity."

"What do you mean by that?"

"They don't look like her." Stephen Phillips didn't even blink when he said it.

That wasn't the answer I was expecting but I knew enough to run with it. "What do you mean they don't look like her?"

Stephen Phillips pointed and shrugged. "You know what I mean."

"No, Mr. Phillips, I'm afraid I don't. Why don't you tell the jury exactly what you mean?"

Stephen Phillips didn't show the slightest discomfort as he said, "She was able to get close to my brother because of the way she looks."

"And how does she look, Mr. Phillips?"

Steve Phillips was too smooth to glare but the weight of his stare certainly became extra. "Like a supermodel. And you know that."

I shrugged. "You mentioned that your brother danced with Ms. Vila the night of the wedding, right?"

"He did."

"He danced with your new daughter-in-law too, didn't he?"

Steve Phillips shrugged. "That was one dance."

"That wasn't my question. My question was, he danced with your daughter-in-law, true?"

"That's true."

"Your wife Paulette danced with Richard too, didn't she?"

"There was a dance for the family and the wedding party."

"Again that wasn't my question, Mr. Phillips. My question was, your wife danced with Richard Phillips the night he died too, didn't she?"

"She did."

"Your wife and daughter-in-law weren't trying to kill Richard, were they?"

"That's a stupid question."

"Please give me the stupid answer."

Stephen Phillips scoffed. "They were not."

"Mr. Phillips, I'm not going to get into your family finances, but is it fair to say that your family is worth billions of dollars?"

Stephen Phillips shrugged. "I can't put an exact number on it because it fluctuates with our company's value but we are worth a fair amount."

"And your family funds charitable trusts, does it not?"

"We do."

"The main trust is called just that, the Phillips Family Charitable trust, true?"

"That's true."

"And that trust in turn donates to various charitable organizations?"

"It does."

"You donate to a variety of afterschool programs, don't you?"

The side of Stephen Phillips' mouth twitched. "*I* don't."

"That's a good correction, Mr. Phillips. I should have said that the Phillips Family Charitable trust donates to a variety of afterschool programs, true?"

"That's true. It's very important to educate our children not to use drugs."

"And this past winter, your family's Charitable Trust donated to the Carrefour Police Recreation League, didn't it?"

"It did."

"That was the first time your family's trust donated to the Carrefour program, isn't it?"

"I wouldn't know."

"Your family also donates to certain political super pacs, true?"

"You'd have to ask our accountant."

"Really? I thought you were the money guy?"

"I recently had to take on more responsibility."

"Well, that's interesting because super pacs and political campaigns have to list who their donors are to comply with campaign finance laws. Do you think we can find your name as a donator to the Republican Party of Carrefour, Ohio?"

Stephen Phillips flicked a hand. "A lot of people ask me for money, Mr. Shepherd. I can't remember them all."

"Okay. Here's a list from last year's disclosure. Is that your name with the maximum contributors?"

He looked. "It is."

"And right below that, is that your wife's name?"

"Yes."

"And then your daughter's?"

"Yes."

"And then your son-in-law?"

"Yes."

"And two separate donations for your niece and nephew?"

"Yes."

"Now the Central Missouri PAC for America? Is that your super pac?"

"It's not mine."

"Your family manages who it donates to, right?"

"We do."

"And that super pac donated to the Carrefour Republican Party too, didn't it?"

"It appears so."

"All of these donations were made after your brother died, right?"

Stephen Phillips shrugged his shoulders. "When we see a need, we address it."

"I see. For example, your family saw a need for an internship program for prosecutors around the state of Ohio, true?"

"We believe in creating opportunities for young professionals."

"So your family's charitable trust funded that prosecutor internship program, right?"

"One of many."

"I see. And one of the many places these paid interns ended up was in Carrefour, Ohio, wasn't it?"

"I have no idea."

"The two interns your family paid to put in Carrefour are working on this case, aren't they?"

Stephen Phillips shrugged again. "We don't control how people use our resources."

I shook my head and walked a little ways away. "Now you mentioned that there were protests surrounding the opening of some of Doprava's land to fracking, true?"

"That's true."

"Out of the five thousand people who protested at Ribbon Falls, there were only eight arrests, weren't there?"

"If you say so."

"Ms. Vila was not arrested there, was she?"

"Not that I'm aware of."

"Mr. Phillips, you're not aware of Ms. Vila threatening your brother in any way, are you?"

"She didn't threaten him. She poisoned him and pushed him until he died."

"That's what you think? That she poisoned him and pushed him until he died?"

"Yes."

I motioned to Danny and a picture popped up on the screen. It was of Liselle and Richard leaning in close together for a picture at the dinner table during the wedding. "Was this picture taken the night your brother died?"

"It was."

Another picture popped up. This one was of Liselle, Richard, Stephen, and Paulette all standing in a row, smiling. "How about this one?"

"Yes."

A picture of Richard leading Liselle onto the dance floor by a hand. "And this one?"

"Yes."

A picture of the two of them dancing and Richard smiling, pressing his lips against Liselle's cheek while she screwed up her face in mock disgust. "And this one?"

"Yes."

A picture of Richard smiling and dipping Liselle. "And this one?"

"Yes."

A picture of Richard and Liselle and the bridal party all with their hands in the air, yelling and smiling. "And this one?"

"Yes."

Finally, a picture of Liselle's head resting on Richard's shoulder and him smiling as they were obviously slow dancing and his cheek was resting on top of her pale blonde hair. "And this one?"

"Yes."

"That's a death struggle, huh?"

"It turned out to be."

"Not like I've ever seen," I said.

"Objection, Your Honor."

"Withdrawn. No further questions, Your Honor."

Victoria flipped her hand at an associate and a picture of Richard popped onto the screen. He had his black tux jacket on but his white shirt was ripped open, revealing a pale chest. He was lying on wrinkled paper sheets and there were leads from the cardioverter machine trailing away out of the picture. Richard's face was pale and his blue lips were frozen in a grimace. "Is this picture from the night of the wedding too, Mr. Phillips?"

"It is. That's my brother at the end of the night in the hospital. They couldn't revive him."

Victoria nodded. "After he collapsed on the dance floor?"

"That's right."

"No further questions. I'm sorry for the loss of your brother, Mr. Phillips."

"Me too," Steve Phillips said and left the stand.

I heard a small noise and I turned. Liselle had her head down and I saw a tear roll down her cheek. I looked up and saw that the picture of Richard Phillips was still up on the screen.

"Your Honor," I said and pointed.

Judge French looked at me, looked at Liselle, and then looked at the screen. "Ms. Lance, are you done with your examination?"

"I am, Your Honor."

"Then perhaps you could turn off your exhibit."

"Certainly, Your Honor," she said and did.

Several jurors were watching Liselle as the picture went off the screen. It was hard to tell what they thought about it but it seemed like a few faces were sympathetic.

"Members of the jury, that concludes our testimony for today," said Judge French. "The prosecution will be wrapping up their case tomorrow. It looks like we will go into next week so please make arrangements with your employers and childcare folks for at least the first part of next week. I'll see you at eight o'clock tomorrow morning. Thank you."

When I looked back down at Liselle, her eyes were dry. She appeared to have gotten herself back under control.

"Eat with us again tonight?" I said.

She nodded.

"Good. Let's head back."

41

That night I drove Liselle back to the office and, since the Black Boar was on the way, we could stop there and pick up our order of Cuban sandwiches and Spanish rice without violating the terms to her release. Liselle was quiet as I parked the car.

"You need to come in with me," I said. "Olivia would have my ass if I left you out here alone."

Liselle looked up. "Isn't it safe here?"

"It's perfectly safe," I said.

She glanced at her ankle. "Oh. Right." And we got out of the car.

It was Thursday so it was crowded. We walked up to the young man at the takeout station behind the bar and I said, "Order for Shepherd."

He looked up, stopped, and stared at Liselle.

I smiled, cleared my throat, and said, "Order for Shepherd, please."

"Uhm, what?" said the young man.

Liselle smiled, then said, "Order for Shepherd, please."

"You bet. Coming right up." He turned, ran into the ice machine, and went back to the kitchen.

The young man came back, and somehow, without ever looking down, took my credit card, processed it, and handed me a pen and a receipt in a tiny plastic tray. I signed it and handed it back. He ignored it and handed Liselle two white plastic bags. "Here you go, Mr. Shepherd," he said.

Liselle smiled. "Thank you, Chris."

Chris began to stutter. "How?"

She tapped the name tag on his chest with a long finger, picked up the bags, and left.

"Bye, Chris," I said.

Chris didn't answer as I followed Liselle out.

We climbed back into the car and continued on to the office. After we had driven a couple miles, I said, "Do you always have stuttering servers?"

She smiled faintly. "Occasionally."

Then Liselle began to cry.

I didn't realize it at first. I thought she was just tired, with her hand pressed against her forehead shielding her eyes, but then I saw that her shoulders were shaking and a drop of water splashed onto her leg.

"Hey! Hey, Liselle. I'm sorry."

She shook her head and her shoulders shook harder. I grabbed a packet of tissues out of the center console of the Jeep and handed them to her. She nodded and opened it and pulled one out and pressed it to her eyes. We came to my office building and I pulled into the lot and we stopped.

"I mean it, Liselle. I'm sorry. I didn't mean anything by it."

"It's not that, Nate." She smiled as she wiped her eyes but the tears were still coming down. "It was those pictures, there at the end? We were having such a good time. We were dancing and we were laughing and..." She stopped and dabbed at the corners. "And then the light just went right out of his eyes, and he was the husk you saw on the screen today."

I listened.

"It was just like one of the trees—he was living a perfectly contented life, everything seemed fine, but under the surface something was boring in that was going to kill him and we didn't even know it. It was awful."

I was so busy focusing on the effect the pictures would have on the jurors that I hadn't really thought about the effect they might have on Liselle. I felt stupid.

"I should've realized," I said. "I'm sorry."

"Why? You're doing your job, which is to keep me from..." Then she couldn't say any more and broke down completely.

I wasn't surprised. Any trial creates pressure. A murder trial creates far more. That pressure can seep out at the most unexpected times.

"You're doing fine," I said, which she actually was. So the two of us just sat there and I let her cry.

At some point, she leaned closer to me and our shoulders touched. The shaking lessened and she leaned a little closer still.

I turned off the Jeep, grabbed the food bags, and said, "Danny is probably starving."

I got out and waited. A couple of minutes later, Liselle got out the other side. She was perfectly composed, with no sign she'd been wracked just minutes before.

We went up to the third floor where Danny was waiting and was indeed hungry. We ate and then got to work preparing for the next day.

∼

The next day was the last scheduled day of the prosecution's case. I don't know what I was expecting but I knew they were planning on this being their big finish, their big push, so I was a little surprised when the first witness they called was the server who handled Liselle and Richard's table at the wedding. Victoria's questioning seemed fairly innocuous but, of course, it wasn't.

"And did you take Mr. Richards' drink order?" Victoria said.

"I did."

"And what was it?"

"Which time?"

"Throughout the night."

"He ordered a Malbec. It started as one bottle and I wound up getting him four."

"Now, why do you remember that?"

"Well, because it was Richard Phillips."

"And why else?"

"Because it was a special kind and we only had four bottles in the cellar."

"Now is Mr. Phillips the one who ordered it?"

"No."

"Who did?"

"That woman."

"Let the record reflect that the witness is pointing at Liselle Vila. Why do you remember that she ordered it?"

"Because each time she ordered, she said it would be the last one. So each time I went down to the cellar, for a special trip, I thought it would be the last trip."

"And you did that four times?"

"I did."

"No further questions."

~

THE STEADY DRIP OF FACTS CONTINUED WITH MORE WITNESSES, none of whom took more than a few minutes.

"And you sat at the same table as Mr. Phillips and Ms. Vila?"
"I did."
"So you ate with them?"
"Not for long."
"What do you mean?"
"I mean as soon as dinner was finished, the band started to play and Ms. Vila stood up, took Mr. Phillips by the hand, and said 'Come on, this is my favorite song.'"
"Why do you remember that?"
"Because we stayed at the table most of the night and I don't think they ever sat back down."

~

"You worked at the bar that evening?"
"I did."
"Did you see Richard Phillips that night?"
"Yes."
"How did you know it was him?"
"Because he ordered two drinks and gave me a one-hundred-dollar tip. It leaves an impression."
"Did you see Ms. Vila too?'
He nodded. "I did. Right after I handed Mr. Phillips the drinks, Ms. Vila came up, took them out of his hands and placed them on the bar, and said, 'Come on. You promised me this dance.'"
"How do you know it was her?"
The bartender shot Liselle a look before lowering his eyes apologetically. "She makes an impression too."

~

"How did you know Richard Phillips?"

"He's my cousin."

"Did you see him at the wedding reception?"

"For a moment or two. He was sweating and breathing a little hard, but he was in good spirits. I hadn't had a chance to talk to him in a couple of years so I was trying to catch up."

"And what happened?"

"We hadn't gotten much past the kids are fine when Ms. Vila came up and said, 'Don't tell me you're too high falutin' for the electric slide.'"

"What happened then?"

"Richard said he would catch up with me later and went out on the dance floor."

"And did he? Catch up with you later?"

"He never had the chance."

∾

"I UNDERSTAND YOU SAW RICHARD PHILLIPS AT THE WEDDING?"

"I did."

"Did you know him before then?"

"I didn't. I'm a friend of Jake's, the groom. We went to college together."

"I see. And how did you come to talk to Mr. Phillips?"

"We were in the bathroom at the same time. He was at the sink wiping his forehead with a wet paper towel. I went to wash my hands and he smiled at me, kind of embarrassed, and said, 'I'm afraid she's wearing me out.' 'There are worse things,' I said. And he smiled and said, 'There certainly are.'"

"Did you know who he was talking about at the time?"

"Of course. How could you not?"

"Why do you say that?"

"I mean, well, look at her. Of course I knew."

"Let the record reflect that the witness is indicating the defendant, Liselle Vila."

Liselle kept her eyes on the table.

∽

ALL TOLD, VICTORIA CALLED EIGHTEEN WITNESSES THAT DAY. None of them took much longer than ten minutes. A few testified that they saw Liselle order red wine for Richard, but most of them related some incident where she led him back onto the dance floor or spun him around so fast that it seemed like their feet were barely touching the floor. The last one was a young woman who had been clearing the discard trays.

"And what's a discard tray?" asked Victoria.

"You know how there's little stands with trays that people put their used glasses on?"

"I do."

"I cleared them and took them back to the kitchen to be washed."

"I see. And were you doing that at the end of the reception?"

"I was."

"And did you see Richard Phillips at that time?"

"I did."

"How did you know it was Richard Phillips?"

"Well, number one, he's a billionaire. And number two, he was handsome, in a dad kinda way."

"And what did you see?"

"He asked if I could get him a bottle of water, and I said that I could, so I did. He gave me a tip, in advance, so I hustled and got the water, and brought it back. He smiled and was about to take a drink when that woman—"

"You're indicating Ms. Vila sitting at the table over there?"

"I am. Ms. Vila came up and said, 'Come on Richard, you

promised me the last dance of the night.' And Mr. Phillips looked at me and he smiled and he said, 'I certainly did' and took a quick sip. Ms. Vila had taken his tie, put it over her shoulder, and started walking towards the dance floor. Mr. Phillips reached out quickly and handed the water back to me, and then he smiled, and I'll never forget what he said."

"And what was that?"

"He said 'That woman will be the death of me.' And then he laughed and followed her."

"You're certain that's what he said?"

"That's not something you forget."

"No, I suppose it's not. No further questions."

∾

I CROSS-EXAMINED ALL OF THEM OF COURSE, SOME LONGER THAN others, but none of it altered the facts of what they saw. And when they were done, all eighteen of them, Victoria Lance stood and said, "Your Honor, that's all I have today. I expect that we'll rest to start the day Monday."

Judge French looked at the clock. "That's all for today then."

And on the heels of that avalanche of testimony, Judge French adjourned us for the weekend.

SEEDS

42

We attacked the case with fresh eyes on Saturday morning. Danny and I were already there when Olivia brought Liselle in to the office. "Can you stay for little bit, Liv?" I asked. "I'm interested in your opinion too." Olivia had been in and out during some of the important testimony.

"All right," she said. "But I have a class at noon."

"Poor bastards," I said. She smiled and she sat and she left her half-mirrored sunglasses on, just like she always did. We all sat around the conference table, everyone in jeans after a week of suits. "We have some decisions to make," I said. "It's their job to prove the case beyond a reasonable doubt. Personally, I think their case is pretty thin and that we made some headway with just about all of their witnesses. I'm interested in where you all think we stand."

Liselle sat straight, hands folded. "You've all done this before. I'd like to hear your thoughts first."

I pointed at Danny. He looked at his notes and said, "They've established that the St. John's wort interfered with Richard's medication. I think you were able to raise some doubt as to whether Liselle saw it, but I'd like more."

"Me too," I said. "So, the four of us know that you didn't see the Lopressor in the bathroom. How else can I show that to the jury?"

There was a moment of quiet before Liselle said, "You mentioned that I could have used the bathroom before him."

"There's another possibility too," said Olivia.

"What's that?" I said.

Olivia looked at Liselle. "You were what, twenty years younger than him?"

Liselle met her gaze. "Almost thirty."

Olivia nodded. "Even better."

I cocked my head.

"Do you really think an older guy wants his younger girlfriend to see his blood pressure medication?" said Olivia.

"I wouldn't think so," I said.

"I bet if you look at the inventory of his possessions there were some little blue pills in there too, right?"

I nodded. "There were."

"I assume he didn't tell you about those either?" Olivia said to Liselle.

Liselle shook her head.

"There you go."

I thought. "I'd have to put Liselle on the stand to establish her lack of knowledge."

"So put me on the stand," said Liselle.

"That's not really an option in this case." I thought about what Olivia had said. "It's their burden of proof. They have to prove, actually prove, that you knew about the Lopressor. I don't think they have. Liv has a good thought though, I might be able to make that argument during closing depending on how the evidence comes in."

I tapped the table. "So I think we can handle the blood pressure medication. I don't think they've established that you knew about it and I like the age difference as an additional argument against your knowledge. What about the St. John's wort though?"

I came back to Danny, who squirmed a little under our attention. "I think there's plenty of evidence that Liselle convinced him to eat and drink things that would spike his blood pressure. That's a problem regardless of the blood pressure medication."

I nodded. "Why?"

"The problem is that Richard shouldn't have been drinking red wine or eating aged meats and cheeses if he was taking St. John's wort. Liselle knew Richard was taking St. John's wort. Therefore, she knew that he shouldn't have had the wine and the high tyramine foods, regardless of the blood pressure medicine." He glanced at Liselle and said, "Sorry."

Liselle shook her head. "Don't be."

"Danny's right," I said. "Why did you let Richard eat and drink those things?"

Liselle shrugged. "I was too."

"What do you mean?"

"I wasn't just making the tea for Richard. We were both drinking it."

"Every time?"

Liselle nodded. "Just about. Certainly every time we were together."

I cursed myself. That was a big angle and I'd totally missed it. "So you didn't think anything of it because you were having the same things?"

Liselle nodded. "You know how those warnings are. I'd never had any trouble with it so I never thought twice about it."

"So the main difference between you and him was the blood pressure medication which you didn't know anything about?"

"And the age difference," said Olivia.

Liselle turned her hands out. "He was a very healthy, active man. Our age never occurred to me."

I nodded and I thought. "I can work with that. What did you think of that last run of testimony yesterday?"

"With the dancing? said Danny. "Individually, it wasn't a lot. Cumulatively, I think it had some traction. So we can't let the jury lose track of just how ridiculous this all is as a murder plot. I just don't think they'll believe that you can dance someone to death."

Olivia's head twitched but with those glasses it was impossible to tell if she was looking at me.

"That's a good point, Danny," I said. "I think I'm going to attack that two ways—I'm going to put on a bunch of witnesses that saw Richard ask Liselle to dance and I'll emphasize in closing that it's a ridiculous theory."

"I think you need to hammer the family throwing their money at this too," said Olivia. "You've got a billionaire family that's used to getting their own way and a prosecutor who's pushing a pretty thin case. I don't think you have to explicitly connect the two. I think the jury will get it."

"Do you?"

Olivia nodded. "I was there for Bre Phillips' testimony. She didn't make the best impression."

I ticked the mental box. "So that leaves us with motive. How did you all think the whole environmental activist evidence played?"

"I think it's the biggest hole in the case," said Danny. "Plenty of people object to fracking on forested land. It doesn't make them murderers."

"What about the violence at the demonstration?"

"There was nothing linking her to it," said Danny. "And even if there was, that's a long way away from premeditated murder."

"Liv?"

"I agree that the fracking demonstration isn't enough," she said.

We were quiet for little bit, then I looked at Liselle and said, "What do you think?"

Light green pools of uncertainty looked back. "I think I'm too scared to think of much of anything. I'll do whatever you say."

I thought a moment, then nodded. "I think we have enough. Now we just have to put it together."

Olivia stood. "That it? My students aren't gonna hurt themselves."

I smiled. "That's it."

"Ready, lady?" she said to Liselle.

"Do you mind if I stay?" Liselle said to me.

I raised an eyebrow. "We're just going to be squirreled up in our offices banging on computers all day."

"I know it's just…" she trailed off and looked away. "I'm alone there. I'd rather do work here. With people around."

I was familiar with months alone in an empty house. "Sure. You can use the spare office."

She smiled in obvious relief. "I brought some work just in case. The ash borers wait for no woman."

Olivia left and we set Liselle up in an office that had once been used by a ruthlessly efficient legal assistant from Minneapolis. Then Danny and I got to work on the case.

~

AT THE END OF THE DAY, I DROVE LISELLE HOME. AS WE PULLED UP to the dark townhouse, she said, "I'm sorry about last night. I don't know what made me break down like that."

"I do. You're in the pressure cooker of a murder trial and you just saw pictures of someone you cared about that were deeply upsetting. Don't worry about it."

"It doesn't seem to bother you. The pressure cooker of a murder trial."

I smiled. "It's my job."

"I know. But it's more. You make me feel like it's going to be okay too."

"I can't promise you that, you know."

"I know. But that's still how you make me feel."

"Good. Good night, Liselle."

Liselle looked up at the house. None of the lights were on. "Would you mind if I came in to work at the office again tomorrow?"

"I have to be in early."

"I don't mind."

"Okay. I'll pick you up at seven-thirty."

She smiled. "Great. I'll see you then." Then she picked up her file and got out of the Jeep. I waited until she was in the house and the light came on and then I left and went home to my own dark and empty house.

∼

WE DID THE SAME THING THE NEXT DAY. I PICKED LISELLE UP AND she worked in Cyn's old office with her files and maps spread out all over the desk. When the day was done, I dropped her off on the way home. Which brought us to Monday, the sixth day of the trial.

43

Monday morning did not start out great.

We were meeting in Judge French's chambers when Victoria said, "Your Honor, we have one more witness."

"I thought you were going to rest," I said.

"We were. But we decided in light of last week's testimony that we needed one more witness."

"Who is it?" said Judge French.

"Professor Hopkins from Washington University."

"An expert?" said Judge French.

"A fact witness, Your Honor."

"Has he been disclosed?"

"It's she. And yes."

"I don't remember seeing her name," I said.

"We disclosed anyone with knowledge of Ms. Vila's academic background or education. We thought she was going to be out of the country, but she's just returned."

"I object to this witness, Your Honor," I said.

"What is she going to testify about?" Judge French said.

Victoria slid a glance at me. "About the defendant's academic background."

"That's it?" said Judge French.

"That's it."

"And then you'll be done?"

"Yes, Your Honor."

Judge French adjusted his glasses. "I'll allow the witness for the limited purpose of the topic disclosed by the prosecution, Ms. Vila's academic background." I started to speak. Judge French raised his hand. "Your objection is noted and will be put on the record, Mr. Shepherd."

As soon as we went back out, I sat down next to Liselle and said, "Do you know a Professor Hopkins from Washington U?"

Liselle's eyes widened a little bit. "Yes."

"Who is she?"

"She was my herbal sciences professor."

Fuck. "Is that as bad as it sounds?"

"Yes."

"Okay."

After the jury was seated, Victoria called Professor Anna Hopkins to the stand. Professor Hopkins had longish red hair and bright green glasses that stood out on her face. I noticed her smiling at Liselle as she took the stand. "Could you introduce yourself to the jury please?" said Victoria.

"I'm Professor Anna Hopkins."

"And what is your degree in, Professor Hopkins?"

"I have two actually. I have a doctorate in biology and one in herbal sciences."

"Do you teach?"

"I do."

"Where?"

"Washington University in St. Louis, Missouri."

"Dr. Hopkins, do you know the defendant Liselle Vila?"

"I do."

"How do you know her?"

"She was one of my students."

"Oh? What class of yours did she take?"

"She took two actually. Introduction to Herbal Science and the following semester, Herbs and Body Systems."

"Are those classes part of a woodland biology degree?"

"No. They do satisfy some biology electives though."

"Do you actually remember Liselle Vila in your class?"

"I do."

"And why is that?"

"I'm the head of our herbal sciences department and I thought that perhaps she was going to pursue a major in it so I took an interest in her."

"Why did you think that?"

"Because she was a very good student."

"I see. And did she pursue a degree in herbal sciences?"

Professor Hopkins smiled. "Unfortunately, no. It was our loss. She's very talented."

"Dr. Hopkins, what do you teach in Introduction to Herbal Science?"

"It's a very basic course. We talk about basic principles of herbal medicine and study the use of botanicals that have been documented through historical times and today."

"By botanicals, you mean what?"

"Plants and herbs. We also talk about the basics of herbal quality control."

"What do you mean by quality control?"

"We discuss how botanicals are obtained and used safely."

"Is St. John's wort one of the herbal medicines that are discussed in your course?"

"It is. We discuss what it's historically been used for and where."

"And do you discuss its contraindications?"

"Not really. This is an introductory course so it's really more of a laundry list of the various herbs that have historically been used and then which ones are still currently used in modern society."

"I see. And you said you also teach a class called Herbs and Body Systems?"

"I do."

"What do you talk about in that class?"

"We talk about the botanicals that are commonly used in Western medicine and their effect on body systems. We also discuss how certain combinations of botanicals are used. Much of that class is focused on disease prevention."

"And is St. John's wort covered in that class?"

"It is. St. John's wort has been used throughout history so we have a brief discussion of how it works."

"Professor, what are contraindications?"

"Contraindications are the reasons you shouldn't take something."

"And are the contraindications for St. John's wort discussed in the Herbs and Body Systems class?"

"They are."

"Is taking beta blockers mentioned as one of the contraindications?"

"It is. In our class, we discussed several medicines that you either shouldn't take with St. John's wort or should consult with your doctor about."

"And Liselle Vila took the Herbs and Body Systems class with you?"

"She did."

"Do you know her grades?"

"She received an 'A' in both courses. That's why I was hoping she would join our department."

"Did you discuss this with her?"

"Joining our department? I did."

"What did she tell you?"

"That she intended to major in woodland biology. She was clearly passionate about the topic and told me that that was the main reason she was taking the class—to have a better understanding of plants and their effect on us and our relationship with the natural world." She smiled, clearly unaware that she was burying my client. "Honestly, it was inspiring to see such passion in a student."

"To be clear, Professor Hopkins, you discussed St. John's wort and its interactions with Western medicine in both of your classes?"

"I did."

"No further questions, Your Honor."

I stood. "Professor Hopkins, how many herbs do you discuss in your Introduction to Herbal Sciences class?"

"I would estimate that there are one hundred and sixty-two."

"And I assume that, in your materials, each substance gets a couple of paragraphs?"

"That's right. Part of what I want to expose the students to is the broad scope of botanical and herbal remedies that exist in our world."

"St. John's wort would have been one of those one hundred and sixty-two?"

"That's right."

"And Professor, in your Herbs and Body Systems class, I assume St. John's wort is again one of many herbs you discuss?"

"That's right. It's only about one hundred in that class, but we also spend time on classifications of herbs and how certain classifications interact with different systems in your body."

"I see. You mentioned that you taught that St. John's wort interacts with certain medications like beta blockers, true?"

"I did."

"If you are not taking beta blockers, St. John's wort is an effective herbal supplement, isn't it?"

"Absolutely."

"Do you teach in your class that it's often used to treat anxiety and depression and insomnia?"

"I do."

"It's one of the most used herbal supplements in the United States, isn't it?"

"It is. People find it to be very beneficial."

"It is commonly taken in tea form, right?"

Professor Hopkins smiled. "There are a variety of teas with St. John's wort that are simply delicious."

"And good for your health?"

"I certainly think so."

"Do you drink herbal tea, Professor Hopkins?"

She smiled. "I do."

"Did you have some this morning?"

"I did."

"Do you know if it had St. John's wort in it?"

She smiled further. "I must confess it did. I figured the calming effects couldn't hurt before testifying. This is nerve-racking."

Most of the jury smiled at that. Professor Hopkins was charming. I smiled too. "You're doing just fine. So the jury is clear, if you are not taking beta blockers, St. John's wort is an effective, healthy, herbal supplement commonly used throughout the United States?"

"Absolutely. Nature provides us with much of what we need and the yellow flower of St. John's wort is a perfect example."

"How would you compare it to Coca-Cola?"

Professor Hopkins scowled. "Soda pop is poison. No one should just drink it. They would be far better off drinking herbal tea."

"With St. John's wort in it?"

"Absolutely."

"No further questions, Your Honor."

Victoria stood. "Professor Hopkins, do you teach in your class that taking St. John's wort while taking a beta blocker can be dangerous?"

"I do."

"Because it can reduce the effectiveness of that medication, right?"

"That's right."

"No further questions, Your Honor."

I stood. "Professor Hopkins, in your classes do you teach that we are all responsible for what we put in our bodies?"

"I do. Everyone has that responsibility."

"Do you teach that if you don't know what's in something, you should ask?"

"Absolutely."

"What each of us take in, as adults, is up to us, right?"

"Right."

"Professor, you're not a medical doctor, right?"

"I'm not."

"Do you teach your students that if they're not sure about a medication's interaction with a supplement that they should ask their medical doctor?"

"I do."

"Do you share your herbal tea with others?"

"Of course," Professor Hopkins said.

"Objection, Your Honor," said Victoria just a hair too late.

"Sustained," said Judge French. "The jury will disregard that last question and answer."

"No further questions, Your Honor."

Victoria decided enough was enough and excused Professor

Hopkins. The professor gave Liselle a little wave as she left. Liselle smiled.

The jury saw it.

"Your Honor, the prosecution rests," said Victoria.

"Members of the jury," said Judge French. "We have some technical things to take care of so we'll have a brief morning break and then the defense will begin its case. Please come back in fifteen minutes.

Once the jury had left, Judge French said, "Counsel, please see me in my office."

Victoria and I looked at each other, shook our heads to indicate neither of us knew what was up, and went back. Judge French sat himself heavily in his chair and said, "What are we doing here, Ms. Lance?"

Victoria looked startled. "What do you mean?"

"I mean what are we doing in the second week of a first-degree murder trial on this case?"

"Your Honor, we think it's clear that—"

"If you're about to say you think it's *clear* that a crime has been committed, you are mistaken."

Victoria shrugged. "We think it is, Your Honor."

"Have you offered a plea deal? For something without intent?"

"We have not, Your Honor."

"Why not?"

Victoria straightened. "We thought it was important to bring the first-degree charge in this case."

Judge French looked at me. "Would you take something less?"

"Given these facts, Your Honor, I don't know how I could recommend a plea to anything that includes jail time."

Judge French nodded. "I understand this is a high-profile case, Ms. Lance, but a high-profile loss is still a loss."

Victoria raised her chin. "*If* we lose, Your Honor. And sometimes we need to bring a case just because it's the right thing to do, regardless."

"That has rarely been my experience." Judge French stared and Victoria Lance returned it until finally Judge French sighed again and said, "Fine."

"We'd like to move for acquittal, Your Honor," I said.

Judge French shook his head. "I'm not going to dismiss the case, Mr. Shepherd. You can put your motion on the record but the grand jury found that there was enough evidence to bring the case so I'm not going to dismiss it, no matter how weak it is." He waved a hand. "All right, are you ready to begin, Mr. Shepherd?"

"I am."

"How long do you anticipate going?"

"Probably no more than a day, day and a half."

"Fine. I'll see you in ten minutes."

44

It was my turn to put on witnesses and I had decided to answer the prosecution's wave of wedding witnesses with one of my own. I put them on the stand, one after another, as rapidly as I could. Just to make the point.

∽

"You saw Mr. Phillips and Ms. Vila at the wedding?"

"I did. I was sitting at their table."

"And you saw Mr. Phillips ask Ms. Vila to dance?"

"I did."

"What did you see?"

"She was eating a piece of wedding cake and Mr. Phillips came over and took her hand and said, 'Don't you dare leave me hanging out here,' and she smiled and excused herself and went out and danced with him.

∽

"And, if you don't mind my asking, how old are you, Mrs. Crandall?"

"I'm seventy-eight."

"And did you see Richard Phillips at the wedding reception?"

"I did."

"When did you see him?"

"I was sitting alone at our table—my husband had recently passed, you see—and Mr. Phillips came up and asked me if I would care to dance."

"And did you?"

"I did. I thought it was very sweet." She paused. "And it made me miss my Franklin very much."

I handed her a tissue.

"Thank you," she said.

"Thank you, Mrs. Crandall."

∽

"You were working at the southeast bar, over by the ice sculpture, the night of the reception?"

"I was."

"And did Richard Phillips order a drink from you?"

"He did."

"What was it?"

"A red wine."

"How do you remember that?"

"He tipped me twenty dollars. I was looking for him to come back the rest of the night."

"Did he?"

"One more time, yes."

"And did he order red wine again?"

"He did."

"One?"

"Yes."
"Was he by himself?"
"He was."
"Both times?"
"Yes."

~

"You worked at the rehearsal dinner?"

"I did."

"I understand you were serving the coffee and dessert after the dinner?"

"That's right?"

"Did you serve Richard Phillips and Liselle Vila?"

"I did."

"Did they have dessert?"

"Yes."

"How about coffee?"

She shook her head. "No. They just asked me to bring cups of hot water."

"Oh? How many?"

"Two."

"One for each?"

"Yes."

~

"What do you mean 'the couples dance?'"

"You know when they have all the couples come out on the dance floor and then they gradually go up with how many years you've been together and you leave until the couple that's been together the longest is the only one dancing on the floor."

"I see, and you and your husband went out there?"

"We did. We've been married for thirty-six years."

"Congratulations."

"Thank you. So as my husband and I were going out, Ms. Vila was pulling Mr. Phillips off the dance floor."

"I see. Did you hear them speak?"

"I did. Ms. Vila kept saying 'But we're not married' and Mr. Phillips said, 'Come on, they won't care.' And she laughed and said, 'No, no, no,' and pulled him off the floor."

"*She* pulled *him* off the floor?"

"It took a few tries but she did, yes."

~

ALL IN ALL, I THOUGHT I WAS COUNTERING VICTORIA'S WEDDING witnesses pretty well and it was all going fine until I got to Beverly Maddox.

Mrs. Maddox was in her sixties and was always in everyone's business except that she was so darned delightful as she did it that no one really seemed to mind. She had been a friend of the Branson family since Ellie and Matt had been small and so naturally had been invited to the wedding. She thought the service was marvelous and the food divine and the guest list just about as noteworthy as one could get in our small town of Carrefour.

"So where were you seated the night of the wedding, Mrs. Maddox?" I asked.

"Well, I wasn't at the head table naturally because even though I'm practically family, I'm not a blood relation and that's the most important thing to have around you at an event like that. No, I was seated at the table right next to the head table along with Dottie Myers and Betsy Frank. The staff served us about the same time as the head table, which I appreciated because I just can't bear to let my asparagus get cool."

I smiled. "I see. So from where you were sitting, you had a clear view of the dance floor?"

"I certainly did. And let me tell you those dance lessons that Jake Phillips didn't want to go to certainly paid off. He practically floated Ellie right around the room."

"Mrs. Maddox, did you know who Richard Phillips was that night?"

"Well, I most certainly did. We might live on the border of Ohio and Michigan, but we're not a backwater. I'd seen him on the news shows and I had read the Forbes magazine article about his family and it was really quite a to do to have them coming right here to our hometown. I thought Carrefour turned it out quite well. Well, you know besides what happened, of course."

"Sure. So you had seen him enough to recognize him?"

"I had indeed. And of course he'd been sitting with the family and he looks just like his brother, Stephen, a little heavier maybe, but the family resemblance was unmistakable."

"And did you know who my client, Liselle Vila, was at the time?"

Beverly Maddox shook a ringed finger. "You know, I didn't when the weekend started, but I took one look at her and my goodness I had to find out. I assumed she must be some sort of model so I was asking around and do you know that it turned out she's a biologist? An actual scientist. Did you know that?"

"I do, Mrs. Maddox. Did you know all that at the time?"

"I did. I'm practically family as I mentioned so I was at the rehearsal dinner and saw her for the first time there. Goodness. She's about as striking a woman as I've ever seen and I once saw Jackie Kennedy no farther away than you to me."

"I see. And did you see Richard Phillips and Liselle Vila at the wedding reception?"

"I most certainly did and, as good a job as the bride and

groom did in their dance, those two danced like they had been doing it together all their lives. I mean they practically floated across the floor. Do you know that at one point they did a waltz? There wasn't even a waltz playing but they totally made it work. It was divine."

"Now Mrs. Maddox, did you talk to Liselle that night?"

"I certainly did. Our table was right next to the dance floor and Ms. Vila saw I was by myself and she came over and sat right next to me. She had been dancing and a woman like her doesn't sweat but she certainly glowed. She sipped a water and she asked me where I was from and how I knew the bride and groom and where I had gotten the beautiful emerald necklace I was wearing." Mrs. Maddox put a hand to her neck where three small emeralds hung at the end of a gold chain. "My Benjamin gave them to me, on our twenty-fifth wedding anniversary, God rest him, but she noticed and it seemed to me that these emeralds were the only thing as green as her eyes in that room."

I exchanged a smile with the jury and said, "What happened next, Mrs. Maddox?"

"Well, we had talked for a time when Richard Phillips came up holding two glasses of wine. And Ms. Vila, she barely takes a sip and sets it aside and Mr. Phillips, he takes a big drink. And Ms. Vila introduced me to him and Mr. Phillips said it was certainly a pleasure to meet someone as interesting and delightful as me and then said, that if I didn't mind, he would like to dance once again with Ms. Vila."

"Let me stop you there for a moment, Mrs. Maddox. So Mr. Phillips brought wine for himself and Ms. Vila to the table?"

"Yes, he did."

"And *he* asked Ms. Vila to go back out and dance?"

"He most certainly did." Mrs. Maddox straightened and she shook her head and, I'm not kidding, she actually clucked. "I understand why you're asking those questions of course,

Nathan. I mean, *Mr.* Shepherd. Mr. Phillips ordered the wine and Mr. Phillips asked her to dance and if you ask me this whole theory that this sweet young woman danced Mr. Phillips to death is just about as silly a thing as I've ever heard. Who in the world would try to dance a man to death? It's not even possible. Waste of everyone's time and money if you ask me. Although it certainly gave me something to look forward to today."

I waited for the objection but it never came. I glanced over and Victoria was just sitting there. I figured she didn't want to cut Mrs. Maddox off and seem rude to the jury.

Mrs. Maddox kept going. "I mean if it was possible, I'd have seen it by now on *60 Minutes* or *To Catch a Killer*, don't you think? It makes no sense. No sense at all."

"Thank you, Mrs. Maddox, I don't want you to talk about other things that you thought about or saw. I just wanted to make sure that you saw Richard Phillips get his own wine and that you saw him ask Ms. Vila to dance. Is that right?"

"Isn't that exactly what I said?"

"Yes, I suppose it is. No further questions, Your Honor."

Victoria stood. "Mrs. Maddox you don't think someone could dance someone to death?"

Beverly Maddox shook her head. "I don't see how they could. This is just a horrible tragedy."

"A horrible tragedy? Just an unfortunate, one-time incident?"

"Exactly."

"No further questions, Your Honor."

I had a very bad feeling. I needed to get Mrs. Maddox off the stand before she did any more damage. Or opened any more doors. "That's all I have for Mrs. Maddox, Your Honor."

"Thank you very much, Mrs. Maddox," said Judge French. "You're excused."

"You may call your next witness, Mr. Shepherd."

One of the hardest things to do in a criminal trial is to rest.

It's the prosecutor's burden to prove its case beyond a reasonable doubt. That means I was free to sprinkle doubt all over my cross-examination of their witnesses. Sometimes calling your own witness can do more harm than good and lead the jury to believe things that they might have doubted before. It's why I had decided not to call a scientist of my own since I'd gotten all the facts that I needed through Victoria's. And it was why I thought the only thing I needed to do was show more positive evidence that Richard Phillips had been exercising his own free will on the night he died. I thought—I was pretty sure; I was almost certain—that we had done enough.

"Your Honor," I said. "The defense rests."

"Very well, Counselors. We are a little early, but this seems like a good time to break for the day and we can do jury instructions and closing arguments—"

Victoria stood. "Your Honor, we have a rebuttal witness."

I really didn't like where this was going, but I had a guess, and I couldn't let the jury hear any of it. "May we approach, Your Honor?"

Judge French waved us up.

When we got there, I said quietly, "Rebuttal to what? All we put on were additional witnesses who saw Ms. Vila and Mr. Phillips at the wedding. The prosecution has literally called more than a dozen witnesses on that."

"Who do you intend to call, Ms. Lance?" said Judge French.

"Your Honor, the prosecution will call Nick Heyward."

I kept a straight face and it was honestly the best poker face I've ever given. Nick Heyward. Liselle Vila's high school boyfriend.

The one she had danced with until he almost died.

45

"Your Honor," I said. "It's getting close to the end of the day. Perhaps we could have a discussion of this witness in chambers?"

Judge French raised his eyebrows. "What is this witness for, Ms. Lance?"

"He's a rebuttal witness, Your Honor."

"I understand that. I didn't see much to rebut in Mr. Shepherd's case, though. What's he testifying on?"

Victoria glanced sidelong at me before she said, "Mr. Heyward is going to testify about certain events in Ms. Vila's past."

"You're going to have to be more specific than that, Ms. Lance."

Victoria turned and stared at me for a moment. "You know, don't you?" she said.

"Know what?"

Victoria turned back to the judge. "Mr. Heyward is going to testify that Ms. Vila danced with him until he was hospitalized and almost died."

"Go back to your tables," said Judge French.

As I returned, I saw Nick Heyward sitting in the back of the courtroom, a square-jawed, blond-haired man in an ill-fitting, blue sport coat with a checked shirt and a striped tie. From the rigid way Liselle was staring straight ahead, I guessed that she'd seen him too.

Judge French said, "Members of the jury, as I mentioned before, we've reached a place where I think that we will break for the day. We are coming close to the end of the case and I expect that we may have one more witness tomorrow and then we will conclude the case and you can begin your deliberations. I ask that you please refrain from speaking to each other about the case and wait until I have charged you to begin your deliberations. In the meantime, have a good evening and I will see you back here at eight o'clock tomorrow."

Judge French banged his gavel and the jury rose and left. As they filed out, Judge French stood, looked at us, and pointed to his office.

I put a hand on Liselle's shoulder. "Are you okay?"

She nodded but didn't say anything.

"I don't want you to speak to him, do you understand?"

She nodded again.

"It's very important. Not a word."

She nodded a third time.

"Danny, take Liselle back to the office now. Don't even stay here to collect your things. I'll get them and bring them back with me when we're done."

Danny nodded and corralled Liselle and, together, the two of them left. I noted with approval that Danny stayed between her and Heyward on the way out.

I hurried into the judge's office and took a seat with Victoria in front of the judge's desk.

"Explain yourself, Ms. Lance," said Judge French.

"Your Honor, Nick Heyward is going to testify that some

years ago in Missouri, Ms. Vila kept him dancing until he ended up in the hospital and almost died."

I started to speak but Judge French raised his hand. "You're going to have to be more specific than that, Ms. Lance."

Victoria nodded. "I don't want to speak for him, Your Honor, but I understand that Mr. Heyward and Ms. Vila dated for a time. After they broke up, they ended up at a party together and took ecstasy along with a group of other teens. While there, they danced for hours and Ms. Vila gave Mr. Heyward so much water that he collapsed and almost died from water intoxication. He was taken to the hospital and, fortunately, they were able to adjust his electrolyte levels in time to save his life."

"Why in the world would you think that I would allow that testimony in this case?" said Judge French.

"Two reasons, Your Honor. First, it shows a pattern of conduct. Second, Mr. Shepherd opened the door."

"How?" said Judge French.

"When Mrs. Maddox told the jury that it was impossible to dance someone to death."

I smiled. "Are you suggesting that Nick Heyward is dead?"

"No. I'm stating that if it were not for emergency medical intervention, he would be."

Judge French nodded. "Mr. Shepherd?"

"There are all sorts of problems with this, Judge. First, if the prosecution was really seeking to enter evidence of a pattern, they should've done it in their case-in-chief, not try to shoehorn it in with an undisclosed witness after our case is done."

Judge French looked at Victoria.

"The testimony of Beverly Maddox opened the door," she said again.

"Beverly Maddox is a chatty gossip, not a forensic expert," I said. "I wasn't using her as an expert to say it wasn't possible to dance someone to death. It was an offhand comment."

"Which I have a right to address," said Victoria.

"You have other objections?" Judge French said to me.

"I do. This conduct supposedly happened in high school. I assume these are juveniles we're talking about. That's hardly relevant to conduct some fifteen years later."

"What else?"

"It's not at all the same situation. I believe the testimony will reflect that the kids had taken ecstasy and that all of them were worried about dehydrating and so all of them were taking steps to avoid it when Mr. Heyward accidentally overhydrated. Unless Ms. Lance is going to present evidence that Ms. Vila was convicted of some sort of crime related to this incident, it seems like awfully vague and unconnected evidence to be entering in this murder trial."

"Was there a conviction, Ms. Lance?" said Judge French.

"No."

"Were any charges filed?"

"No, Your Honor."

"Anything else, Mr. Shepherd?"

"Even if this were relevant, which it is not, this evidence of an accident fifteen years ago is unfairly prejudicial and has to be excluded."

"Ms. Lance?"

"Judge, before I took this case, I would've agreed with Mrs. Maddox that you can't dance someone to death. But this has happened to Ms. Vila not once but twice. It can't be a coincidence."

"First of all, it's only happened to her once," I said. "Second, that kind of haphazard linkage is exactly why this is prejudicial and has to be excluded."

Judge French took his glasses between his thumb and his forefinger, straightened them on the bridge of his nose, and stared at us, expressionless. Finally, he said, "I'm going to consider this overnight. Be here at eight o'clock and I'll give you my ruling. Is there anything besides Mr. Heyward's proposed testimony that's left?"

"No, Your Honor," we both said.

"Fine, then he will either testify or not and then we'll move on to instructions and closing. Have you thought any further about a plea deal?"

"We'll accept dismissal of all charges," I said.

"We'll accept a plea to first-degree murder," Victoria said.

Judge French sighed. "One of you is going to be disappointed. I still encourage you to see what you can do." He waved a hand. "I'll see you both in the morning."

We stood and walked out of the judge's office. I stood aside and let Victoria go through the door first. She stopped as soon as we were out of the judge's hearing. "You know it can't be a coincidence," she said.

"Of course it is," I said. "And you know you're stretching because you have no motive and no murder weapon."

"And you know I'm not because she did it on purpose."

"You've been talking to billionaires too much, Vicki. All that money clouds their perspective."

And that was about as much conversation as we cared to share. The two of us gathered our things and headed out. I saw her associate standing with Nick, speaking to him softly. As I passed, I waved, and he looked at me and nodded. Victoria stared at me, hard.

I didn't care. I left.

∼

A SHORT TIME LATER, I WAS SITTING AT THE CONFERENCE ROOM table eating an Arby's turkey club across from Danny and

Liselle. "What do you think the judge is going to do?" said Liselle.

"I don't know so I have to be ready in case he testifies. Is there anything else you haven't told me?"

"What do you mean?"

"How bad was your break-up?"

"What?"

"I said how bad was your break-up?"

Liselle looked at me without a flicker of emotion. "No break-ups are good."

"I understand that, but I need to know if Vicki is going to get anything out of Nick that would surprise me."

"There might've been some late-night calls."

"After you broke up?"

"Yes."

"And?"

"I might've keyed his truck."

"You're joking."

"I was angry. But we were getting along better by the time of the party."

"Anything else?"

"I told you everything. I was worried that he would dehydrate. Until you told me it was hyponatremia, I didn't know and just assumed that it was dehydration that made him collapse."

"Danny—"

"I know. Research the admissibility of prior similar acts and put together a bench brief for why those acts should be excluded so that you can give it to the judge in the morning."

I smiled. "I don't know who trained you but he did a damn fine job."

Danny smiled. "Some jerk."

"I need to get to work on this cross-examination and closing. Danny, can you call Olivia and arrange for a ride for Liselle?"

"I can wait until you're done," said Liselle.
"Not tonight, Liselle. It's going to be late."
She looked down. "Okay."

I left the conference room then turned around and came back in. "It's okay," I said to her. "Get some rest."

She nodded and that time I really did leave. From my office, I could hear Danny call Olivia and saw Liselle go into the spare office and work on her file for about half an hour until Danny hollered that Olivia was there. She turned off her tablet and waved to me as she left.

～

I SPENT MOST OF MY TIME FINE-TUNING MY CLOSING. IN DOING SO, I came to one conclusion: if Judge French let Nick Heyward testify, we were fucked. No juror was going to believe that both incidents were an accident. We had to keep Nick Heyward out if we were going to win.

Danny gave me a copy of the bench brief before he left for the night. I looked it over and decided that the cases were enough to give the judge a reason to rule our way if that's what he was inclined to do. It seemed to me, though, that there were a couple of other cases that would allow him to rule against us too.

I finished the brief, finished the closing, and drove home.

The house was dark and it was quiet and just a little bit cold for early June. I went straight to my bedroom and slid into bed. The Nick Heyward issue didn't help me sleep but, since it was trial, it didn't prevent me either and I closed my eyes.

～

A SECOND LATER MY ALARM WENT OFF. OR AT LEAST IT SEEMED like a second. I got ready and went straight to court. I arrived at seven o'clock and had to wait for Judge French's bailiff Marty to open the courtroom doors. As soon as they were unlocked, I handed Marty the brief Danny had written to exclude Nick Heyward from testifying. When Victoria showed up a short time later, I handed her a copy too. She smiled, handed me a copy of the brief she'd written last night, and gave a copy of hers to Marty. I leafed through it and saw that she had essentially cited the same cases as me but in reverse order.

"I guess we'll see," I said.

"I guess we will," she said. And the two of us sat down to wait.

~

AT SEVEN FIFTY-FIVE, JUDGE FRENCH CALLED US BACK TO HIS office. The court reporter was poised next to his desk, ready to type. Once we sat, he nodded to the court reporter and said, "We are on the record here in the matter of State versus Vila. The State seeks to call a witness who will testify to an incident that happened approximately fifteen years ago in Missouri in which the defendant Liselle Vila danced with the witness and that witness collapsed and was hospitalized. The Court has reviewed briefs from both parties as to whether this testimony should be permitted. Having reviewed the cited cases and having conducted research of its own, the Court has determined that it will exclude the testimony of Nick Heyward. This witness was not disclosed by the prosecution but, more importantly, the incident he would testify to is remote in time, does not establish an unlawful pattern or practice on the part of the defendant, and frankly is far too attenuated to be of relevance to this proceeding. Even if it were relevant, the Court finds that it would unfairly prejudice the case against Ms. Vila. For that reason, Nick Heyward will not be permitted to testify today."

"Your Honor, may I proffer his testimony for the record?" said Victoria.

"You may," said Judge French.

Victoria then summarized for the court reporter the things she would have asked Mr. Heyward and what he would have testified to. I reiterated my objection that none of that would've been relevant to this proceeding.

When she was finished, Judge French said, "You've made your record. Do you intend to call any other witnesses?"

"I do not, Your Honor," said Victoria.

"Very well then. Are you prepared for closing?"

"I am, Your Honor."

The judge looked at me.

"Yes, sir."

"Very well," said Judge French. "Time for closing arguments."

46

I whispered to Liselle and Danny that the Court had ruled our way, that Nick Heyward would not be testifying. I'm not sure which one looked more relieved and I didn't have time to figure it out since the judge immediately began to speak.

"Members of the jury, thank you for your patience this morning. We had to take care of a few housekeeping matters. I know that at the end of the day yesterday we said that there may be another witness but, due to some rulings from the Court, there will be no more testimony. You are not to make any assumptions based on the fact that this witness will not testify as we have ruled that his testimony is not relevant to either side of the case. At this time, the lawyers will present you with their closing arguments. Ms. Lance, is the State ready?"

Victoria stood. "I am, Your Honor."

"You may proceed."

"Thank you, Your Honor." Victoria looked thoughtful as she walked up in front of the jury and her stance was easy and relaxed as she said, "Liselle Vila killed Richard Phillips. She gave him a drug that blocked his medication. She gave him food and drink that spiked his blood pressure. And then she danced with him until he died. And she did all of it on purpose."

She walked a little to one side. "This is an unusual situation. We don't normally see something this devious and so it took the police a while to figure what evidence to gather and then it took my office a little while more to put it all together but once we did, it all fit. The method she used was unusual, but it's no different than if Liselle Vila had pushed Mr. Phillips into the water and then stood by and watched him drown. It's no different at all."

"You heard the evidence. Ms. Vila is a trained biologist. As part of her training, she took classes that specifically taught her about the effects of St. John's wort. You heard her professor say that Ms. Vila was a gifted student who learned that St. John's wort prevents beta blocker medications from working. And that's exactly the kind of medication that Mr. Phillips was taking when he was killed."

Victoria clicked her remote and a picture of the medication bottle went up on the screen. "There it is sitting right next to the bathroom sink in the hotel room Ms. Vila shared with Richard Phillips. Right where Detective Pearson found it. Liselle Vila *knew* Richard Phillips was taking this medicine. She *knew* the St. John's wort would block it. So what did she do?"

Victoria paused then said, "She prepared a special tea for Richard Phillips that had fifteen times the normal dosage of St. John's wort in it. *Fifteen times.*"

Victoria pointed at me. "Now, Mr. Shepherd might argue that Ms. Vila didn't know that Mr. Phillips was taking a beta blocker. That's not believable. There it is, right there, right there on the sink next to her toothbrush. Right there in her hotel room where a police detective could see it from the hallway."

"But even if you doubt that, we know what else she knew, what she knew for sure. Ms. Vila knew that there are certain things you can't eat or drink when you take St. John's wort. You can't drink red wine and you can't eat aged meats. Why? Because it'll spike your blood pressure like a rocket."

"So what did Liselle Vila do after she had given Mr. Phillips the tea laced with St. John's wort? She gave him red wine and prosciutto and caffeine, all things that would cause a healthy person's blood pressure to spike. All things that would cause a person with a pre-existing arrhythmia to barrel towards a sudden cardiac death."

Victoria walked to the other side of the jury box. "And if that's not enough, if it's not enough that she neutralized Richard Phillips' medicine and she pushed food on him that he shouldn't eat and pushed wine on him that he shouldn't drink, on top of all of that, Liselle Vila pulled Richard Phillips out onto the dance floor and kept him there all night until he literally dropped dead."

"Mr. Shepherd might say that this is ridiculous. He might say that this is a daisy-chain of a scheme that couldn't possibly work. Well, guess what? It did. Mr. Phillips is dead."

"We even have a good idea why." Victoria clicked and the picture of Liselle screaming in protest, fist raised, flashed onto the screen. "Mr. Phillips ran a large successful company and we saw pictures and heard reports that Ms. Vila participated in violent protests against it. She was part of demonstrations against Doprava that ended with arrests and the destruction of property. That might seem extreme but the organizations that Ms. Vila is a part of engage in extreme protests. She would have us believe that just a short time after demonstrating against Mr. Phillips' company, she randomly met him at a charity event and began dating him? What do you think is more likely? That they were suddenly attracted to each other at a charity event? Or that Ms. Vila was angling to get closer to him as part of her scheme?"

"This was a devious plan. And make no mistake it was a

plan. Ms. Vila knew exactly what she was doing, knew exactly what she was preparing, and knew exactly what she was getting Mr. Phillips to do." Victoria turned and looked directly at me. "And she knew exactly what would happen when she danced with him, if she danced with him long enough." She turned back to the jury. "Mr. Phillips suffered a fatal arrhythmia and he died. Just like she knew he would."

Victoria lowered her voice. "Liselle Vila was the murderer. She was also the murder weapon. She neutralized Mr. Phillips' medicine and then did everything she could to make sure his heart gave out. It was murder, the same as if she drowned him or shot him or stabbed him. For those reasons, we ask that you find Liselle Vila guilty of murder in the first degree. Thank you."

As Victoria sat, I took my place in front of the jury and said, "Liselle Vila is one of many people who danced with Richard Phillips the night he died. She's one of many people who handed him a drink. She's one of many people who gave him an appetizer. And we're supposed to believe that that's murder? It's not, members of the jury. It's just not."

"Before he ever met Ms. Vila, Richard Phillips was a fifty-nine-year-old man with a history of high blood pressure and an irregular heartbeat. Those conditions were bad enough that he'd gone to the hospital before and was taking medication to control them. Then, Mr. Phillips came here for a family wedding where he ate and he drank and he stayed up late and he danced and unfortunately, he died."

"This is a tragedy. Fifty-nine seems young. His family is devastated. Although she didn't know him for very long, Liselle Vila feels his loss too. It is a tragedy but it is also something that happens every day. Men Mr. Phillips' age with high blood pressure and heart arrhythmias die. They die running, they die at their desks, they die in their sleep, and, unfortunately, they can die on the dance floor."

I shook my head. "But that's not murder. If it were murder to drink red wine and eat aged prosciutto and drink coffee and drink tea and dance at weddings, our jails would be overflowing."

"The prosecutor has the burden of proving to you that Liselle Vila intentionally killed Richard Phillips. They have fallen so short of that responsibility that I hate to even go over their case. But the fact is that they have not remotely satisfied their burden of proof."

I paced a little. "The prosecution's case hinges on their claim that Liselle Vila knew that Richard Phillips was taking Lopressor, his blood pressure medication. There is not a single shred of evidence that Liselle Vila knew that. Not one. The prosecution relies on a picture of a medicine bottle sitting next to a bathroom sink with absolutely no evidence of when it was placed there. None."

I shook my head. "They want you to assume that Liselle Vila saw it. Ask yourself what's a more reasonable assumption—that a fifty-nine-year-old man tells his younger date that he's taking blood pressure medication or that he hides it from her. The prosecution needs to present you with *evidence* that Ms. Vila knew about the medication and they've given you nothing, nothing but faulty assumptions. There's no evidence that Ms. Vila knew anything about it."

The jurors were listening but I wasn't getting any nods to show they agreed as I continued. "The prosecution also makes a mountain out of the fact that Liselle Vila gave Mr. Phillips tea. That's absolutely true. Liselle Vila made tea. For *both* of them. They drank the tea *together* just like they drank the red wine *together*. There's no evidence that Liselle would've had any idea that it was any more unsafe for him to drink it than it would be for her. And for all of the prosecution's emphasis on the amount of St. John's wort in the tea, there is no evidence that either of them showed any sign of ingesting too much of it. Nothing."

"You heard the testimony of Dr. Wrigley, *their* toxicologist. The strength of the tea depends on how long you steep it and there's no evidence that they steeped it so long that they took a high dose."

"Further, you heard from a parade of witnesses. Not one of them related seeing Mr. Phillips exhibit signs of taking too much St. John's wort—there was no evidence of nervousness or dizziness or agitation or nausea. No, what you heard was evidence of an uncle having a great time at his nephew's wedding—eating and drinking and talking and playing golf and dancing."

"And dancing." I paused and shook my head. "If Liselle Vila is guilty of murder for dancing with Mr. Phillips then it seems to me that they should arrest the bride and the groom's mother and dear old Mrs. Crandall because they all danced with him too. If it was a crime to give Mr. Phillips a glass of red wine, they need to arrest the bartenders who gave it to Mr. Phillips when he ordered it for himself. And if it was a crime to give him prosciutto and cheese, we're going to need a prison bus because there were an awful lot of servers working over that weekend."

I paused for a moment. "Money can buy a lot of things. It can solve a lot of problems, and I imagine the more money you have, the more things you can solve with it. But there are some things that happen to all of us, to all of our families, no matter how much money we have. This is one of those unfortunate things."

"There's a natural tendency to want to blame someone when bad things happen." I looked over into the crowd where Bre Phillips sat. "Especially when we lose a parent or a loved one. But that doesn't mean it's true. And the prosecution's case isn't true here."

"Mr. Phillips had high blood pressure and a heart arrhythmia. He died when he joyfully overindulged over the course of a weekend with his family. *He* ate and drank and danced because *he* wanted to. Liselle Vila didn't make him do anything. And she didn't murder him. The prosecution didn't come anywhere close to proving their case beyond a reasonable doubt. For that reason, we ask that you return a verdict of not guilty of murder in the first-degree for Liselle Vila. Thank you."

As I sat back down, Liselle sat rigidly straight, her hands folded in her lap, her eyes downcast. She glanced up and gave me a quick smile that never touched her eyes and went back to looking down. I sat next to her and listened to Victoria's rebuttal but it was all just more of the same—the tea, the blood pressure medication, the wine, and the dancing. I listened, but it was all ground we had covered before.

Most importantly, there was nothing about an earlier incident, when a high school kid had almost been danced to death.

When Victoria was done, Judge French instructed the jury. It's a long process in which the judge just reads the instructions exactly as they're written with plenty of legalese to go around. It took about half an hour, and when he was done, the jury was dismissed to decide Liselle's fate. When the jury had left, Judge French stood and said, "Make sure you give Marty your cell phone numbers. We'll text you when the jury's back."

"What do we do now?" Liselle said.

"We wait," I said. "It's almost lunchtime. My guess is that they'll order lunch on the Court and then spend a little time eating before they make a decision. We probably have time to get something to eat but we won't go far."

I turned and looked in the first row of the gallery to see that Olivia was standing there. I didn't recognize her at first because she wasn't wearing workout gear; instead it was a black suit and white shirt that offset her spiky, bleached white hair. "Nice job, Shep," she said.

"Thanks."

"Did you come to watch the closing?" said Liselle.

"I did. I also came to take that anklet off you once the jury comes back."

Liselle's eyes lit up. "You're that sure we'll win?"

Olivia teased her bangs down around her glasses. "It'll need to come off one way or the other, Liselle. But I'm hopeful."

Liselle's face fell. "What are our chances?"

I felt like this case was filled with reasonable doubt but I knew better than to tempt the legal gods and say so out loud. "I think the case went about how we expected, Liselle. We have a good chance to win. But you never know."

"But the judge kept Nick from testifying!"

I nodded. "It's one of the reasons I feel good. But you still never know what a jury's going to do."

That didn't appear to be the answer that she was looking for but it was the only one I could give her right then. "Come on. Let's get something to eat."

Liselle had kept her cool throughout the trial. Right now though, she looked very small, and very scared.

I touched her elbow. "Hey."

She looked up.

"Let's get a sandwich. It shouldn't be long."

The four of us walked two blocks from the courthouse to a deli. It was early June so it was sunny and it was warm in that way that made you feel the cool damp of spring had just been put away for good. It felt great.

Liselle appeared to feel the same way. She put her eyes up to the sun and closed them. It didn't take a mind reader to know what she was thinking.

As we walked to the deli, Olivia told us about the new cross training class she was developing and Danny talked about how he owed a whole bunch of nights to his wife and daughter and I prodded them both along with questions about each. Liselle was quiet, as you would expect, and it fell to Olivia and Danny to fill in the silence. We got in line at the deli, which had about four people in front of us, and we had just come to the order station when my phone buzzed. I looked down.

"Well," I said.

"What is it?" said Liselle.

"The jury's back."

"Already?" said Liselle. "You said it would take longer."

"I thought it would."

"Is that good news or bad?"

I stared at the phone. "I don't know. But it means that the jury is certain." I looked at Liselle. "Ready?"

She took a deep breath and nodded.

"Let's go."

∽

THE JURY RETURNED A VERDICT OF NOT GUILTY. IT HAD TAKEN them thirty-seven minutes.

Victoria didn't flinch. She came over, shook my hand, and congratulated me on putting on a great case. I told her she did a great job and that there's no telling what a jury will do sometimes. She gave a half-smile and said she looked forward to the next time we tried one against each other. I was certain that was true.

I heard a rising commotion from the gallery and saw, or rather heard, Bre Phillips making a scene, yelling something about justice and vengeance and pale-haired sluts. A flicker of annoyance crossed Victoria's face and she asked if I would excuse her, which of course I did. Victoria made a motion to the sheriff's deputy who came over and gently took Bre by the elbow while Victoria put her arm around the young woman's shoulders and led her out of the courtroom. When they got to the door, Bre pulled free of them both, turned around, and screamed, "We both know this is the second time you've done this, bitch!"

Victoria and the sheriff hustled the disappointed billionaire out.

I turned and saw Judge French standing at the bench. He looked at me through his black glasses, straightened them and, without changing expression, went into his office and shut the door.

I turned back to Liselle. "You need to go with Olivia and fill out some paperwork so that she can discharge the bond and get that anklet off of you. Danny and I will gather our things and then we'll meet back—"

I was engulfed in a hug. Liselle Vila grabbed me and squeezed, and her shoulders shook, and I realized she was crying.

Her hair smelled like lilacs.

"Hey, hey," I said. I patted her back and let her hang on a moment more before I gently pulled away. "It's okay, Liselle. It's all over."

I handed her a tissue and she wiped her eyes. "It's really done?" she said.

"It's really done. Go with Olivia and then we'll meet up."

She wiped her eyes again and Olivia led her out of the courtroom. When she'd gone, I shook hands with Danny and said, "Nice work."

"You too."

I looked at the litter of notepads and pens and papers and tablets. "Let's clean this shit up and get out of here."

It took us a little bit. As we were finishing up, Judge French walked out of his office, overcoat on, presumably to get some lunch.

He stuck out his hand. "Congratulations, Mr. Shepherd."

"Thanks, Judge."

"You tried a good case."

"Thank you. You manage a good case."

"I like to let the lawyers do their jobs. When they're like you and Ms. Lance, it's easy."

He smiled, took a couple of steps, and then turned back. "I'm not surprised by how this one turned out."

"No?"

"No. Way too much doubt." He looked at me. "Based on the evidence that came in."

I nodded.

"Barring the other potential evidence wasn't a close call. Legally."

"I didn't think so either."

"But practically," he straightened his glasses. "It certainly could change one's view of the situation."

"I understand why you might think that, Judge."

"Have a good weekend, Mr. Shepherd. You too, Mr. Reddy."

Danny started. "Thank you, Your Honor."

"And make him give you a raise." Judge French smiled and left.

We were right behind him.

47

After Olivia and Liselle had taken care of their paperwork and Danny and I had packed up all our trial gear, we met at the cars and decided to go to a late lunch to celebrate. Danny had to be convinced because his wife had done double-duty working and watching their daughter for a couple of weeks but we convinced him that since it was still work hours, he could come out for one drink. We let Liselle pick the place because, well just because, and she picked the Railcar because she wanted to eat outside, because she loved barbecue, and because she'd been unable to go there for months since it was over the state line in Michigan.

We decided not to go to the office and went straight to the restaurant instead. Liselle rode with Olivia, and Danny and I each drove ourselves. I wasn't tired at all, that would come later, but for now I was still wired with adrenaline and awash in relief at having won.

We arrived together at the common parking lot that the Railcar shared with the Brickhouse. Olivia pulled in next to the gym and I parked next to her. As I got out of the Jeep, I heard the continuation of a conversation as Liselle said, "No, you have to show me. And I want to say goodbye to Cade." Olivia relented and showed Liselle into her gym.

I followed them. It was a sunny Tuesday afternoon so there were only five or six faithful but those five or six stared as Liselle and Olivia walked through the rows of equipment to the squat rack on the back wall where Cade was holding a bar with four hundred and five pounds on it, shrugging it up and down as easy as if he were holding a book bag. He glanced back at them, shrugged the weight six more times, then let it drop onto the spot bars. He turned around, held out his hand to Liselle, and said, "Congratulations."

Liselle slapped his hand aside and gave him a hug. "Thanks for your help!"

Cade stayed rigid for a moment before he put one arm around her, straightened so that her feet were off the ground, then set her back down. Liselle laughed.

"Join us for lunch?" I said.

Cade shook his head and pointed at the weights. "I'm going to be a while yet."

"I imagine we'll still be there if you change your mind."

"I'll think about it," he said, which clearly meant he'd already said he wouldn't be coming.

"So show me the rest of the place," said Liselle and Olivia showed her around. When they were done, we walked across the parking lot to the little brick building facing the river and the woods. The pungent hickory smoke made my mouth water.

Liselle practically cackled as she gave a clap. "We have to sit on the patio."

We did. After we asked, the hostess led us out onto the deck and, although it was a little cool in the shade, the breeze and the sound of the river more than made up for it. We ordered beers and brisket.

True to his word, Danny had one beer and then excused

himself to go home. When Liselle gave him a big hug and kissed him on the cheek, Danny just about crumbled with embarrassment before he made his nodding, blushing way out. I kid you not, he *blushed*.

Liselle and Olivia and I got another round of beers when the brisket came and polished it all off—the brisket, the burnt ends, and the sides. Liselle got Olivia talking about her plans for the gym and tried to talk her into setting up a fitness trail with workout stations in the woods. Then she shifted to asking me about my plans which, at the moment, didn't include more than catching up on sleep and on work. Which led us back around to her.

"What about you, Liselle?" said Olivia. "What are you going to do?"

"I could probably get my job back at the Forestry Service but I don't know that I want to stay in the St. Louis area now."

"The Phillips family have you worried?"

Liselle took a sip of beer and nodded. "Living in the same area as a family of billionaires that hates you doesn't seem like the smartest idea. I'm thinking that I'll get the last of the ash borer program set up, make sure it's in good hands, and then move."

"Where do you think you'll go?" I said.

"I'm not sure. Out west maybe. There are a lot of forests that need looking after out there."

I smiled. "You can take the hummingbird tour—flit from forest to forest 'til you find one you like."

Her smile broadened. "I might at that."

That led us to an in-depth discussion of forests and ash borers and replanting and the most amazing waterfalls each of us had seen before Olivia asked, "So when do you leave here?"

"Sunday," Liselle said. "I didn't want to make arrangements to leave until, well, until I knew that I could make arrangements to leave. There are also a couple of things I want to finish up related to my research before I go. I don't have any restrictions anymore, right?"

Olivia shook her head. "You're free as a bird."

Liselle smiled. "That is free." She took another drink and said, "Do you think I could check in on James before I go? I'd like to know how his leg's doing?"

"It's pretty good, but sure. If you're not leaving till Sunday, we could stop over at my parents for lunch and say hello."

"That would be great."

"What research do you need to finish up?" said Olivia.

"I've been piggybacking some of my research off the things that Sarah did here and I want to make one more check of a couple of her sites. I'm thinking about expanding on one of her papers."

"I see," said Olivia and ordered another round.

The conversation devolved from there. The full weight of the trial was lifting from my shoulders and, as heavy as that weight was for me as the attorney, it was even heavier for Liselle as the accused. Soon, we were all laughing and drinking and enjoying the sound of the stream and the sharp, angled light of sunset.

Eventually, we ended with a cup of coffee for me, a glass of seltzer for Olivia, and a glass of red wine for Liselle.

No one mentioned it.

As the three of us left the restaurant, Liselle took a detour to the ladies' room. As I waited by the door, Olivia came right up next to me and whispered, "The same passion doesn't make someone the same person."

I started. "What?"

Olivia kept right on walking to the parking lot. "Night," she said and waved without looking back.

I watched her go until Liselle returned and the two of us piled into the Jeep and I drove her home.

When we arrived at Liselle's townhouse, all of the lights were out and it was dark inside. She sighed. "Only a few more nights in this place."

"You have to be glad to go."

"I will not miss very much in Carrefour." She smiled and it was genuine and bright. "Well, maybe a few things. Can you guess?"

"Hmm. The Railcar?"

"That goes without saying."

"The Grove?"

"Of course."

"That's plenty to miss."

"And my lawyer."

I shrugged. "There are plenty of those out west that are better than what you can find in Carrefour."

"I very much doubt that, Nate Shepherd."

I know there was a streetlight and I know there was moonlight but there was no way I should have been able to see how light green her eyes were as she leaned forward. But I could.

"Thank you," she said.

I smiled, then turned away and got out of the car. I came around to her side and opened the door. She smiled and got out and didn't appear to notice that the door stayed between us. As she walked up the brick path toward the porch, I shut the car door and went back around to the driver side. When the car door snicked open, she turned around, scowled, and tilted her head. "Where are you going?"

"Home."

"Oh."

"Call me tomorrow and we'll set something up for Sunday so you can see James before you go."

The confusion on her face lasted only for a second, then it went cool and she smiled. "Okay. I'll call you then."

"Great," I said and climbed in the Jeep. I paused at the end of the street to make sure that she got in the house and pulled away once an interior light turned on.

All of the trial materials were still in the back of my car. I decided it was too late to take them back to the office and headed for home. I drove into my neighborhood, turned onto my street, and pulled into my driveway. The driveway was empty and the house was dark. I'd forgotten to turn the porch light on.

I unlocked the door, went in, and turned on the lights in a few of the downstairs rooms. Then I grabbed a beer, turned on the TV, and flipped around a little bit to decide on a movie.

I fell asleep before I could order one.

48

I slept in the next day and I enjoyed it. And then when I woke up, I laid in bed and stared out the window and I enjoyed that too.

Eventually I got moving and, a little after noon, went for a run. When I came back, I saw I had missed a call. Liselle.

No, I don't take my phone with me when I run. It defeats the purpose.

I called her back.

"Hey, Nate," she said. "Did you miss me?"

"How could I not? What are you up to today?"

"Enjoying tramping around in the woods. I don't know if I've ever been inside for such a long stretch."

"It looks like a perfect day for it."

"It is. Hey, do you think we could see James tomorrow? I've had to move up my travel plans."

"I'll check with Izzy and Mark, but I'm sure it'll be fine."

"Good. I've made my travel arrangements for tomorrow night so I thought maybe we could meet at the Grove and then head over to see James before I go."

"Sounds good. What's at the Grove?"

"I want to show you something. What time should we meet?"

"How about one?"

"Perfect. I'll see you then." She paused. "Unless you want to get together tonight?"

"I'm sorry, Liselle. I'd love to but I can't tonight."

"I don't know if I believe you, Nate Shepherd."

"I really can't. One o'clock tomorrow sounds good though."

"Huh. Okay. I'll see you then."

"'Bye." I regretted not going to see her but I would regret losing my law license even more. I think. No, yes, I definitely would.

I showered and did a couple of things that needed doing around the house and then decided I needed to restock from the grocery store. One thing about living alone now is that things got pretty bare when I was in trial and didn't have time to take care of it. I stopped at the office on the way to the store to drop off all of the trial materials that I'd left in the car the day before. Without Danny, it took three trips to bring it all in, but to make up for it, I left half the stuff on his desk for him to deal with so that he would know that he's a valuable part of the trial team. I took a quick look through my mail, made sure there weren't any emergencies lurking in it, and started to leave when I saw the tablet and brown file in the spare office where we'd set Liselle up during trial. I knew she'd want her work to take home with her so I went over to gather it up.

I didn't intend to look at it but the name "Sarah Shepherd" caught my eye and I saw a topographical map with dates and circles moving outward from Detroit. It was a map of the progression of the emerald ash borer from where it had started in Detroit. The port where it was believed to have arrived was marked with a green dot and dated rings moved outward from there, including the ring that encompassed Carrefour and the Grove. The date on that ring matched the time Sarah had gotten involved. The map ended at northwest Ohio and northeast Indiana but I knew the borer had just kept going, to Missouri and beyond.

I was curious if there was any other work from Sarah in the pile but I didn't see anything. Instead, it mostly just looked like shipping manifests from the late 1990s and early 2000s. I gathered them into the folder, closed it, and took it back to my car.

I stopped at the grocery store and I was in aisle number twenty-three, right between the soups and the macaroni and cheese, when it hit me. The shipping manifests.

I hurried through the rest of the trip and pushed my rattling cart back to the Jeep. I left the groceries right there by the side of the car and pulled the file out of the backseat. I looked again to see if I was remembering what I'd seen correctly. I was. I threw the file back onto the seat and loaded the groceries. I hustled home, left the groceries in the Jeep, and hopped online to the Missouri Secretary of State's office to check its corporate filings.

An hour later, I went back to my car and brought in the groceries. My ice cream had melted.

∾

THERE'S AN OLD RULE IN CROSS-EXAMINATION THAT YOU NEVER ASK a witness a question that you don't know the answer to. There's a similar but slightly different rule for clients—don't ask a question that you don't want to know the answer to.

I picked Liselle up a little before one o'clock the next day because I'd promised that I would. I was quiet as we drove out to the Grove and when Liselle asked if something was wrong, I said I was still tired from the trial. We parked the car and walked up the path toward the center of the Grove, past the white pines and the sugar maples and through the black cherries that were just dropping the last of their blossoms.

When we came to the ash trees, still barren and stark like a field of burnt bones, Liselle took my hand and pulled me off the path. I let her. We'd gone about twenty-five yards into the dead trees when she said, "Look."

I looked. "I'm sorry, what?"

"Here," she said and pointed. I saw a tiny sapling, no more than two feet high, planted between two dead ash trees.

"What is it?"

"An accolade elm." Liselle was beaming. "We planted fifty of them yesterday. I wanted to show you."

I looked around and saw that there were indeed saplings planted at regular intervals between the dead ash trees. Liselle's enthusiasm was apparent as she led me from one to another and said, "During all this time up here, I was able to get a grant from the Forestry Foundation. They're going to pay for planting five hundred saplings in the Groves over the next five years, which should go a long way towards revitalizing this section. They've done studies and found that the accolade elms thrive in the same soil as ash trees and they turn bright yellow in fall. As the dead ash trees come down, these can grow up to take their place. It'll take some time of course but all good things do—"

I broke the rule.

"I learned about Five Gen Shipping today," I said.

Liselle didn't look away from the sapling. "There's still a risk of fire, of course."

I continued. "Five Gen is a Chinese shipping company that runs container ships from China to US ports."

Liselle looked around. "Especially from lightning."

"Including Detroit."

"There's no way to avoid fire with all of this deadwood."

"It was the company that shipped the containers that had the emerald ash borers in them."

"But fire is a natural process too."

"Five Gen appears to be a Chinese company."

"Fire is a cleaner. Nature's cleaner."

"It's not though. The company is a shell."

"The flames destroy the diseased, the rotten, the corrupt."

"It's a shell for the Doprava Company."

She looked at me then. "So that what's good has room to grow."

I locked in on eyes that were the lightest green I had ever seen; eyes that I now knew saw the world much differently than me. "Doprava is the one who shipped the containers with the ash borers here," I said. "Richard Phillips was the one who set up the shipping company. Stephen even mentioned it at the trial, that Richard had figured out a way to cut their costs and ship products direct from China."

Liselle reached out and touched the tiny sapling she'd planted the day before. "I told you that Richard was an inspiration, that instead of struggling against a problem, he'd find a way to work with it." She stroked a leaf of the sapling with her thumb. "There's nothing more powerful than nature's lifecycle. You can see it clearly in the woods, you can hear its heartbeat in the forest. We ignore the world around us and then use our science to try to make nature match the beat that *we* want, to force it into an artificial rhythm. But nature's rhythms, its innate beat, is too powerful. It resists our efforts to shape it and always brings us back to the unavoidable cycle. Sometimes we just have to get out of the way and let it happen. Like with these elms." She stroked the tiny sapling one more time then stood and put one hand on the trunk of an eighty-foot-tall, barren ash tree. "And these ash trees."

I didn't say anything.

Liselle waved a hand at the row of saplings. "I'm so happy, I really didn't think we'd get the grant and be able to plant before I left." She stepped closer and took my hands in hers before she raised her face to mine with a joyful smile, and said, "I'm so happy, I could dance."

In that moment, I understood why Richard Phillips found that invitation to be irresistible. But he didn't know what I knew.

I stepped back and pulled free of her hands. "Let's go, Liselle," I said and walked back towards the path.

She came up beside me. "Are we going to see James then?"

I looked at her. "I don't think that's a good idea."

She stopped and now there was anger in her face. "I thought you'd appreciate what I did."

I think she meant the trees.

"I do."

"It's what your wife would've wanted!"

I looked at the rows of saplings. "That's true."

"She would've done the same thing!"

I stared at her. "With the saplings," I said. I turned back to the path. "Come on. I'll take you home."

"Don't bother." She pulled out her phone and her thumbs flurried to send a text.

"What are you doing?"

"Getting a ride."

"In the woods? I'll take you home."

"I'd rather spend time with someone who appreciates what I'm doing."

We walked back toward the parking lot. We didn't say anything. At one point, Liselle's phone buzzed and she texted back.

It took twenty minutes or so to get back to the parking lot and by the time we got there, a Ford truck was pulling into the lot.

I didn't see an Uber or Lyft sticker. "Do you know this person?""

"It's how I'm getting home."

"I thought you were flying?"

"You thought I was flying. I never said I was flying."

The truck pulled in and I saw a man with reddish-brown hair and a bushy brown beard. He seemed of an age with Liselle.

As the truck stopped, Liselle held out her hand. "Thank you for everything you've done. *I* appreciate what *you've* done for me."

I took her hand and shook it. "You're welcome."

"Send me pictures as the trees grow."

"Sure," I said.

She waved to the man in the truck and he got out and approached us. He was good size, about the same as me, and smiled as he approached. "I want you to meet the man who helped me plant all of those saplings yesterday," said Liselle.

The man came up and shook my hand, pumping it with smiling exuberance. "You did a great job, man. Great work on the trial."

"Thanks."

"Nate Shepherd," Liselle said. "This is Jeremy Raines. An old friend of mine."

I kept my face straight. "Nice to meet you."

Liselle smiled even sweeter as she turned to Jeremy. "We're going to get going a little early, Jeremy. Nate has a family gathering to get to."

"Awesome. We'll make it home by dark. Nice to meet you, Nate."

"You too, Jeremy."

Liselle went to my car, grabbed her folder and tablet, and put them in Jeremy's truck. As she did, she said, "Oh, I almost forgot." She reached over into the truck bed and pulled out a sapling. She came back and handed it to me. "I thought you could plant this one in your yard. To remind you of Sarah's work. And mine."

When I took the sapling, Liselle gave me that same sweet smile, a smile that was probably the last thing that Richard Phillips ever saw, then put her hands over mine and kissed me on the cheek. "Thanks again, Nate." She looked me in the eyes. "I never would've made it without you."

Then she climbed into the truck and the two of them drove away.

I held the sapling, bearing the unexpected weight of it, feeling the grit of its dirt coating my hands. I stood that way for some time. Then I climbed into the Jeep, put the sapling on the passenger seat, and headed to Mark and Izzy's house.

I was anxious to see how James was doing.

EPILOGUE

Little James was doing just fine.

He was still not allowed to run and he was a little unsteady as he came out of his house but he looked great. He gave me a hug and he asked me if the hawk lady was coming and I said no. He looked disappointed but the look was fleeting because kids bounce back fast.

Izzy followed him out. She gave me a hug and asked if the hot woodland biologist was coming. I said no and Izzy looked disappointed, but then conceded that since the hot woodland biologist was accused of murder, it was probably for the best.

I saw Olivia later that week. She asked if Liselle had left town and I said that she had. She asked if we were going to keep in touch and I said that we were not. Olivia rifled a hand through her hair, said Liselle was no Sarah, and that it was probably for the best. I agreed on both counts.

I received a postcard a few weeks later. It was a picture of the Roh National Rain Forest in Washington State. There was no message and there was no address, which was probably for the best.

It took me a little while to decide what to do with the

sapling. It was a reminder of Sarah's work but also of the person who had continued it. In the end, I decided that you have to take the bad with the good and planted the accolade elm along the back tree-line of my yard. It took root and by fall it had grown at least half a foot. I didn't know if it would thrive, but it certainly appeared to have a chance which, really, was all that I could ask for.

THE NEXT NATE SHEPHERD BOOK

Blind Conviction is the next book in the Nate Shepherd Legal Thriller Series. Click here if you'd like to order it.

FREE SHORT STORY AND NEWSLETTER SIGN-UP

There was a time, when Nate Shepherd was a new prosecutor and Mitch Pearson was a young patrol officer, that they almost got along. Almost.

If you sign up for Michael Stagg's newsletter, you'll receive a free copy of The Evidence, a short story about the first case Nate Shepherd and Mitch Pearson were ever on together. You'll also receive information about new releases from Michael Stagg, discounts, and other author news.

Click here to sign up for the Michael Stagg newsletter or go to:

https://michaelstagg.com/newsletter/

ABOUT THE AUTHOR

Michael Stagg has been a trial lawyer for more than twenty-five years. He has tried cases to juries and he's won and he's lost and he's argued about it in the court of appeals after. He still practices law so he's writing the Nate Shepherd series under a pen name.

Michael and his wife live in the Midwest. Their sons are grown so time that used to be spent at football games and band concerts now goes to writing. He enjoys sports of all sorts, reading, and grilling, with the order depending on the day.

You can contact him on Facebook or at mikestaggbooks@gmail.com.

ALSO BY MICHAEL STAGG

Lethal Defense

True Intent

Blind Conviction

Printed in Great Britain
by Amazon